ELENA LOPEZ
began with a lie
and became a legend.

Mary Ellen Lawrence had possibilities. Anthony Duke, entrepreneur, promoter and scoundrel, saw them. She would never gain fame as a ballet dancer, but if she assumed a new name and a new glamorous identity, he promised, she could become the most famous woman of the era.

That was how Elena Lopez was invented. Anthony Duke told the story, and soon all London believed. The raven-haired beauty with the sapphire blue eyes became, at his word, a celebrated Spanish dancer banished from Spain because of her dangerous intimacy with a crown prince. Duke's friends filled the newspapers with tales about her to promote her London debut. Her debut caused a sensation and Elena (nee Mary Ellen) was the toast of London. And her fictional past was just a preface to her scandalous tour of the world, her amours with monarchs, her romances with composers and writers, her pursuit of fame and her search for love.

In this, her first novel since LOVE'S TENDER FURY, Jennifer Wilde finds a heroine and an era worthy of her spell-binding story-teller's art.

Dare to Love

Jennifer Wilde

WARNER BOOKS

A Warner Communications Company

WARNER BOOKS EDITION

ISBN 0-446-81826-7

Cover art by Tom Hall

Warner Books, Inc., 75 Rockefeller Plaza, New York, N.Y. 10019

A Warner Communications Company

Printed in the United States of America

Not associated with Warner Press, Inc., of Anderson, Indiana

First Printing: March, 1978

10 9 8 7 6 5 4 3 2 1

With love to Patricia,
Pam and Barbara, who know
the reasons why.

CORNWALL

1844

I

They still stared and whispered to themselves as I walked down the street. Three years had passed since I was home last, but the village hadn't changed at all, nor had the people. At eighteen, I was no longer a child, but to the villagers I was still the Lawrence girl, the subject of scandal. It pleased me to find that I was not affected by the stares, the whispers. What these people thought simply didn't matter any more. They would never again be able to cause the anger, the pain, the resentment that had marred my childhood.

My blue-black hair fell to my shoulders in waves, and I wore a dusty rose cotton frock trimmed with lace. My manner of dress shocked the villagers, as did my cool, self-possessed attitude. I should have been wearing black, with my head covered and bowed with grief. Aunt Meg had been buried less than a week ago, and the very fact that I dared appear in public so soon afterwards was an affront to the good citizens. They couldn't know that Aunt Meg had begged me never, never to wear mourning for her, had begged me not to grieve.

"Remember me with a smile," she had whispered in that hoarse, fading voice. "Forgive me, darling, for my inadequacies, and remember only the good things. You're strong. I've seen to that. You're strong and gifted and intelligent, and you'll survive. Forgive me, darling, forgive me—"

I hadn't understood at the time. Aunt Meg had devoted her life to me. She had given me everything—love, security, the very best education. She had given me comfort and compassion when I was a child, and when I began to study dancing she had given me the gift of her faith in me. What could there possibly be to forgive her for? It was only after the funeral that I learned that all the money was gone, that Graystone Manor was to be taken in payment of debts. The house and everything in it would be sold within six weeks if I was unable to raise ten thousand pounds. The sum might as well have been ten million.

The ballet school in Bath had been very expensive, but Aunt Meg had never let me suspect her financial difficulties. She had continued to pay my tuition and to send spending money, money for new clothes. On my visits home she had put on a splendid front. Unable to conceal the fact that all the valuable pieces of furniture had been sold one by one, all the good paintings and all the silver, she had explained it away lightly, by saying that she was expecting a huge sum any day now from the sale of the Northumberland property and that I was not to worry about it. She wanted me to tell her about my progress, the recitals, my adventures at school, to absolutely banish thoughts of anything so trivial as money.

The money was gone, and in six weeks I would be homeless. John Chapman had generously allowed me the six weeks. He had also allowed me to keep the fifteen pounds. Aunt Meg had pressed into my hands before her death. Chapman was forty years old, a bachelor, a large, strapping man with rugged good looks, bronze-red hair and shrewd gray-green eyes. He was most understanding of my plight, most reasonable. He felt certain we could come to some kind of agreement, make some kind of arrangement. His voice had been deep and husky when he told me that, and there had been a gleam of anticipation in his eyes. I knew what kind of arrangement he had in mind, and I refused even to think about it.

Slowly, I strolled past the row of shops that had been standing since the days of Good Queen Bess. Sunlight sparkled on the worn brown cobblestones, and even this far inland there was a salty tang in the air. This small inbred Cornish village had once represented the world to me, a world in which I was an outcast, a pariah because

10

of the circumstances of my birth. But I had since discovered another world, and its horizons were boundless. That was one of the reasons I felt immune to the villagers and their opinion of me. They were to be pitied, not feared.

Jamie Burns stood lounging against the wall of the pub up ahead talking to a husky friend at his side. Jamie was the blacksmith's son. He had been the ringleader of the gang of children who used to taunt me whenever they had the chance. Hands joined, they had danced around me like so many demons, yelling, "Gypsy brat! Gypsy brat! Gypsy brat!" hoping I'd cry, hoping I'd strike out at them, but I had never cried, and after a while I learned not to strike out, either. How many times had I gone home with bruises and cuts, my pretty dresses ruined, my pigtails all undone? How many times had Aunt Meg taken me in her arms and soothed me and told me I was foolish to let it bother me, that I was better than any of them? Those memories were still vivid in my mind, but they no longer caused anguish.

Jamie and his companion watched me approach. Both wore muddy boots, tight trousers, and coarsely woven white shirts. Jamie wore a loose leather jerkin, as well. His dark brown hair was unruly; his face, fox-like, wore a crafty smile. His cold eyes seemed to glitter as I drew nearer. I had seen that look in the eyes of several men, but it had never blazed so openly. I recognized Jamie's companion now, Billy Stone, a heavy lad with blond hair and the face of a wicked choir boy. His blue eyes were alight with the same male hunger, his wide mouth curling at the corners in a lewd grin. Neither of them spoke as I passed, but I could feel their eyes on me as I moved on down the street.

The bell over the door at the pharmacist's shop tinkled, to announce my entrance. The smell of roots and herbs and straw assaulted me as I moved past the rows of colored bottles to the wooden counter in the back of the shop. The pharmacist wasn't in, but Evan Peters, his assistant, came out of the back room. Adjusting the thin black leather apron that covered his shirt and trousers, Evan looked at me and from his expression I could see that he recognized me immediately. His

11

daughter Molly had been one of the circle of tormentors during my childhood. His light hair was beginning to gray at the temples. His face was thin, and the brown eyes were hard. They passed immediate judgment on me as I stopped in front of the counter.

"Good afternoon, Mr. Peters," I said.

"Mary Ellen Lawrence, ain't it? Couldn't be anyone else. You've grown up."

"I'd like some medicine for a cough."

"You've changed," he said, ignoring my request. "You were a tall, skinny kid when you left, all elbows and eyes. Hear you went off to a fancy school in Bath. Hear you been studyin' dancin' with some Eye-talian fellow there."

"That's right. Do you have something for a cough?"

"Heard about your aunt's death. Consumption."

I was silent, trying to keep my face expressionless.

"Head over heels in debt she was, I hear. Stack o' unpaid bills when she died and Graystone Manor going to John Chapman. Hear he's gonna foreclose. Reckon you'll be in a tight spot when he does. Reckon you're in a tight spot already. You got money to pay for the cough medicine?"

I took a pound note out of my pocket and placed it on the counter.

Peters grinned and stepped through the door back of the counter, returning a few moments later with a small brown bottle filled with a thick liquid. Instead of handing it to me, he set it on a shelf behind the counter. Picking up the pound note, he carried it over to his cash box and began to make change. He moved with deliberate slowness, hoping I would show some sign of irritation. But I was determined not to reveal my impatience.

"My Molly done married Bertie Green and moved out ta the farm. Bertie owns it now that his folks passed on. Molly already has two young 'uns."

"That's splendid, Mr. Peters."

He counted the change very slowly. "Molly, she knows her place. She don't put on airs like some. You're a fine young lady now, ain't cha? Speak like a bloody swell, ever so refined. Guess they put a lot of ideas in your head at that fancy school."

"They did indeed," I replied.

12

"Reckon you wantin' to be a dancer comes natural. I remember when you used to run across the moors to spend time with them gypsies that camped in the meadow. Hear you learned all them gypsy dances. I wouldn't let a child of mine go near that scum."

"I'm sure you wouldn't."

"Your aunt believed in lettin' you do whatever you took a mind to. I reckon she felt you had a lot in common with them gypsies, seein' as how you're half-gypsy yourself. You even kinda look like one with those dark blue eyes and that long black hair."

He clearly hoped to insult me. He failed. I was proud of my heritage on both sides. I had been born as the result of a great love, and if that love had been wrong in the eyes of the world, if it had caused a tempestuous scandal and ended in tragedy, I was still proud to know I was the product of it. It hadn't always been that way, of course. As a child I had been terribly ashamed, bitter even, but I had grown up.

"We run them gypsies off a couple o' years ago," Peters continued. "Sly, thievin' bunch, the lot of 'em. Hear tell they're comin' back for th' fair in Claymoor. If they got any sense, they won't come around *here* no more."

Peters finally set the medicine on the counter before me. Picking up the bottle, I slipped it into the pocket of my dress along with the change.

"I hear that your aunt's maid is stayin' on with you. Fanny. I suppose the cough medicine is for her. You certainly look healthy enough."

"Fanny is staying with me, yes."

"Noble of 'er, seein' as how she ain't been paid in over a year, seein' as how you'll both be out in th' cold soon as Chapman forecloses. What you plannin' on doin'?"

I looked at him with cool politeness and smiled.

"That, Mr. Peters, is none of your bloody business."

Turning, I started toward the door before he could detain me any longer. His comments had irritated me far more than I cared to admit. I hadn't been to the village even once during the past three years, avoiding it whenever I returned to Graystone Manor for holidays. As I left the shop I vowed I would never come again.

Any provisions we might need, Fanny could come for, as long as the fifteen pounds held out. I wouldn't have come today had she not desperately needed the medicine. I no longer cared what any of these people thought about me, but there was no reason to expose myself deliberately to the kind of mentality Peters had displayed just now.

My skirt rustled over my petticoats as I moved back down the street toward the old stone church and the road that led away from the village. Jamie and Billy were no longer in sight, and I was relieved. No doubt I could have put them in their place with a few well-chosen words, but after the encounter with Evan Peters I didn't want to speak to anyone. I merely wanted to be left alone. These people led such barren lives, their world confined to a few square miles. How could I ever have let their opinion of me matter?

Passing the bakery shop, the livery stable, the tiny inn with its mortar-and-timber-facade and thick glass windowpanes, I was conscious only of the grief that still surged inside me. Aunt Meg had begged me not to mourn, but I did, I couldn't help it. I had stayed in my room for two days after the funeral, crying quietly, refusing to eat, refusing to answer Fanny's knocks on the door, and finally I had found the strength to face reality, to face the loss and accept it. I would be strong as she had taught me to be, and I would try to remember her with a smile, but the grief would always be a part of me.

Passing the old graystone church at the edge of the village, I paused to look at the tall spire of tarnished copper. Tall oak trees grew on the right, their heavy boughs shading the toppling marble tombstones in the cemetery behind the low graystone wall. Aunt Meg was buried beside her parents in Claymoor, but my mother was here, her grave unmarked. My grandparents had refused to let mother be buried in the family plot in Claymoor. On impulse I pushed open the gate in the wall and moved down the uneven flagstone walks. It was dim here, everything in shadow, and the air was cool. The cemetery hadn't been kept up at all. Many of the stones had fallen over; the damp marble was green with moss. I finally located the unmarked grave near the

14

back wall. It was covered with grass, with acorns scattered all around.

My mother had been only a year older than I am now when she died. The Lawrences had been the most prominent family in the district, Graystone Manor a fine mansion. My grandfather had owned vast properties, and he had been proud of his aristocratic blood, his connections with royalty, however tenuous they might have been. His two daughters had been a disappointment, for naturally he had wanted a son to carry on the line. The oldest, Meg, a serious, bookish girl, seemed destined for spinsterhood, but he hoped to make an important match for Alicia—wild, impetuous Alicia who was so very beautiful, so willful, so gay. While Meg read her books or sat lost in daydreams, Alicia had suitors by the score, but she wanted none of them. They were far too tame.

Alicia, my mother, preferred to race across the moors on her stallion, sometimes not returning until very late at night. When my grandfather learned that she was spending her time at the gypsy camp, he was outraged and forbade her to return. Alicia paid no heed to him, for she was passionately in love with a man whose fiery spirit matched her own, and nothing was going to keep her from him. With his powerful connections, my grandfather was able to have the gypsies banished from the area. When they left, my mother left with them, riding off in one of the brightly painted caravans with her Ramon.

My mother had done a watercolor of her lover, a watercolor which Meg had carefully preserved all these years. Ramon was tall and dark and dashing, his black locks unruly, his brown eyes ablaze with savage fires. Moody, mercurial, frequently violent, he had loved his aristocratic mistress with a fierce, possessive love that caused him to seethe with jealousy if another man so much as looked at her. One night, in Kent, Ramon's brother Juan had displayed too much interest in the lovely blonde who shared his brother's caravan. A violent quarrel ensued. Knife blades flashed in the firelight. Juan was killed. Ramon died two days later of wounds his brother had inflicted. The gypsies blamed Alicia for turning brother against brother and causing the deaths.

15

She was thrown out of the camp. She was five months pregnant at the time.

She arrived in Cornwall two weeks later, pale, penniless, broken with grief. Her father refused to take her in. He forbade his wife and daughter to have anything to do with the shameless creature who had given up all right to be called a Lawrence. But Meg slipped out of the house and went after her sister. She gave Alicia all of the money she had carefully hoarded, enough money to allow the girl to take a small cottage and hire a midwife as her time drew near. Meg continued to defy her father, slipping off to visit her sister, trying to give her comfort, trying to console her in her grief.

Three and a half months later, I was born. It was a difficult birth, taking over thirty hours, and serious complications set in afterwards. My mother had lost all will to live, and she died four days after I was born. She was buried here in this unmarked grave, and I was placed in an orphanage, for my grandfather adamantly refused to take a gypsy's bastard into his home. He died of a heart attack six years later, just days after my grandmother succumbed to lung fever, and it was only then that Meg was able to take me out of the orphanage. It was an unconventional thing to do, of course, and the county was scandalized. My aunt didn't care that the gentry no longer called, that the villagers held her in contempt. Still unmarried, heiress to all her father's estate, she devoted herself to me, to doing all she could to compensate for those first six years.

A gentle breeze ruffled through the oak leaves overhead. Pale shadows played over the grave of Alicia Lawrence. Once, long ago, I had hated her, had blamed her for those six years spent in the bleak gray orphanage, for the cruelty and the taunts of the village children after I came to live at Graystone Manor, but I understood her now, and I felt only sadness. She had loved unwisely, perhaps, but she had loved with all her heart, and I knew it would be that way with me, too. A faded watercolor and an unmarked grave were all that remained of my parents, but their blood was alive inside me, and after years of hurt and bitter resentment I had learned to be proud of it.

16

II

Closing the cemetery gate behind me, I walked on down the road leading out of the village, and soon there was nothing on either side of me but wide open land. To the west the land extended for several acres to the edge of the cliffs that plunged down sharply to the waters below, and on the east, beyond the low graystone wall, there were flat fields spotted with towering haystacks. The road curved inland, disappearing below a slope, appearing again atop the slope beyond. I could see a small open carriage far away, heading in my direction, a tiny black toy in the distance, horse and driver barely visible. The sky stretched overhead a luminous gray-white barely stained with blue. The air smelled of salt and sea. I could hear the waves crashing against the rocks below the cliffs, and seagulls crying out as they dipped and soared. After Bath with its elegant Georgian buildings and narrow streets and formal gardens, Cornwall seemed like a foreign country, bleak, brooding, with a stark, primeval beauty all its own.

Despite the grief so heavy inside me, I responded to the land and its harsh beauty. I longed to clamber over the rocks below, again, and feel the sea mist stinging my cheeks, as the waves slammed against ancient stone and sprayed geysers of water into the air. I longed to rush across the moors once more with the wind tearing my hair, to feel again that wild, untamed feeling that had possessed me when I used to race to meet the gypsies and dance the savage, sensual dances they had taught

17

me. Three years at the academy and ballet school had given me polish and poise, but behind the demure, well-bred facade the lonely, restless spirit remained the same. I could never be like the other girls at school, no matter how much I tried. Perhaps that was why dancing meant so much. In dance I could express all those surging emotions. Even in the carefully stylized steps of ballet, I felt a release.

Walking slowly down the road, surrounded by country air and sunlight, I thought of Madame Olga and the ambition she had inspired in me. The once renowned Russian ballerina had come to the academy to give lectures on the dance. She was ancient, a tiny woman with wrinkled skin and enormous black eyes that seemed to burn. Her hair was sleeked back, fastened in a tight bun on the back of her neck, and she was swathed in sables. She wore a gigantic emerald on one finger of her scrawny hand, the huge stone glittering with greenish-blue fires. A quarter of a century before, she had been the toast of Europe, and one heard that kings had vied for her favors, that the Czar had given her a fortune in jewels, that an English duke had committed suicide when she refused to return his affections.

I was dazzled, and so nervous I could hardly contain myself when, after the lectures, she watched us go through our paces. She scowled disdainfully all the while, making acid comments to poor Miss Brown, who had worked so hard to get us into shape. Later on, though, Madame Olga admitted that at least one of us showed promise. "The little girl with the raven hair and dark blue eyes, the one with the high cheekbones, she's not so bad," Madame confided, and when Miss Brown relayed the comment to me I was ecstatic. I wrote to my aunt at once, begging to be allowed to leave the academy and rush off to London.

At the time, I was only sixteen, and Aunt Meg was naturally too sensible to allow any such rash action. I must finish my training at the academy first, she informed me. I could continue my dancing classes there, along with all my other studies, and if when I graduated I still wanted to go to London, well, we would see about it. I studied harder than ever, learning everything Miss

Brown could teach me. I also took private lessons from a retired Italian ballet master who had a shabby studio in Bath near the academy. Giovanni, who had known Madame Olga during her heyday, wrote to her about me, recommending me in the highest terms, just this month. And she had written back, agreeing to take me on as a student in September.

I was unbelievably happy. Madame Olga was the best teacher in all England. She took only a select number of students each year, and after studying with her almost all of them were placed in important companies. I was going to be one of those students. I was going to be a famous ballerina as Madame Olga had been. I would become the toast of Europe and drink champagne, and men would fall in love with me. The future was aglow with glorious possibilities, and life seemed magical. I seemed to walk on air, so great was my elation, and then I received the urgent message from Doctor Reed. I arrived back in Cornwall only hours before Aunt Meg passed away.

A light gust of wind caused my skirt to flap and sent my long hair fluttering. My magical future had vanished in one great swoop, and I was faced with stark reality. Things couldn't have been worse, yet for some reason I refused to worry. I was strong. I would survive. Somehow or other. I had six more weeks before Chapman would foreclose and all Aunt Meg's goods would be sold at auction. Stubbornly, I clung to the conviction that something would happen during those weeks. What I felt couldn't be defined as optimism. It was, rather, a steely refusal to give up. I wasn't ready to admit defeat, not yet.

I suddenly had the feeling I was being watched as I passed one of the haystacks. I paused, vaguely disturbed, for the sensation was powerful, impossible to mistake. I could almost feel the eyes boring into my back. Another gust of wind lifted my skirts. I turned. Jamie Burns and Billy Stone were moving away from the haystack, both grinning wide grins. Jamie waved and leaped over the low stone wall. Billy called my name. I watched them saunter toward me, and my heart skipped several beats. They had known I would be coming this way. They had come ahead of me, had hidden themselves behind the haystack. Every instinct told me to flee, to run down the road as fast as I could, but I knew that would be pointless. They would overtake me in moments. I must be very, very calm. That was my only hope. They sauntered across the road, arrogant in their youth and superior strength.

"Well, well, well," Jamie drawled. "What 'ave we 'ere?"

"Look at 'er," Billy said. "Ain't she somethin'? Never seen such a ripe 'un in all my born days."

I stood very still, trying to control my breathing, telling myself I mustn't panic. My pulses were leaping, and my knees seemed to go weak. I held myself erect through sheer willpower and stared at them with my chin held high, eyes cool and haughty.

"Always wanted to 'ave me a gypsy wench," Billy remarked. "I 'ear they're real special, all fire an' fight. Reckon I'll find out this very afternoon."

Jamie's cold gray eyes glittered. His lips twisted into a leer. Shoving a lock of unruly brown hair from his brow, he stepped nearer. There was hatred in his eyes, hatred and lust that seemed to smoulder. Billy came up beside him, slinging a powerful arm around his friend's shoulders. My heart was pounding. My throat felt dry. Waves of panic threatened to sweep over me. I held them back, willing myself not to show the least sign of fear.

"What'd they teach ya in that swell school you been to, Mary Ellen?" Jamie asked.

"They taught me not to be intimidated by oafs like you."

My voice was surprisingly calm. Another gust of wind swept across the flat, open land. My skirts billowed. My hair blew across my cheek. I pushed it back, holding myself straight and distant.

"I reckon they musta fed you real good at that school, Mary Ellen," Jamie said. "You're all growed up." He nodded. "Yeah, you're all growed up. Real ripe an' juicy."

The panic was very near the surface now, and I was trembling inside. I felt so weak, so vulnerable. They

20

were both as strong as oxen, hard with muscle, and I would be powerless against them. Rape was jolly sport for youths like these, any nubile lass their natural prey. How many maidens had they forcibly deflowered? Like animals bursting with energy and appetite, they thought of nothing but release. Right and wrong failed to exist for them. It would be useless to plead, useless to fight.

"Soon as I saw you prancin' down th' street so 'igh an' mighty, I knew what I was gonna do," Jamie snarled.

He moved another step nearer, eyes glittering, his face tight, a mask of hostility. He seemed to seethe with it. I drew back, my composure slipping fast. My heart was beating louder and louder, so loud I felt sure they both could hear. I moved back another step, almost stumbling. Billy chuckled and shoved Jamie aside with rough amiability.

"You're scarin' 'er," he said. "I keep tellin' ya, Jamie, you gotta gentle 'em a little, gotta feel 'em up and get 'em in th' mood. 'Ere, I'll show ya 'ow it's done."

"Don't touch me," I said hoarsely.

Billy shook his head. Dark blond waves spilled over his brow, and the almost-pretty face seemed to glow with pleasure. The blue eyes were merry and lascivious, and he smiled a tender, taunting smile.

"Come on now, wench," he said. His voice was husky and seductive. "Don'tcha wanna be friendly? Me an' Jamie, we're a couple o' swell fellows, really know 'ow to make a wench 'appy. Ask Daisy Clark. Ask Mollie Jeffers. Ask any uv th' girls. They're all just pantin' to 'ave us come a-courtin'."

That taunting smile widened, pink lips curling up at both corners, and the eyes were aglow with anticipation. As he seized my arms and pulled me toward him, everything seemed to whirl in a blazing haze of fear and fury. I struggled violently, trying to pull away, and he laughed a rumbling laugh and held my arms even tighter, his fingers biting into my flesh. I cried out and kicked him, slamming my toe against his shin with all the force I could muster. There was a mighty yell, but it wasn't Billy. It was Jamie. Jamie yelled, and Billy's eyes widened in dismay.

Neither of us had heard the horse and carriage, that

21

carriage that had seemed so tiny when I had seen it in the distance. It was standing but a few yards away, and Jamie was struggling with a man in a dark blue suit. They seemed to be hugging each other, rocking to and fro, and then they broke apart and Jamie staggered backwards and shook his head as though to clear it. Then he charged at the stranger like an enraged bull. The stranger stepped to one side and, smiling a tight smile, stuck his foot out to send Jamie crashing to the ground with a terrible thud.

Billy was still dismayed, unable to believe what he saw. It had happened in a matter of seconds, and he was still gripping my arms. His face tightened now, and his eyes flashed with rage. He gave me a forceful shove that sent me reeling backwards. I stumbled and fell, landing with shattering impact that knocked the breath out of me. My head began to spin, and black wings seemed to flutter all around, closing in on me, blocking out the light. Several moments passed before I was aware once again of the stomping, shuffling, thudding noises around me. Palms flat on the ground, I managed to sit up. Everything was shimmering, out of focus, and my head was still spinning.

Jamie was on the ground on the other side of the road, groaning, and Billy and the stranger stood a few feet apart, the stranger cool and apparently unconcerned, Billy panting, his chest heaving. A moment passed and then Billy hurled himself toward the stranger and swung his arm in a wide arc, his fist flying toward the stranger's jaw. The stranger smiled and made a smooth half turn, and as the fist flew past his shoulder he seized Billy's wrist in midair and gave it a wicked twist, swinging Billy around in front of him and thrusting his arm up between his shoulder blades.

Billy yelled in anguish, and the stranger thrust his arm up even higher and gave a mighty push. Billy stumbled forward, tottering, and finally fell to his knees. Jamie moaned and climbed to his feet, rubbing his jaw, staring at the stranger with glazed eyes. The stranger stood there with his fists resting lightly on his thighs, a half smile on his lips. He waited, daring Jamie to make an aggressive move. Jamie shook his head and

22

staggered back a few steps, clearly unsure of himself, and then he turned and moved hurriedly back down the road toward the village. Scrambling to his feet, Billy rushed after his friend. The man in the dark blue suit smiled, watching them depart. They were almost out of sight before he finally turned his attention to me.

He stepped across the road, reached down, and took my hand to help me to my feet. He was still cool and unconcerned, showing not the least sign of exertion. There was a glint of amusement in those dark brown eyes. Awry half smile played on his lips.

"Brence Stephens," he said. "At your service."

And that was the beginning.

III

He was very tall, with the lean, muscular build of an athlete, all supple grace and strength. His navy blue suit was superbly tailored, the trousers snug, the jacket emphasizing broad shoulders and a slender waist. He wore a maroon and white striped waistcoat, his maroon silk stock neat, unruffled by the fight. His black knee boots were highly glossed. He had a deep tan, and his hair was jet black, rich and abundant. There was a tautness about his cheekbones, the skin stretched tight. His mouth was wide, the lower lip full and smooth and shell pink, undeniably sensual.

"Are you all right?" he inquired.

I nodded, brushing dust from my skirt.

"Lucky I happened along when I did," he said.

His voice was deep and melodious with an appealing huskiness. Despite his gentleness with me, I sensed that he was accustomed to giving orders, accustomed to having them obeyed. There was a certain hardness about him that suggested a military background. He had clearly enjoyed the fight that had sent both strapping youths running with little or no effort on his part, yet he was unquestionably well bred. He would be as much at ease in an elegant drawing room as on a raging battlefield, always in command of the situation. He was without question the handsomest man I had ever seen, that strong virile beauty strangely augmented by the patina of hardness.

"I should have taken my horsewhip to those two,"

he remarked. "Ruffians like that shouldn't be allowed to roam free."

Having regained my composure, I pushed a lock of hair from my cheek and looked at Brence Stephens. The unpleasant encounter with Jamie and Billy might never have happened.

"No harm was done, Mr. Stephens."

He lifted one smooth, finely arched brow, registering surprise at my accent. Obviously, he'd taken me for some country wench, and my cultivated voice made him look at me with new interest. A familiar assessment glowed in his eyes; he found me intriguing, and he found me desirable, too. That was quite plain.

"I must say, you seem terribly calm about the whole thing," he said. "Most young women would be hysterical."

"I find hysterics quite unattractive."

"I was rather hoping you'd throw yourself into my arms, sobbing uncontrollably."

"Indeed?"

"Then I'd be able to comfort you. I'd enjoy that."

He spoke lightly, teasing with a smile on his lips, and it was impossible to take offense, yet I was on guard just the same. I had never met a man so utterly attractive. His features might have been chiseled by a master sculptor. He might have materialized from some school-girl's dream, and that made me uneasy. Feeling terribly young, terribly inexperienced, and disoriented by my reaction to him, I sought refuge in a cool, haughty manner that he seemed to find amusing.

"I'm at a disadvantage," he said. "You know my name. I don't know yours."

"I'm Mary Ellen Lawrence."

"Mary Ellen," he said.

He made it sound like music. He looked at me with dark brown eyes that seemed so wise, so knowing, and my disorientation grew. My cool manner didn't deceive him at all. I sensed that he knew exactly what I was feeling and why, even if I was unsure about it myself. Why should I have this pleasurable glow inside and this tremulous fear, both at the same time? I wanted to reach up and touch that full pink mouth with my fingertips, but I wanted to run away, too, before it was too late.

"I'll drive you back to the village," he said.

"I don't live in the village."

"No? Where do you live?"

"Graystone Manor," I replied.

"Graystone Manor? I'm afraid I don't know the place. This is my first visit to Cornwall, you see. I'm staying with my cousin, Lady Andover. She and her husband live in the next county. Perhaps you know them?"

"I know of them."

"I wanted to see something of the countryside. That's why I'm so far afield. Beth, Lady Andover, spends every afternoon playing cards with her cronies, and Freddie seems to devote twenty-four hours a day to his gun collection. I wanted to get out, get some fresh air. I borrowed this rig. It's lucky for you I did."

"I—I suppose I should thank you."

"You should," he agreed. "It isn't really necessary, though. I love a good fight. Not that those two ruffians offered a real challenge."

"You handled yourself extremely well."

"I've had plenty of practice. In India."

"You're a soldier?"

"I was. That's behind me now."

A slight frown creased his brow, and his lips lifted at one corner in a show of distaste. Military life had obviously palled for him. I sensed a certain restlessness in him and a steely determination to succeed which fascinated me. I also had a vague, disturbing feeling that was almost like a premonition of danger. It was as though I had come face to face with my fate, and my instincts were warning me to flee.

"I—I'd better get back," I said.

"I'll drive you."

"That isn't necessary. I'll walk."

"You'll ride," he told me.

His voice was pleasant, yet his tone made it clear that he would brook no argument. Touching my elbow, he led me over to the carriage and helped me up onto the upholstered seat. He swung up beside me with athletic

27

grace. As he gathered up the reins, I was acutely aware of his nearness. The carriage was a light open rig, designed for intimacy, the seat quite small. I could smell the clean male smell of him—it was heady and rather upsetting.

"A mile or so back I passed a large gray house surrounded by overgrown gardens," he said. "Is that Graystone Manor?"

I nodded. Brence Stephens clicked the reins and turned the carriage around, his strong, capable hands applying just the right amount of pressure on the reins. In moments we were heading back down the road. The horse moved at a leisurely pace, its glossy coat gleaming dark, tail and mane rippling like silk. Seagulls circled against the pearl-gray sky, crying their shrill cries, and dazzling sunlight bathed the open land. I could see the ocean beyond the edge of the cliffs, a surging blue-gray expanse that melted into a misty steel and gold horizon.

Neither of us spoke. The man beside me seemed oblivious of my presence. Lost in thought, he might have been alone in the carriage. I studied his profile, noticing the stern set of his jaw, the full curve of his mouth. His cheeks were lean, with faint hollows beneath those taut cheekbones, and his rich black hair made a striking contrast with his evenly tanned complexion. He would have acquired that tan in India, I thought. I had the feeling that he had just recently returned to England.

Several moments passed in silence broken only by the steady clop of horse hooves on the road and the cry of the gulls. Brence Stephens finally sighed and gazed at the open land with critical eyes.

"Interesting place," he remarked.

"You don't like Cornwall?"

"I've been here a week, and I've rarely been so bored. There's not all that much to do, and Beth and Freddie aren't the most stimulating company. I felt obligated to visit, for Beth's my only living relative, and she begged me to come. I had some time on my hands, so—here I am."

"You said you're no longer with the military."

28

"I resigned my commission. Military life can be extremely limiting. One can go just so far, climb just so high. I'm going into the diplomatic service. It was arranged by . . . uh . . . a friend of mine before I left India. In a few weeks I'll be leaving for Germany as aide to the English ambassador of a tiny state you've probably never heard of. It's an insignificant post, but it's a beginning."

"I'm sure you'll go far."

"I intend to," he said firmly.

I suspected that the "friend" who had arranged his post was of the feminine gender. Probably the wife of some official, I thought, an older woman with a pouting mouth and worldly eyes who sought a return to youth in the arms of younger men. A woman like that would find Brence Stephens impossible to resist, and I suspected that he would have no qualms about using his male allure to achieve his own ends.

"I suppose you're engaged to some local squire," he said.

I shook my head. He lifted an eyebrow in surprise.

"No? I should have thought you'd have been long since spoken for. There must be suitors by the score."

"There are no suitors, Mr. Stephens."

"I find that hard to believe."

"I'm sure Lady Andover will be able to explain things to you. Once, long ago, she was a—a friend of my aunt's."

"Ah," he said, "so there's a mystery."

"There is no mystery," I replied.

He didn't pursue the matter, but I could tell that he was intrigued. Undoubtedly, he would ask his cousin about me and, undoubtedly, she would tell him that I was the bastard daughter of an aristocrat and her gypsy lover. Lady Andover knew all about me, and by this evening Brence Stephens would, too. Some of the old resentment returned, but I banished it immediately.

The horse followed a curve in the road. In the distance I could see the towering oak trees and the large graystone house surrounded by shabby gardens wild with a riot of flowers. Directly behind the house the moors began, ground covered with grayish-brown grass faintly touched with green, gradually rising in a series of small hills. The terrain was ancient, windswept, savagely beautiful. Beyond those barren hills there were more moors leading to the grove where the gypsies used to camp.

For a moment, thinking about the camp, I forgot the man beside me. I could see the little girl with pigtails rushing across the moors. I could see the painted caravans, the campfires that blossomed among the trees as twilight fell, and I could see those dark, exotic men and women who were fierce and volatile but so very kind to me, taking me in, making me a part of that intimate, tempestuous family. But that was all in the past. I was grown now. Never again would I be a part of that vibrant world.

"You love this land, don't you?" Brence Stephens said.

"It's part of me," I replied.

"You must teach me to love it. My cousin tells me I must see Land's End. It's not far from here, I understand."

"A mile or so," I said.

He tugged on the reins, stopping the horse in front of the gate set in the low gray wall that surrounded the property. The gardens were ablaze with color, and the towering oak trees cast long, heavy shadows over the road; the house was only partially visible behind the low hanging limbs. Brence Stephens climbed out of the carriage with indolent grace and reached up to help me alight, his hands encircling my waist. His fingers tightened, lifting me, drawing me toward him. When he set me on my feet, he maintained his hold for several seconds, peering into my eyes. His own dark eyes were inscrutable.

"I'd like to see you again," he said.

"I—I don't think that would be wise."

"No?"

He let go of my waist. I felt relief and disappointment at the same time. He continued to look into my eyes, and again I had a desire to reach up and touch those full, finely carved lips. The premonition I had felt earlier returned, even stronger this time. Every instinct told me that this man was a threat to me, and somehow that made him all the more alluring.

"You're afraid," he said. "It's there in your eyes."

"You're imagining things, Mr. Stephens."

"There's loneliness, too, and sadness."

"I must go inside."

"Don't be afraid, Mary Ellen."

His voice was gentle and persuasive, husky, like music. It was beautiful, and he was beautiful, too, aglow with rugged vitality. Disturbing new emotions blossomed inside me, unfolding like petals, and I tried to hold them back. I didn't want to feel them. I didn't want to step over that invisible threshold that beckoned. I drew back, wishing he would leave, wishing I had never gone to the village. His eyes held mine, compelling me to accept those things I tried desperately to deny.

"I'll call on you tomorrow," he said.

"You mustn't come here."

"Then I'll meet you. Tomorrow afternoon, at two o'clock. I'll be at Land's End. You'll come."

"No."

"You'll come," he promised.

He left then, climbing into the carriage without another word, without so much as a backward glance. I stood by the gate, watching him drive away. I stood there long after the carriage had disappeared from sight. Something had happened to me, something irrevocable. I thought of my mother and her Ramon, and for the first time I fully understood what had happened to her so many years ago and why she had been willing to sacrifice all for love.

IV

I did not go to Land's End the next afternoon. I wanted to. With all my heart, I wanted to see Brence Stephens again, but I knew that it would be a mistake, that it could lead to nothing. He probably hadn't shown up himself, I reasoned. After he talked with his cousin and learned of my background, he had probably shrugged his shoulders and put me out of his mind. I was trying to put him out of mine. It wasn't easy. I was strangely discontented in a way I had never been before.

I forced Fanny to take her medicine and to stay in bed while I did the necessary housework. I tried to read George Sand's new novel, but it was all about love and, much as I admired her work, I found the emotional passages much too disturbing. Two days passed, and on the morning of the third day after the encounter on the road, John Chapman came to see me. Fanny showed him into the drawing room and creaked slowly up to my bedroom to announce his presence.

"I'll be down shortly," I told her. "Offer him a glass of sherry."

Fanny nodded, coughed, and left the room. Putting away my book, I removed the blue cotton dress I was wearing, folded it up and set it aside, in no hurry to join my guest. He could wait. It would be good for him. John Chapman wasn't used to waiting. Wearing only my petticoat, I sat down at the dressing table and began to brush my hair. When I was finished, I lingered in front of the mirror for a moment, examining myself with critical eyes.

I wished that I were beautiful, but that I would never be. Beauty meant delicate features and clear blue eyes and soft blond curls. My hair was the color of a raven's wing, tumbling to my shoulders in dark waves that gleamed with blue-black highlights. My eyes were a satisfying deep sapphire blue, but my cheekbones were too high, my mouth too full. The girls at the academy had called me "The Spaniard," teasing me about my rich coloring. They had teased me about my figure, too. It wasn't proper for a respectable young woman to have such a slender waist, such voluptuous curves.

The dress I slipped into showed off those curves to advantage. It was a pale violet silk printed with tiny dark blue and pink flowers. Aunt Meg had delighted in buying me clothes, and I possessed an extensive wardrobe, with dresses far more sophisticated than those ordinarily worn by girls my age. The violet silk had short puffed sleeves, and the low-cut bodice emphasized my bosom. It was tight at the waist, and the long skirt was very full.

Stepping back from the mirror, I turned this way and that, studying the effect of the dress. I was pleased with what I saw. I might not be a demure English beauty, but I had something that men seemed to find much more intriguing than mere beauty. Brence Stephens had been aware of it immediately, and John Chapman was aware of it, too, acutely aware. This intangible quality was as yet untested, but I sensed that it was a valuable asset, a weapon to be discreetly employed in the struggles ahead.

I had never been concerned about my looks the whole time I was growing up. I had thought only of dancing, working for hours on end, consumed by an ambition that left room for nothing else. A change had taken place in me, and with it had come a new wisdom, something I knew must be instinctive with every woman. I didn't welcome it. I fervently wished I could return to being an innocent schoolgirl, but I had grown up. Aunt Meg's death had awakened me to the grim realities of life, and the meeting with Brence Stephens had awakened something else, something I had sensed fleetingly in the past but never fully realized until I looked into those dark, knowing brown eyes.

I was a bit nervous as I started downstairs to the drawing room, for I was going to have to handle John Chapman very carefully. He had agreed to give me six weeks before turning me out, and I needed that time. I had to make some kind of plans for the future. I had no idea what I would do, but perhaps I would find some solution during the time allotted me. Until now I had been too grieved by Aunt Meg's death to give much thought to what was going to happen to me.

Pausing at the foot of the stairs, I braced myself for the meeting with Chapman. I was fully aware of the kind of "arrangement" he wanted to make with me, even though he had yet to express it in words. I had no intention of agreeing to it, of course, but I didn't want to offend him. Not yet. He could turn me out tomorrow if he chose to, and if I annoyed him, he wouldn't hesitate to do just that.

John Chapman had come to Cornwall six or seven years before, new-rich, self-educated, an upstart who seemed intent on taking over the whole county. Not only did he own tin mines, but he had been buying property right and left, ruthless in his quest for power. The villagers detested him, but those not actually in debt to him depended on their jobs at the mines in order to survive. The gentry looked down on him, but all felt obligated to give him at least a token acceptance. None dared snub him outright.

He was very rich, and he was powerful, by far the most powerful man in this part of Cornwall. He had drive and determination and a complete lack of scruples. Men like Chapman were taking over England. Wealth was supplanting lineage as the symbol of authority, and blue blood didn't mean nearly as much as money in the bank. The old order was knuckling under, unable to withstand the force and vigor of the new breed.

Chapman stood up as I entered the drawing room. Setting his empty sherry glass aside, he looked at me with gray-green eyes that took in every detail of my appearance.

"Good morning, Mr. Chapman," I said. "How kind of you to call."

"I was passing by, thought I'd stop and see how you're getting along."

He still studied me, as though I were a piece of property he considered buying. He was a large, sturdily built man, well over six feet tall, all hard muscle. Forty-two years old, still unmarried, he had red-bronze hair and broad, rugged features. The jaw was strong, the mouth full but hard. Certain women would find him quite attractive, for he had incredible presence, exuding vitality and an aura of brute strength. He was actually rather striking in his polished brown knee boots, snug tan breeches, and dark pinkish-tan corduroy jacket, a strong, ruthless figure who made the room seem much smaller.

"You're looking lovely."

"You're being gallant, Mr. Chapman."

"I'm being frank. You're a lovely girl, Mary Ellen."

I lowered my lashes demurely, a faint blush coloring my cheeks. I was acting the part to perfection.

"I hear you had a little trouble at the village the other day. I understand a couple of the village boys tried to be familiar."

"It was nothing."

"You shouldn't go out without a chaperone, you know."

"Indeed?"

"A lovely girl like you—it isn't safe."

"I can take care of myself, Mr. Chapman."

"If you want to go out, let me know. I'll be happy to come by for you in my carriage. You need to get out, get some fresh air. I'd be glad to take you for a drive any time, any time at all."

"I wouldn't want to put you to any trouble, Mr. Chapman."

"Trouble? It would be a pleasure."

His lips were slightly parted and his eyes were dark with male hunger. He looked as though he wanted to crush me in his arms, as though it took great effort to restrain himself. It gave me a curious sense of power, but I was apprehensive, too. This was all so new to me,

36

and I felt ill-equipped to play the games I knew I would have to play.

"Have you thought any more about the future?" he inquired.

"I—there hasn't been much time."

"Of course not. Your aunt's death was a great blow."

"Fanny has had a letter from her sister in Devon. She wants Fanny to come live with her. Fanny said I could go with her. Perhaps I could find some kind of employment in Devon. I could teach dancing, or perhaps I could be a governess."

"Ridiculous for a girl who looks like you to worry about such things. You have youth, beauty, charm—" He hesitated, a husky catch in his voice. "The future shouldn't concern you at all."

"I have no money," I said.

"That needn't bother you."

"In just a few weeks I'll have no home."

"That needn't bother you, either."

"But—"

"I don't want you to worry, Mary Ellen."

Drawing his brows together into a stern line, he moved nearer. He was so very large. I was in his power, he thought, and that pleased him, gave him a feeling of superiority. I took a step backwards, my eyes apprehensive. He liked that. He smiled a satisfied smile, male, masterful, savoring his power over the weak female.

"I think you know what I'm suggesting," he said.

"I—I think so."

He took my hand and drew me toward him. Tilting my head back slightly, I looked up into those eyes that were so hungry. I longed to draw back and slam my hand across his face, to slap that smug, arrogant half smile off his mouth, but I didn't. I lowered my lashes again, the demure maiden I knew instinctively he wanted me to be.

His fingers tightened over mine. "I'm prepared to be very generous, Mary Ellen."

"It—it's all so confusing."

It was the perfect thing to say. Chapman nodded, releasing my hand. He stepped back, tugging at the lapels of his jacket, finally resting his hands at his sides. I moved over to the window and gazed out at the pale blue sky, feeling him behind me, feeling his eyes taking in my profile, the curve of my throat, the line of bare shoulder. I touched the faded brocade drapery, holding it back a little, letting the sunlight caress me. After a moment I turned and looked at him, a resigned look in my eyes.

"I'll consider what you've said, Mr. Chapman."

"Good."

"I'll need time."

"Of course. I said I'd give you six weeks."

"You're very . . . considerate."

He smiled. He felt very good now, very sure of himself.

"I won't press you, Mary Ellen. I realize you've had a great blow, losing your aunt, learning the true state of her finances. You must feel as though the bottom's dropped out of your world."

I nodded, my lower lip trembling.

"I think you'll find our . . . uh . . . arrangement quite satisfactory, Mary Ellen."

With that, he smiled again and said he must be off now to his business. I accompanied him to the front door and nodded politely as he stepped outside. Chapman took my hand and lifted it to his lips and kissed my palm for a long, lingering moment, and I tried not to cringe. Releasing my hand, he gave me a final, triumphant smile and strode confidently toward the gate. As I watched him climb into his carriage and drive away, I wondered if all men were as easy to manipulate. Chapman thought he had won, but the victory was mine. I wished I could feel better about it.

V

I had no destination in mind. I simply had to move, to be out, alone with my thoughts. As I walked, the breeze caught and toyed with the skirt of my pale violet silk dress. It wasn't a sensible garment to wear for taking a walk, but I had been too upset to bother changing. The encounter with Chapman had been disturbing even though I had won the time I needed. Afterwards, anger had set in, anger at myself for playing the game, anger at him for assuming he could do with me as he pleased. After the anger came sadness, and for the past hour I had been fighting tears.

Life was so unfair, so very unfair. I had been on the brink of realizing all my dreams when Madame Olga had accepted me as a student. And then everything had vanished with Aunt Meg's death. Darling Aunt Meg. How she had sacrificed for me. How she had loved me. No, no, I mustn't allow myself to think of her. I couldn't, not yet. I had come to terms with my grief, and now I must come to terms with reality. I had to banish every trace of self-pity. That would only hinder me. I was going to do more than survive; I was going to cling stubbornly to my dream of success. Somehow, I would make it materialize for me.

Skirt whipping, hair tousled, I walked across the dusty fields that ran to the edge of the cliffs, thinking about the immediate future and trying to formulate some plan. Fanny wanted me to go to Devon with her, and at the moment that seemed to be the only solution. I certainly couldn't hope to find any kind of employment here in Cornwall, and any kind of arrangement like that Chapman had in mind was out of the question.

There were many wealthy families in Devon. Perhaps I could indeed become a governess, temporarily, at least until I saved enough money to finance classes with Madame Olga. I would keep up my exercises, my practice, keep my body in shape. Somehow I would get to London, and if it took an extra year or two, I would simply have to wait. But I wouldn't give up, wouldn't even acknowledge the possibility of defeat.

I walked across the fields until I reached the edge of the cliffs, and then I followed the line of cliffs, stepping over small rocks. The land began to slope downward, the waves were closer, and I saw Land's End ahead. I had not consciously planned to come this way, but now it seemed right. When I reached the rocky stretch that jutted out into the water like a giant brown paw, I walked to the farthest point and sat down on one of the boulders.

Shelves of jagged brown rock surrounded the area on three sides, spreading fan-like into the water below. I watched the waves splattering, plumes of misty spray catching the sunlight. The gulls swooped lower, investigating, hoping I might have brought food. There was a small outcropping of rock in the water directly ahead, and beyond that nothing but ocean, stretching endlessly, merging into a mist-shrouded horizon. This was the westernmost tip of England, and across the ocean was America, hundreds and hundreds of miles away.

Gazing toward that blurry violet line where sky melted into sea, I wondered if I would ever see America. It was vast and rugged, I had read, with huge mountains and great deserts where red Indians still roamed wild. There were large cities, as well, and thousands of towns filled with people ready to give an enthusiastic reception to anyone English, anyone European. Singers and dancers and actors were beginning to tour America, returning with tales of exuberant crowds and fantastic energy and incredible wealth. Many artists who had considered the place barbaric before were planning to cross the ocean in hopes of garnering some of that wealth.

I smiled a rueful smile. Here I sat, imagining myself touring rugged Western towns, dancing before wildly applauding mobs, and I had never even danced before a real audience. The recitals at the academy didn't count. Madame Olga had said I showed promise, but I knew it would take many more years of hard work before I would be ready for actual performances. I was prepared to work, to wait, to experience the inevitable frustration, for I was determined it would all happen one day despite this temporary setback.

As I gazed at the plumes of water splashing violently against the rocks below, my mood gradually turned pensive and I began to think about the man I had vowed not to think about. I remembered the handsome face, the easy charm and the patina of hardness, and I remembered the curious premonition that Brence Stephens represented danger, presented a threat. I felt it in my blood, even as I longed to be near him once again.

A strange new emptiness inside made me feel curiously incomplete, as though something important were being denied me. It was absurd, of course. I would get over it. I wasn't in love with him. How could I possibly be in love with him? It was just that I knew that I *could* fall in love with him, so easily, just as my mother had fallen in love with the handsome gypsy. Something told me that falling in love with Brence Stephens would be just as disastrous for me as falling in love with Ramon had been for my mother.

Being in love seemed to be the most important thing in the world to most of my classmates at the academy. They had chattered of nothing else, had bragged about conquests made during the holidays, talked about handsome suitors and moonlit lawns and kisses stolen in rose gardens. Twice a month there had been carefully chaperoned dances at the academy with a guest list of "suitable" young men. My classmates had been all atwitter, flirting outrageously, but I had found the dances tedious. The young men had been terribly attentive to me, had filled my dance cards promptly, had vied with each other to fetch me punch and escort me out for fresh air in the gardens, but all of them had seemed frightfully immature and clumsy. Their rough caresses had left me cold. I had earned a reputation for being icy and aloof, but that hadn't bothered me in the least.

The other girls took affairs of the heart so lightly, falling in and out of love at least twice a month, but it could never be that way with me. I knew there were depths of emotion inside waiting to be aroused, and it would take more than a schoolboy to stir them. Brence Stephens had made me aware of those emotions.

The waves crashed against the rocks and, immersed in thought, I didn't hear the footsteps until they were quite near. I turned to to see him approaching, and a wild joy seemed to flood my soul, joy that was totally unexpected and impossible to deny.

He was incredibly handsome, so handsome it hurt, and I felt a stab of pain that was pleasure as well. His carriage was standing in the distance, the horse contentedly grazing on the short grass. He had come. Deep down I had known he would, just as I knew my coming here was no casual thing.

"Hello, Mary Ellen," he said.

"Hello."

There was no joy in my voice. The joy sang inside, but there was fear as well. I felt I was standing on the edge of an abyss, precariously balanced, about to fall.

"I thought you might be here," he said. "I've come each afternoon."

"Have you?"

"I think you knew I would."

"Perhaps I did."

He stood there in the sunlight tall and splendid, his hands resting lightly at his sides. His eyes were no longer remote, no longer filled with detached amusement. His expression was grave, and he looked vulnerable, unsure of himself and stubbornly determined not to show it. I suddenly realized that he was lonely.

"That first day I was very disappointed," he said. "I waited for three hours, and when you didn't come, I was angry, at first, and then I began to fear I'd offended you. You see, it's been a long time since I've been around a young woman like you. I've been away from England for several years, and the women I met in

42

India—" He hesitated, searching for the right words. "They—they weren't like you. I was—well, I suppose I was a bit forward the other day, and I'm sorry for it."

I could tell that he was sincere. He was certainly complex, a man of many moods. I suspected that the stern authority and self-assurance he had displayed before were part of an invisible shell he wore in order to protect the man inside, a man frequently besieged by self-doubts and afraid to expose the tenderness that was part of his makeup.

"Apologies don't come easily for me," he said. "I'd rather face a band of howling natives."

"I imagine you would."

"You're making this very difficult, Mary Ellen."

"Am I?"

"You know you are."

"Did—did you ask your cousin about me?" I inquired.

He nodded gravely. "She told me all about your parents, your birth, your upbringing. Did you really expect that to make any difference, keep me from coming?"

"I . . . I wasn't sure."

"I want to get to know you, Mary Ellen. I want to spend time with you. The other afternoon . . . I felt something. I'm not sure I've ever felt it before. When I saw you standing there in your dusty rose dress, your hair all dishevelled, so beautiful, so vulnerable . . . something happened."

He had lowered his eyes, and now he looked up at me, expecting a reply. I made none. The abyss yawned before me, and I seemed to sway dangerously, even though I stood perfectly still. He misinterpreted my silence. He frowned, his eyes dark and moody, filled with disappointment and something almost like resentment. A long moment passed, and then he stepped over to the edge of the rocks and peered down at the waves.

Several moments passed before he turned to face me.

"I suppose I've made a fool of myself," he said.

"No, Brence. Something happened to me, as well. I . . . I was afraid, and that's why I didn't come before."

He was puzzled. "Afraid?"

"Of you, of myself, of . . . what might happen."

"You mustn't be afraid," he told me. "Surely you know I wouldn't hurt you."

His voice was gentle, his manner grave, protective. I felt that he needed me, and I needed him as well. I knew that if life was to have true meaning I must dare to live. I must dare to love. I took that fatal step, and Brence was there. I was no longer alone. I knew that I loved him, that I was committed. There could be no turning back.

VI

It was late afternoon when we reached the fairgrounds at Claymoor. The sun had slipped out of sight on the horizon, leaving behind a blaze of gold and orange banners that slowly faded against a darkening blue sky. Brence helped me out of the carriage and handed a coin to the little boy who appeared, eager to watch after the horse. We moved past the other carriages, strolling toward the booths and stalls and tents. The annual fair was a major event for people in these parts, and there was a big crowd. Most of the important business had been transacted earlier on, and now that the bartering and trading was over, the crowd was intent on enjoying themselves. An atmosphere of raucous gaiety prevailed.

"I wonder where the gypsies are," I remarked. "I don't see the caravans."

"We'll find them," he promised. "You're really quite eager to see them, aren't you?"

"It's been so long. I don't even know if they'll remember me. I hope Inez is still with them, and Rudolpho, and Julio, of course. He used to tease me and pull my pigtails every chance he got. He was a dreadful little boy, actually, two years older than I and very proud of his masculinity."

Brence smiled, guiding me past the stalls. Children ran to and fro, marveling at the puppet shows and the carousel with its brightly painted horses that bobbed up and down as the calliope played. Dour farmers drank tankards of ale while their wives timidly examined the hand-made lace and the copper pans. Robust lads swaggered about pretending to be men, and girls in their best print dresses laughed together and flirted with the lads. There was a wooden dance floor with Japanese lanterns strung above it, where couples danced country dances while the fiddles played and the colored lanterns swayed in the breeze, casting red, blue, purple, and gold shadows. It was all vital and exciting, noisy and colorful, but I was interested only in looking for the caravans, fearing that perhaps the gypsies hadn't come after all.

We passed the booths loaded with wares and the roped-off enclosures where the livestock was kept, passed the carousel and the shooting gallery and the ring where wrestling matches were being held, a boisterous crowd urging the combatants on with lusty shouts and cheers. People stared as we made our way over the grounds, for gentry rarely attended these affairs and we were obviously out of place. Brence looked cool and elegant in his navy blue suit and glossy black boots, and I wore a deep pink frock printed with tiny black polka dots. It was one of my favorites, sophisticated and quite fetching; the skirt was adorned with row upon row of ruffles.

As we passed the benches and tables where food was being served, I caught sight of John Chapman. He was standing at one of the stalls, a tankard of ale in his hand, talking to two farmers who had worried expressions on their faces. His own expression was sternly indifferent as the farmers pleaded with him. He probably held mortgages on their farms, too. Chapman glanced up and saw us, and I hesitated nervously. Brence looked at me, arching a brow inquisitively.

"Something wrong?" he inquired.

"John Chapman, the man I told you about. He's over there. He's seen us. I'd just as soon not speak to him."

Chapman set his tankard down, brushed past the farmers, and headed toward us. As he approached, a pretty brunette in a vivid red dress hurried over to him and caught hold of his arm, a radiant smile on her lips. Golden hoops dangled from her ears. She obviously knew him quite well and expected a warm reception, but Chapman said something in a sharp voice and shoved her

46

away with unnecessary brutality, his eyes flashing angrily. The girl stumbled and almost fell.

"Charming chap," Brence remarked. "He has a real way with the ladies, I see."

The girl recovered, bit her lower lip, and then hurried away. I could see that she was unable to comprehend Chapman's violent rejection. As Chapman joined us, Brence's mouth grew tight; the tautness about his cheekbones became very pronounced.

"Miss Lawrence," Chapman said. "Fancy seeing you here."

"Hello, Mr. Chapman. I—this is my friend Brence Stephens. Brence, John Chapman."

Brence nodded curtly. Chapman ignored him.

"I stopped by to see you yesterday afternoon," he informed me. "You weren't home. The maid said she had no idea where you were."

"That's right," I replied.

"I stopped by last Thursday, as well. You weren't home then, either. It seems you've been busy."

I didn't have to explain myself to John Chapman, and I had no intention of doing so. He expected me to, however, and stood there waiting for me to speak, while I gazed at him with a polite look in my eyes. Moments passed. The knot of flesh above the bridge of his nose tightened, and his nostrils flared. Brence slipped his arm around my waist, gazing at Chapman with a look of cool boredom that was somehow also frightening.

"She's been busy," Brence said.

The two men sized each other up. I prayed there wouldn't be a fight. Chapman was larger, with a sturdy build that suggested the strength of a bull, but I had reason to know Brence's prowess when it came to fighting. I remembered the way he had routed Jamie and Billy. I shivered. His arm tightened around my waist. Chapman scowled.

"We must have another talk soon," Chapman said. "We have quite a lot to discuss."

I gave him a polite nod. He hesitated a moment, still scowling, and then he turned and walked away, arms swinging, shoulders rolling beneath the corduroy jacket. I sighed with relief, and Brence removed his arm from my waist. His manner was extremely casual, but the look in his eyes was lethal as he watched Chapman depart.

"Chap could use a few lessons in deportment," he said lightly. "For a minute there, I thought I might have to give him one. It would have been a pleasure, I assure you."

"He makes me very uneasy."

"You needn't worry about John Chapman, Mary Ellen. Shall we resume our quest?"

I nodded and Brence smiled, and a moment later I forgot all about John Chapman, for as we turned the corner of a row of stalls I saw the gypsy encampment ahead. Assembled on the outskirts of the fairgrounds were at least a dozen painted caravans and a shabby purple tent adorned with faded gold stars and half-moons. A small crowd milled about, examining the rugs and baskets and strands of beads and other wares the gypsies displayed. Swarthy men attended fires as the shadows gathered. I felt a rush of excitement, remembering, and it must have shown on my face, for Brence laughed as he led me toward the encampment.

I was a child again, hastening to join my friends, eager to belong, to be a part of their bright, colorful world. How glorious it was going to be to see Inez and Rudolpho and Julio and all the others. I moved from caravan to caravan, filled with expectancy, but I saw no one I knew. It was the same tribe, I knew that, for I recognized the caravans, however sadly their colors had faded, but I saw not a single familiar face. It was almost dark now. The fires were crackling, orange and yellow-orange flames leaping, and someone was strumming a guitar. More and more people were coming to the encampment in anticipation of the dances. Brence and I paused in front of the fortune-teller's tent. He smiled, a fond look in his eyes, but I could tell that he was merely indulging me.

"I don't know any of them," I said.

"It's been a long time, Mary Ellen. Tribes change."

I felt a terrible disappointment, and then the flap of the tent opened and the fortune-teller stepped out to stare at the gathering crowd with disdainful black eyes. Her long red and blue skirt was shabby, her red cotton blouse slightly soiled. Yards of tarnished gold beads hung from her neck, and a purple bandana covered her hair. She was very old, her face the color of mahogany, seamed and lined. Her eyelids were painted pale blue, and her cheeks were highly rouged. Her thin lips were a vivid scarlet, curling in a cynical smile as she watched the people milling about the camp. The cloying perfume she wore failed to conceal the odor of garlic and sweat.

She turned to look at Brence and me. Coal-black eyes glowed with greed and barely concealed malice.

"I tell fortune!" she snapped. "Pay first."

Brence shook his head. The fortune-teller shrugged and started to step back into the tent, and then she hesitated, a deep frown creasing her brow. She stepped nearer, studying me closely. We recognized each other at the same time. Inez wailed and threw her arms in the air, and we fell upon one another, holding, hugging, rocking together. When she finally held me at arm's length to get a better look, I had to fight back the tears.

"My Mary Ellen," she growled. "Ess really you. All grown up."

"I was so worried. I couldn't find you, couldn't find Rudolpho or Julio or anyone I knew."

"Some leave, abandon zee tribe. New ones join us. Julio ess still vith us. Chasing some wench, I fear, instead of helping his poor mother. Rudolpho ess here, too. Rudolpho!" she shrieked. "He ess lazy as ever, shiftless, strumming his guitar instead of finding chickens and fresh milk. Rudolpho! Come at once!"

Rudolpho came hurrying around the corner of the tent, plump, jolly, exactly as I remembered him. He recognized me at once, his black eyes widening in amazement, and then his lips spread into a wide grin and he swept me up in a tight bear hug that almost cracked my ribs. He whirled me around and set me down and then whirled me around again, laughing gleefully all the while.

"Enough!" Inez barked. "Leave her be!"

"Rudolpho," I said breathlessly. "It's so good to see you."

"You remember, eh? You remember Rudolpho and all the things I teach you? I show you how to pick a pocket, no? I show you how to look forlorn and hold out your hand for coins. I teach you all the dances."

"Zut! Zut! Leave her be! She and I, we have things to talk about. We go into zee tent."

"Inez, I—I'd like you and Rudolpho to meet my friend Brence Stephens. He was kind enough to bring me today."

They looked at him, Rudolpho with a friendly grin, Inez with narrowed eyes that were openly suspicious. Brence nodded politely. Inez placed her hands on her hips and looked him up and down.

"Ess beautiful," she observed. "Ess good for you? Zat is zee question. You take charge of him, Rudolpho. Show him zee camp. Get him out uv zee way for a while."

Brence gave me a good-natured smile and let Rudolpho lead him toward the caravans and crackling campfires. Inez's eyes narrowed again as she watched them leave. After a moment she muttered something under her breath and took me inside the tent where a candle, burning in an old pewter holder, cast a soft golden glow. There was no crystal ball, but a pack of soiled Tarot cards set on the rickety table and a series of faded cabal signs hung on the purple tent walls. The smell of garlic and damp cloth was almost overwhelming, but I was so happy to be with Inez that I hardly noticed.

"Sit down," she ordered. "We talk."

"There's so much to talk about I don't know where to begin," I said, taking one of the chairs. "Tell me about you, Inez. Tell me about you and Rudolpho and everything you've been doing."

Sitting down across the table from me, Inez propped her elbows up and made a face, shrugging her bony shoulders.

"Gypsy life always zee same. We steal chickens. We sell zee trinkets and tell zee fortunes. We move from place to place. Gypsies come and go. Nothing changes. I hear you go to fine school, study dancing."

I told her about the school in Bath, describing my classes, and when I told her about Aunt Meg's death, I was unable to conceal my grief. Her face was like carved mahogany as she listened, black eyes glowing.

50

There was a moment of silence after I finished. When Inez spoke, her voice was a harsh growl.

"Zis man. He help you forget your grief?"

"He's been . . . marvelous, Inez."

She grimaced and began to toy with the Tarot cards, turning up first one, then another, her expression fierce. For some reason, she didn't like Brence, but she undoubtedly still saw me as a child and still had a protective feeling toward me.

"These past twelve days have been the happiest days of my life," I told her. "We—every afternoon I go to Land's End, and he meets me there. I've taken him to all my favorite places—he's a stranger to Cornwall, you see. We've been to the haunted caves and to the Druid stones. One afternoon we had a picnic on the moors, and another day we went to one of the small fishing villages down the coast. A fisherman showed us how to mend nets and took us out on his boat."

Inez slapped another card down and again made a face.

"Several times we just rode in the carriage," I continued, "taking any road we happened to fancy, exploring, talking, getting to know each other and just—just being together."

"You luff him?"

"With all my heart. I never knew such happiness was possible, never knew I could feel so close to another person. It's as though I'm truly alive for the first time, as though life before Brence was a kind of dream and I'm only now awake."

"He luffs you?"

"I think so. He's so considerate, gentle, attentive. He treats me as though I'm the most important person in the world to him. Sometimes he's silent and moody, and—sometimes he seems remote, but I think he's in love with me, Inez. I want him to be. I want it more than anything in the world."

The flap of the tent flew back, and two giggling young girls in cotton print dresses flounced in, accompanied by a hulking lad with straw-colored hair and an embarrassed expression. Inez pressed her mouth into a thin red line and waved an arm at them, her eyes flashing.

51

"You wait! I busy now!"

The trio backed cautiously out of the tent. Inez muttered a curse under her breath, and then she looked up sharply.

"You are still virgin?" she asked bluntly.

I was taken aback, and it was a moment before I replied.

"Brence has been . . . quite gallant and . . . and casually affectionate," I said hesitantly, "but he's never attempted to take any liberties. He's never even kissed me. He's been the perfect gentleman."

"Zut."

"He respects me. He doesn't want to rush me or frighten me."

Inez studied me with shrewd eyes, her lips curling disdainfully. She began to toy with the Tarot cards again, scattering them over the table and placing them face down.

"He knows all about my background, Inez," I told her. "That doesn't matter to him. He's courting me anyway. He's going into the diplomatic service and he'll need a proper wife, and . . . I believe he wants to marry me."

Inez did not reply. Instead she began to turn the Tarot cards face up, one by one. The purple cloth walls billowed gently, and the candle flame danced, casting soft shadows. I realized that she was reading the cards for me. I sat silently, vaguely apprehensive. After a while she turned up the last card. She studied it for a long time, and then she swept the cards aside abruptly, her eyes dark with worry.

"What did you see, Inez?"

Inez stood up. "Ess nothing. I read zee fortunes. I tell zem what zey want to hear. Ess all a gypsy hoax."

I got up, too, and Inez glared at me angrily, hands on hips. The flap of the tent flew back again. A plump, nervous farmer's wife stepped inside, clutching her purse tightly. Seeing the expression on Inez's face, the poor woman turned pale and hurried back out. Inez sighed. Her anger had vanished, and suddenly she looked very old, very tired.

"My poor Mary Ellen, my little chick who has grown into such a lovely young woman—no longer zee little girl with zee pigtails who wants to become gypsy, too. Already you know such grief when your aunt die. Zhere will be more, my child."

"But—"

"You will travel, many trips, many countries. You will know many men, and—and zhere will always be zee one. You will have great fame and glory and zhere will be riches, but zhere will be pain as well, such pain. You must endure and go on, and one day—" She hesitated, a frown furrowing her brow. "One day, eff you are strong enough, you will find zee happiness you seek."

"Will Brence ask me to marry him? Will—"

"Ziz ess all I tell you!" she snapped impatiently. "Zey wait for me! I must make zee money! You go now—and remember what I say. Zee strength is zhere inside. You must draw on it. You will need it, my child."

VII

When I stepped outside the tent, the sky was blue-black and frosted with stars, but the campfires burned brightly. Leaping flames cast shadows over the caravans, and guitars were strumming. A crowd was already gathering to watch the dances. Brence was leaning against a nearby caravan waiting for me, his arms folded across his chest. Seeing me approach, he straightened up and smiled a warm smile, the way an indulgent parent might smile at a capricious child.

"All finished?" he inquired.

I nodded. "Did Rudolpho show you around the camp?"

"Every inch of it. Fascinating experience," he added dryly. "Shall we leave now?"

"Not yet," I protested. "We must see the dances."

People had formed a wide circle around the clearing in front of the caravans. Clasping my elbow firmly, Brence shoved and nudged until we were standing at the front of the crowd. Two fires burned, wood crackling as the flames danced, washing the ground with wavering orange patterns. Three gypsies in colorful attire strummed guitars, and another slapped a tambourine. The music was sensual and savage. The crowd was restless, eager for the spectacle to begin.

Brence put his arm around my shoulders and looked down at me with a half smile playing on his lips, but I had the feeling he was preoccupied and only pretending to give me his attention. He sighed and gazed at the fires, and although his arm rested heavily on my shoulders, he might have been completely alone. These moments of remoteness occurred frequently, as did the moody silences, but they never lasted long. He had confessed that this interim period before he began his new career was difficult for him, and I knew that he had a great deal on his mind. I only wished that he would share it with me. My life was an open book to him, but Brence had been extremely reserved about his own life, giving only the briefest of sketches.

Born into the aristocracy, Brence had been a pampered child, but his father had lost the family fortune while Brence was still a boy. As a result, he had always been on the fringes of things, included in all the activities but, because of lack of money, never really able to participate. At Eton and later on at Oxford he felt like an outsider, never able to entertain in his rooms, never able to indulge in boyish larks. His mother died when he was in his teens, and when he was twenty his father succumbed to a heart attack, leaving him alone and penniless. Brence left Oxford and took a commission in the army, departing for India almost immediately.

Was it this early deprivation that explained his consuming ambition, his determination to make a name for himself in the world? He needed to prove something, and that need was a kind of obsession. Sometimes I felt he was very vulnerable, for all his strength, for all his confidence. I longed to comfort him. I longed to be everything to him. As we stood waiting for the dancers to appear, I wondered how long it would be before he stopped treating me with such respect and casual affection, and started treating me like a woman. Only then could I give him the support and assurance I sensed he needed.

The music built to a crescendo, stopped abruptly, and there was a moment of silence. Castanets began to click. A gypsy girl stepped into the clearing, her long black hair wild and tangled, her sullen mouth blood-red, dark eyes glaring at the crowd with open hostility as she moved around the circle with the grace of a tigress, clicking her castanets all the while. The music began again, the melody slow, matching the movements of her body. She wore a faded green dress with bodice cut low to show off a magnificent bosom. A tarnished gold belt encircled her slender waist, and the rows of silver and gold braid that adorned the full green skirt were tarnished as well. Golden hoops dangled from her earlobes. She swirled around, and the music swirled, too, growing louder, throbbing with passion.

As I watched, I remembered, and my body seemed to vibrate to the music. It was difficult to stand still. The girl swayed back and forth, her arms above her head, the castanets chattering. She threw her head back and hissed, vicious, passionate, a beautiful animal eager to engage in fierce combat with the lover who had not yet appeared. She stamped her heels on the hard-packed earth, looking this way and that, scowling impatiently, and when the gypsy youth stepped into the clearing she hissed again, pretending to despise him.

She whirled around, her back to him, and the youth bared his teeth and flashed dark, dangerous brown eyes, stalking her as a panther might stalk his prey. His tall, slender dancer's body was clothed in tight black breeches and a white shirt open at the throat, its long full sleeves gathered at the wrist. A vivid red sash was tied around his waist. Perhaps twenty years old, he had shiny black hair that covered his head in a rich cluster of curls, and his features were harsh, dramatic, the mouth a savage pink slash. He circled around the girl, moving to the music in a lithe, muscular stride.

The dancers' movements brought them near to where Brence and I were standing. When the youth turned and scowled, he saw me, and then he stood still, forgetting the music, forgetting the dance. Those dark eyes stared into mine, and when the girl caught hold of his arm and tried to pull him back, he gave her a hard shove without even looking at her. She stumbled backward and losing her balance, fell on her backside with jolting impact. She cursed him loudly, but he paid no attention. Mouth turned down at the corners, brows pressed together, he stared at me, and I recognized him. That face had been younger, thinner the last time I had seen it. The surly boy had grown into a savagely handsome man.

"You remember?" he growled.

"I remember," I whispered.

"The dance? You remember how it ends?"

"I think so. It—it's all right, Brence," I said quickly as he began to tense.

Julio seized my wrist and pulled me into the clearing, and I moved to the music, becoming a part of it, my body a supple instrument. I was a gypsy, all fire and fury, caught up in the dance I had learned so many years ago. I whirled around, my dark skirt swirling above my knees, the ruffles fluttering. Julio smiled fiercely, circling me as I swayed. The gypsy girl leaped to her feet, flying toward us with claws unsheathed. Julio caught her and snarled a threat between his teeth, tearing the castanets from her fingers and pushing her aside. She turned away, casting venomous glances at me over her shoulder. I took the castanets from him and fastened them on my fingers, missing not a beat, and the crowd applauded, thinking it all a part of the performance.

The music was fiery and flamboyant, ringing with a sensuous melody that caught me up, became a part of me. Julio backed away from me, and I followed, hips swaying, castanets clicking provocatively. He stopped. He snarled. I threw my head back, hair flying free, spilling over shoulder and cheek, and I stamped and stepped, shaking my skirt, easily recalling each movement. He turned his back to me, folding his arms across his chest, and I circled around him, enticing him, brazen in my beauty, aware of my power. He looked up, nostrils flaring, teeth bared, desire beginning to stir, beginning to burn in his eyes as I smiled and swayed and whirled.

I danced the dance of love, executing each movement as expertly as I had in the past, but now I understood them and each movement took on new meaning. The demure young woman in the sophisticated frock became a seductive creature, for I was dancing for Brence, not Julio, smiling for Brence, telling him in dance what I could not tell him in words. Julio came to me and wrapped his arms around my waist and we swayed together, to and fro. I dipped backwards, supported by those steel-strong arms, my hair brushing the ground, and he swung me in his arms, to the left, to the right, my body limp, liquid, melting to the music. He released

58

me, and I whirled away from him, faster, faster, and he pursued me, crushing me to him in a passionate embrace as the music abruptly ended.

The crowd applauded vigorously. Julio let me go and smiled the old arrogant smile, all male superiority as he looked me up and down.

"You'd make a good gypsy, little sister. The fire is there. With practice you'd make a good gypsy, good partner."

He strolled over to the musicians and took an old felt hat and began to move around the circle of people, collecting coins, much too superior to engage in further conversation with a mere female. I removed the castanets and gave them to one of the guitarists. He grinned broadly and nodded in approval. Smoothing my hair back and adjusting my bodice, I joined Brence. His expression was noncommittal.

"You were quite good," he remarked.

"I used to know all the dances."

"Shall we go now?"

"I suppose so. I've seen my friends, and . . . one can never recapture the past. I'm an outsider here. I suppose I was back then, too, but they were so kind to me—"

I was in a pensive mood as we drove away from the fairgrounds. For a few minutes, caught up in the magic of music and movement, I had been vibrantly alive, but now I felt a curious deflation. Brence was silent and remote, which didn't help at all. Had he understood the message I conveyed with the dance? Had he been pleased, displeased, shocked? I had no idea. Thousands of distant stars twinkled like diamond chips against the smooth black sky, and the fields on either side of the lonely road were the color of old pewter. As we rode near the edge of the cliffs I could see the ocean and hear the waves slapping the rocks far below.

I thought about what Inez had told me, trying to remember her exact words. There would be many trips to many countries, she had said. As a diplomat Brence would naturally travel a great deal, and as his wife I would naturally accompany him. I would know many men, but there would always be the one. The one would be Brence, of course, and the others—the others would be the diplomats and ambassadors whom I would meet as I performed my duties as official hostess. Fame and glory would come as Brence reached the pinnacle of his career, the riches a part of it. The pain . . . I supposed she meant there would be a number of setbacks, disappointments, and I would need to be strong, always encouraging him.

Lost in thought, I was surprised when I looked up and saw Graystone Manor ahead. A lamp burned downstairs, making a yellow-gold square in one of the windows. Fanny would be waiting up for me, worried, unable to sleep until I was safely inside. Brence tugged gently on the reins and stopped the carriage in front of the gate. He hadn't said a single word since we left the fair, and he didn't speak now. Climbing out of the carriage, he reached up to encircle my waist with strong hands and help me down. The gate creaked noisily when he opened it, echoing in the silence as we walked toward the house together.

When he reached the door Brence turned and gazed at me. His face was all shadow and planes in the moonlight, the cheekbones taut, the lips slightly parted. He was so near, so tall, so handsome. I felt a hollow ache inside as he gazed at me; moments passed, and the ache grew unbearable. Would he finally take me into his arms? Would he finally kiss me, tell me all the things I longed to hear? Leaves rustled in the breeze. Moonlight and shadow made dancing patterns over the ground.

Brence sighed and reached up to brush a stray lock of hair from my cheek.

"You're incredibly lovely, Mary Ellen. I wonder if you have any idea how lovely you are."

His voice was soft, melodious, a husky drawl. I stood very still, barely able to breathe, yet I was trembling inside. Brence took hold of my bare shoulders, his fingers squeezing my flesh with a gentle pressure.

"Lovely," he said, "unspoiled. So innocent and yet so wise, so eager."

His fingers tightened their grip. He tilted his head slightly and studied me as a connoisseur might study a priceless work of art. I looked up into those dark, gleaming eyes, waiting, wanting to speak, unable to say a word.

"Shall I be the one?" he mused. "The temptation is strong. Shall I be the cad and satisfy my instincts, or shall I be the gentleman I'd like to be and leave now, before it's too late?"

I held my breath, and the moment that followed seemed to stretch into an eternity. He finally sighed and gave my shoulders a painful squeeze, and then he released me.

"There are things we need to settle, but this is not the night. You must be very tired. I'd better go now."

I was still unable to speak. Brence smiled.

"Tomorrow, Mary Ellen," he said.

He spoke lightly in that gentle, husky voice that was so like music, so persuasive. Tomorrow. As I watched him walk back toward the carriage, I wondered if I could bear to wait for tomorrow to come.

VIII

Leaving our horse and carriage under the shade of the trees, we started across the brownish-gray moor, walking slowly, moving down sloping ground, climbing over occasional boulders, large gray stones lightly streaked with bronze and green. There was a light breeze, and the short, stiff grass rustled, whispering, while above the sky arched an endless blue, pale and pure. We could smell the pungent moor smells of damp earth and dust, of rock and root and grass mixed with the tangy smell of salt. The landscape was wild, primitive, savage grandeur surrounding us, swallowing us up.

"How far is this secret waterfall?" Brence inquired.

"At least another mile. There's a small valley fed by the spring, and the grass is greener there. There are mossy banks covered with tiny purple wildflowers and huge gray rocks, much larger than these. It's not a *large* waterfall, but it's lovely."

"You're quite attached to these moors, aren't you?"

"I love them. They—they seem to speak to me. They make me want to dance. I suppose you think that's foolish."

"I think it's delightful. You never fail to intrigue me, Mary Ellen. Sometimes I wonder what the final shape will be."

"What do you mean?"

"You're clay, my dear, beautiful clay, malleable, not yet fully formed, not yet baked in the kiln of life. One moment you're innocent, expectant, so very young and vulnerable, and the next moment you're sad, serious, wise beyond your years. The woman is there inside the girl, and I've a feeling she'll be a magnificent creature."

"Indeed?"

"I had a glimpse of her last night when you were dancing."

"That wasn't me, not really. That was just music and mood and a part I played."

"You played it well. You were superb."

"Thank you."

"You've told me about your dancing, of course, but I never realized you were so accomplished."

"Last night wasn't really dancing—I mean, it wasn't ballet. All the gypsy dances I learned are merely for amusement. It's ballet that I love. So many years of study—" I paused, remembering the sweat and the aching muscles, the burning pain required to make a light, graceful movement seem light and graceful.

"You had your heart set on studying with this Russian woman in London, didn't you? What was her name?"

"Madame Olga. The chance to study with her meant . . . it meant everything. She takes only a few students, and only those who have already made great progress. I'd never have been accepted had Giovanni not written to her, recommending me. Ballet was going to be my life—"

"Was?"

"And then I met you."

"Then you met me," he said.

His voice was quiet, reflective. His mood was pleasant, attentive, as casually affectionate as ever, yet I sensed a tension that hadn't been there before. Something in the set of his jaw, the tight curve of his mouth suggested a steely determination and, at the same time, a curious reluctance. I was sure that he was going to declare himself today, ask me to marry him, and that wouldn't come easy to a man like Brence Stephens.

He walked beside me with a long, casual stride, wearing a pair of shiny black knee boots, snug black breeches, and a loose white silk shirt opened at the throat, the long sleeves full, billowing slightly in the breeze. His hair was windblown, and his dark brown eyes were moody, contemplating inner visions I could only guess at.

We walked for several minutes in silence, moving down another gentle slope. As we drew nearer the underground springs the grass began to lose its brownish-gray hue, gradually turning a dusty jade green. The ground became softer, spongy underfoot, and there were many more boulders now, huge, hulking stones of varying shapes. Patches of wildflowers began to appear, pale purple, purple-blue, deep royal purple, white. It was a strange, mysterious place that cast a peculiar spell. I fancied the ghosts of the Druids who had once dwelled here watched us as we passed, invisible specters that whispered in faint voices.

I wore a dark blue frock with a full, flaring skirt. As I walked the skirt billowed, revealing glimpses of the ruffled white petticoats beneath, and my hair tumbled about my shoulders in loose waves. I was filled with a heady anticipation, but there was apprehension as well. What if I disappointed him when he finally took me into his arms and kissed me? What if I were awkward and gauche? I was so very inexperienced, knew so little about these matters despite all my worldly reading. I wished that I were indeed the seductive temptress of the dance, instead of a nervous girl unsure of herself.

"Your maid looked upset when I called for you," Brence remarked.

"She was. She's leaving for Devon tomorrow, and she's reluctant about leaving me alone."

"Oh?"

"She didn't plan to join her sister until—until things were settled, but she received another letter. Her sister's going to take a short trip and wants Fanny to come early so she can look after the cottage. Fanny didn't want to, but I insisted. There's really no reason for her to stay."

"So you'll be all alone in the house."

"For at least three more weeks. Then Chapman will foreclose and all the furnishings will be sold at public auction. I—I don't know what I'll do then."

"You're not to worry, Mary Ellen."

He'd said that before, and it was very comforting. Brence was going to take care of me. What did it matter if the house was lost, the furnishings sold to strangers? We would be leaving Cornwall, sharing a bright new future together. The thought was elating. I felt that glorious rush of happiness, aglow inside, shimmering, making me light-headed.

Surrounded by boulders as large as houses, I led the way along the narrow path that twisted among them, Brence following patiently behind. The sound of splashing water echoed among the stones, and there was the smell of moss and mud. The stream was a glittering silver ribbon that appeared and disappeared. We caught glimpses of it as we followed the path that finally led into the small clearing I remembered so well. A thin waterfall tumbled over the face of a rough gray boulder, branching into three small streams that fell into a pool with mossy banks. An oak tree spread shadows over the ground, and the purple wildflowers grew in profusion.

"So this is the famous waterfall," Brence said.

"I told you it wasn't large. It's lovely, though."

"Lovely," he said, but he was not looking at the waterfall.

"I used to come here as a child. I used to sit on that rock by the pool and lose myself in daydreams."

"What did you dream?"

"I dreamed I belonged. I dreamed everyone liked me, that I was pretty instead of plain, that I had loving, respectable parents and a definite place in the scheme of things."

"You must have been a sad child."

"Not sad, at least not often. Defiant, feisty, proud, especially when the other children taunted me. My aunt loved me inordinately, and because she loved me so she didn't hold too tightly. She let me roam wild, gave me a great deal of freedom."

I moved over to the flat gray rock by the water and sat down, spreading out my blue skirt. Brence came to stand behind me, and I tried not to tremble. The back of my head was level with his chest. He rested his hands on my shoulders, fingers gently squeezing my flesh. I could see our reflections in the pool, silvery, shimmering, distorted by the ripples. Several moments passed in silence, and then Brence lifted my hair and stroked the nape of my neck.

"And what are you dreaming of now?" he murmured.

"I—I'd rather not say."

"You're trembling."

"I can't help it. I wish I were older. I wish I didn't feel so—so nervous."

"There's no need to be nervous, Mary Ellen."

"I know."

"What a bewitching child you are. Child, woman, a bewitching combination of the two. The moment I laid eyes on you, I knew this was meant to be. I've tried very hard not to fall in love with you."

He continued to stroke the nape of my neck. A delicious languor began to swell inside, spreading through me with a prickling sensation, glorious torment that grew and grew.

"I never meant to fall in love with you. There's no place in my life for love just now. I have things to accomplish, things to achieve, and any kind of attachment could only be a distraction. I've fought it. I've tried to deny it. You've bewitched me, Mary Ellen."

I watched the shimmering reflections in the water, listening to that deep, melodious voice that seemed to caress me just as his hands caressed, and I turned, looking up into his eyes. They were dark, glowing with need, with warmth. His lips parted, curving into a lovely smile. He pulled me to my feet, drawing me into his arms. How many times had I dreamed of this moment?

"I should have left Cornwall immediately," he said. "I should have known what would happen. I love you. I've never loved before. I've had many women, and I enjoyed each one, but none of them meant anything to me. They were mere diversions. Would that you could be merely a diversion, too."

His arms went around my waist, clasping me loosely against him, his head tilted to one side as he peered down into my eyes. My heart seemed to stop beating, and the languor inside turned into an ache, the torment unendurable, unendurably sweet. I rested my palms on his shoulders and looked up at him and held my breath,

67

afraid to breathe, afraid reality would dissolve into a hazy blur and I would awake to discover that this, too, was a dream.

"I love you, Mary Ellen. I never thought I'd say those words."

"I—I've waited."

"If only you weren't so young. If only you weren't so damned vulnerable. You've never known a man, have you?"

I shook my head.

"Of course you haven't. You've probably never been kissed."

"Not—not really. There were schoolboys at the academy dances. They used to take me into the gardens. One of them—one of them tried to kiss me, but I didn't let him."

"I'll bet you slapped his face."

"Hard," I said.

Brence chuckled, and then he sighed, and then his arms drew me closer and he leaned down until his lips were almost touching mine.

"I'm glad I'm the first," he crooned.

His mouth covered mine, moist, firm, lightly brushing at first, skin caressing skin with gentle pressure. I tilted my head back and he held my waist with one arm. His lips pressed mine, probing, demanding response. As the ache spread into the marrow of my bones and sensations burst into life, I slid my arms around his back, palms rubbing soft silk, feeling the warm skin beneath the cloth, resting on his shoulders and then clinging desperately as he parted my lips with his. I seemed to be drowning in sensation as he prolonged the splendid torture.

He drew his head back, and I felt dizzy, and would surely have fallen had he not clasped me. Smiling, brown eyes glowing, dark with desire, he kissed my shoulder, the curve of my throat, and I tried to control my breathing, wanting to cry out as the rapturous sensations possessed me. Brence sank to his knees, drawing me down with him, lowering me onto the mossy bank. The waterfall splattered and splashed, making bright music, and the scent of the wildflowers was a heady perfume as he slipped his hands inside my bodice, pulling it down until my breasts sprang free. He held them with his hands, fingers encircling the soft mounds of flesh, touching, caressing.

I tensed. In spite of myself, my need, I grew rigid, suddenly possessed with the age-old fear born into every woman. I tried to sit up. He shoved me back down, and I cried out, but he smothered my cry with his lips, kissing me with an urgency that communicated itself to me, became my own, and I held him to me, trembling beneath him as his hands lifted my skirts. He raised himself up on one elbow to adjust his own clothing, and then he planted his knees between my legs and spread them by gently touching my thighs.

"There'll be pain, Mary Ellen. Only a little."

"This—this isn't—"

"Relax," he ordered.

"No. Please. I—I didn't intend—"

The shock of his entry galvanized me, and I struggled wildly, in vain. He pinioned me to the ground with the weight of his body, probing deeper with firm control, meeting the resisting membrane, pressing against it, driving through it with a brutal thrust that caused me to cry out. The pain burned for only a moment and then, inexplicably, it melted into pleasure, pleasure such as I had never imagined possible. My flesh was velvet, softly shredding as that hard warmth caressed and filled, lifting me into an incredible realm of feeling. I spiraled to dizzying heights, each level more exhilarating than the one before, and then, for one brief moment, I hung suspended, clinging to him in wild desperation as we swayed in space and then fell hurtling into a void of shattering ecstasy.

As we drove back over the lonely road toward Graystone Manor, Brence was silent and remote. The carriage bowled along, wheels spinning, the horse moving at a steady clip. I was silent, too, holding a bouquet of purple wildflowers in my lap. My blue skirt was stained with moss, as were the petticoats beneath, and I still felt the radiant glow that was the aftermath of love. Brence had taken me a second time, and there had been no pain, only bliss. He had been gentle, considerate, tender, kissing every part of my body. It was only as we walked back across the moors that he grew remote, drawing into himself.

The remoteness was merely one part of his nature, something I would have to learn to live with. It made the charm, the engaging smile, the tenderness all the more effective in contrast. I toyed with the wildflowers, thinking about what had happened. I had finally crossed the last threshold into womanhood, leaving the girl behind. There was a new wisdom, a new maturity, and I would never again see things in quite the same way. My love for Brence was even stronger, an integral part of me now, and the joy inside was shimmering beauty.

A man on horseback appeared in the distance, riding toward us, and as he drew nearer, I recognized the corduroy jacket, the red-bronze hair. John Chapman drew his horse over to the side of the road and stopped, watching us approach. His face was a brutal mask, his gray-green eyes blazing as we drove past him. Brence gave no sign that he had even seen him. I promptly dismissed John Chapman from my mind. He was unimportant. I was going to marry Brence Stephens. Though he hadn't asked me to this afternoon as I had believed he would, I felt that after the intimacy we had shared the question itself was a mere formality.

IX

The gardens were shabby and overgrown, but there was still a profusion of roses, large, velvety smooth, salmon pink with a faint blush of gold, and white, pale and lovely. Selecting those with the longest stems, I clipped carefully and removed all the thorns before placing them in the wide, shallow basket that swung from my arm. Today was going to be a very special day, I sensed, and I wanted everything to look perfect. A vase of roses would brighten up the parlor. I had the feeling I would remember today for the rest of my life, and I wanted to be sure of a proper setting for the occasion.

Two weeks had passed since our afternoon on the moors, and Brence hadn't once mentioned marriage, but for the past three or four days he had been restless, unusually moody, a great deal on his mind. Last night, before he left, he had looked at me for a long time as though he were trying to make some kind of decision, and finally he had sighed and told me he would be here early this afternoon. I knew it was almost time for him to leave Cornwall, and there was just enough time for us to marry and have a brief honeymoon in London before he would take his post in Germany to begin his career in the diplomatic service.

I was married to him already in my heart. With Fanny gone, Brence came to the house each day, bringing food and wine. No longer did we roam all over the countryside, exploring. With the exception of an occasional stroll on the beach nearby, we stayed inside. I prepared the food he brought, and we ate, we talked, and, as the afternoon waned, we went upstairs to my bedroom and made love until the room was dark and moonlight streamed through the windows and the cool night air caused the curtains to rustle and stir. I treasured each touch, each caress, and I returned them with a fervor that matched his own.

It didn't seem possible that my love for him could have grown, but it had. Each day it grew stronger and stronger until it seemed there was nothing but this joyous feeling that dominated every waking moment and became glorious dreams when I slept. I belonged to him heart and soul, and he belonged to me. How wonderful it was just to watch him as he sat silently in the parlor, brow creased in a frown, and how wonderful to rub the frown away with my fingertips and stroke his cheek, rub my thumb over the smooth curve of his lower lip, teasing him out of his mood and driving away his private demon with skill that came naturally to me.

How wonderful to linger in his arms after love, to watch the moonbeams making silvery patterns on the ceiling and feel those strong arms holding me close, to rest my cheek on his chest and feel his heart beat and revel in the warmth of him, the smell of skin and sweat and hair. As the room grew cooler, as the curtains billowed like silken sails, what delight to run my fingernails lightly over his naked ribs and feel him stir, see him smile lazily before he turned and rolled heavily atop me and took possession of me once more, to lead me into that paradise the two of us shared and would go on sharing for the rest of our lives.

How lost, how alone I felt when finally he climbed out of bed and began to dress. Love meant everything to me, but in my new wisdom I realized that it was different for men. Men were preoccupied with making a living, making a name for themselves, succeeding, and love for them was a separate entity to be savored only when time permitted. I knew that Brence was concerned about his new career, that his career would always take priority. I understood and accepted it. I would be there to aid him, to encourage him, and when he needed the diversion of love I would open my arms and, for a while, make him forget everything else.

Now, basket filled with roses, I slipped the clippers into the pocket of my skirt and went inside. The front foyer looked bleak and bare with all its finery stripped away. The long Sheraton table was gone, as was the blue and gray Aubusson carpet with its pink floral patterns. All the fine things that had been sold in order to pay for my schooling and my ballet lessons and a magnificent wardrobe that would make the other girls envy me. The wardrobe, my books, and a few personal effects would be all I would take with me.

John Chapman would auction off the rest of the furniture, and then he would sell the house. It didn't matter. I had grown up here in Cornwall and I loved it, but already it was part of the past. I doubted that I would ever return. Brence and I would travel all over Europe, going from one exotic place to another. There would be hardships, too, as Inez had predicted, but we would weather them together.

Putting away the clippers in the musty garden room back of the kitchen, I took down a tall blue vase and arranged the roses in it, then carried them into the parlor. The French windows stood open. Rays of wavering silvery yellow sunlight streamed in. The white marble mantel was polished to a shine. Even if the nap was worn on the dark blue sofa, if the mahogany sideboard was losing some of its veneer, the flowered pink and gray wing chairs still looked good, and the oval mirror in its gilt frame added a touch of elegance. I set the vase of roses down on the sideboard and then rearranged them, touching the velvet-soft petals carefully.

It was after twelve o'clock. Brence would be here soon. How would he phrase it? What would he say? Would he be cool and matter-of-fact, or would he draw me into his arms and look deep into my eyes and tell me once again that he loved me? He might not even ask the question. He might simply say that he had made all the arrangements and tell me to start packing my bags. Lost in delicious speculation, I stood there by the sideboard with my fingertips touching the roses, and then, catching sight of myself in the mirror, I realized that I still wore my morning dress.

I hurried upstairs to my bedroom and, opening the wardrobe doors, examined the profusion of dresses hanging inside. Which one should I wear? I spent several minutes in indecision, rejecting first one and then another, and finally, smiling, I took down the dusty rose cotton frock I had been wearing the first time we met. It wasn't particularly elegant, but he had found it quite fetching . . . How long ago that seemed.

Spreading the dress out on the bed, I took off the frock I had on and, wearing only my petticoat, sat down at the dressing table to brush my hair until it was shining with blue-black highlights. Finally satisfied, I applied a touch of subtle perfume behind my earlobes and in the cleft between my breasts, and then I slipped on my dress. Standing in front of the mirror, I adjusted the bodice, ran my hands around the snug waist, and smoothed the skirt over my petticoats. I wondered if he would remember the dress.

As I left the bedroom I could hear his carriage approaching the house, and I smiled, feeling the familiar rush of excitement. I started down the staircase, and suddenly, halfway down, my knees seemed to give way and I had to grab hold of the bannister for support. Everything shimmered in front of me, blurring, spinning, and there was a faint buzzing in my head. I was unable to breathe properly, and my pulses were leaping. Nerves. I had never in my life been so nervous. Terrible doubts assailed me, and there was a moment of sheer panic while I stood gripping the bannister so tightly that my knuckles grew white.

The carriage stopped and I heard the sound of his footsteps coming up the path. Panic still held me in its grip, and I was frozen, unable to move, as Brence knocked on the front door. Several seconds passed and then the buzzing stopped, the dizziness vanished. I took a deep breath, let go of the bannister and moved on down the stairs, composed now, that dreadful moment of apprehension behind me. I opened the door. He stepped inside. He was wearing his navy blue suit and a long black cloak, a traveling cloak. The hem almost swept the floor.

74

Smiling, I took his arm and started to stand up on tiptoes to kiss him. His expression held me back. His mouth was tight at the corners, his brows drawn together, his eyes dark and determined as though . . . as though he had a very unpleasant task to perform.

"You're early," I said lightly. "I just finished dressing."

I stepped back and whirled around, displaying the dress. If he recognized it, he gave no sign. Why was he wearing the cloak? He'd never worn one before. Why was he so very grim? I felt a tremor of alarm, the merest tremor, but I refused to acknowledge it.

"I—I see you didn't bring any food," I remarked. "That's all right. There's enough in the pantry to do."

I led the way into the parlor, feeling light-headed, trying to still that tremor inside.

"I'll make us an omelet later on. I can't cook, not really—it wasn't included in our curriculum at the academy, but Fanny taught me how to make omelets. Aren't these roses lovely? I cut them this morning. I wanted everything to look nice because—because I knew today was going to be special, and—"

I cut myself short, unable to go on, unable to keep up the pretense. He stood there in the middle of the room with the cloak draped back over his shoulders, his mouth drawn into a tight line. I turned my back to him, praying it wasn't so, praying fervently.

"I have something to tell you," he said.

I knew. Already I knew, and I didn't think I was going to be able to face it.

"I was going to write a letter. I was going to send it after I left, but I couldn't. I had to come myself. I'd rather face a firing squad, but I had to come."

I turned to look at him. Why did I feel this terrible calm that was like a kind of death?

"You're going," I said.

"My train leaves at three. My bags are in the carriage."

"I see."

"I'm sorry, Mary Ellen. I didn't mean for it to happen this way. God knows I didn't. I've done you a terrible wrong, and I'll regret it for the rest of my life."

"Will you?" My voice seemed to be coming from someone else.

"I fell in love with you, Mary Ellen. Against my will, I fell in love for the first time in my life. I should have left as soon as I realized what was happening, but I didn't. Would to God that I had."

The sun still shone through the window, but it wasn't nearly as bright as before. The draperies stirred as a gust of wind swept in. Petals dropped from the roses, making a velvety pile all around the tall blue vase.

"I thought you were going to marry me," I said.

"I'm sorry."

"I thought you were going to marry me and take me away with you. I thought we were going to live happily ever after. I actually believed it. How naive I was. How naive."

"Mary Ellen—"

"I loved you, Brence. How I loved you."

He frowned, uncomfortable, eager to be done with it, eager to go. Another gust of wind made the draperies blow inward. The sunlight continued to fade. The blue sky was turning a soft gray, and clouds were building. I stepped over to the French windows and closed them.

"It's going to storm," I said. "You've never seen one of our famous Cornwall storms. They blow up out of the blue, without warning, and sometimes they can be quite fierce—"

"I have to do this, Mary Ellen. I have to think of my career. Marrying you would—" He frowned and left the sentence unfinished.

"Marrying me would endanger it," I said. "When you take a bride, she will be very proper, very aristocratic, probably very wealthy, as well. Am I right? It wouldn't do to marry the—the bastard daughter of a gypsy. It wouldn't do at all. I understand, Brence."

"I wish things were different. I wish—"

"Go. Please—just go."

He reached into his breast pocket and pulled out a long envelope.

"I intended to send this along with the letter. There's enough money here to keep you for a year. You can set yourself up in a modest cottage. You'll meet some nice young man. You'll marry. You'll have children, and you'll forget all about this summer."

"You don't really believe that, do you?"

"Take the money, Mary Ellen."

"I shouldn't. I should throw the money in your face, Brence, but I have the feeling I've earned it."

Brence didn't say anything. He placed the envelope on the sideboard beside the vase of roses and then he adjusted the folds of the cloak about his shoulders. He turned to look at me. The skin was stretched tightly over his cheekbones, and his dark brown eyes were full of regret.

"Goodbye, Mary Ellen," he said quietly.

I didn't move. Brence hesitated for only a moment, and then he walked briskly out of the room, the cloak belling out behind him. His boots rang on the floor of the foyer, and I heard him open the front door and close it behind him. I heard him driving away in the carriage, driving out of my life. I sat down on the sofa, watching the room grow dim and gray as the storm approached. I wanted to cry, and I couldn't. Why couldn't I cry? I prayed for the tears to come.

Time passed and all sunlight faded and there was a rumble of thunder in the distance. Colors melted into gray and the room grew darker, and still I sat, unable to feel the anguish, completely numb inside. Brence was gone. I would never see him again. Never again would he take me into his arms and hold me and smile and kiss me tenderly as I wrapped my arms around his shoulders and grew weak with love. He was gone. Gone. It wasn't true. I couldn't bear it. I would wake up. This terrible nightmare would be over, and everything would be all right.

I lost all track of time. The thunder grew louder. The windows rattled violently. Soon the first drops of rain would splatter against the panes. Brence had long since boarded his train and it was speeding away, and he was beginning a new life and I was alone. Alone. There was no one. I couldn't face it. I knew that. I couldn't go on. Thunder rumbled and the wind howled around the house, and then there was a dreadful calm, the calm before the storm began in earnest.

Suddenly, I heard a horse neighing in loud protest, footsteps coming up the pathway. I stood up, startled, and then joy flooded me and I ran into the foyer, fighting back the tears. He had come back. He couldn't do it. He couldn't leave without me. He couldn't leave me behind because he loved me. The front door opened, and I was ready to dissolve into tears and throw myself into his arms.

"Brence," I whispered. "Brence—"

John Chapman stepped inside. He closed the door behind him. It was dim in the foyer, but I could see his face, could see the look in those gray-green eyes.

"He's gone," Chapman said. "I was at the station on business. I saw him board the train. Your lover is gone."

"You—"

"It seems he's deserted you."

"You—have no right to come here!"

"I've come to take what's mine. I've waited, Mary Ellen. I've waited far too long. I saw you with him in the carriage that afternoon. I saw the way you looked. I knew what happened. It was written all over you."

"Get out."

"I've seen his carriage out in front of the house every afternoon, every night. I suppose he told you to send the maid away so the two of you could use the house. Nice for him. He had it real nice, and now it's my turn."

I backed away, and Chapman chuckled, enjoying my alarm. A clap of thunder sounded. The whole house seemed to shake. The wind began to howl again, blowing furiously.

"Blood will out," he said. "You might have a fine education, might give yourself fine airs, but you're your mother's daughter just the same. Stephens sensed that immediately, just as I did."

"Get out," I repeated.

"No, Mary Ellen. You're the one who's going to get out. You're leaving tomorrow at noon. There'll be a boy with a wagon to take you and your bags to the station. I don't know where you'll go or what you'll do, but I imagine you'll manage. You can always sell it on the streets."

"You're vile."

78

"I had plans for you, Mary Ellen, such fine plans. All your problems would have been solved, but you toyed with me, strung me along, playing me for a fool. I don't like that."

He scowled. His red-bronze hair gleamed darkly, and his eyes were full of male hunger. He stood with legs apart, fists planted on his hips.

"I don't like to be toyed with, Mary Ellen."

He moved toward me, and I backed into the parlor.

"Don't—don't come any closer," I warned.

"You don't seem so sure of yourself now. You don't seem so high and mighty. What's the matter, Mary Ellen? Are you afraid?"

"Stay away from me."

He laughed. He closed the distance between us in three long strides, throwing his arms around my waist, crushing me to him. I struggled frantically, raking my nails across his cheek, drawing blood. Chapman bellowed and gave me a vicious shove. The back of my legs banged against the sofa. I lost my balance and tumbled onto the cushions. The windows rattled noisily as the wind slammed against them. Chapman stood over me, breathing heavily.

"Tomorrow you leave," he growled, "but tonight is mine."

X

The air was fresh and clear and invigorating, the sky a vivid blue without a single cloud. Radiant sunlight spilled from above, becoming silver sunbursts on the water, sparkling on brown cliffs, and making everything sharp and clear. The storm had washed the earth, and the day was bright and pure. I walked carefully, picking my way along the edge of the cliff.

The boy with the wagon wouldn't arrive for at least another hour, and my bags were packed, standing ready in the front foyer. They contained all my clothes with the exception of the dusty rose cotton. Early this morning after Chapman had gone, I removed the dress and destroyed it. I could never have worn it again. I had bathed and scrubbed my body and deliberately forced the nightmare out of my mind. It was over, part of the past. John Chapman would get his just reward one day. I couldn't afford to think about him any longer. I was going to begin a whole new life. I was already a different person.

Walking helped. I hadn't been able to bear the house a moment longer. Bags packed and waiting, I would return just in time to meet the boy coming to take me to the station. I would wait by the wagon while he fetched the bags. I would never set foot inside the house again. It was no longer the house where I had grown up under Aunt Meg's loving supervision. It was the house where I had been betrayed and abandoned

81

and violated. I was glad to be leaving. I couldn't have stayed a day longer.

Only my clothes, my books, the watercolor of my father, and a few other personal items would leave Cornwall with me, and I would never again return to this part of England. Brence Stephens had given me the means of escape. I wasn't going to move into a modest cottage, nor was I going to meet a fine young man and marry and bear his children and live the dull life women were expected to live, shallow, subservient, shut off from the world around them. I was meant for something else. I had a destiny, and I intended to fulfill it.

Land's End jutted out into the water ahead. I had come here deliberately. I had to see it one more time before I left. Walking out over the rock to the farthest point, I stood there with nothing but air in front of me, jagged rocks and tempestuous waves below. Misty spray shot into the air, dampening my cheeks. The wind tore at my skirts, silk and petticoats lifting, billowing behind me, my hair swirling about my head.

I allowed myself to weaken. I allowed myself to think of Brence, and the anguish and grief swept over me as the waves swept over the rocks, threatening to demolish me. I loved him. I loved him still. He had used me and then abandoned me, but the love was still alive inside me, a constant torment. How could I go on without him? How could I endure life without the promise of his arms folding around me and his lips closing over mine? Brence. Brence. Why? I would never be able to forget him, never recover. Tears brimmed over my lashes and spilled down my cheeks, and I let them flow for several minutes, and then I brushed them away.

From somewhere within me strength came, and I hardened myself and held to that hard core, forcing the pain back down into the dark recess where it would remain, tightly contained. I wouldn't give in to it, and I wouldn't give up. I was going to survive. I was going to succeed. For Brence Stephens I had been ready to compromise, ready to give up my dream of glory for the dream of love. But I had been a fool, a naive fool, and I had only myself to blame. Never again would I compromise. Never again would I depend on someone else for happiness. Standing there at the tip of Land's End, the wind tearing my hair, the waves surging below, I made these vows.

I was going to London to study with Madame Olga. There was enough money in the envelope to pay for a year of study if I was careful, if I lived in the cheapest lodgings, if I watched every penny. A year with Madame Olga would make all the difference. I was going to work and work and work, practice until I dropped from exhaustion. I was going to become the greatest ballerina in all Europe, bathed in glory, a glamorous figure imbued with a special radiance, and Brence Stephens would see me and remember and beg me to be his. One day, I vowed, the tables would be turned. I clenched my fist, filled with steely resolution. I was going to make that dream come true, and nothing on earth was going to stop me.

LONDON

1845

XI

We gathered backstage like a cluster of nervous flowers, pink, white, and red tulle skirts billowing. Sarah remarked that she felt silly as hell being a rose and added that, if rose she must be, she'd rather be a red one. White didn't suit her at all. Theresa, leaning down to tighten the ribbons of her ballet slippers, complained that all those *tours jetés* Madame expected us to do were too bloody much. She fully expected to go crashing against the brick wall on the other side of the stage and end up being crippled for life. When Jenny remarked that that might be a blessing, Theresa gave her a look that should have killed.

"What kind of crowd do we have?" Sarah wondered.

"It's a sell-out," Theresa informed her. "Madame's productions are always a sell-out. You'd think the old witch would pay us a pound or two."

"We do it for the experience," Jenny said. "How many students have an opportunity to perform before a live audience a full week every month?"

"Get her," Theresa snapped. "She's almost as bad as Mary Ellen, serious about the dance, *dedicated*. My calves are killing me, and we haven't even started yet. These dreadful slippers don't fit!"

Glancing around to make certain that Madame wasn't in sight, Sarah hurried across the empty stage to peer through the peekhole in the dusty velvet curtain. All of us were tense. The monthly ballet performances created a terrific strain on the nerves, but we realized they were invaluable experience. Madame Olga took only twenty students at a time, and only girls who had years of study behind them. Classes were held in the rehearsal hall of the theater that Madame owned, and each month she presented a new ballet, which she had choreographed herself, featuring her students. Every important producer in the world of English ballet attended these performances to scout for new talent, and over the years many of the girls had received contracts to appear with leading troupes. Half the *corps de ballet* at Convent Garden were graduates of Madame Olga's school.

Sarah looked up from the peekhole and motioned for me to join her. I hurried over, my red tulle skirt floating like gossamer petals. I knew what she was going to tell me.

"He's out there," she whispered.

"Again?"

"Second row, center aisle, the same seat he was sitting in last night. He doesn't give up, does he?"

I touched the curtain carefully and leaned forward to peer through the tiny hole invisible to the audience out front. Anthony Duke was there, all right, sitting in the seat Sarah had indicated. He wore formal attire, black satin lapels gleaming, white tie slightly awry. A half smile played on his full lips, and his dark blue eyes seemed to dance with mischief. He sat slumped down in his seat, toying with his program, completely at ease, exuding an aura of cocky self-confidence.

The musicians were beginning to fill the pit. As Sarah and I rejoined the other dancers, I could see she wanted to question me, but fortunately Madame appeared and there was no time. Small, regal, wearing a long black gown that fell in a straight line, Madame Olga examined us with dark eyes that seemed to smoulder with criticism. Her hair was sleeked back over her skull and fastened in a tight bun. Her lips were a bright red. Diamonds and emeralds flashed at her eyes and throat. Not quite five feet tall, she was fierce and formidable, crackling with magnetism.

"Tonight, young ladies, you are roses," she said in her thickly accented, guttural voice. "You are not fat dairy cows clumping around in a pasture. You are roses, delicate and fragile and airy."

"I feel more like a weed," Theresa quipped.

"What was that?" Madame growled.

"Nothing, Madame," Theresa said sweetly.

"You are a garden of roses touched with dew, bathed in moonlight, and as the sun comes up you open your petals slowly and celebrate the new day with joy and elation."

Sarah sighed. Madame's little talks always exasperated her.

"You are artists," Madame continued. "You are creating an illusion of beauty. When the curtain rises, something mystical and magical will happen. You will be responsible for it. I might add that someone very important will be looking you over. One of you girls will be leaving me at the end of the week for Covent Garden. Which one has not yet been decided."

"Marvelous," Sarah whispered. "Just what my nerves need."

"You haven't a prayer," Theresa said.

"Bitch!" Sarah hissed.

Madame's eyes flashed menacingly as Regina came rushing toward us, pink skirt flying, soft blonde hair spilling from her carefully arranged topknot. Breathless, blushing, Regina smiled a nervous smile and blinked her large blue eyes. Madame threw her hands up and rolled her eyes heavenward. Regina giggled. Theresa kicked her. Jenny stepped over to pin up Regina's topknot as Madame moved her lips in silent prayer, begging for patience.

"I lost one of my slippers," Regina explained. "I couldn't find it anywhere."

Madame glared. "I expect perfection. Nothing less will do. You will be perfect. I will be watching you out front, and I will see all of you tomorrow morning at ten, in the rehearsal hall."

There were several groans. But when Madame's brows shot up, and her mouth became a hard, tight line, blood red, the groans subsided immediately. Resigned glances were exchanged. A great spirit of camaraderie prevailed among Madame Olga's girls. All of us, victims of her stern tyranny, presented a united front; we were exclusive martyrs who paid dearly for the abuse she handed out.

"The music is beginning. Please, young ladies! You are not a gaggle of silly geese thinking of nothing but men and hair ribbons. You are artists! You are roses, beautiful roses, pink and white and red!"

We hurried across the stage, ballet slippers pattering with a soft, muffled sound. Sinking to the floor, we spread our skirts out and folded ourselves up, seven pink roses stage right, seven white roses stage center, six red stage left. The lights dimmed and the music of Chopin filled the auditorium, lovely, melodic, subdued. There was a rusty, metallic creak as the heavy curtain lifted and parted. We were suddenly bathed in a hazy silver-blue light. The crystal spangles scattered over our skirts sparkled like dew in the moonlight.

He was out there again tonight, the third night in a row. I had snubbed him properly the first night he approached me in front of the theater. He had merely grinned. Overhead, now, the haze of blue vanished and the silver grew brighter, melting into gold. I lifted one arm, slowly, moving it with the music. Last night he had been waiting for me again, and I had told him in no uncertain terms that I wasn't interested in his proposition, that I knew a scoundrel when I saw one and would summon a Bobby if he didn't leave me alone.

I lifted my other arm, both arms caressing the sunlight, gold melting into white, my head still bowed. He would be waiting for me tonight as well, no doubt, top hat tilted on his head, satin-lined opera cape falling from his shoulders. He would be leaning against the wall just outside the foyer, humming to himself, tapping his cane on the pavement as he watched the traffic pass up and down the street in front of the theater. His impudent blue eyes would light up as I stepped outside. That cocky grin would form on his lips. I would walk right past him, ignoring him completely.

I raised my head, slowly, slowly, shoulders down, neck a long, graceful line, and I swayed from side to side, lifting layers of red tulle, the stage a garden of roses bathed in morning sunlight, pure white light, dew sparkling. He was very good-looking. Not handsome, no. The mouth was too large, the cheekbones too broad, the nose slightly crooked as though it had been broken and reset improperly. He had the face of a wicked choir boy. He was thirty or so, I judged, tall and lean and very attractive and much too charming. Pink roses stood, swayed, and danced across the stage as the Chopin melody swelled.

I wasn't at all interested in Mr. Anthony Duke. Ballet girls were all the rage this year, and every roué in London felt he must possess one. Madame Olga's girls were not yet professionals, but they were highly prized, possibly because she kept such a close watch over us, sternly forbidding us to go out with any of the men who attended the performances. During the past year at least a dozen men had made advances to me, but I had snubbed them all. Sarah and Theresa found this amusing. The white roses were dancing now, moving around in circles with the pink, celebrating the bright white sunlight.

He was just another man-about-town, eager to have his ballet girl to squire around and show off to his friends. I didn't believe for a minute that he was connected with the theater. An entrepreneur, he called himself, formerly with Fleet Street. Knew everyone worth knowing, he claimed; wanted to make me a star. A child of twelve would hardly fall for that old chestnut. He had the looks of a natural born liar, a rogue who breezed through life on his charm, his wits, his dashing appearance. Pink and white roses circled around the red, beckoning us to rise, to celebrate the morning and savor its beauty. We swayed, red petals rising, floating, arms reaching for the sunlight.

I was lonely. I had never known such loneliness. Though I was friendly with the other dancers, I was close to none of them. I hadn't the means to associate with them outside the theater, and my pride prevented me from accepting the invitations they handed out so casually. I had no friends at all except Millie, and she kept such odd hours that I rarely saw her. It would be nice to go out to a restaurant with a man, to attend the theater with him on one of the nights when we weren't dancing. But not a man like Anthony Duke, not a rake who hung around outside theaters pursuing women who wanted nothing to do with him.

"Jesus!" Sarah hissed. "Get up, Mary Ellen!"

I looked at her, startled. The other red roses had already unfolded and were standing on tall stems, swaying as the white and pink wove in and out. Sarah floated past. Rising a good thirty seconds after the others, I whirled about, pretending it was part of the choreography, joining in step, but I was unnerved. What on earth was the matter with me? I had never done anything like that before. I was always part of the music, part of the magic, my own identity thoroughly submerged. I moved across the stage on point, bending, swaying, whirling.

I made no more errors, but all the while I was conscious of the lights, the sea of faces, the hundreds of eyes watching, of one pair in particular. The dance was supposed to be a liquid flow of expression, but tonight I was acutely aware of each step, each movement. I felt stiff and mechanical, a separate entity going through my paces with little feeling.

Red and pink roses danced offstage while the white remained to do their special interlude. I moved around a coil of rope and stood beside a stack of flats that leaned against the wall to watch. Mattie, the wardrobe woman, rushed over to hand each of us a towel, and we carefully patted away perspiration. Regina's topknot had begun to spill down again. She giggled as an irritated Theresa shoved soft blonde waves back in place and jabbed hairpins into them. I was out of breath, and every muscle in my body felt sore. For the first time I was afraid, afraid I wouldn't remember the steps when the red roses did their specialty, afraid I would blunder.

Applause filled the auditorium as the dancers in white tulle sailed offstage as though carried on air. The pink whirled on, skirts making full circles as the dancers spun on point. Sarah seized a towel from Mattie and moved over to join me, patting her face and shoulders.

"What's the matter with you tonight?"

"I . . . I don't know."

"It's that man, isn't it? He's upset you."

I shook my head. "That isn't it, Sarah. It's . . . it's a lot of things. I just . . . can't seem to concentrate."

I had exactly ten pounds to my name. I had been extremely frugal, but after a year the money had simply vanished. I hadn't paid Mrs. Fernwood for three weeks, and I knew she wouldn't hesitate to turn me out of my room if I didn't pay up soon. For the past month I had been skipping breakfast and dinner, eating only lunch, trying to economize even more. I needed new ballet slippers. I needed a new cloak before winter. I would have to pay Madame again at the end of the month, and I simply didn't have the money.

Loneliness wasn't the worst of it. Doubts had begun to besiege me about my dancing. Madame Olga took only those students who showed great promise. I had been very promising, but after a year I was no better than I had been when I began her classes. Deep down I knew that. I worked harder than any of the others. Many an afternoon after classes were over I remained behind to practice in the deserted rehearsal hall, but it seemed to do no good. The ability was there, the technique, but that special quality was missing, the quality that set a dancer apart and enabled her to shine. Would I ever have it? Not without more hard work, and how could I continue to study with Madame Olga if . . .

"You look faint," Sarah said.

"I'm all right."

Her blue eyes were filled with genuine concern. "But Mary Ellen, this isn't like you. You—oh, you're not pregnant, are you?"

"Of course not."

"I didn't think so. You and Jenny are about the only ones who don't have a man on the string. Something's bothering you, though. I can tell. Look, if I can help in any way—"

I squeezed her hand. "I'm all right," I repeated. "I— I've been trying to lose weight, and I just felt a little weak."

Sarah was thoroughly exasperated. "For heaven's sake!" she snapped. "Of all the—you go home tonight and get something to eat! You'd better get in line now, our *pas de six* is about to begin. And try not to disgrace us."

I smiled again, amused. Sarah's friendly abrasiveness had been exactly what I needed. I got in line with the other red roses who, listening to the music, awaited their cue. I detested self-pity, and I had come very close to it tonight. For a year now I had pushed myself with drive and determination, ignoring the loneliness, the emptiness inside, ignoring the hardship, fighting the bitterness and the pain that swept over me each time I thought of Brence Stephens. I had been strong, but the strain had finally gotten to me. As the dancers in pink whirled off-stage, I felt a new strength, a new resolution.

I would find some sort of employment that would still permit me to continue with Madame Olga. I would serve food in a restaurant. I would even sweep floors, if necessary. I wasn't going to admit defeat. I would work and work, and that quality, that charisma, would materialize and I would become a great prima ballerina one day. I had to believe that, for that dream was all I had. It was all that kept me going. Without it, I would be utterly lost and the anguish I had been holding at bay would destroy me.

I moved onto the stage, on point, floating on air. I was one with the music now. I was part of the magic, a rose caressed with bright white sunlight. One *tour jeté*, two, perfectly executed. The pink roses joined us, surrounded us, and then the white, and we whirled, carried on air by the breeze in the garden. The music grew softer, slower, and the sunlight melted into gold, dark gold, fading into silver, silver-blue, dimming into darkness as we sank to the floor, petals folding.

The music ended. The curtain fell on the same tableau the audience had seen when the curtain rose. We maintained our positions as the curtain rose again, fell again, and then we hurried backstage to the sound of enthusiastic applause. The stage was bathed in blazing light. The heavy velvet curtain rose again, and we took our curtain calls just as Madame Olga had staged them. We were relaxed and elated, smiling as the audience continued to show its appreciation with hearty enthusiasm. Then Madame Olga moved regally on stage and acknowledged the applause with an imperious nod.

As Madame Olga left the stage, the curtain fell for the final time and the house lights came on. We adjourned to the dressing room. Though it was small and cramped and poorly ventilated, an atmosphere of bright frivolity prevailed. It was always like that after a performance. The dancers chattered vivaciously and laughed and dashed about like lovely, exotic birds, turning their costumes over to Mattie, changing into their street clothes, gossiping merrily as they sat at the mirrors lining the long dressing table. The air was heavy with the smells of sweat and powder and perfume. The two small windows opening onto the alley in back of the theater permitted only an occasional suggestion of fresh air into the room.

Taking off my costume, I handed it to Mattie and grabbed a towel from the stack she had placed on one of the benches. I patted myself dry, put on my petticoat, and sat down at the dressing table to unfasten my hair, letting it cascade about my shoulders. I removed my stage makeup and dried my face. Bone weary now, but in a much better mood than I had been earlier, I felt determined once again to succeed against all odds. This was my world, my life, and no amount of adversity was going to defeat me.

"I think it went very well," Theresa exclaimed. "We were marvelous, just marvelous! All except Mary Ellen, of course. It's encouraging to know even she makes an occasional error, and it was a dilly!"

"I was terrible," I admitted.

"That's all right, pet. I almost landed on my backside twice tonight. All right, who's got my rouge? First someone steals my box of powder, and now my bloody rouge is——"

"It's right there in front of you," Jenny told her. "I'd be very careful how I use it. Madame might still be around, and you know how she feels. Only prostitutes wear makeup offstage, she says, and her girls must be above reproach."

95

"You'd think she was running a bloody convent," Sarah complained. "My brother brought me to the theater this afternoon, my brother, mind you. Madame saw us and I got such a lecture. Her young ladies must conserve all their energies for the dance—"

"I didn't know you had a brother," Theresa said.

"She doesn't," Jenny remarked.

"I do as far as Madame Olga is concerned. He's ever so nice. Dreamy brown eyes, dark red hair, and such shoulders! He's rich, too. Let me borrow a spot of your rouge, Theresa. I'm meeting him tonight."

"I'm meeting my cousin," Theresa informed us. "He's an Earl. At least he says he is. Has a divine flat in Kensington, servants and everything."

"Is he the one who gave you the diamond bracelet?"

"That was my uncle, pet. The bastard went back to his wife two weeks ago, before I even got a necklace to match!"

The others burst into gales of merry laughter. I smiled and continued to brush my hair.

"Speaking of relatives," Theresa said, "that man was out front again tonight, Mary Ellen. You know the one I mean, the divine-looking fellow who's been pestering you."

"She saw him," Sarah told her. "She's not interested."

"I wish he'd pester me," Theresa sighed. "I'd give up my cousin in a minute. Who is he, Mary Ellen?"

"His name is Anthony Duke."

"Duke?" Regina trilled. "Did someone say there's a duke backstage?"

Sarah, Theresa, and Jenny groaned in unison. Regina wasn't noted for her towering intellect. The others treated her with a combination of patience and weary resignation.

"It's the Prince of Wales," Sarah said.

"Oh? I'd love to meet him."

"I bet he'd just love to meet you, too. He's almost five years old. You'd have so much in common."

"What does this Anthony Duke do?" Theresa asked.

"He claims he's connected with the theater," I replied.

"He looks like a bounder to me," Jenny observed.

"They're the best kind. You're really not interested, Mary Ellen?"

"Not in the least."

"I suppose you'd rather practice your dancing," Theresa said dryly.

"It wouldn't hurt you to practice a little more yourself," Jenny remarked. "If you keep on clumping about like you've been doing for the past couple of nights, Madame's going to put you out onto the street. I've no doub you'd feel right at home there."

"Absolutely, pet."

All three of them laughed in bright, silvery peals, Theresa the loudest. They continued to chatter, but soon forgot Anthony Duke and went on to another subject. Tuning them out, I brushed my hair and gazed at my reflection in the mirror, noting the changes a year had made. I was thinner, and my eyes were a darker blue, dark with the knowledge of life and loss and loneliness. My lids were brushed with faint violet shadows. My cheekbones were still too high, my mouth too large, too dark a pink. The features were the same as those of the eighteen-year-old who had gazed into her mirror a year ago, but there was a new maturity, a patina of disillusionment. The girl had vanished. The woman who had taken her place looked much older.

Putting the brush down, I turned around on the stool, slipped on my high-heeled violet pumps, and got up to dress. My blue-and-violet-striped cotton frock had long sleeves, a square-cut bodice, and a tight-waisted skirt that fell over my slim petticoats. It accentuated my full bosom and my slender waist. With my hair tumbling about my shoulders in rich, abundant waves as blue-black as a raven's wing, I looked like a dark, exotic gypsy with a curiously aristocratic demeanor. Not beautiful, but undeniably striking.

"I'm off!" Theresa cried. "Wish me luck with my cousin, girls. He's promised me a special treat tonight."

"Let me guess," Jenny said.

The dressing room began to empty out as the dancers departed, silks and satins rustling. In a flurry of excitement, Regina left, assuring her friend Martha that the

Prince of Wales was waiting backstage. Discreetly rouged, sumptuously gowned, Sarah sighed wearily and bade the rest farewell. Jenny took down her cloak and told me she'd best get home to dear old Mum. Within a few minutes I was alone in the dressing room. The bright litter the girls had left in their wake glowed in the lamplight; soft gray shadows played over the damp tan walls.

I lingered for a while, putting away my brush and makeup in the drawer assigned to me, checking to see if my extra pair of ballet slippers was still in my locker. Finally, when Mattie came in to put out the lights, I left the dressing room and moved quickly past the backstage area, which was like a huge semidark cave festooned with bizarre black shadows. Hurrying down the narrow hall on the side of the auditorium, I ignored the stage door and stepped into the front foyer. The lobby had a shabby elegance about it with its worn red carpet and cream-colored floral wallpaper patterned in flaking gold leaf.

The chandelier was still ablaze. Todd stood in front of the doors, key in hand, face lined with weariness. Todd, caretaker of the theater and assistant stage manager, had his living quarters in the basement and he waited to see us all out every night.

"Evenin', Miss Lawrence. You're the last of the lot again."

"Sorry, Todd. Mattie's still backstage."

"I know. She an' me're gonna stroll 'round the corner for a quick nip when she finishes up. Can I fetch you a 'ansom?"

"I think I'll walk home, Todd."

"You take care now, ya 'ear? It's mighty late for a pretty young lady like yourself to be wanderin' about alone."

He held the door open for me. I smiled and thanked him, stepping out into the recessed area beneath the marquee. Carriages and hansom cabs rumbled up and down the street. Elegantly dressed pedestrians walked along the pavements, talking, laughing, enjoying the warm night air. Lamp lights created a soft golden haze, and there was no fog. Anthony Duke was nowhere in sight. I felt a wave of relief . . . and something absurdly akin to disappointment as well.

I started down the street in a pensive mood, a faint melancholy stealing over me as I thought of the lonely room that awaited me and the memories that invariably came to haunt me whenever I was alone and unoccupied. I had tried to fight them off for twelve months now, but still they came to torment me. The pain was still potent, the bitterness as strong, the longing worst of all. I hated Brence Stephens for what he had done to me, hated him with all my heart, and yet I longed to be in his arms, longed to know again that wild splendor we had shared.

As I reached the corner and paused to let a carriage pass before crossing the street, I heard the footsteps running toward me. I turned to see Anthony Duke hurrying toward me, his opera cape billowing behind him like dark wings, satin lining flashing. Reaching the corner, he stopped and grinned that audacious grin that was so engaging.

"I almost missed you," he said. "I popped into the club to have a drink, struck up a conversation with a chap from the opera and completely lost track of time. Bet your heart sank when you didn't find me waiting."

"Hardly," I retorted.

"You on your way home?"

"That's none of your—"

"Of course you are," he interrupted. "You never go anywhere else. I know. I checked it out, made inquiries. I know all about you, luv."

"Mr. Duke—"

"I'll just walk along with you. Who knows what evil these dark streets conceal? You'll feel much safer with a big strong chap like me at your side. You might even invite me up to your room."

"If you don't—"

He seized my arm and, cutting me short, said, "If I don't stop bothering you, you'll call a Bobby. Right? Wrong. I'm a very persistent fellow, Mary Ellen. I always get what I want. I've been patient up till now, but my patience is fast running out. If you don't behave, I'm likely to throttle you."

He removed his hand from my arm and grinned again.

I slapped him across the face, a resounding blow that stung my hand. Anthony Duke make a clacking noise with his tongue and slowly shook his head.

"Oh, luv," he said. "You really shouldn't have done that."

XII

He made no attempt to restrain me as I started across the street, nor did he follow me. Halfway down the street I turned to look back. He was still standing at the corner, rubbing his jaw, and his expression seemed thoughtful. The incident disturbed me more than I cared to admit. I had difficulty getting to sleep that night, for once not thinking of Brence, thinking instead of the audacious stranger who had come into my life so recently, who seemed to believe he could simply take over, order me about, treat me as though I were his own personal property.

At rehearsal the next morning, I was still thinking of him as we began our exercises. We wore black ballet slippers, black tights, and black cotton practice costumes that resembled petticoats with full skirts that swirled just below the knees. The rehearsal hall was warm and we were all perspiring. Madame was in a demonic mood, snapping orders in a chilling voice, clapping her hands together angrily, stamping her foot. She wore a long blue smock with full, flowing sleeves. Ropes of opals hung around her neck, purple, violet-blue, opal pendants dangling from her ears. She was very unhappy with us, dark eyes flashing, blood-red mouth tight with disapproval.

She was particularly displeased with me today. I could tell that. Madame Olga knew I was dedicated, that I devoted far more time to practice than the others. She approved. Never friendly with any of us, she had always treated me with a modicum of respect which, though barely perceptible, was there nonetheless. This morning her manner had been frigid when I greeted her. Those great eyes had been afire with disapproval. She had not returned my greeting, but nodded curtly, instead, and clapped her hands and ordered us to get in line.

She had noticed my slip last night, of course. She watched every performance with eagle eyes, noting even the slightest discrepancy in movement and line. I assumed that she was furious with me, and rightly so, that I would have to work even harder to make up for it. Tonight I would dance better than I had ever danced before, but this morning I was finding it hard to concentrate. Madame's harsh, icy manner upset me. And, no matter how much I tried to put him out of my mind, I kept thinking of Anthony Duke when I should have been thinking of the music.

Though I stumbled twice, Madame did not comment. Ordinarily when one of us made an error she stopped the rehearsal and flew into a rage, giving the offender a severe tongue-lashing. She did just that when Theresa missed a step. Ordering the pianist to stop, she upbraided Theresa with unusual venom and made us start all over again. It was almost one o'clock in the afternoon before we finally finished. Madame swept out of the room without a word, her blue smock flowing, opal pendants swinging. I was exhausted and, in the mirror behind the practice bar, I could see that my cheeks were pale.

We retired to the changing room like a flock of blackbirds whose wings had been clipped. We towelled ourselves dry, removed our practice clothes, and took our street clothes out of the lockers. There was none of the merry frivolity and chatter that took place in the backstage dressing room. We were beaten down, dispirited, bodies aching from the ordeal Madame had put us through. Everyone had seen me stumble, but no one commented on it, not even Theresa, who had every right to feel resentful. I changed into my yellow cotton dress, eager to get home, to bathe, to rest until it was time to come back for the evening performance.

Sarah caught up with me as I was leaving.

"Your friend was here this morning," she said.

"My friend?"

"Anthony Duke. I got here early, before any of the others, God knows why. I suppose my clock was fast. Anyway, just as I was passing Madame's office the door opened and he stepped out."

"He—he'd been in her office?"

Sarah nodded. "Evidently they'd been having some kind of conference. He looked very pleased with himself."

I felt a sinking sensation in the pit of my stomach.

"He swaggered on down the hall, humming to himself. He's very attractive, Mary Ellen, and much too charming. It's none of my business, of course, but—well, I'd be wary of him. Anthony Duke looks like a scoundrel to me."

"I got the same impression," I said dryly.

"He *is* connected with the theater," she continued. "William and I stepped into the club last night for a drink after the performance—William's the 'brother' I mentioned. Duke was at the bar, downing Scotch and holding forth with some out-of-work tenor. He dashed out a few minutes after we arrived, and I asked William about him. He told me quite a lot."

"He knows Duke?"

We stepped into the foyer and paused beneath the chandelier. Rays of sunlight streamed in through the glass door panels, making bright squares on the red carpet and causing the gold leaf on the walls to glitter. Sarah touched her hair and gave me a wry smile.

"Not socially, but he knows about him. Duke's connected with the Dorrance Opera Company. It's a far cry from Covent Garden, but it's still a professional company, however second-rate. Some of the best singers appear there between engagements at Covent Garden and La Scala."

"I've heard about the company."

"The sets are shabby, the costumes laughable, but the orchestra's supposed to be tolerable. Dorrance will hire one good soprano to bring in the paying customers and surround her with has-beens and competent amateurs, and she'll carry the evening. Dorrance isn't the only company that does that, of course. Even if the tenor's asthmatic and the baritone a drunk, opera lovers will endure any kind of production as long as they can hear their favorite hit those high C's."

"What does Duke do?"

"He handles the promotion. He's chummy with the lads on Fleet Street; used to write for one of the papers himself, I understand. No matter how bad the production, he can always get plenty of coverage—spicy stories about the prima donna, backstage gossip about feuds, and so on. It's sensational and tasteless, but it sells a lot of tickets."

"I imagine it does."

"He's also in charge of the entertainment between the acts, William said. It's Duke's job to get some singer or juggler or acrobat to keep the audience occupied during the intermissions. I hate to think what kind of talent he's able to find."

Sarah shook her head, sighing wearily. "Anyway, Mary Ellen, you don't want to get involved with Mr. Anthony Duke. I'd keep right on snubbing him if I were you."

"I intend to. I . . . I wonder what he wanted with Madame."

"God knows. Whatever it was, it didn't cheer her up. I've never seen her in such a bitchy mood. The way she jumped all over Theresa, I thought she was actually going to draw blood!"

"She was unusually rough," I agreed.

"Rough isn't the word for it. Well, I'm off to the flat and a hot bath. I'll see you tonight, and try to remember all your cues. We don't want Madame committing mass slaughter."

The sinking sensation persisted as I started back toward the rooming house. Carriages and lorries rumbled down the street. Hawkers cried their wares. A bell pealed from one of the churches. London was alive and bustling with all its customary noise and color, but the activity and the ever-changing drama of the streets held no fascination for me. Ordinarily, I would have paused to examine a store window, to inspect the wares on a cart, to watch pigeons circling an ornate spire, or watch a group of children at play. Today I walked briskly, a frown creasing my brow, a dreadful fear spreading inside me.

What could Anthony Duke possibly have wanted with Madame Olga? I could think of no logical explanation. Madame was far too grand to have anything to do with the Dorrance Opera Company. She would pale at the thought of one of her dancers appearing there. But Anthony Duke had come to see her about me, I was sure of that. His visit had upset her, and that was the reason she had been so cool toward me. I was Madame's favorite student, everyone accepted that, and yet this morning she had treated me as though I didn't exist. What had he told her that had caused her manner toward me to alter so abruptly?

Anthony Duke was persistent, and he was ruthless, too. His good looks and charm couldn't conceal that. It was evident in the set of his jaw, in the curve of his mouth. He might be able to cause dozens of women to swoon just by cocking his eyebrow and flashing that boyish grin, but I had no doubt that he could be utterly unscrupulous if occasion demanded. Duke was the kind of man who would stop at nothing to get what he wanted, and he wanted me. All that talk about putting me on the stage was merely an attempt to attract me.

I was upset, and angry as well. How dare he invade my life? I had enough to worry about without any new threats. Unless I found some sort of employment, I would be penniless within a few weeks. I hadn't made nearly enough progress with my dancing, despite all my hard work. I needed at least another year before I would be ready for employment as a professional dancer . . . and this handsome, arrogant stranger with mocking blue eyes and breezy, determined manner had forced his way into my life, into my thoughts, adding yet another worry.

I was still angry as I reached the square where the grim brownstone rooming house I lived in stood amid a row of identical houses. Situated just off Marylebone Road, it was within walking distance of the theater. There were elegant squares nearby where the wealthy dwelled, but here children played noisily in the unkempt gardens beyond the wrought-iron fence, and everything had the mellow patina of age. Though the neighborhood was only semi-respectable, it wasn't a slum. I was fortunate to have found a room here, and I only hoped I would be able to keep it.

Climbing the flat white marble steps stained with neglect, I peered into the dimly lit foyer with its abundance of dusty green plants. Mrs. Fernwood's marmalade cat peered back at me from the top of the refectory table, lounging indolently across the unclaimed mail and ignoring the chipped blue saucer of meat tidbits his mistress had placed nearby. I adored animals, but this particular creature had taken on the hateful, proprietary disposition of its mistress. His eyes seemed to accuse me as I moved toward the steps. I felt like an intruder and, remembering the unpaid rent, silently prayed Mrs. Fernwood wouldn't hear me.

"There you are!" she cried.

Having made it up only four steps, I stopped as Mrs. Fernwood shuffled into the foyer. Stout, stolid, wearing a loose blue-and-gray-flowered wrap that only emphasized her girth, she tottered a bit before catching hold of the refectory table to steady herself. The cat hissed. Mrs. Fernwood chuckled, her dark eyes bright with malice, her plump cheeks flushed. A bright red paint coated her thick lips, and her hair, worn in short sausage ringlets, was a highly improbable shade of brassy gold. Millie claimed that the woman had once been the proprietor of a notorious brothel near the waterfront. It wouldn't have surprised me in the least.

" 'Ear you're movin' soon, ducks," she said.

"Mrs. Fernwood, I know my rent's overdue, but—"

"Oh, don't worry 'bout *that*, child. Your friend paid, paid for th' rest of th' month, too, 'e did, even though you'll be leavin'. Charmin' lad, that 'un. Cheeky as they come. Teased me somethin' awful, slapped me on th' fanny as 'e was leavin'."

I stood very still.

"When—when was he here?" I inquired.

"Couple-a 'ours ago. 'Andsome devil. You're a lucky lass. A chap like 'im, 'e can take care o' all your needs. Must be a regular demon in the 'ay, all fierce an' greedy. I knew you'd find yourself a man sooner 'r later. All them fine airs never fooled me for a minute."

106

Patting her brassy curls, Mrs. Fernwood smiled. It was actually a leer. Scooping up the cat, she began to stroke its back. It hissed warningly, one paw slashing out at the sleeve of her wrap.

"I suppose 'e'll be settin' you up in a grand flat," she mused. "I knew it'd 'appen. Well, luck to you, luv. Treat 'im real nice. 'E's a prize, an' you could just as easily be walkin' the streets like your chum Millie. I know all about 'er. None o' my affair, though, not as long as she pays 'er rent."

"Why don't you go have another glass of gin, Mrs. Fernwood?" I snapped.

" 'Magine I will, ducks. Just thought I'd pop out an' say ta-ta 'fore you leave. I see so many of 'em come an' go. Young, pretty, ambitious, they don't stay long. There's always a man. You've stayed far longer than most, but then you're choosey. Guess it paid off. Got yourself a real prize—"

I left her rambling on and climbed up the four flights to my floor. So he had paid my rent. Thoughtful of him. That was one less thing I had to worry about, at least until the end of the month. Stepping into my room, I shut the door with a slam. I knew what he expected in return, and he wasn't going to get it. The rent was paid. Fine. I wouldn't have to creep up and down the stairs like a burglar, afraid Mrs. Fernwood would come pouncing out with palm extended. But Anthony Duke would never see a penny of the money again, nor would he receive any other kind of compensation. He was quite mistaken if he believed I would feel a sense of obligation to him.

Unable to rest, I straightened my room and went through my wardrobe, wondering how much longer my clothes would last. I still had many fine dresses, but they were beginning to show wear. I had not bought a single new outfit since arriving in London. I had lived frugally, counting each penny, yet the money had still vanished. I wasn't going to worry about that just now. My rent was paid, thanks to Anthony Duke, and as long as I was paid up, I might as well order a hot bath. Mrs. Fernwood charged extra for baths, of course, but luxuriating in a hot tub would do wonders for me.

Stepping out into the hall, I caught sight of Jessie

washing the windows at the end of the hall and asked her to prepare a tub. She scurried away, her enormous brown eyes full of concern. Jessie was a dear thing with her patched black stockings and faded gray dress, her pale blonde hair always spilling down from her topknot. Millie and I tipped her as much as we could for her pathetic services, and the child always looked as though she wanted to burst into tears. I found it cruel that a girl barely thirteen should have to polish bannisters and carry out slops and haul in buckets of coal, but Millie claimed Jessie was one of the lucky ones; when she was thirteen Millie was already on the streets.

I soaked in the bath for over an hour and washed my hair as well. It was almost six before I returned to my room. I would have to leave for the theater in an hour or so. Wearing only my petticoat, I sat in front of the dressing table and brushed my hair. Sunlight slanted in through the windows, pale and silvery, making bright patterns on the faded rose carpet and gilding the surfaces of the old mahogany furniture. The shabby room was comfortable enough with its flowered chintz curtains, its overstuffed olive chair and worn rose satin bedcovers. My books, which were all I had brought with me from Cornwall besides my clothes, helped to make the room my own.

I was still brushing my hair when I heard footsteps in the hall and a light knock on the door. "Yes?" I called, and Millie stepped into the room, looking bright and sunny in a yellow muslin dress embroidered with tiny brown and gold flowers. The cut was exceedingly girlish with its puffed sleeves, form-fitting bodice, and full, swirling skirt. Millie's long golden curls, pert pink mouth, and freckled cheeks might have been those of a demure young girl fresh from the country were it not for the deep-blue eyes. They were dark with worldly wisdom, eyes that had seen far too much for a seventeen-year-old. Tough, resilient, outrageously saucy, Millie was fiercely independent and invariably good-natured, determined to make the best of things no matter what the circumstances.

" 'Ow do you like it?" she exclaimed, whirling around to show off the dress.

"It's enchanting, Millie."

"Made it myself. Just finished 'emmin' the skirt this afternoon. Don't I look winsome?"

"You look charming."

"No feather boas or flashy paste jewelry for me, luv. No rouge or powder, either. The men fancy a sweet young lass with a delicate air, and I aim to please. I've been practicin' my blush for weeks!"

"I'm sure you'll be a sensation."

"Oh, I don't wanna be that. I just wanna keep on makin' ends meet, if you know what I mean." She smiled her saucy smile, delighted with her *double entendre*.

Millie had been orphaned at twelve and sent to live on a farm with her widowed uncle and his two strapping sons. When she was twelve and a half, her uncle had raped her, and shortly thereafter she was servicing his sons each night as well. Figuring that if she was going to spend so much time on her back, she might as well get paid for it, Millie had stolen a pouch of coins from her uncle and headed straight for London. The city was a treacherous place for a young girl alone, but Millie had faced all adversities with self-assurance, retaining her high spirits and the cheerful disposition that made her so endearing.

"Thought I'd pop down and 'elp you dress," she said. "Looks like you're gonna need a 'and with your 'air, too."

"It really isn't necessary, Millie."

"Oh, I love doin' it. What'll it be tonight?"

"I really hadn't given it any thought."

Millie had already opened the wardrobe door and was inspecting the clothes with a critical eye.

"Mmmm, let's see—not the pink silk, and this blue taffeta is beginnin' to look frayed. I'll 'ave to work on that 'un, maybe add a row of ruffles or somethin', Do you feel like velvet? Too dressy? You don't 'ave anything red. You'd look smashin' in red, luv. With that gorgeous black 'air you'd look like a dream. So many pretty things. I'd be in 'eaven if I 'ad clothes like this. 'Ere it is! This lovely pearl gray. Watered silk, it is, and all these ruffles of coral lace—"

Millie took the dress from the wardrobe and spread it

out on the bed, handling it tenderly, smoothing the skirt. She loved to help me take care of my clothes. Talented with needle and thread and an inventive seamstress, she had kept my things in marvelous condition. Millie had a way with hair, as well, and adored doing mine up for me, attempting new styles. Fussy, particular, with instinctive taste and a critical eye, she would have made a superb lady's maid. I told her so.

"Oh, I'd like that," she said, "but who'd 'ire a 'ore, luv? Not any of the fine ladies I've seen sashayin' about London. Dear me, they'd be appalled at the very idea."

"You mustn't put yourself down, Millie."

"I don't," she retorted. "I do what I do 'cause I 'ave to. Some girls might choose to starve, but me—I 'ave more spunk. It's not so bad, really. I 'ave my regulars—pleasant chaps, most of 'em, quite fond of me. I've always been particular. I'm lucky. I could be sellin' it in Soho every night like those other poor wretches."

Millie stepped over to the dressing table, took the brush from my hand, and began to arrange my hair.

"I've been puttin' a little aside, too, luv. Most-a the girls blow their earnin's on gin or give it all to some man who clips 'em on the jaw by way of thanks. Me, I never touch liquor, and I'm not about to let any man boss me about."

"You're very wise."

"I 'ave to be, luv. It's Millie against the world, and I don't mind tellin' you, the world can be rough when you're all alone."

"I've noticed."

"You've 'ad your share o' knocks, too, but you've got class and education. You're going to be rich an' famous one of these days. I can feel it in my bones. 'Ere now, we're finished."

She fastened another hairpin in place, frowned, and stepped back to admire her handiwork. Soft ebony waves swept back from my face, were caught up in back and fell in a rich cascade over my shoulders. Millie studied the coiffure critically for a moment and then smiled and snapped her fingers and began to rummage through the ribbon box, finally coming up with a long coral ribbon of soft velvet. She affixed it to the back of

110

my head in a large bow, gave my waves a final pat, and pronounced herself satisfied.

"It looks lovely," I told her. "It always does when you do it."

"I reckon I 'ave a talent with 'air," she admitted. "It's time we got you dressed, luv. Wouldn't want you to be late to the theater. Wish I could come watch you dance again, but I've got an appointment at nine. Wonderful chap. Always gives me a generous tip—"

The gown was one of my loveliest, much too elegant to wear to the theater, but Millie had her heart set on it, and I wasn't going to disappoint her. It had narrow sleeves and a modest scooped neckline that exposed an ample amount of bosom. The bodice was form-fitting, the waist snug, and the full pearl-gray skirt was adorned with row upon row of coral lace ruffles. Millie helped me dress, spreading the skirt out over my voluminous petticoat and fastening the bodice in back.

"You look like a bloomin' duchess," she declared. "All them chaps 'angin' 'round the stage door are gonna be knocked right off their feet."

"There's just one," I replied, "and believe me, I'd love to see him take a spill."

"That 'andsome chap with brown 'air and wicked blue eyes?"

"You've seen him?"

" 'E was 'ere today. I was just comin' down the stairs as 'e was biddin' old Ferny adieu. 'E gave me the eye. That sort always does. Not that 'e was really interested, mind you, just lookin' over the goods outa 'abit. 'E was givin' Ferny a 'andful o' bills."

"My rent. He was kind enough to pay it."

"Smashin'. I 'ope you're not plannin' to pay 'im back."

"Not a chance."

"Good for you, love," she said, fetching the long coral velvet gloves that went with my gown. " 'Ere, might as well put these on while you're at it. Seein' 'im might not be a bad idea."

"What do you mean?"

" 'E might 'elp you forget the other one."

"How did you—"

"Oh, you've never mentioned 'im, luv, never said any-

111

thing about your past, but I knew the minute I met you. Knew you were tryin' to forget some man. It was written all over you. Still is. You're never gonna be able to forget 'im long as you stay in your room an' brood. This chap might be just the tonic you need."

I pulled on one of the gloves, smoothing it over forearm and elbow. "I doubt it," I said wryly.

"Oh, I'm not sayin' you should fall in love with 'im. God forbid. That sort'd break your 'eart, steal your money, an' laugh 'is 'ead off as 'e walked out the door. I'm just sayin' it might do you good to go out with 'im an' 'ave a bit o' fun."

"I'd rather read a good book."

Millie gave me an exasperated look. "All these books —they can't be good for you. You're young, an' you're a gorgeous creature, luv. It seems such a waste."

I finished pulling on the other glove and began putting my things in the gray silk reticule that matched the dress. Millie brushed a long gold ringlet away from her temple and stepped over to the mirror to admire the cut of her gown. It accentuated her slender waist and well-rounded bosom.

"We 'ave to learn to use men, luv," she said. "If we don't use 'em, they're bloody well gonna use us, and me, I like to be the one who calls the shots. It's much nicer that way. Think about it."

"I will," I promised. "I'd better leave now. I don't want to be late, and it's a long walk. It's warm out. I don't think I'll need a cloak."

Millie went downstairs with me and walked me to the front door, making a face at Mrs. Fernwood's cat as we passed the table. We said goodbye on the front steps, and I started down the street, feeling rather foolish in the elegant gown and the long velvet gloves. If I were going to meet a man or, at least, take a carriage, it wouldn't be so bad, but I was dressed for a grand party and didn't even have enough money in my reticule to pay for a cab. I smiled, amused at the thought, amused, too, by Millie's matter-of-fact philosophy concerning men. She was probably right, I reflected. Brence Stephens had certainly used me.

It was a lovely evening, the sky a pale gray, not yet

black, and there was a misty haze in the air. The gas-lights, just coming on, looked like soft silvery blossoms glowing dimly through the haze. Turning into one of the better squares, I moved past a row of elegant houses, white marble steps gleaming, where an atmosphere of luxury prevailed. Behind the wrought-iron fence the flowers in their neat beds exuded a fragrant smell, and a bird warbled throatily in one of the trees. I was glad I had given myself time enough for a leisurely walk, so I could enjoy the evening.

A large closed carriage turned the corner at the end of the street and stopped. The horses stood patiently at the curb. I sauntered on, paying it no attention, but when I neared the carriage the side door opened. A man climbed out and stood on the pavement watching me approach. His hands rested lightly on his thighs, and as his opera cape belled out in the light breeze, I saw a flash of the white silk lining. My heart skipped a beat, and I stopped.

Anthony Duke moved toward me.

"You—"

"I intended to pick you up at your front door," he explained, "but as we turned the corner I saw you coming down the street and told the driver to pull over. I always seem to be running a little late. It's one of my worst faults."

"If you—"

"No arguments now, luv. Be a good girl. Just come along peacefully."

"I'm not going anywhere with you."

Anthony Duke took hold of my arm.

"Oh, but you are," he said.

XIII

His voice was pleasant, even playful, but there was nevertheless a steely edge to it. In the glow of the gaslight, I could see his lean and angular face, the cheekbones too broad, the nose slightly crooked, its imperfections making it even more attractive. The wide mouth curled in a boyish grin, and the blue eyes were full of merry mockery and an undeniable determination. He was so tall I had to tilt my chin up to look into those eyes. His fingers tightened on my arm, hurting me.

"Let go of me!" I ordered.

"Promise to behave yourself?"

"I promise to slap you senseless if you don't let go this instant."

"Spirit. I love a lass with spirit."

"I'm going to be late to the theater!"

"Oh, but you're not going to the theater tonight. Didn't I tell you? You're coming to my digs. We're going to have a lovely dinner together, just the two of us."

"You're out of your mind!"

"It's all arranged. When I spoke with Madame Olga, I told her that you'd no longer be studying with her. In fact, I told her we were going to run off together and live in delicious sin. She was quite upset. She called me several colorful names, all heavily accented."

"You're mad!"

"My man has everything set up—a gorgeous dinner, luv, champagne in a silver bucket. Pheasant. Oysters, too.

115

It's all waiting. I've given him the night off for the sake of discretion. I'll serve it myself."

I tried to pull away, but his fingers tightened even more, and I gave a little cry. He chuckled softly. So, I kicked his shin. He gave a cry considerably louder than mine had been. A face appeared at one of the windows, and he let go of my arm. Seizing the opportunity, I tried to dart past him, but his arm encircled my waist, pulling me up against him. I screamed, and he immediately clamped a hand over my mouth. While all this was going on, the driver sat impassively on his perch in front of the carriage, toying with the reins and paying not the least bit of attention to us. The face at the window disappeared.

"Let's be sensible about this, luv," Duke begged, but I continued to struggle.

Cautioning me to stop, his hand clamped tighter over my mouth, and he pulled my head against his shoulder. I managed to open my mouth wide enough to get one of his fingers between my teeth and bite him. He let out a yowl that rang up and down the street. Breaking free again, I whirled around to slam my reticule across his face, then started to run. He moved quickly to tackle me and I pitched forward, landing on the grass with him on top of me.

"There's such a thing as too much spirit," he grumbled.

"Help!" I screamed. "Help!"

"Oh, shut up!" he snapped, climbing to his feet, dusting his trouser legs.

He reached down and swept me up into his arms. Though I kicked my legs and pounded at his chest with my fists, he merely looked disgusted and continued carrying me toward the carriage. Nearby a door opened, and two men and a frightened housemaid appeared on the steps of the closest house.

"Lover's spat," Duke called. "Nothing to be alarmed about."

"He's a white slaver!" I yelled.

Duke kicked open the carriage door and hurled me inside, toppling me onto the cushioned seat in a jumble, ruffled skirt and petticoats all aflutter. I had barely managed to sit up and smooth my skirts down when Duke plopped down beside me, slamming the carriage door shut. "Home, Benson!" he yelled, and the carriage began to rumble down the street. Frantically, I reached for the door on my side and tried to open it, Duke slapped my hand and locked the door.

"Can't you see that I'm doing this for your own good?" he protested.

"You're abducting me! That's a criminal offense!"

"Not so loud. I've got a crashing headache, and my shin hurts something awful. My finger's bleeding, for Christ's sake!"

"Serves you right! You're insane. That's the only explanation. You are out of your mind! Dear God, for all I know you might really *be* a white slaver! If you don't stop this carriage immediately—"

"I must warn you, luv. I was a champion pugilist at Oxford, famous for my dynamic right. If you don't stop this caterwauling immediately, I'm going to slam that dynamic right across your pretty jaw. You'll be out cold for hours."

"You probably would!"

"No doubt about it."

"I don't believe you ever went to Oxford."

"Only stayed a couple of years. Got frightfully bored. All that Latin. Silly nonsense. I had other fish to fry."

"Beautifully put," I snapped. "Did you make up that particular phrase?"

"You *are* a shrew," he grumbled. "We'll play on that. All famous 'artistes' have lots of temperament. Fiery. That's the word. Fiery. But The Fiery Mary Ellen Lawrence? That name's impossible, luv. Much too refined. We'll work on it."

"I have no idea what you're talking about!"

"I'm going to make you a bloody *star*! Can't you get that through your thick skull?"

I was terribly upset and angry, but not nearly as upset and angry as I should have been. In some peculiar way I was actually enjoying myself, and I had rarely felt so alive. Anthony Duke was outrageous, completely outrageous, but I had the feeling some mystic fate had brought him into my life for a purpose I wasn't aware

117

of yet. He had ruined me with Madame Olga. I knew she would never forgive me. But deep in my heart I also knew that it would have been futile to continue my studies with her. I was in a strange mood, bold, uncaring, resigned.

"You're a lousy dancer," he said chattily. "Oh, you've got everything down pat, all the steps, all the movements, but you're mechanical. You've got no spirit, no élan. There's no poetry in your dancing, no—"

"Thanks so much! And you're going to make me a star?"

"Not in ballet. You'd fall flat on your shapely little behind. They'd laugh you off the stage. Oh, you might eventually do in the back row of the *corps de ballet*, but—"

"Just what gives you the right to—"

"I'm an authority, luv. Now shut up and let me finish. You've got no gift for ballet, but you've got something else, something much rarer. You've got presence. You've got incredible magnetism. I spotted it immediately. You might have been stumbling around like an awkward heifer, but—"

"Stop this carriage!"

"—but there wasn't a man in the audience who didn't want to take you to bed. You made the other girls disappear. There you were, vibrant, alive, seething with a sensuousness that poured across the footlights in waves. Despite the prissy steps. Despite the schmaltzy music and arty lighting effects. What you have, Mary Ellen, not to put too fine a point on it, is the ability to make every able-bodied man want to commit delicious sin with you. I've never seen anything like it."

"How dare you talk about me that way!"

"You're not aware of it. That's the dandy thing. You're not consciously seductive, not even coy. You're elegant and refined, aloof, and that makes it twice as potent. It's the damnedest thing I've ever seen. We'll have to use that carefully, have to present it in just the right way. Ballet is out. Can you sing?"

"I—"

"Probably not, and besides, singers are a glut on the market. Have you ever tried to act?"

118

"Never," I retorted.

"Not to worry, luv. We'll think of something. You're going to be the most sensational thing that's ever hit this town. You're going to take London by storm, then Europe, then—"

"You are mad," I said. "I knew it."

"The right act, the right costumes, the right presentation, and you'll be a smash. We'll have to start from scratch, create a whole new personality, give you an exotic background."

"Mr. Duke, I really feel this has gone far enough. Are you ready to stop the carriage now? I have no intention of sitting here and listening to your nonsense."

"You'll do exactly what I say from now on," he informed me, "and if you don't, I'll clout you. I've no compunction at all about striking a woman. You'll discover that beneath this dashing, charming facade I'm quite hellbent on having my own way."

"I discovered that the first time I laid eyes on you!"

"Good. Then we understand each other. You're going to hate me during the next few weeks, for I shall be utterly merciless, but you'll be grateful for the rest of your life."

"I doubt it!"

"Take my word for it."

The carriage slowed as it passed through two stone portals and clattered over the rough cobblestones of an ancient inner courtyard. When it had come to a complete halt, Anthony Duke sighed and opened the door. He climbed out, turned, and reached for my hand, but I drew back. With a vicious jerk forward, he pulled me out of the carriage to land against him. He whirled me about and wrapped one arm around my throat. Holding me in front of him, he lifted his head to speak to the driver.

"That'll be all for tonight, Benson. I won't need you tomorrow until two, when you'll drive me to the theater."

"Righto, guv'nor," Benson said.

He turned the horses around and drove out of the courtyard. We were in a very old part of the city. Ancient brownstone buildings reared up on three sides. Facing the street was a tall brick wall with the portals on either side of the narrow entrance way. The carriage barely scraped through as it rumbled out. Lights glowed in several of the brownstone windows, soft yellow squares against the stone, and there was the smell of age, mossy, mellow, not unpleasant. A cat yowled from the top of the wall.

Duke had his arm still crooked around my throat, and I could feel his strength. He might have the jaunty, breezy manner of a vagabond, but his body was hard and trim, his responses as finely honed as a professional athlete's. I found myself wondering what he would be like in bed, and I was appalled at myself.

"All calmed down now?" he inquired.

"Not at all," I retorted. "If you don't let go of me this instant, I'm going to let out a scream that will—"

His arm tightened about my throat, cutting me short. "I shouldn't," he said. "I did some wrestling at Oxford too; famous for my death grip. Put a number of chaps out. Took hours to revive 'em properly. Be delighted to do the same to you."

I tugged at his arm, and he released me with a chuckle. Coughing, I turned around to give him an angry glare, but he just grinned that lovely, engaging grin. I wanted to slap him.

"It seems you've quite a lot of accomplishments!" I snapped.

"You've no idea, luv. I'm a man of many talents, as you'll soon discover." He clamped his fingers around my wrist. "Come along now, the champagne is waiting. Oh, by the way, there are quite a few stairs, but you're young and able-bodied. I'm sure you can make it."

He opened the door and pulled me inside. We were in a narrow, dingy foyer with a battered table, a dimly flickering oil lamp, a closed door to the right and, directly in front of us, a flight of wooden steps. He started up the steps, still holding my wrist, dragging me along and chatting breezily as we climbed.

"Chap who paints posters has the first two floors, woman who gives piano lessons has the third—noise drives me berserk. I'm constantly fighting with her. I have the top two floors, living quarters and studio. Nice

120

digs. Cheap, too. Your room is on the top floor, right next to the studio. Has its own bathroom."

"*My* room?"

"You're going to be living here. It will be much handier that way, since we'll be working night and day."

I saw no reason to comment. The idea was altogether too outrageous. I was still stunned by all that had happened, but I was no longer upset. This utterly ludicrous episode was not to be believed. It was some mad whimsy, completely divorced from reality. The other students were getting ready to go onstage at this very moment, and I should be with them. The fact that I wasn't didn't bother me at all. Following Duke up a second flight of stairs, I realized that I was actually enjoying myself, and that startled me.

"Don't lag. You look a mess, incidentally. Your hair's all undone, and you've lost your ribbon. You've got grass stains on your skirt, too."

"That's your fault!"

"Shouldn't have given me so much trouble. Anything I can't stand, it's an obstinate woman."

"I'm sure most of them leap at the chance to do your bidding."

"Matter of fact, they do. They just can't seem to get enough of me. Don't usually have to abduct 'em off the street, though. My fatal charm doesn't seem to work with you. No idea why."

"I'm immune."

"You'll come 'round," he promised, dragging me up a third flight of stairs and stopping in front of a door. He fumbled in his pocket for a key, found it, and inserted it in the lock. His hair was all atumble, and his opera cape was askew on his shoulders. The lock resisted his efforts. As he stood there puzzling over the keys he looked delightfully comical, and extremely appealing. I wanted to smile, but I wouldn't give him that satisfaction.

"Damnation! What the bloody hell is wrong? Oh, wrong key. Here we go."

When the door opened at last, he pulled me inside, closed the door, and locked it again. He slipped off his cape and tossed it over a chair. It fell to the floor in a heap. His evening clothes were elegantly cut, tails just

121

the proper length, waistcoat of white satin embroidered with darker white silk floral designs, but he wore them casually, as he might wear an old suit. His white silk tie was even crooked.

"Here we are. All snug and comfy."

"I may still scream."

"Scream your bloody head off. No one's likely to hear. You're at my mercy. Might as well relax and enjoy yourself."

"Do you plan to rape me?"

"Not really, luv. My interest in you is purely professional."

"Oh?"

"Sorry to disappoint you. Personally, I lean toward bosomy blondes or occasionally, a redhead."

"I see."

"Don't look so crestfallen. I could make an exception in your case."

"Please don't bother."

The large room was filled with an attractive clutter of old furniture, awash with books and magazines on the theater. Lamps glowed brightly. Colorful entertainment posters in narrow black frames hung on the walls, and cheerful yellow brocade adorned the wide windows. The windows were open, and I could hear and smell the river. Looking out, I saw that the building backed onto the Embankment. A table in the center of the room, which was laid for dinner, held a silver bucket of champagne. Duke sauntered over to the table to examine things, lifting covers off of food, humming to himself as he did so.

"Cleeve did a dandy job," he announced. "Shouldn't have worried. He always does. Cleeve's my valet, fine chap, absolutely devoted to me. Has his own rooms down in the basement. Must remember to pay him his salary one of these days."

I stepped over to the large mirror that hung in an ornate and slightly tarnished gold frame. My hair was indeed all undone; with the ribbon missing it fell in thick waves that gleamed blue-black in the lamplight. My eyes were cool, my expression composed, but there was a faint pink flush tinting my cheeks. During the struggle with

122

Duke, the bodice of my gown had slipped precariously low, revealing even more bosom. I adjusted it, and as I smoothed the skirt down I noticed that one of the pink lace ruffles was torn. Millie would have to do some repair work. I wondered what could be used to remove the grass stains.

"You've wrecked my gown," I announced.

"Lovely gown," he replied. "Not to worry. A few months from now, you'll have dozens of gowns, much more elegant. Come sit down. Take off your gloves."

"I will," I said, moving over to the table, "but that's *all* I'm taking off."

Anthony Duke lifted the bottle of champagne out of the bucket and began to inch out the cork. "You keep dropping these hints. I'm beginning to think you've a yen for me."

"Don't flatter yourself!" I snapped.

I removed the gloves and sat down at the table. He grimaced, still struggling with the cork, his brow furrowed. "Bloody hell!" he cried, and the cork popped out with a loud explosion and hit the ceiling as champagne bubbled all over his hands and onto the floor. He muttered something under his breath and poured champagne into two elegant crystal glasses. He handed me a glass, sat down, brushed the hair from his brow, and grinned.

"Not usually so clumsy," he informed me. "Hope I didn't get you all wet."

"At this point it would hardly matter."

"Oh, come now, you're enjoying yourself. You know you are."

"I should be onstage this very minute. I should be dancing. Madame will never forgive me."

"You don't need her any more, luv, now that you've got me to look after you. I told you, I'm going to make you a star. We've got three months before your debut."

"Three months!" I decided to play along.

"Dorrance is presenting *The Barber of Seville*. New production. It's going to be a disaster. I've got to come up with an absolutely sensational attraction to entertain the paying customers between the acts. You're it!"

"I'm going to wow them?"

"Believe me. Forget the opera. They're going to come

123

pouring into the theater to see you. Tons of advance publicity—my chums on Fleet Street will help out there. You're going to be colorful, and exotic—a personality."

"I can't sing. You assure me I can't dance. I certainly can't act. What am I supposed to do?"

"Don't worry about it. We'll figure something out. Drink your champagne."

"You're utterly preposterous, you know."

"Am I? I think fascinating might be a better word."

"An absolute scoundrel."

"I don't deny that. Everyone loves a scoundrel."

"You're conceited and arrogant and—"

"Mean as hell," he interrupted. "I'd as soon slap you as look at you. Keep on in that vein and I'll smack you good and proper and enjoy doing it. Hate a lippy woman. Drives me berserk."

I took another sip of champagne, forcing back a smile. "You're not nearly as fierce as you pretend to be."

"You think it's just jaunty banter?"

"Most of it."

He grinned. "Maybe so, but don't push me too far. Here, let me pour you some more champagne, and then I'll tell you all about myself, hold you spellbound."

He poured the champagne. I sipped it. We ate the oysters and the pheasant and the asparagus with hollandaise sauce, and as we ate Anthony told me about himself, exuding that boyish charm that so nicely complemented his robust virility. If not exactly spellbound, I was at least relaxed, studying this overwhelming male creature with cool objectivity.

"We were gentry," he said. "You know—big house, servants, private pew in church, all that rot. My father was a gambler—stocks and bonds and investments, not cards—who lost almost everything. We barely managed to hold onto the big house, the servants, the private pew. I was an only child and deplorably spoiled. All the womenfolk fussed over me. I had a grand childhood, roamed all over the countryside, playing pirates, imagining myself a red Indian, launching surprise attacks on any unfortunate neighborhood child who happened to pass my way. I was a bit of a bully, I'm afraid."

I arched an eyebrow in mock surprise. "Oh?"

124

"The despair of my parents. Always getting into scrapes. Both of them sighed with relief when it came time to send me off to school. Eton, mind you—my father had connections. Got into even more scrapes there, bloodied many a nose, twisted many an arm, pulled many a prank. Fascinated?"

"Fascinated," I said dryly.

"Thought you would be. Finally made it to Oxford, a handsome scamp, the answer to every maiden's prayer. Got my nose busted in a boxing match. No longer so handsome, but even more interesting. Added character, that broken nose. At Oxford I boxed and I wrestled and I rowed and I spent as little time as possible with my masters. Hated Latin. Hated history. I joined the dramatic society and began to act in plays. You should have seen me as Iago."

Flashing that charming grin, he poured more champagne into my glass and then bounded off to fetch another bottle. He moved with supple male grace, his gait long and loose and bouncy. The fresh bottle of champagne was placed in the silver ice bucket and swirled around. An inexperienced drinker, I had had far too much champagne already, and I was beginning to feel it. I felt gloriously free and relaxed; my cares had vanished. I couldn't remember when I had enjoyed myself so much.

Anthony Duke slipped back into his chair, a thoughtful look in his eyes now, a certain tautness in his facial muscles.

"My parents died of influenza within days of each other. The big house was mortgaged to the hilt. The servants hadn't been paid in months. In short, I hadn't a penny and I had to leave Oxford. Just as well, I suppose. The place didn't suit me at all. I came to London to become an actor. With my looks, charm, personality, I figured I'd take the West End by storm."

"And you didn't?"

"Flopped dismally, luv. I'll be the first to admit it. There were a couple of very lean years, with only one or two small roles. I played an assassin in the court of Cesare Borgia, looked smashing in maroon tights and purple velvet tunic embroidered with black and silver. The part had two lines, 'Aha, I've caught you,' and 'Die,

125

you Venetian dog!' I was to let out a diabolical laugh as I plunged the dagger into his throat. The laugh was a great success, very diabolical. I also got to play a dandy in a Regency drama. Didn't say anything, just sat at a gambling table shuffling cards."

He sighed and shook his head. "Afraid that's the sum total of my thespian career. I learned a lot, though. Learned that it took technique and training to become a good actor, and that most actors starve, good or bad. Not my style at all. I discovered that if you want to make money in the theater, it's better to work behind the scenes. I became a promoter, did a stint on Fleet Street, learned all about advertising. That eventually led to my position with Dorrance. I promote, help out with the production end of things, get together the *entr'acte* specialties."

"It sounds very interesting," I conceded.

"Fascinating work. Loads of responsibility."

"I take it you think the company would fail if it weren't for you."

"Probably would, if *The Barber of Seville* is any indication. We don't even have a name singer, just some garish sets and moth-eaten costumes rented from an outfit that's going out of business. You can see why I've got to come up with a stellar attraction."

"Me," I said.

"You."

"You really are mad, Mr. Duke."

"Anthony, luv. Tony if you're feeling chummy. The minute I saw you, I knew you were it. You've got star quality, Mary Ellen. Got it in abundance. Couldn't take my eyes off you. I saw the possibilities immediately. More pheasant?"

"I couldn't."

"More champagne," he said, refilling my glass.

"You're trying to intoxicate me."

"Get you nice and tipsy so I can have my way with you? I wouldn't dream of it. When I have my way with you, and I shall, it'll be because you want it as much as I do."

"Don't hold your breath, Mr. Duke."

"Anthony. Drink up. Tell me about yourself."

126

"You seem to know everything already."

"I did do a lot of investigating," he admitted. "I know you come form Cornwall, no living relatives, know you've been studying with Madame Olga for a year, working hard, getting nowhere, buoying yourself up with false hopes. Know you're flat broke, been skipping meals, walk to and from the theater because you can't afford a cab. You never go out. There are no men in your life. The future looks bleak."

I was silent. He grinned.

"*Looked* bleak. That's all changed now. Anthony Duke has discovered you. He's going to be your personal manager. He's going to make you a star. Have faith in me, luv."

"Why should I?"

"Because I have faith in you. I know what you've got. I know it's a very rare commodity. That kind of presence, that kind of sensuousness is far more valuable than talent. The fact that you're a gorgeous woman makes it even more valuable."

"I'm not a gorgeous woman."

"You're not pretty," he said. "Thank God for that. You don't have a pink-and-white complexion and clear blue eyes and pale blonde ringlets. You don't look like an aristocratic milkmaid. You don't meet the current standards of beauty at all. You're individual, exotic, and, believe me, you're going to make the men in this city forget all about pretty blonde milkmaids."

"I want to go home," I said.

"You're not having a good time?"

"I'm sad."

"You've had too much champagne."

"I know. I'm sad. You've ruined me with Madame Olga and wrecked my career in ballet in one fell swoop. Everything you said about my dancing is true. I've never admitted it to myself. I hate you. My head is spinning. Why did you do it? Why me? I tried so hard. I worked so hard. I'm not used to champagne."

"You're not going to cry, are you?"

"Of course not."

"Anything I hate, it's a teary-eyed woman."

"I can't help it."

"Everything is going to be fine, Mary Ellen."

His voice was gentle and melodious as he got up from the table and came around to where I was sitting. Standing behind me, he began to massage my shoulders, kneading the flesh, his strong fingers easing the tension. I closed my eyes, and my head whirled around and around. Then he was pulling me up and holding me against him, his arm around my waist, and I felt warm and secure and safe, and my head was against his shoulder and he was stroking my hair.

"Brence," I whispered.

"Easy, luv. Christ, you're smashed."

"It's your fault. It's all your fault."

"Absolutely smashed, and we haven't even begun to *discuss* things. I can really pick 'em. Got a bloody innocent on my hands."

"I . . . I don't know what happened."

"The champagne. It hit you all at once."

I was spinning in darkness, delicious darkness, and his arms were so very strong and he was so tall, so gentle, holding me, stroking my hair, tender, comforting, protective. It was marvelous to have someone holding me again after such a long time. Suddenly, I was limp, falling, falling, and he swept me up into his arms. I opened my eyes, but the room was spinning, a blur of shapes and colors that whirled around and around.

"What are you—"

"I'm putting you to bed, Mary Ellen."

"Help!"

"Jesus Christ!"

"I know what you're going to do."

"You weigh a ton! Stop kicking!"

He stumbled and hurtled forward and muttered a curse and dropped me, and I landed on something soft and bouncy. We were in another room. I was on the bed. Standing over me with a disgruntled expression, his brows pressed together, he muttered another curse. I closed my eyes and my head seemed to spin and the darkness returned and I welcomed it, the delicious dark. Someone was pulling off my shoes, having a very difficult time with it. I smiled and floated away into the darkness.

128

XIV

The dazzling sunlight seemed to be drilling into my
brain. I groaned and struggled to sit up, but it took far
too much effort. Watery reflections danced on the walls
and ceiling, shimmering silver bright amidst the yellow
sunlight. Pressing my hands against my temples, I took
a deep breath and tried to sit up again. I managed it.
Just. There was a horrible crash overhead, a series of
dull thuds. My head seemed to explode. I shuddered.
Another crash occurred. Bits of plaster flaked off the
ceiling and came drifting down like dusty snow.

Several minutes passed. When the sunlight no longer
hurt my eyes, I looked around the bedroom, an undeniably male abode. A cane leaned against a chair, a
black silk top hat perched jauntily atop it. The room
was cluttered and untidy and bore the unmistakable
stamp of its occupant. Newspapers and clippings were
piled on the desk. Theatrical posters leaned against the
wall in a heap. A half-eaten apple lay in a chipped blue
saucer. A sleazy periodical devoted to wrestling was on
the bedside table, and a pair of old and oily boxing
gloves hung from a nail on the wall. Though my slippers
were on the floor beside the bed, I was still wearing my
pearl-gray watered silk. It was deplorably crumpled.

I put on my shoes and stood up. My head felt as
though it were caught in a vise, and my stomach was in
an even worse condition. Not certain that I wasn't on the
verge of death, I stumbled over to the mirror. What I
saw was not at all reassuring. My cheeks were flushed.

My hair was a wild tangle. My bodice had twisted down, almost uncovering one breast. I pulled the sleeves up, adjusted the cloth, and reaching for the ivory-backed brush on top of the dressing table, I began trying to put my hair in some kind of order. Each stroke of the brush was like torture.

A door opened and closed with a deafening retort. I fought back a scream. Bright, bouncy footsteps sounded in the next room. Anthony was humming merrily as he appeared in the doorway, looking dapper in a brown-and-white-checked suit and a topaz satin waistcoat. The impudent blue eyes were bright and mischievous, the boyish grin playing on his wide lips. I glared at him, not trusting myself to speak.

"How do you feel?" he inquired.

"Wretched."

"Really shouldn't drink so much. If you can't handle it, leave the stuff alone."

"What happened?"

"You passed out on me."

"I—how did I get in here?"

"I carried you in, dumped you on the bed."

"And then?"

"I removed your shoes. Spent the night on the sofa myself. Dreadfully uncomfortable. Lumpy. Wouldn't want to make a habit of it. A drunken woman sprawling all over my bed, snoring something awful, and me trying to get a few honest winks on a sofa two feet too short—"

"I did not snore!"

"Touchy, aren't we?"

"You *plied* me with champagne. I knew what you had in mind. I'm not naive. I've heard all about men like you. Will you wipe that disgusting grin off your face?"

His expression sobered immediately. "Sorry, luv."

The grin sprang back of its own volition. The blue eyes sparkled. He sauntered over to the bed and smoothed down the dark tan counterpane. I put down the hairbrush and winced at the noise as it touched the dresser.

"Glad to see you up and about," he remarked. "I was

just on my way to roust you out. Today's an important day. Can't have you sleeping till all hours."

"What time is it?"

"Two o'clock. When you sleep, you sleep."

"Two o'clock! I don't believe it."

"Take my word for it. I was up bright and early myself, on the move before the first cock stopped crowing. Accomplished wonders. Got all of your things packed up, got 'em moved in upstairs."

"My things?"

"The old harpy with the brassy hair and gin on her breath was very obliging, gave me the key, didn't give me a bit of trouble. Wanted to come up and help me pack. I thought I was never going to get rid of her. Cleeve and I packed everything up. Never could have done it without his help. All those bloody books!"

"You—you took my things?"

"Moved 'em in upstairs. Told you last night. You have your own room, with bath. Right next to the studio where we'll be working. Thought you understood that."

"I'm going to be very calm," I said firmly. "I'm not going to be angry. Anger would be wasted on you. I'm going to go downstairs and go outside and find the nearest Bobby and have you arrested."

He looked hurt. "Whatever for?"

"I simply refuse to believe any of this. Last night—last night was like a hazy dream. I scarcely remember what took place. I must have been insane to let you bring me here."

"You put up a splendid fight," he reminded me.

It was foolish to try to argue with him, and I was in no mood to do so, in any case. I had a lot of thinking to do, serious thinking, and I needed a clear head. Coffee was what I needed. I told him so, and he grinned, looking very pleased with himself.

"There's a pot waiting. A place all set for you at the table. Buttered toast and jam, too. Had Cleeve set everything up for you. You see, I can be thoughtful and considerate. Don't believe in starving my women, not as long as they behave themselves."

I followed him into the next room. A place had indeed been set, and there was coffee in a slightly tarnished silver pot, a rack of buttered toast, a small silver dish of strawberry jam, and a single long-stemmed red rose in a slender crystal vase.

"Nice?" he inquired.

"Nice," I agreed.

"I'm a cruel taskmaster," he informed me, "and I've a wretched temper, but you'll discover that I can be a very likable chap, given half a chance. Sit down and drink your coffee."

I sat. I poured coffee into my cup. The aroma was rich and fragrant and lovely. Duke stepped over to the mirror, tugged at the bottom of his rich topaz waistcoat, and straightened the lapels of his brown-and-white-checked jacket. Finally satisfied with his appearance, he turned and began to pull on a pair of dark brown gloves.

"What was that dreadful noise I heard?" I asked. "I thought the whole ceiling was going to come crashing down."

"I dropped a couple of cartons of books. Damned heavy, almost broke my back carrying them up the stairs. Everything you own is upstairs in your room, waiting to be put away. I decided to leave the putting away to you."

"How thoughtful."

"When you finish your coffee, go up and have a look at your new home. I've got to pop round to the theater on very important business, but I'll be back in an hour or so. Oh, Cleeve's lurking around somewhere. Don't be alarmed if you run into him."

He left then. I could hear his footsteps as he hurried downstairs like some exuberant schoolboy. When I finished my coffee, I poured a second cup and ate two pieces of toast. The pain in my head began to recede. I felt very sober now, frightfully so. Sunlight spilled through the opened windows. I could smell the river. My coral-pink velvet gloves were thrown across the back of a chair where I had left them last night. Last night seemed to have happened a very long time ago. Here I sat in a strange room, wearing my most elegant gown—one coral ruffle dangling, dark grass stains soiling part

132

of the skirt—calmly drinking coffee. In fact, I was calmer, it seemed, than I had ever been in my life.

Anthony Duke had burst into my life and taken it over, just like that. Madame Olga would never forgive me, never take me back, so he had wrecked my future in ballet, but I wasn't even angry. I accepted it. What he had said was true. I had been buoying myself up with false hopes. I wasn't a good dancer. I would never be. Desire and determination were of no avail if that certain brilliance was missing, and it was, would always be. I didn't have it. Today, as the breeze from the river ruffled the curtains and sunlight spread over the carpet, I could face the truth. For a year I had been deceiving myself, working frantically, refusing to allow that tiny seed of doubt to take root.

I would never get on in ballet, no matter how long I studied with Madame Olga. I had no money, as Anthony Duke had pointed out, and there were very few respectable jobs open to a woman of my age, with my background. Giving dancing lessons sounded all very well, but there was an abundance of failed ballerinas in London and teaching positions were avidly sought. The chances of my obtaining one would be slim indeed, particularly as I could no longer use Madame Olga as a reference. I could become a governess, perhaps, but my youth and my physical appearance would be definite drawbacks, and I had no desire to moulder away in some dim attic nursery.

Facing this reality, without false hopes, without illusions, I realized there was nothing I could do but go along with Anthony Duke. He wanted to make me a star, he said. The man might be an out-and-out scoundrel, but he was no fool. He knew the theater, knew the public, knew what they wanted, and he believed I had a special quality that would appeal to them. Surely, he wouldn't have started all this unless there was a hefty profit in it for Anthony Duke. He thought he could make money, a lot of it. He certainly wasn't after my body. A man as attractive as he had to do no more than snap his fingers to get almost any woman he wanted. He had made no effort to seduce me last night—had candidly informed me that I wasn't his type. His interest in

133

me was professional, and if he believed he could make something of me, then I must believe it, too.

I felt strangely stimulated, almost excited. I should have been depressed, of course, should have been grim and despondent and angry, but I wasn't. This past year had been long and hard and, for the most part, bleak. I had done nothing but work and hope and dream. The months had been gray with loneliness and worry, a constant struggle to hold back the sadness that threatened to overwhelm me, and Anthony Duke had come charging in with breezy determination, splashing color all around. I had to admit to myself that I had enjoyed last night, the lovely meal, his ebullient manner, his cocky chatter. If I formed an affiliation with Anthony Duke I would be letting myself in for anger and irritation and all sorts of conflicts, but things would never be dull and gray.

"Finished, miss?"

I turned, startled. A tall, very thin man with graying hair and a sober expression stood in the doorway, holding an empty tray. He wore a butler's uniform that, though spotless, had seen better days, jacket and trousers both a bit shiny with age. His face was long, his mouth thin, his pale blue eyes patient and weary.

"Oh," I said, "you must be Cleeve."

He nodded. "I'll just clear the table."

"I'm Miss Lawrence."

"I know," he said. "You read a lot."

"You helped Mr. Duke move my things."

He nodded again and moved over to the table.

"I—I suppose you're accustomed to that. Moving a lady's belongings upstairs, I mean."

Cleeve shook his head, placing the tray on the table and reaching for the empty coffeepot. "Mr. Duke has entertained many young ladies," he informed me, "but you're the first he's let move in."

That's encouraging, I thought. Cleeve stacked the dishes on the tray, slowly, patiently. He had to be well over sixty, I reasoned, and I had the feeling he had been with Anthony Duke for a very long time. When I asked him, he nodded again.

"All his life," he said. "I was with the family before

Master Anthony was born. When his parents died and the big house was sold, I accompanied him to London. Can't say that I liked the idea, but someone had to look after him. He's always needed a great deal of looking after. Disorderly, Master Anthony is. Always has been."

"You must think a lot of him."

Cleeve looked at me with weary eyes. There was no need for him to reply. I could see that he would have gone to the stake for Duke without a moment's hesitation. I found that reassuring. A man who could inspire such devotion and loyalty couldn't be a thorough villain.

"I'll just take these things down," Cleeve said. "My kitchen's in the basement."

"You cook, too?"

"I do all the cooking," he replied. "Someone has to. Master Anthony can't afford to pay a cook wages. Can't afford to pay me, truth to tell, but we manage."

"He's very lucky to have you," I said gently.

"Thank you, miss. I'll be going now."

After Cleeve left, I stood there for several minutes, lost in thought, and then, picking up my gloves, I went out into the hall and climbed the final flight of stairs to the studio. The door was standing open, and I stepped inside, amazed at the size of the room. Brilliant sunlight streamed in through a skylight that slanted down from the ceiling, creating an airy, open effect.

The room was enormous, so enormous that it looked bare despite the furniture. A battered-looking piano stood in one corner, a brightly colored Spanish shawl with tangled fringe draped over it. There was a rickety table nearby piled high with papers and books and opera librettos, and standing against the wall, a moth-eaten sofa covered in threadbare burnt orange velvet. There were lamps and straightback chairs and a low table scattered with books of costume design, two swords and two fencing masks, and yet another pair of worn boxing gloves. The floor was a vast expanse of bare polished hardwood, agleam with sunlight. The studio, which was obviously used as a rehearsal hall, smelled of sweat and smoke and leather, exceedingly masculine.

I could imagine Duke rehearsing his specialty acts, snapping orders, making criticisms, boisterous and bullying. He had probably held many a rowdy party for his theatrical colleagues up here as well, parties with laughter and loud talk, lots of wine, impromptu boxing matches, and fencing forays. No doubt, he and his friends would behave like noisy schoolboys. There was still much of the schoolboy in his nature, I reflected, noting the boxing gloves.

My heels rang on the floor as I crossed the room and entered the bedroom that adjoined it. It was small and snug, its plaster walls painted a very light blue; one tiny window looking out over the river. A violet-blue counterpane covered the bed. The headboard was painted white, as were the bedside table, the dressing table, and the wardrobe. The wardrobe was much too large for the tiny room, and so was the overstuffed chair covered in rather garish purple velvet. A lamp stood on the bedside table, and a white vase on top of the small bookcase held a bunch of fresh violets that had been hastily crammed into it. He must have bought them this morning in hopes of pleasing me.

My clothes were piled on top of the bed in a tangled jumble, and all my other possessions sat in boxes around the floor. Two boxes of books had fallen over, books spilling out over the faded gray carpet with its barely visible violet floral patterns. This room was directly over his bedroom. A narrow door led into a tiny but quite modern bathroom complete with large zinc tub. Putting down my gloves, I wondered where to begin. I would have to smooth all the clothes out and hang them up in the wardrobe, place the books in the bookcase, and put the rest of the things away in the drawers of the dressing table, but first I would wash up and change into something sensible.

I removed the rumpled silk gown and performed my ablutions in the bathroom, sponging myself thoroughly. Then I donned a dusty-rose cotton frock patterned with tiny blue forget-me-nots. The dress was old and too tight at the waist. The snug bodice had been modest enough when I was sixteen years old and the dress brand-new, but Millie had mended the neckline and it

136

was now a good two inches lower, revealing more than I ordinarily cared to reveal. This afternoon, however, I was pleased with the plunging effect.

Because Anthony Duke claimed that I wasn't his type, I had a purely feminine inclination to prove otherwise, if only to have the satisfaction of rebuffing him. Retrieving my cosmetics from one of the packed boxes, I sat down at the dressing table and applied a hint of soft blue shadow to my lids and heightened the natural pink of my lips with dark pink lip rouge. With my hair tumbling about my shoulders, I thought I had a certain wild splendor that suggested windswept moors and stormy emotions. Was that the special quality he had referred to? He said that I had the ability to make every able-bodied man want to commit delicious sin with me. Well, I might not be his type, but he was certainly an able-bodied man.

As I shook my dresses out and hung them up in the wardrobe, I wondered at the change that had come over me. Change? Perhaps that wasn't the right word. Anthony Duke made me feel like a woman, and I hadn't felt that way for a very long time. For the past year I had been serious and dedicated, entirely devoted to my dancing, leading a drab, nun-like existence outside the theater. I had coolly rebuffed all advances from the men who flocked around the theater, had denied all the emotions and instincts that Brence Stephens had unlocked and nourished with his manhood. I had shut that part of me off. Now, another man had appeared, and he made me feel vibrant and alive and attractive. Although I had no intention of going to bed with him, it was nice to experience the subtle glow he had awakened.

Hanging up the last dress, I began to fold the other clothes and put them away in the drawers. That done, I arranged all the books in the bookcase and stopped to rearrange the violets in their white vase. A cheap bouquet of violets was a cheap bouquet of violets, hardly overwhelming, but the fact that he had thought to buy them was rather touching. I stroked one of the soft petals, and then stopped, forcing myself to curb the warm feeling the flowers had summoned up. What was

137

it Millie had said? That sort would break your heart, steal your money, and laugh his head off as he walked out of the door. Millie was right. I was going to have to be on guard constantly.

There were two more boxes of my things left to unpack. As I picked them up and set them on the bed, I heard footsteps crossing the studio floor, and a moment later Anthony Duke was standing in the doorway, observing me. He noticed the dress, and the neckline. He didn't say anything about it, but he noticed. His blue eyes glowed with appreciation, and his lids drooped slightly, giving him a sleepy, sensual look. A half smile curved on his lips. I knew what he was thinking, and I was pleased with myself for having scored a small triumph. Ignoring him, I began to remove things from the boxes.

He looked at me, wanting me, and then he sighed and shook his head and assumed his customary stance of cocky self-assurance. He folded his arms across his chest and leaned his shoulders back against the frame of the door, lounging there like some idle ruffian.

"See you've decided to stay," he remarked.

"It would seem so."

"Good. Thought you might put up another fight."

"I really haven't much choice, Mr. Duke. You saw to that."

"Indeed I did. Dastardly conduct, mine. I'm doing you a favor, though. You'll discover that soon enough."

"We'll see. At least I'll have a roof over my head."

"I say, did you notice the violets?"

"Violets?"

"Over there on top of the bookshelf. I bought 'em this morning, paid a fortune for 'em. Outrageous what that old crone charged me."

I glanced toward the bookshelf. "How sweet."

"You don't like violets?"

"Not particularly, but it was thoughtful of you to buy them."

He scowled irritably. "Shouldn't have wasted my money," he muttered. "Women. Damnable creatures."

I repressed a smile. He strolled over to the bed and began to poke about in one of the boxes, taking out my

138

castanets, examing them, putting them down and reaching for the framed watercolor of my father, the one my mother had painted such a long time ago. He studied it intently.

"Striking chap," he said. "Quite handsome in a fierce sort of way. What kind of costume is that he's wearing?"

"It—it's not a costume. He was a gypsy."

"Friend of yours?"

"My father."

He arched one brow in surprise. I took the picture from him and put it in the drawer of the bedside table.

"His name was Ramon. My mother ran away with him. He was killed in a knife fight. My mother was an aristocrat, very beautiful, and she scandalized everyone by falling in love with a gypsy. Her family disowned her. I was born out of wedlock."

"Happens to the best of people," he said casually. "So you've got gypsy blood? Hmmm, that's very interesting."

"I'm quite proud of it. I knew the gypsies well. I used to run across the moors to their camp. They were . . . they were warm, wonderful people. They taught me all the gypsy dances, and—"

"Dances?" he interrupted.

"Spanish dances."

"With castanets? Heels, stamping, guitars strumming, flamboyant, uninhibited?"

I nodded. He looked suddenly excited.

"You remember 'em?"

"The dances? Of course I do."

He snapped his fingers, nodding vigorously. "I'm beginning to get something, luv. Gypsies, castanets, knives flashing in front of a blazing fire! I'm beginning to see a picture in my mind. You're wearing a Spanish outfit. The skirt has lots of different-colored ruffles. You're stamping your heels and clicking your castanets and—"

He grabbed up the castanets and seized my wrist and moved toward the studio, dragging me after him. I stumbled. He shot me an impatient look, pulled me over to the piano, and stood there frowning, blue eyes intent on his own thoughts. Then he focused on the brightly

139

colored Spanish shawl and nodded to himself again, his fingers still clamped tightly around my wrist.

"Gypsies are out, love," he said. "No offense, but the picture isn't quite right. Spanish. That's what you'll be, an exotic Spanish dancer, fierce, fiery, seething with passion. They'll love it!"

"I don't speak a word of Spanish," I protested.

"Doesn't matter. You can learn a few phrases. I think we might just be able to pull it off. Your hair's the right color, and your eyes—well, who said all Spaniards have to have dark, flashing eyes? With the right makeup, the right kind of costumes—"

"You're hurting my wrist!"

"Stop caterwauling! We'll invent a colorful background. Doesn't matter what we say. Who has any idea what's going on in Spain? You could have royal blood. No, no, that sounds a bit stuffy. I have it! You're a notorious Spanish temptress, a celebrated dancer expelled from Spain because of your dangerous liaison with a crown prince."

"Does Spain have a crown prince?"

"Who knows? Who cares? Don't bother me with details. I'm a promoter. That's my business, and no one does it better! With my ideas and my connections I could make a star out of a mud fence. In your case I have considerably more to work with."

"Thank you," I snapped.

Anthony Duke grinned and let go of my wrist. I reminded myself again to be wary. The grin was disarming, yes, and the boyish enthusiasm very appealing, but beneath that attractive facade was a hard, ruthless man with very few scruples and, I suspected, very potent masculinity. I was acutely conscious of his virility, and it alarmed me.

"We're going to work beautifully together, you know, and we're going to make lots of money. Here, take the castanets. Do one of your dances for me. I need to get some idea of what you can do. After seeing your ballet performances, I'm not too optimistic, but your dancing isn't really what we'll be selling."

"I couldn't," I said modestly.

"Couldn't what?"

"Dance. Not here. I—well, there isn't music, for one thing, and I—I'd be frightfully embarrassed."

"Don't be absurd."

"I have to be in the right mood. I have to—"

"Dance!" he ordered.

I took the castanets and stepped out to the center of the floor, painfully conscious of his eyes watching me. Sunlight streamed in through the enormous skylight. I needed starlight and fires glowing in the darkness and painted caravans looming out of the shadows. I needed raucous laughter and husky voices and hands clapping in a savage beat, but here there was only this ponderous, expectant silence. Folding his arms across his chest, he leaned against the piano and looked at me with impatience. I began to move, slowly, hesitantly, very ill at ease.

As I clicked the castanets and swayed, I began to remember, and the sunlight seemed to melt into darkness. I saw the caravans, the fires, the faces of my friends. The memories came rushing back, now, and I was very young again, elated to be with these people, free, uninhibited, belonging, dancing, really dancing, the music in my mind growing loud and lively and fierce. I stamped, I swayed, I swirled, I was afire with feeling, tossing my head, my hair flying, my skirts whirling up and around, the music growing louder, the laughter more raucous, an old excitement in my blood. I danced, forgetting Anthony Duke, caught up in the wild rhythm that seemed a part of me.

I danced for several minutes, but gradually the music slowed and the hands no longer clapped, and the sunlight was there again and I was in the studio. Out of breath, my bosom heaving, I stopped dancing and brushed my hair back from my face. He was still leaning against the piano, arms folded, his head tilted slightly to one side. He wore a bemused expression.

"Well?" I said.

"You've got something, luv."

As I moved over to the piano to put the castanets down, Duke studied me carefully, examining me with an intense scrutiny I found most disconcerting. I could smell the musky male scent of his body, and I had a

141

perverse longing to reach up and rub my fingertips across that lean cheek, to touch that full pink mouth that turned up thoughtfully at one corner.

"Still need a lot of work," he told me. "You're rough, but the fire's there, the feeling. What we need now is passion."

"Indeed?"

"You a virgin?" he inquired.

I was startled, too startled to reply.

"Don't look so offended. My reasons for inquiring are purely professional. If we're going to create a passionate, tempestuous woman seething with sensuality, it'll be much easier to do if you know what it's all about."

"I know what it's all about," I said dryly.

"Thought I might have to give you a few lessons. There's a lot of allure there already. After seeing you dance—" He hesitated, eyes sparkling. "If I weren't such a gentleman, we'd be over there on that sofa this very minute."

"You think so."

"I know so. I can be very persuasive. Don't worry, I won't try to seduce you. I promise."

"It would be wasted effort, I assure you."

"That a challenge?"

"Mr. Duke—"

Grinning, he thrust his hands deep into his trouser pockets and strolled away from the piano. He began to pace back and forth across the floor, shoulders hunched, head lowered, a thoughtful expression on his lean, attractive face.

"We'll have to start work on your Spanish immediately," he said. "I'll hire a chap to tutor you. Lessons every day. The language isn't all that important, it's the accent. Spanish music—I'll find some. I'll accompany you on the piano myself. No need to worry about guitars and such at this point. We'll start work tomorrow."

He paced, frowning now, immersed in thought. "We've got to have a name. Something striking, easy to remember, dramatic. Mary Ellen Lawrence is out. Something Spanish, of course. Marie Elena? Sounds

142

like a nun. Elena. Hmmm, I like that by itself. Elena what? Elena ... Elena ... I've got it!"

He stopped his pacing and rested his hands on his hips and looked at me with a triumphant glow.

"Elena Lopez! That's it. It's got the right ring. It's got allure! From this moment on Mary Ellen Lawrence ceases to exist. From this moment on you're an exotic creature who drives men mad. Fiery, tempestuous, smouldering with passion! You're going to be a sensation! Elena Lopez will be the most exciting thing this town has ever seen!"

"Will she?" I said doubtfully.

"She will indeed, luv," he exclaimed. "Take my word for it."

XV

Hyde Park was green and spacious and lovely with great open spaces bathed in sunlight. Above us, the pure, pale sky had only the faintest suggestion of blue. Millie and I strolled past neat flowerbeds, squares of violet, white, and blue with dramatic touches of red. In the distance we could hear children playing and water splashing and carriages rumbling up and down the drives, but here all was serene, with only a few people strolling across the wide lawns. About noon, I had fetched Millie in a cab and we had lunched at an inexpensive restaurant and come here afterwards. It must be well after three now, I realized.

I should be studying my Spanish. Anthony Duke had left at eleven, saying he wouldn't be back until six. So, instead of poring over the Spanish grammar and practicing my accent, I had decided to see Millie. I was determined not to feel guilty. For the past few weeks I had been working night and day, it seemed, and I felt entitled to an afternoon off. If Duke found out about it and objected, that was just too bad. He was a merciless slave driver, making incredible demands, and the nervous tension was almost more than I could bear. I needed some relaxation and, most of all, I needed a few hours of freedom.

"The 'ole set-up seems fishy to me," Millie announced. " 'E 'asn't made a single advance?"

"Not one," I replied.

" 'Asn't touched you?"

"Oh, he's touched me, all right. Yesterday he seized me by the arms and shook me until I thought my head would snap off, and he slapped me last week. I slapped him back, of course. He grabbed me by the throat and bared his teeth and said that if he hadn't invested so much time and money in me already he'd choke the breath out of me. He becomes a monster when things don't go well."

"So it would seem."

"Most of the time he's very patient, but—well, I get very tense, and he gets tense, too, and these little explosions happen. They don't mean anything. He's usually rather considerate. He's hard on me, but then he's very hard on himself as well. He *believes* in me, Millie, and he's staked everything on my success."

"I see."

"He's already gone into debt, and he'll have to spend a lot more before I make my debut. If I fail, he'll lose everything. These past few weeks have been like a living nightmare in many respects, but in some ways they've been the most exciting weeks of my life. He's very dynamic, very forceful. When he's working, he's all business—that breezy charm entirely vanishes."

" 'As you eatin' outta 'is 'and, don't 'e?"

"Not at all," I retorted. "I've no illusions about him. He's doing this for himself, because he believes I'll make his fortune. If I'm successful, he can give up his position with Dorrance and devote himself to being my personal manager. He'll be rich, but I'll be rich, too, Millie. And famous."

"That matters a lot to you, don't it?"

I nodded. "I have my reasons."

"You wanna show that man, the one who abandoned you. You were goin' to be a famous ballerina an' 'e was goin' to see you in all your glory an' regret what 'e did, an' now you're goin' to be this fiery Spaniard who makes strong men weak and 'e's goin' to feel even worse."

"That isn't my only motive."

"I've an idea it's the main one."

"Perhaps," I admitted. "I really haven't had much time to think about Brence Stephens."

146

"You've another man in the picture now. A new man always makes a girl forget the old."

"Anthony Duke isn't 'a new man,'" I said firmly. "Our relationship is purely professional."

"Oh?"

"We're working toward a mutual goal. I'd be a fool if I allowed there to be anything else between us. You warned me about him, remember? I took your warning to heart. I know very well that anything more would be disastrous."

"The flesh is weak, luv, an' this Duke chap is terribly 'andsome. 'E's so tall an' lean, so dashin'. 'E looks like a merry pirate with that broken nose and them archin' eyebrows and those devilish blue eyes. 'E ain't *my* type, but not many girls'd be able to resist 'im."

"I find it frightfully easy."

Millie gave me a knowing look and reached up to her golden curls, a pixie smile on her lips. She was convinced that I was infatuated with Anthony Duke, and nothing I could say would change her mind. Millie might affect a hard, cynical attitude, but she was a romantic at heart. She brushed a fleck of lint from her vivid yellow skirt and paused to gaze at a bed of larkspurs that blazed blue in the sunlight.

"'As he taken you out?" she inquired.

I shook my head. "He's keeping me under wraps, he says. He doesn't want anyone to see me just yet. When the time is right, he'll launch me with considerable fanfare, but for now—" I let the sentence trail off, realizing I sounded wistful.

"You just stay up there in that studio every night?" she asked.

"Studying," I reminded her. "I go over my Spanish lessons, and sometimes I practice my dances."

"And 'e's out every night."

"He goes to the theater," I said defensively. "It's his job."

We moved on down the lane toward the large iron gates that opened onto Oxford Street. Trees on either side threw shadows across the pathway, flickering blue gray patterns dancing on the ground. Leaves rustled overhead, and birds sang throatily, darting to and fro.

The sounds of children playing grew distant as we neared the gates. The skirt of my blue-and-violet-striped cotton frock fluttered in the gentle breeze. Pulling open the string of my violet silk purse, I checked to be sure I had a few coins left inside, enough to pay my cab fare back to the studio.

"I suppose you know 'e 'as a lady friend," Millie remarked.

"I—" Taken by surprise, I hesitated. "I assumed as much. Sometimes he doesn't come in until very late. He makes so much racket that I always hear him. Once he didn't get in until three in the morning. . . . Of course he has a woman. He's an extremely virile man. Men like that always—"

"She's a blonde," Millie interrupted. "I saw 'im with 'er. I was in a cab, on my way to see one of my regulars, and we were passin' the theater an' it was just lettin' out an' there 'e was, big as life. 'E was standin' at the edge of the street, tryin' to wave down a cabbie, not 'avin' a bit of luck. 'E was wearin' that opera cape, 'ad a silk top 'at on 'is 'ead. I recognized 'im at once. Couldn't fail to, 'im bein' so tall an' dapper-lookin'."

Millie paused. I refused to question her, affecting an indifference I did not feel.

" 'E 'ad 'is arm curled around 'er shoulders. Cool, she was, 'aughty. One of them tall, silvery blondes with perfect, icy features. She 'ad on an ice-blue velvet gown an' looked very put out at 'avin' to stand there while 'e fetched a cab. 'Ave you met 'er?"

"Indeed I haven't."

"Don't think you'd care for 'er," Millie informed me. "Way 'e was 'uggin' 'er shoulders, looked like 'e was very fond of 'er. Looked like 'e knew her mighty well."

"I'm not at all interested, Millie. What Anthony Duke does is none of my business. He could have a whole string of women, for all I care, and knowing him, he probably does."

"Wouldn't surprise me in the least," Millie agreed. "Regular tomcat, that one. The tall, lean ones always are. Just watch yourself, luv. I'd 'ate to see you get 'urt again."

"I'm not going to be, I assure you."

148

We passed through the gates, leaving the park behind. Traffic was heavy on Oxford Street, with carriages and vehicles of every description moving up and down, wheels rumbling, horse hooves ringing on the stones. I began to look for a cab, a bit worried about the time. It wouldn't do for Anthony Duke to get back before I did.

"I've missed you," Millie said. "The place don't seem the same without you."

"I've missed you, too. This afternoon's been nice. We'll have to do it often. You've been well?"

"Well as can be, dear, still 'opin' to meet the right man, the one who is goin' to reform me and set me up in my own place. Trouble is, the chaps I meet 'aven't got reformin' me on their minds."

She laughed merrily, looking like a naughty school-girl in her yellow dress, her golden ringlets gleaming in the sunlight. I hailed a cab, and as it pulled over, I gave Millie a quick, impulsive hug. I felt a great rush of affection for this saucy minx who bore her lot with such gallant aplomb. The Millies of this world are rare indeed.

"You take care now, luv, you 'ear?"

"I will," I promised, opening the door of the hansom. "You do the same."

I gave the cabbie the address and, closing the door, settled back against the dusty leather seat. As the hansom pulled into the heavy stream of traffic, I thought about what Millie had told me. Anthony was seeing a blonde. I wasn't surprised. Why should I be? I certainly didn't care. He could see a different woman every night of the week, as far as I cared. Ours was a business relationship, nothing else, and if he wanted to make a fool of himself over some icy, silvery blonde, that was no concern of mine.

I was fond of him, true, in my way. I had to admit that much. It would be impossible not to be fond of him, even though he was an outrageous bully, barking orders, pushing me until my head spun. He was easily wrought up, particularly after we'd been working for hours nonstop. But his outbursts were merely an outlet for all that nervous energy that built up inside. Heaven knows, I'd had a few outbursts of my own, as bad as his.

I smiled, remembering the time I had hurled a vase at his head, just missing, remembering his startled expression.

He might be a bully, but he was marvelously stimulating, and his bullying tactics had been highly successful. He had decided that I was to do two dances, one fast and fiery, the other slow and sensuous, and now I had both down to perfection. He had choreographed them himself, basing them on my original gypsy dances. Though I might not have been terribly good at ballet, I was very, very good at these dances, primarily because he refused to let up, kept after me until I thought I would collapse. It was the same with my Spanish. He drove me ruthlessly, forcing me to repeat my lessons over and over again long after my tutor had departed. As a result, my accent was almost perfect, even though my vocabulary left much to be desired.

He was fierce and determined, incredibly demanding, and I had to admit that it was exciting to work with him. I enjoyed every minute of it, even the tantrums. When he was pleased, the bully vanished and the charming rogue returned with that lovely, engaging grin on his lips. Then, he was delightful. He was rarely pleased, though, because he was a perfectionist. Elena Lopez was his creation, and she was going to be a sensation, set the stage afire, have all London at her feet. He would have it no other way.

The hansom shook as we rounded a corner. Through the window I could see a newspaper stall, a small boy in ragged clothes standing in front of it waving a paper. Elena Lopez wasn't a sensation yet, but there had already been more than one article about her in the papers. Anthony had arranged it, of course. He had brought his friend David Rogers up to the studio and they had plotted their campaign together. Both were hearty, enthusiastic, and noisy. Ignoring me, they argued with each other, creating a flamboyant and exotic fictional personality for the fascinating Elena.

Rogers, a ruggedly built, good-natured young man, looked as though he spent most of his time on a soccer field. He had strong, even features, lively gray-green eyes, and thick sandy brown hair brushed rather

150

severely to one side. Heavier than Anthony and not as tall, Rogers exuded an aura of good health and boundless vitality. The two men had become friends when Anthony was working on Fleet Street, and they had kept in close touch ever since. Rogers did feature articles for one of the large newspapers, supplied items for several of the columns, wrote theatrical criticism and, naturally, was writing a play. Anthony had appointed him official press representative for Elena Lopez, and he was to be in charge of all dealings with the gentlemen from Fleet Street. He was also the only one of Anthony's colleagues who knew the truth about the temptress from Spain.

A relatively short "factual" article had appeared two weeks ago, informing readers that the celebrated dancer Elena Lopez had been expelled from Spain because of political unrest caused by her relationship with an unnamed "crown prince." The crown prince, it seemed, had been squandering a fortune on "the dark, sensuous beauty" and had given her jewelry that belonged to the State. The State had demanded she return the jewels. The dancer had refused. The police had broken into her apartment and retrieved the jewels by force. The crown prince had been officially admonished. The dancer had been banished as "an unhealthy influence." When she left Spain she still had three pieces of the jewelry the prince had given her, a diamond bracelet, a diamond and ruby necklace, an exquisite diamond brooch. All three had been gifts to Queen Isabella I from Ferdinand V on the occasion of their first wedding anniversary. The jewelry had been craftily concealed in a pair of shoes before the police burst into the dancer's apartment.

A second article had appeared last week. It stated that Mr. Anthony Duke had recently returned from Paris after lengthy negotiations with the Spanish dancer Elena Lopez, who might possibly give her first public performance in exile under the auspices of the Dorrance Opera Company. The dancer was described as "difficult, unreasonably demanding, tempestuous." Mr. Duke doubted that they would be able to come to terms, as the dancer had no particular desire to resume her stage

151

career. She had allowed Duke to examine the famous jewels, the article continued, but when he questioned her about them, she had snatched them out of his hands, claiming that she had earned them and adding that the whole of Spain could go up in flames for all she cared. The jewels would never be returned.

The article had generated considerable interest and caused a spate of angry letters to the press, letters that crackled with moral outrage, and vehemently protesting the dancer's appearance in England. Rogers and Anthony had spent several uproarious hours composing the letters, vying with one another to see who could be the most incensed. Their original letters had prompted several sincerely outraged citizens to write in as well, and both men were delighted. Their campaign was working splendidly. Elena Lopez had already created a small stir, and, with Anthony's assistance. Rogers was currently working on a long "exposé" article that, they assured me, would have all London talking about the notorious Spanish temptress.

As the cab rumbled over a bridge, I could smell the river and knew we were nearing the studio. Elena Lopez had already taken on a life of her own in the pages of the newspapers. Elena Lopez was living in Paris, drinking champagne, wearing velvet gowns, flashing her jewels, and Mary Ellen Lawrence was being jostled about in a shabby old hansom with dusty interior, wearing an old blue and violet striped cotton dress and wondering if she had enough coins in her purse to pay the cabbie. The fiery creature who was already flesh and blood in the minds of many had nothing to do with me. Elena Lopez was a brilliantly conceived hoax, and I wondered if I would be able to carry off my part of it without mishap.

The horses stopped and the cabbie leaped down to open the door for me. Counting out my coins carefully, I could see that there were just enough, not even one left for a tip. The cabbie, looking disgruntled, grumbled to himself as he got back up on his perch and drove away. I stepped into the dim foyer and began to climb the stairs, wishing fervently that the studio were on the ground floor. No wonder Anthony was so lean and trim, I thought. All these stairs would keep anyone in shape.

I passed the door to his private quarters and moved on up to the studio. The door was standing open, and I stepped inside, startled to find Anthony pacing up and down, hands clasped behind his back, his jaw thrust out angrily. When he saw me, he stopped and glared. Looking unusually handsome in glossy black boots, dark maroon trousers and jacket, and a waistcoat of dark cream satin embroidered with darker cream leaves, his eyes seemed to snap with blue fire. His cheeks were flushed. A heavy brown wave fell across his brow.

"Something wrong?" I inquired.

"Where have you been?" he thundered.

I didn't like his tone. "Out."

"Where have you been?"

"Now just a minute—" I began.

"I'm in no mood for games, Mary Ellen! Tell me!"

"I went to lunch with a friend, and then we went for a stroll in Hyde Park."

"You've been with a man!"

Could he possibly be jealous? The idea enchanted me. I moved airily toward the door to my bedroom. He sized my arm, his fingers tightening brutally.

"Answer me!"

"I wasn't aware you'd asked another question."

"You've been with a man, haven't you?"

"If indeed I have, Mr. Duke, it's no concern of yours."

His eyes flashed. His brows were lowered menacingly. His mouth was a tight, terrible line, and his nostrils flared. I had never seen him so angry. I felt a small, triumphant thrill, and decided to be angry, too, but in a cool, ladylike way. I pulled my arm free and stared at him with frosty composure.

"You don't own me," I snapped.

"What ingratitude!"

"I'm supposed to be grateful?"

"I'm spending a bloody fortune on you! I'm up to my ears in debt already, and the real expenses haven't even begun. Your clothes, your costumes, and your hotel suite are going to be the best, mind you, the best suite

153

in the best hotel. Elena Lopez can't receive the press in a tattered cotton dress, in a shabby garret studio. I've fed you! I've put a bloody roof over your head! I've—"

"You've fed me, yes!" I was beginning to feel real anger. "You've had Cleeve bring up a tray. We haven't dined together once since that first night. Not once. You've never taken me to a restaurant. You've kept me shut up here in this—"

"I'm keeping you hidden! No one must see you. No one must know about you. When Elena Lopez finally comes to London—"

"I'm getting weary of Elena Lopez!"

"You bloody little—"

"I'm warning you, Anthony. If you strike me, if you dare raise a hand to me, I'll walk out that door and—"

"Try! Just you try!"

"I've gone along with your bloody scheme, Mr. Duke. I've worked until I thought I'd drop. I've let you scream at me. I've let you bully me. I've let you treat me like— like an old shoe you could kick around, but I happen to be a human being! I happen to have a few feelings. It's all very well for you to go out every night, not coming in until the small hours of the morning, but when I decide to spend a few hours with—"

"Who is he?" he interrupted.

"That's—"

"I want to know who he *is!*"

I stared at him defiantly, refusing to answer. Anthony fumed, eyes blazing, his right hand balled into a tight fist, wanting to hit me. He finally emitted a loud curse and slammed his fist into the palm of his left hand. It made a very loud impact, and he winced and shook his left hand vigorously to relieve the smarting sensation. I couldn't help smiling, and he gave me another murderous look. Marching over to the piano, he took a deep breath. Though he had his back to me, I could see him fighting to control himself.

"I didn't know you'd be in so early," I remarked casually.

He turned around to face me, his brows still lowered. "That's bloody obvious! How long has this been going on?"

"How long has what been going on?"

"How long have you been sneaking out to meet this—this man! You were supposed to be studying your Spanish."

"I didn't feel like it today."

"Don't press your luck, Mary Ellen. I'm in control of myself now, but you've no idea how close I came to hitting you. I'm calm now and prepared to be reasonable, but don't press your luck. You're not to see him again."

"That's a decision I'll make for myself."

"You're not to set foot outside this bloody building unless I'm at your side. That's an order! If you know what's good for you, you'll bloody well obey it. I don't know who this fellow is, but you can forget him right now. We've come too far, we've worked too hard. One tiny slip could wreck the whole plan."

"You're really worried, aren't you?"

"You're bloody right I am! David's article appears next week. Elena Lopez appears in London the week after that. We've got to be very careful from now on, and we've got to work like hell."

"I know the dances," I pointed out. "My Spanish accent is as good as it'll ever be. I'm *tired*."

"You're just on edge, luv," he replied, relaxing a bit. "You'll feel much better once we've done the press interview and you've made your debut. You'll be splendid, just splendid."

"Thanks!"

"You want to be squired about? Taken to restaurants? There'll be enough of that, once you've become Elena. Every man in London'll be eager to shower you with attention."

"I can hardly wait," I said dryly.

He grinned. He brushed the thick brown wave back from his forehead and came over to me and squeezed my arms affectionately. I felt a delicious tremor inside, and I felt angry, too, as angry as I would have been had he patted me on the head. I pulled away.

I could feel the tears rising, and I fought them back, turning away from him. I moved over to the window and stared at the buildings across the way. I refused to cry. What was wrong with me? A deep sadness stole over me, and I felt alone, so very much alone; there was a painful emptiness inside. Usually, I was strong, beautifully in control of myself, but of late my emotions seemed to be getting out of hand. I seemed to be living on nervous energy, and the tensions continued to build day by day. I closed my eyes and took a deep breath, fighting the tears, willing them not to come.

"You all right?" he asked.

I nodded. I could hear his footsteps behind me, feel him approaching me. He stood directly behind me, and I thought my nerves would snap. I didn't dare turn. He put his arms around my waist and drew me against him.

"You sure?" he said.

"I'm all right, Anthony."

"Look, I didn't mean to carry on like that. I never *mean* to. It's just this vile temper of mine. I'm very fond of you, actually. I'd never do anything to hurt you, and I'd kill any bloke who did."

His arms tightened around my waist, forcing me to lean against him. I could feel the warmth of his body, every fiber of my being seemed to stretch taut with tension. I tried not to tremble.

"One of these days I'll show you my gratitude," he said. "One of these days you'll be glad you joined forces with me. That's a promise. You're not going to regret any of this, Mary Ellen."

He gave me a tight squeeze, and then he released me, abruptly. Moving back over to the piano, he picked up a pair of gloves. I watched him pull them on. He picked up his maroon top hat, stepped over to the mirror and placed it on his head, arranging the tilt just so. Reclaiming the long gray cloak he'd tossed over the sofa and swirling it in the air, he draped it over his shoulders. He hadn't been wearing a cloak when he went out earlier. I suddenly realized that he had changed to an entirely different outfit.

He was obviously getting ready to go out again, and it was much too early for him to be going to the theater. He shook his shoulders to make the cloak hang properly, adjusting the heavy folds.

"I came home early to change," he said. "I forgot that

I had an appointment tonight. I won't be going to the theater. They can do without me for one night."

I did not comment.

"I promised to go to a party with a . . . friend of mine. It's outside London, a long drive. We'll have to leave early. Probably won't be back until almost dawn."

Why was he telling me this? He owed me no explanation. Was it because he felt guilty?

"When I found you weren't here, I got frightfully worried. Cleeve had no idea where you'd gone. I really *was* worried, Mary Ellen."

"Oh?"

"Guess that's why I got so worked up."

He stood in front of the mirror, admiring himself, the splendid male peacock fancying his plumage. Finally satisfied, he sighed and reached for the slender black cane he frequently affected.

"These little spats are good. They bring out your spirit. There's an awful lot of gypsy blood beneath that demure facade. We're going to have to work on that a bit. Elena's tempestuous, temperamental. You're going to need a few acting lessons."

"Am I?"

"Not too many. You *do* have a temper, luv. I've a feeling that if you really got worked up you could be formidable indeed. Mary Ellen is all cool dignity and poise, but there's a lot of Elena in you, far more than you realize."

He grinned. I wanted to slap him.

"Must hurry. I'm late already. You get some rest tonight. Forget about the Spanish. Cleeve'll bring you up a nice hot meal. I'll expect you to be fresh and feisty tomorrow."

He sauntered across the room, the cloak swaying from his shoulders as he moved. At the door he turned, tipping his hat jauntily. I watched him go, picturing the "friend" he was going to meet—a cool, aloof blonde, wearing ice-blue velvet. Seizing the tall Chinese vase sitting on the table nearby, I examined it with great interest. I heard a door slam far below and heard a carriage pulling up in front of the building. I looked at the vase. It was lovely, pure white etched with exquisite orange and gold flowers. The carriage drove away. I hurled the vase against the opposite wall. It crashed with a great explosion, sending a hundred jagged pieces clattering to the floor.

XVI

I gazed into the mirror, and Elena Lopez gazed back at me. My brows and lashes had been darkened with mascara, my eyelids coated with soft violet shadow. Rouge emphasized my high cheekbones, and my lips were a darker red. The makeup had been applied subtly, with great care, and the effect was most satisfying. My eyes seemed darker, a deep violet-blue, and I looked far more sophisticated, even exotic. My ebony hair was pulled back sleekly, long plump curls dangling between my shoulderblades. The makeup and hairstyle had been decided upon only after considerable experimentation.

Anthony had wanted me to wear a beauty mark, but I had refused. We had argued. He had finally given in. After a few acting lessons, I felt I knew Elena Lopez through and through, her voice, her gestures, her reactions, even her thought processes. Some of her rebelliousness had worn off on Mary Ellen. I wasn't nearly as malleable and easy to manage as I had been before. Though certainly I was not as tempestuous and temperamental as Elena Lopez, I could be exceedingly stubborn, as Anthony Duke had discovered.

I toned down the rouge a bit and then, finally satisfied, rose from the dressing table. Trying to appear calm and composed on the surface, actually I was a mass of nerves. In precisely one hour Elena Lopez would be checking into her hotel. It would be her first public appearance, and David had already warned us that several of his colleagues from the newspapers would be waiting for us in the lobby, hoping to scoop each other before the official press reception. It was going to be an ordeal, and I was very apprehensive. At the moment, I desperately wished I had never agreed to be part of the hoax.

David's article had appeared a week ago. It was a lurid piece of fiction that had caused a sensation, revealing, as it did, that Elena Lopez was the illegitimate daughter of the notorious Lord Byron and a Spanish beauty whom he had adored briefly and abandoned heartlessly upon discovering she was with child. Elena was fourteen when her mother died. She began to dance in cantinas, sponsored by an immensely wealthy Spanish nobleman who kept her plentifully supplied with jewelry and used a horsewhip on potential rivals. Abandoning the nobleman, Elena had journeyed to Russia, where she became the mistress of Alexander, son of Czar Nicholas and the future sovereign of all Russia. She had ridden wildly over the steppes surrounded by her own entourage of fiery Cossacks, had been the cause of a duel to the death between two important Russian diplomats, had given rowdy all-night parties for Alexander and his friends. A young Russian poet had shot himself when she refused to bestow her favors on him. He had been a poet of the people, and his suicide had almost caused a full-scale revolution. When her carriage was stoned by angry serfs, Alexander had been struck on the forehead by a rock. Finally, Czar Nicholas, himself, paid her a large amount of money in order to rescue his son from her clutches and get Elena out of Russia for good.

On her return from Russia, the article continued, Elena had begun her affair with the Spanish crown prince, the affair that resulted in her being banished from Spain. Queen Isabella's jewels were mentioned once more, described in detail, the story of Elena hiding them in a pair of shoes repeated. During her recent stay in Paris, Elena had fallen under the hypnotic spell of the concert pianist and composer Franz Liszt, as famous for his love affairs as for his music. Theirs had been a flamboyant affair, marked by fierce battles and physical violence. Liszt had locked her out of their hotel room. Elena had climbed through a window and, seizing a knife, had ripped all his clothes to shreds. He had attempted to strangle her. Liszt had finally fled to Germany to escape the raven-haired beauty who drove him to distraction. Elena, still seething over his cowardice, claimed that he was by no means the superb lover he was reputed to be. The meekest of her Cossacks could best the great Franz Liszt when it came to passion.

I thought about the article as I dressed. I found it utterly preposterous, but the public seemed to find it fascinating. Both David and Anthony were elated with the results. All London was talking about Elena Lopez —waiting to see her in the flesh. The opera was sold out for weeks and weeks, and people who cared nothing for music were still clamoring for tickets. The fact that Elena was supposed to be Lord Byron's daughter would explain my blue eyes and English features, Anthony assured me, and as for the Russian material, who would bother to disprove it? I was exceedingly dubious about the Franz Liszt episode. Liszt was very much alive, very much in the public eye, but Anthony laughed at my worries. Liszt was infamous for his affairs, he informed me. If by chance Liszt happened to see the article, he would probably be amused. He certainly wasn't going to deny having an affair with the celebrated Elena Lopez. Real or not, an affair with her could only add to his reputation.

I seriously doubted that the pianist would appreciate Elena's remarks about his prowess in the bedroom. The whole tone of the article disturbed me. Elena Lopez was a reckless adventuress, totally unscrupulous, and Mary Ellen Lawrence was her opposite in almost every respect. It was true that I had captured her spirit, her flair, but that was just acting, and I still had reservations about my ability to carry it off successfully. Anthony didn't, or so he claimed. He insisted that I would be superlative, but I suspected he had secret reservations of his own. He had grown increasingly tense and edgy of late, his breezy manner replaced by a grim determination that made me all the more apprehensive.

As I smoothed my velvet skirt down over my petticoats and adjusted the bodice, I thought about the quarrels we had had over my wardrobe. Anthony had seen Elena as flashy, flamboyant in her dress, and I had seen her as exquisite and elegant, though bolder than fashion dictated. I had won, but not until after some fierce arguments. A prim little woman with dusty complexion and apologetic brown eyes had arrived at the studio one day to take my measurements. I had assumed she was measuring me for my costumes and nothing more was said. But this afternoon I had opened my wardrobe to find it totally empty. My dressing table drawers were empty of garments, too. Except for what I had on, every stitch of clothing had been whisked away. Anthony had arrived with several boxes containing the outfit I would wear tonight—shoes, undergarments, gown, gloves, hat. Blithely, he informed me that my things had been packed by Cleeve and taken to a home for the needy. I was appalled, naturally, until he explained that Elena Lopez's wardrobe would be delivered to the hotel in brand-new trunks covered with gray leather.

"Only the best for La Lopez," he said.

"But my clothes—"

"They belonged to Mary Ellen Lawrence. Elena Lopez wouldn't be caught dead in any of them. Don't worry, luv, you're going to be very pleased with your new things. You damn well better be. They're costing me a king's ransom."

Remembering our arguments, I was extremely upset that he had taken it upon himself to select all my new clothes. I opened the boxes expecting to find flashy garments all aglitter with spangles and frills, only to discover elegant black slippers, lovely beige silk undergarments, black lace gloves, a magnificent hat, and the gloriously elegant purple velvet gown I was now wearing. Anthony had beamed with pleasure as he watched me opening the boxes. He admitted that he had been mistaken, that Elena would have perfect taste in her offstage attire, saving the flamboyance for the footlights. He assured me again that I would love the rest of the garments as well, those arriving in Elena's trunks.

I was eager to see them, but first I would have to get

through the ordeal of arriving at the hotel, checking in, fending off the gentlemen of the press. Thinking of that, I shivered inside. Anthony would be at my side, lending me some of his strength, however, and David would be there, too. David planned to meet us in the lobby after bringing Millie to the hotel and checking her into her own private room, which I had insisted be near my own. Millie was to be my personal dresser and maid. She was elated at the idea of "going respectable," thrilled at the prospect of being a part of my new life. Anthony had balked at hiring her, claiming that he couldn't afford to pay her a salary, that he was going to be bankrupt as it was, that I could bloody well dress myself, bloody well do my own hair. But I stood firm, coolly informing him that unless Millie were given the job, Elena Lopez would never set foot in London. He had carried on, accusing me of blackmail, but he had given in at last, and I had won another small victory.

Ever since the night Anthony had sallied off to take his friend to the party, I had been much harder to handle. Ever since the moment I had smashed the vase against the wall, I had been deliberately temperamental, questioning his judgment, arguing with him, insisting that I have my own way on a number of occasions. I found myself aggravating him intentionally, and Anthony was easy to aggravate. I'd spent hours and hours each day creating Elena Lopez under his tutelage, and it seemed that I was actually taking on some of her strength and self-confidence.

Standing before the mirror now, I admired the woman who was reflected in the glass. She was indeed exotic, not Mary Ellen at all. The gown was a rich velvet of deep royal purple. It had long tight sleeves and a form-fitting bodice with a square-cut neckline that left most of my shoulders and a considerable amount of bosom exposed. The skirt fell from the very tight bodice in gleaming folds over ruffled mauve petticoats. It was a regal garment, simple, incredibly elegant. I pulled on the delicate gloves with gossamer-like floral patterns of black lace. My hat was a great cartwheel of purple velvet with an enormous brim that slanted down in front. Black, white, and purple ostrich plumes spilled down on one side. I adjusted the brim, fastened the long black pin in place and stood back to admire the total effect. I had never worn such beautiful things. They seemed to give me confidence. I actually felt that I was an exceedingly attractive woman. Perhaps I could carry the whole thing off, after all. I felt like Elena Lopez, a glamorous creature who could have any man simply by crooking her little finger.

"Ready, luv?" Anthony inquired.

I turned, startled. I hadn't heard him approach. He stood in the doorway, a bit subdued, looking wonderfully handsome in his formal attire. There were faint smudges beneath his eyes, a tightness at the corners of his mouth. I could sense his tension, and I wanted to take his hand and squeeze it and assure him that everything was going to go smoothly. I felt a great rush of warmth and affection for this man who had bullied me and treated me so abominably and made these past weeks so unnerving and so very exciting.

"I suppose so," I replied. "I'll just need to fetch my fan."

"You look spectacular," he said. "I'd like to hurl you on that bed and make love to you until you screamed for mercy."

His expression was grim, his voice flat, but his words were thrilling nevertheless. I picked up the fan, fastened it around my wrist, and glanced around the room for a final time.

"I don't suppose I'll be seeing it again," I remarked.

"It's very unlikely. Cleeve will pack all your personal belongings tomorrow and bring them to the hotel."

"Make sure he doesn't deliver them to a home for the needy. I'm still upset about my clothes."

"Look, luv, I'm rather on edge. Let's not get into that again."

"I was just making conversation—"

"Don't," he snapped.

Even though I realized he was under a great deal of strain, I was offended. There was no need for him to be so abrasive and cold. He turned and strode through the studio in brisk, determined strides. I followed more slowly. I would miss this vast room with its huge skylight and shabby furniture and Bohemian atmosphere. It had been the scene of so many arguments, so much frustration and anger, so much elation. As I said goodbye to it, I realized I was saying goodbye to a whole part of my life. I would never be the same again. As soon as I entered the hotel as Elena Lopez I would be starting a completely new phase. I was sad, frightened, too. I hated to leave, to move on.

"Are you coming?" he called impatiently.

I followed him down the stairs, silent, offended. The carriage was waiting for us in the courtyard. As he opened the door, helped me inside, and climbed in beside me, he remained grim, so very grim. The driver turned the carriage around and, passing through the portals, started down the street. We were on our way. The confidence I had felt earlier ebbed away. It was his fault. He sat there with his arms folded across his chest, his chin tilted down, his eyebrows lowered in a straight, solemn line. Anthony Duke was a man of many moods. The charming, whimsical fellow who had carried me off to his studio might have been another individual altogether.

"We'll want to put on a good show," he said. "We'll ignore the press, refuse to speak to any of them, but we'll want to put on a good show nevertheless."

"Of course," I said coldly.

"You're Elena Lopez. Remember that. Remember it at all times. You're a stunningly beautiful, tempestuous *femme fatale*."

"I'll try."

"You'll do more than try."

"Don't worry, Anthony. I have quite a lot invested in this little project, too. My whole future."

"You needn't be snippy," he growled.

"You needn't be so bloody aloof."

"Something's been bothering you, luv. I can tell. You haven't been yourself these past couple of weeks. You've been stubborn, unreasonable, demanding. It's almost as though you've been trying to get back at me for something I've done."

"You're imagining things."

"Maybe so, but I don't like it. I don't like it at all."

165

"That's just too bad," I retorted.

Fortunately, he lapsed into stony silence again. We were both spoiling for a fight, and it wouldn't do to give vent to our hostilities at this particular moment. The carriage rumbled over a bridge and passed through a sordid slum district. I clenched my hands tightly, growing more and more tense. The urge to cry was still with me, but I refused to give in to it. Anthony would have no patience with tears. Anthony had very little patience to begin with. He was harsh and hard and completely unfeeling.

We left the slums behind, and rode through a park, green lawns spread with soft shadows from the trees, lovers strolling hand in hand along the flowered pathways. Out of the park, the carriage slowed down because of heavy traffic. We were nearing the Strand. The sounds of the city assailed my ears, and through the window I could see the crowded sidewalks, elegantly attired men and women strolling past expensive shops and restaurants. As we drove through Covent Garden, a labyrinth of majestic old buildings, the narrow streets littered with wilted flowers and cabbage leaves, I gazed at the opera house, grand and imposing with its tall white columns. A few moments later we were moving down the Strand at a snail's pace.

When the carriage stopped, my heart seemed to stop with it. Anthony climbed out and turned around to take my hand. Our eyes met. His expression was still grim, his blue eyes dark with worry. He had staked everything on this, I suddenly realized. His whole future depended on the next few moments. If I failed, if they even suspected I wasn't genuine, he could lose everything. He helped me out of the carriage, holding my hand very tightly, his fingers crushing mine together. He seemed to radiate nervous tension. I had been grossly unfair. He had worked so hard, had invested all his money, had gone deeply into debt, because he believed in me. I couldn't fail him. I couldn't let him down.

"This is it, luv," he said.

I nodded and stepped into character. Mary Ellen Lawrence vanished, her worries and apprehension evaporating. I was dark and exotic and gorgeous in my

166

purple gown and beplumed hat. I was spoiled, accustomed to much pampering, and I was sensual, accustomed to turning every male eye. I had had a tedious, bumpy crossing from Calais to Dover, an even more tedious ride in a stuffy railroad carriage, and I was in a testy mood, concerned about my trunks. Elena Lopez took over entirely, possessing me. I saw with her eyes. I felt with her emotions. Gazing at the lovely facade of the hotel with open disdain, I spoke with a heavy Spanish accent.

"So thees eez zee oh-tel. Elena Lopez eez accustomed to pal-aces. I do not like thees place. Zhere eez no red carpet!"

I glared at him with angry eyes. Anthony was taken aback, and then he was delighted. I could see his spirits rising. He gave my hand another tight squeeze. Pulling my hand free, I tossed my head. This English menial was altogether too familiar. I allowed him to take my elbow and lead me toward the entrance where a doorman in gray uniform festooned with gold braid held the door open for us. Moving past the doorman without a glance, my chin tilted haughtily, my red lips forming a pout of disapproval, I looked over the spacious lobby, all gold and crystal and gleaming white. A group of men in poorly fitting suits were clustered near the front desk, talking loudly. One of them turned and saw us. He let out an exclamation of glee, and the whole pack charged us.

They all began to talk at once, eager, excited voices and rapid-fire questions merging together and creating one vast roar. I recoiled in horror, my eyes flashing. They were like a pack of leaping, yapping hounds, and I wanted to slash them with a riding crop. Anthony gripped my elbow tightly, shoving the men back with his free hand. David joined the group. He helped Anthony subdue the pack.

"Later!" David cried in his robust voice. "Give her room! Let her pass!"

"How do you like London?" a thickset redhead bellowed. "What do you think of English men?"

"Is it true that Franz Liszt locked you out of your room?" a strapping blond yelled.

"Are you really Lord Byron's illegitimate daughter?"

"Did the Russian poet really commit suicide because you wouldn't—"

"Back!" David thundered.

"Don't shove me, mate! Hands off! Who the bloody 'ell do you think you are? I just want a minute of your time, Miss Lopez. I just want to know if—"

I stood stony still, ignoring the noise, the confusion, the flushed, hearty faces, the overwhelming stench of cigar smoke and sweat. David and Anthony finally managed to drive the pack away from me. Anthony told them I was exhausted, far too exhausted to talk with them now. David promised that they would all be invited to a reception in my suite, later. I would talk freely then, and there would be food and drinks. The men grumbled menacingly. One of them called David a traitor but he ignored the remark. Finally, the pack withdrew, huddling together near the elegant staircase to stare at me angrily.

"Who are zees men?" I asked as Anthony rejoined me.

"The press," he replied.

"Zee big man with zee shoulders and sandy 'air, who eez he?"

"David Rogers. He's working for us. He'll handle all our relations with the press. We've already arranged for your suite, Miss Lopez, but you'll have to sign the register."

The gentlemen from Fleet Street were listening intently. They watched with hostile eyes as I followed Anthony over to the desk and signed the register. The desk clerk, looking both embarrassed and appalled that such a commotion had taken place, handed a key to a youth in a gray-and-gold uniform and told him to take us up to my suite. The men continued to grumble among themselves. I didn't like their mood. I decided to do something about it. I might not be able to answer their questions just yet, but I wanted to win them over immediately. I looked at them with a great deal of interest, a woman sizing up potential bed partners.

"Why do I need someone to 'andle zees men for me?

168

Why can't I speak vith zem? I deedn't know zey were vith zee press. I thought zey were ardent admirers who wanted to sleep vith me."

"Uh, Miss Lopez—" Anthony began uneasily.

"Are all English men zo 'andsome?" I asked.

The men were listening and watching me intently. I continued to study them, my lips slightly parted, my eyes straying from man to man.

"Zat big redhead, he is good-looking, no? He eez big and tall with zee strength of a stallion. Zat blond, he has zee smouldering eyes, he is very good vith zee women, I can tell. Zey are all virile. Zey remind me of my Cossacks. I will ask zem up to my room. I will answer zeir questions and give zem champagne."

"Later, Miss Lopez," Anthony said nervously. "Mister Rogers has arranged a reception. You can talk with them then. You're tired. You've had a very uncomfortable journey, and—"

"Zey are disappointed," I interrupted. "Zey will go back to zair papers and zey will write unkind things about Elena Lopez. Zis big man with zee shoulders and zee sandy 'air, he does not tell Elena Lopez when to speak to zee men from zee press!"

"The reception is all arranged. You see, that way every one of the men will have an equal opportunity to speak with you. No one will be short-changed. They'll all be able to get a good story."

"I see. I will invite zem to my reception."

"Mister Rogers will inform them as to—"

"*I* vill ask zem!" I said defiantly.

As I started toward the group of men, Anthony grabbed my arm, trying to restrain me. But I jerked my arm free and gave him a blazing look that should have incinerated him on the spot. I moved over to the staircase and stood in front of the men. Their attitude had changed completely. They were no longer hostile toward me. David and Anthony had become the villains, and Elena Lopez was their champion. I smiled at them. David shot Anthony a frantic look.

"Gentlemen of zee press," I said slowly, trying very hard to speak proper English. "I want you to come to a party. We will have champagne and I will answer all your questions. Elena Lopez loves zee gentlemen of zee press. Zey are always so charming."

They grinned. They beamed. They adored me.

"You," I said angrily, pointing to David. "Zis oh-tel 'as a place where zey serve drinks? Yes? Please, you will take all zee gentlemen zhere and buy zem drinks. Elena Lopez pays. Zey put it on her bill."

Three or four of the men actually cheered. David frowned and looked at Anthony but shrugged his shoulders and led the way into the adjoining bar. The men followed eagerly. I waved to them. Anthony gripped my elbow and led me up the stairs, the uniformed youth hurrying ahead of us. I felt a glow of triumph. It had been so very easy. I hadn't been nervous at all. Instinctively, I had thrown myself into the role with complete abandon. As we followed the youth down a long, wide plushly carpeted corridor, I found that I was actually enjoying myself.

"Where are my trunks?" I demanded as we stopped in front of a door. "Where eez my jewel case? I gave it to my maid? She eez here? Elena feels na-ked without her jewels."

Anthony gave me a grim, exasperated look as the youth opened the door and led us into a spacious, beautifully appointed sitting room done in tan and deep maroon and pale blue. An enormous crystal chandelier hung from the ceiling. Deep maroon draperies framed the tall windows. The young man opened a door and showed us the bedroom and indicated the adjoining dressing room and bath. Anthony, tipping him generously, told him everything was satisfactory and showed him out, closing the door behind him. He took a deep breath and leaned against the door, staring at me, his arms crossed over his chest, his face expressionless.

"I like it," I said.

"At these prices, you'd bloody well better."

"I've never seen such luxurious rooms."

"Only the best for Elena Lopez."

His face was inscrutable, and he kept staring at me as though I were a stranger. Had I done well? Had I gone too far? I moved across the deep tan carpet. I took off my hat and laid it on a sofa upholstered in pale blue. He continued to watch me, his lids drooping slightly.

"Where's Millie?" I asked.

"She's probably in her room. It's at the end of the hall."

"My trunks?"

"They'll be here."

"I don't care what *you* think," I said testily. "*I* think I was magnificent."

"You do?"

"Absolutely magnificent!"

"You're bloody generous with my money. Do you know how much those chaps drink? They drink like fish. That little gesture of yours is going to cost me a bloody fortune, and you know what?"

"What?"

"I don't even care."

I looked at him, surprised. His eyes began to sparkle and his mouth spread into a wide grin. Bounding across the room, he caught me up in a great bear hug that almost broke my ribs. He squeezed me tightly, rocking me to and fro, and then he actually whirled me around, as exuberant and lusty as a soccer player who has just won a big game. He set me on my feet and seized both my hands and squeezed them and grinned and grinned.

"The style! The flair! I should never have worried! I should have known you'd be tremendous. What an entrance! You had them eating out of your hand! Christ, you were marvelous! Marvelous!"

He hugged me again.

"For a minute there, I actually believed you were Elena Lopez!"

He released me, and I caught my breath. Then he grabbed my hands again.

"I couldn't believe it. I was stunned! That accent! Those flashing eyes! What instinct! You knew just what to do, just what to say. You've got the press on your side already, luv, and the rest is going to be a snap of the fingers. You were fantastic!"

"Thank God," I said.

171

XVII

Anthony insisted that we do it again. So we did, and when we were finished, the men in the orchestra sighed and shifted their instruments. I stood onstage with my hands on my hips, tapping my foot impatiently. Everyone was on edge. Tomorrow night Elena Lopez would make her debut. This afternoon was our last chance to rehearse. Anthony was like a demon, hard on the orchestra, even harder on me, making impossible demands. He climbed out of his seat now and strode up and down the aisle. His footsteps rang loudly in the vast, empty auditorium.

"You're going to hate me, I know, but I'm going to ask you to do it one more time. The fast number's fine, all fire and fury, music and movements in perfect harmony, but the slower number—"

He shook his head. Several men in the orchestra groaned. Several more cast angry glances in his direction. They were here to play Rossini, not to indulge an upstart entrepreneur who clearly wouldn't know what art was if it bit him on the neck, and they resented him. They felt sorry for me. They had expected fireworks from the notorious Elena Lopez, but she had been meek, patient, polite, never once complaining during any of the rehearsals. She had been friendly to each and every one of them, greeting them warmly in her thick Spanish accent, and giving them apologetic looks when she failed to satisfy the bully.

She was tapping her foot now. She was bone weary.

Her nerves were raw and jangling. If he kept on pushing her and riding her, those fireworks were going to materialize.

"One more time," he pleaded. "Remember, men, this music is sensual. It's not Mozart. It's not Rossini. It's a Spanish love song, slow and moody. Think of hot summer nights in Madrid. Think of a lovelorn youth and a seductive temptress who is trying to make him forget the fair maiden he loves. Think of—"

"I'm thinking of my backside," one of the men protested. "I've been sitting in this bloody chair, propping up this bloody violin, for four hours straight."

Anthony ignored the remark. He strolled down the aisle, moving nearer the stage. He was wearing dark plum-colored trousers and a white cambric shirt opened at the throat, sleeves folded up to his elbows. His brown hair was casually disarrayed. I tapped my foot more rapidly now, my nerves near the snapping point.

"Miss Lopez," he said, "kindly remember that you are attempting to seduce a beautiful youth with burning eyes. You want him. Your movements are slow, sensuous. You are smouldering with desire."

I looked at the conductor. I looked at the men in the pit.

"Who eez thees man?" I asked.

"What's that?" Anthony said.

"Who *eez* thees man! He thinks he can tell Elena Lopez about passion? He thinks he can treat her with—with this pa-tron-izing condescension? She has been zee angel, right? She has not complained. She has let heem browbeat her and work zeez poor men to death. No more! She eez finished for zee day."

"Now hold on, luv."

"Finished!"

I stomped my foot, tossed my head, and I stalked offstage. The men in the pit applauded noisily. As I headed toward my dressing room, stepping over coils of rope, moving past stacks of flats leaning against the bare brick walls, I could hear Anthony clambering up onto the stage in hot pursuit. Reaching the rusty iron staircase that wound up to the less important dressing rooms above, I whirled around to face him. When he saw the expression on my face, he hesitated, biting back the angry words he'd been about to speak, realizing he was going to have to use a different approach.

"Look, luv—" he began.

"Not one more word!" I snapped.

"This is our last opportunity to—"

"I am exhausted! So are those men! The theater's like an oven, not a single breath of fresh air, and you've been a heartless slave driver! You're lucky I'm not sprawled out onstage in a dead faint! You expect me to perform tomorrow night? I won't be *able* to perform tomorrow night. I'll be in some hospital bed in a state of complete collapse!"

"The accent, remember the accent. Someone might overhear."

"Go to *hell!*"

He shook his head and gave me a weary, patient look.

"I want you to stay in character as much as possible, but this is overdoing it."

His voice was patient, too. He might have been speaking to a rather simple-minded child. I could feel the anger boiling up inside me. Smiling, he patted my arm, all warmth and understanding now. He started to say something gentle and consoling, but when he saw my flashing eyes he decided against it. He stepped back and thrust his hands into his pockets and shrugged his shoulders. I stormed past him, angry tears burning in my eyes.

Millie was waiting for me in the dressing room. Observing the state I was in, she didn't bother to speak, but fetched a glass of cool water and handed it to me. I sat down in front of the mirror and drank it. Sprinkling cologne on a cloth, she patted my temples and forehead with it. I took a deep breath, willing myself to simmer down. After a few moments I took the cloth from her and finished wiping my face. Millie gave a sigh of relief.

"I'm sorry, Millie."

"You just got a bit wrought up," she said. "It's all this tension and strain."

"I suppose so."

"You'll be fine once tomorrow night's over with.

You're gonna' be a sensation, just like you were when you gave the reception for them fellows from the newspapers. They loved you—just look at the things they've been writin' about you—and the audience is going to love you, too."

"You're beginning to sound like Anthony."

"God forbid."

"I don't need reassurance. I just need—I just need a little peace and quiet."

" 'Course you do, luv."

Millie handed me a towel and set a ewer of water on the dressing table. I slipped out of my rehearsal gown and bathed my neck and arms. Millie helped me into a robe, and when I sat back down she began to brush my hair. Millie took her job very seriously. Dressed in a simple dark-blue cotton dress, a ruffled white organdy apron tied around her waist, her golden curls caught up in a loose French roll on the back of her head, she was determined to be the best lady's maid in London. Now that she had gone respectable, she was respectable with a vengeance, watching her language, trying not to drop her h's.

"You 'aven't—*haven't* said anything about the roses," she remarked. "A boy brought them a couple of hours ago. Cheeky lad, thought he could get fresh. I put 'im in 'is place quick enough."

The roses stood on the bureau in a tall white basket. They were a vivid red, gorgeous, and there must have been at least three dozen of them. I knew who had sent them without even glancing at the small white card nestling amidst the stems. Mr. George Dorrance had sent me roses every single day since I began rehearsals at the theater. He had asked me to dine with him on three different occasions. I had refused each time. Dorrance felt obligated to sleep with all the attractive female guest artists who performed with his company. As he was rich and important and very attractive, his success was generally a foregone conclusion. Elena Lopez presented quite a challenge.

"They're lovely," I said, unimpressed.

"He doesn't give up, does he?"

"Not easily."

176

"He's been most attentive."

"Most," I said.

When Millie finished with my hair, it was lovely, all sleeked back, long curls dangling, the Elena Lopez style that a few of the women who had encountered me here at the theater were already beginning to imitate. I touched up my makeup as Millie took down my dress, a street dress that happened to be silk, maroon and black stripes, very thin. It was sumptuous, as were all the outfits Anthony had purchased. Elena Lopez had a fabulous wardrobe. The gowns all had a certain style, too, a look created for the seductive Spanish dancer, current fashions be damned.

I slipped into the dress, and Millie had just finished buttoning me up in back when someone knocked on the door. I frowned. I guessed who it would be. Anthony never knocked, he just barged right in. Millie had a good idea who it would be, too. We exchanged looks, and she stepped to the door and opened it. Dorrance strolled in, smiling. The dressing room was quite large, but he was so big that his presence made it seem much smaller.

"And how did the rehearsal go?" he inquired.

"Eet went very nice-ly," I replied.

"I see you got my roses."

I nodded. He smiled. Dorrance was in his late thirties, a tall, heavily built man, a large man who carried his size with ease. He had dark, wavy hair and deep brown eyes that were much too sincere. The drooping lids and the wide, full lips betrayed a highly sensual nature. He was much too aware of his good looks, and I found his manner heavy-handed, calculating. Dorrance saw himself as a great womanizer, which indeed he was. His easy success with women had given him a confidence I found most unappealing. I was neither overwhelmed nor flattered by his interest in me, merely bored. It was difficult not to show it.

"Everything is satisfactory?" he asked.

"Veree."

"Duke's been treating you all right?"

I nodded again, wishing he would leave.

"We're very honored to have you with us," he continued. "To show my appreciation, I'd very much like to take you out to dinner tonight."

"I am veree tired," I said.

"It would do you good, you know. You need to relax, unwind a bit before the big night. I could show you a very good time, Miss Lopez, a very good time indeed."

"I'm sorree."

He smiled. "I'm not going to take 'no' for an answer. I'm going to be at your hotel tonight at eight. I've a feeling you'll change your mind. If not—well, I'll simply dine alone, with deep disappointment. Until tonight, Elena."

He took my hand and, turning it palm upward, lifted it to kiss, Continental style, his lips pressing against the two small mounds of flesh. He held it a little too long, and it was all I could do not to pull my hand away. Still holding my hand, he gave me a heavy, seductive look with lids drooping and squeezed my hand hard. I was supposed to breathe deeply and melt with longing, but I did neither. Releasing my hand he nodded and left. Millie made a clucking sound and shook her head.

"He thinks you're in the bag, luv."

"I know. He's wrong."

"He *is* terribly good-looking—charming, too."

"Too good-looking, too charming."

"What are you going to do when he arrives at the 'o— *ho*tel?"

"I'm going to be indisposed."

Slipping on my black lace gloves, I turned as the door opened and Anthony stepped in. He had put on his jacket and waistcoat now, tied a brown silk neckcloth at his throat. Ignoring him, I asked Millie to go see if our carriage was ready. She left, giving Anthony an impudent look as she moved past him. They didn't get on well together. He resented having to pay her a salary, and she resented his cavalier attitude toward me. Millie was nothing if not fiercely loyal.

"That girl's altogether too uppity," he said.

"I'm sorry you think so."

"You feeling better?"

"I'm fine," I said coldly.

178

"Still a bit frosty, I see."

He glanced at the roses.

"Dorrance still in hot pursuit? I saw him leaving the dressing room a minute ago. Looked very pleased with himself. You finally agree to go out with him? I assume he asked."

"He asked me to dine with him tonight, yes."

"Might not be a bad idea, luv. Good publicity value. Dorrance has quite a reputation with the women, and the papers would leap on it immediately. We'd get some nice coverage."

"That's all you can think of, isn't it?"

"Every time your name's mentioned in the papers, it's more tickets sold, more money in the bank. Besides, you need to get out of that hotel room. It would take your mind off tomorrow night."

"You think so?"

"Sure it would. Uh . . . I'd take you out myself, but I've got a very important engagement. Go out with him, let him feed you oysters and champagne. Have a good time. Can't do any harm."

"I doubt his intentions are honorable."

"I know damn well they're not, but you can handle yourself, and I feel sure you can handle George Dorrance, too. Poor man lays a finger on you, he'll get instant frostbite."

"He's very attractive."

"You're much too bright to be taken in by that heavy-handed seductiveness. I'm not a bit worried."

Would he worry if he thought I was attracted to Dorrance, if he thought there was a possibility I might succumb to the man's advances? I wondered. Anthony stepped over to the mirror to adjust his ascot. Satisfied, he moved toward the door. I looked spectacular in the black-and-maroon-striped silk, and he hadn't even noticed, had hardly glanced at me.

"I just thought I'd pop in and see if you were all right. That little temper tantrum of yours had me worried."

"Good."

Anthony grinned. "You really were quite spectacular out there, stamping your foot, storming around with

179

your eyes ablaze. I wouldn't be at all surprised if the papers didn't hear about your outburst. It might be worth a column. Temperament's always colorful."

He sauntered out, leaving the door wide open, and Millie appeared a moment later to inform me that the carriage was waiting. My mood was black as we left the theater, and the joggling, uncomfortable carriage ride didn't help. People stared as Millie and I got out in front of the hotel, and others stared as we moved through the lobby and up the grand staircase. It was difficult for me to realize that I was already a celebrated figure in London, easily recognizable thanks to the Elena Lopez "look" we had worked so hard to achieve.

Millie went on to her room, and I entered the expensive suite that was so very beautiful, so cold and unwelcoming. Even though I had scattered my books and personal belongings about, it felt impermanent. Every night I sat here, alone, like a prisoner amidst all this splendor. Millie might come in to chat for a while, but when she left the feeling returned, worse than ever after the brief respite. I had not gone out once, not even to dine in the restaurant below. Not daring to brave the restaurant and the stairs without a male escort, I had my meals brought up to the room.

Anthony had come to see me only twice, to discuss the contracts he was negotiating with Dorrance on the first occasion, to have me sign them on the second. What did it matter to him that I was lonely and nervous and disoriented? He cared not a jot. I had signed a contract to appear at the Dorrance Opera House for one month, and I had signed a contract authorizing Anthony to act as my personal manager and collect all monies and handle all business affairs, and that was all that mattered to him. If I paced up and down in this elegant suite, if my nerves were about to snap and my disposition was growing steadily more shrewish, what did he care? My "little temper tantrum" had amused him. He would use it to advantage. I had no doubt I would read all about it in tomorrow's papers.

Stepping into the bedroom, I tossed my reticule on the bureau, slipped off my gloves, and looked at myself in the full-length mirror. The skin seemed to be stretched

180

taut across my cheekbones. There were faint shadows beneath my eyes. The strain was clearly visible there in my face, in my body. I glanced at the clock. It was shortly after seven. How many hours would I pace? How many hours would I spend in bed, tossing, turning, unable to relax, unable to sleep? How was I going to endure one more night, wrought up, on edge, frightened out of my wits at the thought of appearing before hundreds of people? He should be here to give me strength and comfort, to reassure me. But he had a very important engagement tonight, and I could go hang.

Something hard and rebellious tightened inside of me. I pulled a silken cord to summon the maid, and when she appeared I ordered hot water for a bath. I bathed and a few minutes later I was at my dressing table, touching up my makeup, doing my hair, not wanting to call Millie. Millie wouldn't approve. Millie thought George Dorrance was a fool, pompous and pretentious, laughable with his conceit and self-conscious seductiveness, and I did, too, but I couldn't stay in this room alone one more night. Dorrance would take me to an expensive, plushy restaurant, where there would be music and laughter and other people, and perhaps I could relax and forget about tomorrow night and what it would bring.

I chose my gown with great care. It was a vivid scarlet silk with puffed sleeves that fell off-the-shoulder and an extremely low-cut neckline and a full, flaring skirt that swirled over the multilayered skirts of my petticoat. It was a spectacular garment, just the sort of thing Elena Lopez would wear. I put it on. Elena Lopez looked stunning and fiery and tempestuous, and Mary Ellen had never in her life been so tense, so angry and resentful.

I left the suite and moved slowly down the grand staircase, scarlet silk rustling crisply. Everyone stared, but I ignored them, and when George Dorrance stepped forward to greet me at the foot of the stairs I gave him a cool, curt nod and let him lead me across the lobby and out to the street where a carriage was waiting. I felt cold and hard, barely able to contain my impatience as he spoke in a deep, playful voice and employed his seductive manner and bored me with his transparency. Sensing my mood, he was silent during the carriage ride, a half smile playing on his full lips. He was filled with anticipation. He was certain of success. Whatever had possessed me to come out with him? I had a headache, and it grew steadily worse.

The restaurant was exactly what I had expected, plush, frightfully expensive, spacious, the walls a pale ivory, the carpets gold, the chandeliers dazzling with crystal pendants. It exuded an atmosphere of wealth and luxury and privilege, and I hated it, and I hated the way Dorrance preened as the headwaiter led us past the banquette and down three gold-carpeted steps and into the main dining room, seating us at a prominent table where everyone in the restaurant could see us. No secluded, private room for Dorrance. He wanted to be seen with me. He wanted everyone to think he had made another conquest.

"Champagne?" he said.

"Of course."

"Oysters?"

I nodded.

"Caviar, too. This is an occasion."

"Sí," I answered in a flat voice.

He talked. I listened, nodding occasionally, replying when it was absolutely necessary. I sipped the champagne, ate a few oysters, took a spoonful of caviar, bored, so very bored, tense, too. Why had I come? My headache was excruciating and everyone was staring, and this man kept smiling, employing all his charm, lids half-lowered over seductive eyes, voice seductive, too, and very confident. The main course came. I toyed with my food, unable to eat. Dorrance was so intent on wooing me that he didn't even notice.

"—very generous terms," Dorrance was saying. "I must say I fought him, but after I read all the stories in the newspapers—"

"I—I'm sorry. What were you saying?"

"Duke drives a hard bargain. He demanded top salary. I'm paying you more than I've ever paid an *entr'acte* performer, more than I usually pay the best

182

prima donnas. But Duke was right, you're worth every penny."

"Mmm." I was distracted.

"He looks dapper tonight. Celebrating, I suppose."

Dorrance was staring across the room, toward the steps, and I turned to see the headwaiter leading Anthony and his companion to a table. Anthony was wearing his formal attire, and he did indeed look dapper, his mood positively jovial as he took his seat and leaned across the table to say something to his companion. She smiled a cool smile. She was beautiful, far more beautiful than I could ever hope to be, her features perfect, her eyes a clear blue, her hair a pale, silvery blonde. I stared. I felt nothing. I seemed to be numb. Dorrance was saying something, but I didn't hear a word.

Anthony must have felt the intensity of my stare. He turned and saw me. He looked surprised, then alarmed, then sheepish, and then he grinned and gave me a little wave, but I continued to stare until he grew uncomfortable. Dorrance was still talking. I forced myself to look away from that table across the room, to concentrate on what this pompous, conceited fool was saying. It was difficult.

"—good working relationship with all my performers. I want them to be happy. To feel pampered and secure. I want them to know I'm behind them all the way—"

I didn't care. He could have a different blonde every night of the week for all I cared. I wasn't his type. He had told me that on more than one occasion. He had made it very clear. I wasn't his type, and he certainly wasn't mine. He was a rogue, a scoundrel—handsome, yes, and breezy and charming, and any woman would be a fool to trust him for a minute and I couldn't care less what he did. He could go straight to hell. I hadn't any illusions about him. We had a business arrangement. He had transformed a pathetic little ballet girl into a colorful personality and we were both going to make a great deal of money, and that was all that mattered to him.

"—like to give you a little token of my esteem. It's not much, but I hope you'll be pleased."

Reaching into his vest pocket, Dorrance took out a flat white leather box. He looked deep into my eyes as he opened the box. The diamonds gleamed and glittered, silvery-blue, silvery-violet, flashing brilliantly as he held the bracelet up for my approval. I hardly noticed. The waiter had brought champagne to their table, and Anthony was pouring it for the blonde, who took her glass and smiled another cool smile and Anthony was saying something to her and Dorrance was dangling the bracelet, diamonds shimmering, and I was no longer numb. I could feel my fury rising.

"—a mere bauble compared to the jewels you've already received from admirers, but—"

A very important engagement, he had told me. I'd take you out myself, but I've got a very important engagement. Busy all the time. You know how it is. He had a very important engagement with a blonde iceberg when I was going to make my debut tomorrow night. I had needed him tonight, but he sat there grinning and having the time of his life, and I was supposed to take it calmly and act as though nothing had happened.

"Something wrong?" Dorrance inquired.

"Excuse me," I said, forgetting the Spanish accent.

I stood up. Dorrance leaped to his feet, startled, still holding the diamond bracelet. Everyone in the restaurant watched as I marched over to Anthony's table, my silk skirt crackling loudly in the sudden silence. Anthony stood up, a worried expression on his face. His eyes were filled with alarm.

"Uh . . . uh . . ." He looked at the blonde, looked back at me. "This is Elena Lopez. She . . . uh . . . she doesn't speak much English. I'd like you to meet Elizabeth Clark, Miss Lopez."

Elizabeth Clark and I exchanged venomous nods.

"Fancy seeing you here tonight—" Anthony stammered.

He sank back down into his chair, still looking upset. A large platter sat on the table. It was white, rimmed with gold. I picked it up. Anthony grinned a foolish grin and shook his head, silently begging me not to do what he knew I was going to do, and I slammed the platter down on top of his skull. The fine porcelain shattered into a dozen pieces that clattered noisily as they fell. Anthony cried out. People gasped. A waiter rushed over, horrified. Anthony staggered to his feet, stunned, but not really hurt.

"Temperament's always colorful!" I snapped.

I turned and moved briskly toward the steps. George Dorrance, catching up with me, took my arm, but I pulled free and shoved him away. I moved up the steps and through the door, until I was standing outside on the edge of the street, signalling for a hansom. I gave the driver the name of my hotel and climbed inside, still seething with anger, fervently wishing I'd broken Anthony's skull instead of the platter.

XVIII

I paced up and down the sitting room, trying to calm myself, horrified at what I had done to Anthony in the restaurant but, at the same time, wishing I had hit him harder. Half an hour had passed since I returned to the hotel, and I was still filled with conflicting emotions, though anger dominated. I wanted to scream and beat my fists against the wall, and I wanted to sob uncontrollably to let loose the flood of tears dammed up inside. It wasn't just tonight that had put me in such a state. I had been building toward it for weeks and weeks.

Someone knocked on the door, a loud, insistent knock. Who could it be? Millie always tapped lightly. I was in no mood to see anyone. I ignored the knock, and after a moment it sounded again, louder, even more insistent. I flung open the door. Anthony stood there with his top hat in his hand and a grin on his lips, looking inordinately pleased with himself. I tried to slam the door in his face but he shoved me roughly out of the way and stepped inside.

Tossing his top hat onto the sofa, he looked at me with sparkling blue eyes.

"Bravo!" he said, as he unfastened his cape.

A slender blue and white vase sat on the table beside me. I seized it. Anthony dropped his cape and, moving quickly toward me, grabbed my wrist, giving it a brutal twist. The vase fell to the floor, rolling unbroken across the carpet.

"Christ!" he exclaimed, "I've created a monster!"

187

There was merriment in his voice, in his eyes. I kicked his shin viciously. Swearing, he let go of my wrist. As I drew my hand back to slap him, he caught me and whirled me around and held me in a tight bear hug. I lifted my foot and ground the heel of my shoe into his left instep. He swore again and released me, and I dashed over to the mantel, my fingers closing around a figurine.

"No!" he cried. "That's Dresden! It costs a fortune!"

I hurled the figurine. He ducked. As the figurine crashed against the wall, I grabbed its companion piece and hurled it, too. My aim was better this time. The figurine smashed across his knee, breaking into a thousand pieces. Anthony ducked again as I threw a silver box at him. Sailing over his head, it crashed into a mirror and the glass exploded. As he dodged the small golden clock I threw next, I suddenly realized that he was enjoying himself, and I wanted to kill him.

When I reached for the heavy silver candelabrum he gave a cry of genuine alarm and leaped across the room to restrain me. We fought and my anger knew no bounds now; I hardly knew what I was doing. He had a difficult time controlling me, but he was finally able to lock his arms around me, crushing me against him. Then the rage inside me seemed to boil over, all the fight went out of me, and I stopped struggling. Anthony hesitated for a moment and then, cautiously, released me and stepped back.

He shoved a lock of hair from his brow. "Christ," he said, "I need a drink."

"Get out," I told him.

Stepping over to the liquor cabinet, he took out a crystal decanter of whisky and a glass. I watched him pour the drink, and although the violent rage had dissipated I was still angry enough to hope he'd choke on the liquor. His neckcloth was rumpled, his hair unruly. He looked marvelously, wickedly appealing, and that made me feel even less charitable toward him. Surveying the debris, he shook his head, and then he smiled and raised his glass.

"To Elena," he said.

"Go to hell."

"That's what I intend to call you from now on. Elena. Mary Ellen is gone. It's finally happened. That transformation I was praying for has taken place. That fire, that fury, those magnificent gestures—they were all genuine. You weren't acting!"

"Will you please leave?" I snapped.

"I drove you, taunted you, kept you in a state of nervous tension, all with a definite purpose in mind. I watched you grow testier, watched Mary Ellen Lawrence change from a sad and desperate little ballet girl into a fiery, tempestuous woman."

"I hate you!"

"No, you don't, luv. Tonight, in the restaurant, you were superb. I told a couple of my old mates from Fleet Street you'd be there, told 'em there might be fireworks, and both of them were there. What a story it's going to make."

"How could you possibly—"

"Dorrance always takes his women there. I knew you'd be nervous and restless and unable to spend another night pacing around in this suite. I knew you'd see red when I walked in with Elizabeth. I hoped you'd do something, but I never dreamed it would be quite so spectacular!"

"You—you set it up!"

"Indeed I did. It was all carefully staged. Dorrance didn't know anything about it, of course, but he played his part to perfection just the same. That diamond bracelet was just the right touch. You should have accepted it. We could've hocked it."

"You're despicable."

"Shrewd, merely shrewd. The story'll be in all the papers in the morning, and it'll be sensational. Shame we didn't have an audience just now. You were even better hurling things."

I could feel the rage stirring inside again. Deliberately, with great effort, I suppressed it. I wasn't going to let him provoke me again. Moving over to the unbroken mirror, I toyed with my hair. It had come all undone, spilling down about my shoulders in tumbling blue-black waves. I pushed at it but, finally, let it go, realizing it would be futile to try to restore order. Smooth-

189

ing the red silk over my waist and adjusting the bodice that had slipped dangerously low during our tussle, I examined my reflection as though I were alone in the room. Despite the disheveled hair, I managed to look cool and composed, my eyes a dark, serene blue.

I turned to face him. "I think you'd better go now," I said calmly.

Anthony ignored my remark. Taking a final sip of whisky, he put the empty glass down. He was looking at me with a peculiar intensity, his eyes half veiled. I felt a tiny alarm spring to life. I knew that look and what it signified. He had never looked at me that way before, had never allowed himself to look at me that way before. The air that only moments before had been filled with an aura of crackling anger was suddenly tinged with a new aura, even more palpable, its message undeniable.

"You look gorgeous," he said.

There was a husky catch in his voice. My guard went up immediately.

"Red is definitely your color."

"I'm very tired, Anthony. I want you to go."

"That isn't what you want, luv."

His eyes were filled now with desire. I looked at him, trembling inside, because I knew all at once just how much I wanted him, and I knew it would be a disastrous mistake to let him make love to me. I had no illusions about him, none at all, and he already had far too strong a hold on me. Summoning all my strength, I gazed at him coldly, and when I spoke my voice was crisp.

"I suggest you go back to Miss Clark," I said.

"Elizabeth? She means nothing to me, never has. She was available. I wanted you and didn't dare risk endangering our project by taking you."

"Oh?"

"Surely you realized that?"

I said nothing. I felt cold inside, and hard, and I clung to that cold, hard core, knowing it was my salvation, knowing I mustn't give way to the emotions that were stirring, demanding release. How attractive he was in his elegant formal attire, tall and lean and rakish with the slightly twisted nose and that curious half smile

190

that played at the corners of his mouth. But he was unscrupulous, a rogue through and through, the facile, boyish charm never quite concealing his ruthless drive, his determination to get ahead through fair means or foul. I knew all this, just as I knew I was not immune to that charm, must fight it with all my strength.

"I've wanted you from the first moment I laid eyes on you," he said. "But I knew all my energy, and all yours, had to be concentrated on turning you into Elena Lopez."

He folded his arms across his chest, propped his shoulders against the wall behind him, and looked at me with those dark, gleaming eyes. His face was all sharp planes and angles, hard, the skin stretched tautly across broad cheekbones. The lamplight burnished his hair, making it a darker, richer brown, and those errant locks spilled down over his brow once again.

I wanted to brush them back. I wanted to rest my palm against his cheek, stroke those full lips with the tips of my fingers. I wanted those strong arms to draw me to him, to hold me tightly, and I wanted to release the feelings that grew more and more demanding, captive inside, denied for such a long time. Brence Stephens had awakened them, giving them shape and texture, tight buds that blossomed into fullness at his touch, and I had shut them away, disowning them, refusing to acknowledge their urgent demand because I was afraid. I was afraid now, for I had loved once, loved fully, without reservation, and anguish and loss had been my reward.

"It's time, Elena."

"Don't call me that."

"You are Elena. You've become the creature I envisioned. The little ballet girl is gone forever."

"No."

"You're a woman, a gorgeous woman, far more passionate than you realize. I was aware of it from the first. All that passion seething beneath the cool, refined surface. It shows in your dancing, in your angry outbursts."

"If I've had angry outbursts, it's because you've driven me to them."

"Quite true. I did it deliberately. It was all part of the

191

awakening process. I saw your potentials, saw what I could do with them."

"And now you want to make love to me," I said in an icy voice. "I suppose you think that would be the crowning touch, complete the process."

"That isn't the reason."

The room was in semi-darkness, only one lamp burning, the bedroom beyond in darkness. I stood near the sofa, refusing to recognize those emotions surging inside as I watched him saunter over to extinguish the lamp. There was a moment of pitch darkness, and then silver began to seep in through the windows, soft, misty silver that spread slowly. Anthony came toward me. I stiffened. I willed myself to remain cold, distant, because I wanted him but I knew he would use me and, when the time came, abandon me without a moment's hesitation, blithely moving on to new adventures.

"No," I said sharply.

"You want me, too, Elena. Don't try to deny it."

"Get out."

"This was inevitable. We've both been waiting."

Drawing me to him, he put one arm around my waist and the other around the back of my neck. I struggled, but his lips found mine and he kissed me for a long time, gently at first, those firm, warm lips caressing my own, pressing and probing tenderly. Gradually the tenderness gave way to urgent demand. As his arms tightened and he made a moaning noise deep in his throat, sensations sprang to life inside me, driving away will and resolution, and my arms went around his back, palms stroking the silky texture of his jacket, touching the nape of his neck as he forced my lips apart and his tongue lashed mine aside.

My head seemed to spin, and as the dizziness grew I seemed to be on a rack, sweet torment pulling me apart, his arms holding me tighter until I was molded against him, melting into him, overpowered by his strength. He drew his head back, peering down at me, and in the moonlight I could see his eyes dark, determined. I was trembling. I shook my head. He planted his lips on the curve of my shoulder and they burned my flesh as they moved toward my throat and breasts.

192

I tried to push him away, my palms pressing against his chest, but he fastened one hand around my wrist and moved toward the bedroom door, pulling me after him. I fought him desperately, but Anthony didn't even seem to notice. Catching hold of the doorframe, I tried to hold on to it. He gave my arm a savage tug, propelling me into the bedroom. Moonlight poured through the windows, gilding the furniture, gleaming on the satin counterpane that covered the bed.

His hand still held my wrist, his fingers like iron bands crushing skin and bone. I was filled with panic, afraid because reason had fled and my whole body was taut. Anthony ignored my efforts to break free. I might have been a troublesome child, he a severe adult. I kicked him. He let go of my wrist and slapped me across the face, a blow that sent me spinning into darkness, reality dissolving as the pain shot through me and I fell into his waiting arms. Several minutes may have passed, or it may have been merely seconds, for when I opened my eyes they were wet with tears and my cheek still burned where he had slapped me, but the panic was gone. He was holding me tenderly and saying sweet words in an incredibly tender voice.

He kissed me again, his lips caressing mine. I touched his cheek, and ran my fingers through his thick, luxuriant hair that was like heavy silk. He drew his lips away and looked at me with tender desire, with longing, his arms cradling me loosely, and I lifted my hand to touch his mouth, running my index finger along the soft, firm curve of his lower lip. Both of us were possessed now with the same need, but the urgency seemed to have vanished, turning into a delicious languor that stole through our limbs with painful slowness, warm, honey-sweet. Anthony smiled, and I tried to smile, too, but there was too much sadness in my heart. For even as I gave way to the languor, I knew it was folly, but I was past the point of caring.

Clumsily, he began to unfasten my gown, muttering a little curse as he freed my arms from the sleeves and pushed it over my hips. After I stepped out of the circle of red silk, he removed my undergarments one by one until, finally, I stood naked in the moonlight, trembling

193

slightly, resigned but exultant, too, filled with a wild joy that seemed to sing in my veins. Stepping back, he looked at me, and his eyes darkened with something almost like reverence. For the first time in my life I felt completely beautiful, and I was glad, so very glad that I could be beautiful for him.

Resting his hands on my shoulders, he gazed into my eyes for a long moment, his own conveying a silent message that caused the music inside to swell. He caressed my shoulders, my throat, touching me gently, reverently, his fingers sliding slowly over my flesh. His hands encircled my breasts, his fingers stroking the soft, fleshy mounds. My eyes closed as waves of sensation swept over me, carrying me into a void where there was nothing but this man, this moment, these feelings that swelled and surged and threatened to drown me. With one hand lightly at my waist, he bent to kiss each nipple, his lips moist and warm, and I caught my fingers in his hair, almost fainting with desire.

It had been so long, so long, that I had denied myself, denied this part of me. Now as he caressed me, kissed me, drew me into his arms, I shivered, and Anthony, thinking I was cold, folded me closer, murmuring soft words. He caught my lips with his; his mouth worked slowly, savoring mine, his lips spreading and forcing my own to part. That kiss seemed to last forever, sheer torture that combined agony with bliss, and, naked, I clung to him as his silk shirt pressed against my bare breasts.

Finally, lifting me into his arms, he carried me to the bed, lowering me onto the satin counterpane, and he knelt over me and kissed me again and again, on my temple, my throat, my breasts, my thighs. The feeling inside me grew more and more tormenting. Anthony moved away from the bed, and I felt lost, alone, incomplete, craving his touch, craving his body and the musky smell of him that was like heady perfume. He stepped into the shadows away from the windows, and I could see his dark form moving and bending as he removed his clothes. As I watched, his neckcloth floated to the floor like a silky moth.

I closed my eyes and stretched on the counterpane,

its satin smooth and cool beneath me, emptiness above, space that must be filled with muscle and bone and weight and warmth and wonderment. Need mounted to agony as I opened my eyes and saw him step out of the shadows and into the moonlight, naked now, looking like a magnificent statue suddenly imbued with life. He stood there for a moment bathed in silver, moonlight rippling over that perfect body, and then he smiled a wicked smile and I raised my arms as he moved across the floor to the bed.

The mattress sagged and the springs creaked noisily as he climbed onto the bed, and he looked so startled by the sound that I laughed, and Anthony laughed, too, gathering me to him. The weight of his body crushed me, heavy, hurting, glorious. It was lovely, lovely, and I struggled beneath him; for a few moments we were like two children playing a naughty game, wrestling together on the slippery satin counterpane, limbs entwined, and then his face, inches from my own, grew stern, almost savage, and his lips sought mine with bruising force and a wild, tumultuous fury possessed us both. He was fierce and forceful, uninhibited, and I was uninhibited, too, returning each touch with equal ardor, clutching him to me as senses shredded like silk tearing and we soared as one to a dizzying height and plunged together into a shattering paradise where ecstasy exploded again, again, and again.

XIX

The music of Rossini swelled, fast, merry, slightly frenzied, ringing loudly through the wings and down the hall, into my dressing room as I checked my makeup. Through the closed door it was like the frantic buzzing of a swarm of insects, and soaring over it was the voice of the soprano, who was much too shrill. A capacity crowd filled the theater. Every seat was taken, and dozens of people were standing in back. In twenty minutes the first act would be over and I would step out in front of the footlights and all those hundreds of people would be staring at me, waiting for Elena Lopez to dazzle them. . . . I forced the thought from my mind, concentrating on the face in the mirror. The perfect, sultry face of Elena.

Millie was fidgeting around like a nervous cat, making a terrible racket, dropping things, and I was the one who should have been nervous. I wasn't. I was resigned. I felt much older, and wiser, too. Last night had been explosive, and it had been satisfying, but, somehow, it had merely underlined my loneliness. I had made love with Anthony Duke, but I could never love him, could never depend on him. He was as mercurial as quicksilver and as elusive, bright and glowing and impossible to hold. I was wise enough to know that, wise enough to realize that no matter how many times we made love it could never be more than physical gratification.

"—wants to take me out," Millie was saying. "Altogether too fresh, he is, thinks he can take liberties. I'm respectable now and I intend to stay that way, though I must admit it gets a bit tiring. He is very good-looking in a rough-and-tumble sort of way. What do you think?"

"I—I'm sorry, Millie. I wasn't listening."

"David Rogers. He wants to take me out tonight after we finish up 'ere. Has *plans*, he does. Thinks I don't know what he's after. Do you think I should go out with him?"

"You'd probably enjoy yourself."

Millie brushed a stray tarnished gold curl from her temple. "I probably would," she admitted. "I suppose you can carry this respectability bit too far. A person needs to have a little fun, wouldn't you say? I just might let him take me to dinner. . . ."

She flashed the old pixie smile and, glancing at the clock, took down my costume. As I stood up, I slipped off my robe, and Millie helped me into the bold, dramatic garment designed for Elena Lopez. The blue satin bodice had full off-the-shoulder sleeves and was cut extremely low, over it a black velvet corselet, laced down the front, fitted snugly over bosom and waist and the top of my hips, flaring then into a skirt composed of row upon row of silk ruffles, red, blue, violet, and white, ruffles that billowed and blew as I moved. It was provocative and revealing, and when I danced the skirt would lift and whirl, exposing my legs.

"I feel naked," I said.

"You look smashing. The men are going to go out of their minds."

"What time is it?"

"Ten more minutes," Millie informed me. "You nervous?"

"Not really. Resigned might be a better word."

"You're going to be sensational," she promised.

"I have to be," I said. "My whole future depends on it. I don't intend to fail, Millie. I can't."

At the hard, determined note in my voice, Millie gave me a curious look. I was frightened, terribly frightened, but I wasn't going to acknowledge the fear. I wasn't even going to entertain the possibility of failure. I had to succeed. I had to make money, to make some kind of life for myself. If I couldn't be a celebrated ballerina, then I could be Elena Lopez, and Elena was going to be a spectacular success. I stood in front of the mirror, smoothing the dress over waist and hips, willing myself to be strong and self-assured.

"Are you ready?" Millie asked, as she took my hands and squeezed them and then gave me a quick hug. I hugged her back, and then I picked up my castanets and left the dressing room.

The music of Rossini swelled to a crescendo, and as I closed the dressing room door behind me there was one brief moment of paralyzing fear, a moment of incredible grief and loss that seemed to stab at the very core of my being, but I quickly pulled myself together and moved down the hallway past stacks of painted flats and a rack of shabby, fading costumes.

Moving past the rusty iron staircase, I stood in the wings beside a huge pile of boxes. The music rose, swirling higher and higher as the final notes of the first act were sung. The stage was brightly lit, the strong lights somehow enhancing the cheap set and making the costumes seem almost rich. Magic was taking place out there, a golden illusion being spun, however poor the performers, however shabby the production. Here, beside the boxes, it was dark and dusty. High above, men in shirtsleeves stood on catwalks, ready to work ropes and pulleys the moment the last note was sounded. In a few moments I was going to create my own magic. I was going to convince that vast crowd of people sitting in the darkness that I was indeed Spanish and seductive.

A sudden draft of cold wind eddied backstage as someone opened the stage door that led into the alley. My costume left much of my bosom and shoulders and almost all of my back bare, and I shivered as the icy wind swirled past dusty brick walls and besieged me, causing the ruffles on my skirt to flutter. The door closed. Footsteps approached. Anthony materialized out of the darkness and, seeing me standing there, moved toward me with that long, jaunty stride.

"Here you are," he said.

"Hello, Anthony."

"I didn't realize it was so late. I've been in a mad rush all day. It's almost time, isn't it?"

"It's almost time," I said.

He looked resplendent in his formal attire, dark satin lapels gleaming, white silk tie perfectly knotted, his manner breezy and casual as ever. I hadn't seen him all day. He had dressed and slipped out while I was still sleeping. He hadn't even bothered to leave a note. Last night might never have happened.

"I suppose you saw the papers today," he remarked, toying with his top hat.

"I saw them."

"That incident in the restaurant made terrific copy, luv. It caused a whole new rush on the box office. Dorrance was delighted, by the way. No hard feelings. They spelled his name right."

I said nothing.

"Say, I . . . uh . . . I hope you weren't upset about my leaving like that this morning. I guess I should've awakened you, but . . . well, you were sleeping so peacefully I didn't want to disturb you."

"You needn't apologize."

"I had things to do, very important things. I had a meeting with some chaps I know. We're going to make an awful lot of money, luv, and money means responsibility. You have to know how to handle it, how to invest it for the best returns. These chaps are involved with the railroads. They're looking for investors, a few smart men willing to double, triple their investments in a matter of months. They explained the whole thing to me, and it's a chance in a lifetime—"

Aware that I wasn't paying attention, he cut himself short and shook his head, and then he gave me an apologetic smile.

"Sorry. I guess I got carried away. I should've realized this isn't the time or place to discuss business. You don't want to be bothered with details, anyway. I'm the manager. I'll manage, and you just concentrate on being a sensation."

As the words left his mouth the music ended. The men above worked frantically, hauling on the ropes. The heavy gold velvet curtains rang down, slowly,

200

smoothly, sending thin clouds of dust backstage. The audience applauded, and members of the chorus hurried offstage and up the staircase to their dressing rooms. A stagehand held the curtain back so the principals could step out in front of the lights for their curtain calls.

Anthony took my hand and squeezed it tightly.

"I'm not going to wish you luck, luv. You don't need it. You're going out there and you're going to dazzle 'em. I've known it all along. I knew it from the first."

"Indeed?"

"From the first."

He squeezed my hand again and grinned that engaging grin, and even though I knew him for what he was, I couldn't help responding. I did so ruefully. Anthony Duke was the kind of man women would forgive over and over again, each time against their better judgment. As I pulled my hand free and fastened on my castanets, Anthony thrust his hands into his pockets, looking pleased and proud.

The principals were still taking their curtain calls, milking applause now, the soprano outrageously grateful, smiling, bowing, blowing kisses, while behind the curtains in the darkness men were dismantling the set quickly and quietly. I left Anthony and moved nearer the stage. I was much calmer than I had any right to be. Perhaps it was a kind of numbness. The soprano took one final call to tepid applause, and then the baritone seized her wrist and pulled her back behind the curtain. The audience grew silent. Moments passed. The air seemed to be charged with tension. They were out there waiting, filled with expectancy, growing more and more restless as they stared at the brilliantly lighted gold curtain.

The orchestra began the first strains of the Spanish melody, slow and sensuous music that suggested hot sunlight and cool balconies and smouldering passions. The curtain rose slowly to reveal a bare stage with a blue silk backdrop. As I waited, I thought of Brence Stephens. If I succeeded tonight he might one day come to a theater and see Elena Lopez and remember the girl he had abandoned. As the music grew warmer, more persuasive, I realized that I had done all this for him, to show him, to have revenge on the man who had given me such happiness and then brutally destroyed it.

As the music swelled, I moved onstage with the grace of a panther, hips swaying, colored ruffles billowing. Proud, passionate, disdainful, I pouted my lips and glared at the audience and then tossed my head, giving them exactly what they wanted, wooing them even as I scorned them. I could feel their awe, their admiration, but I was Elena and it was no more than my due. I raised one arm, then the other, and I stared at the dark sea of faces and imagined a handsome Spanish youth with soulful eyes who must melt before me as I began my sinuous dance of love.

Movement and music seemed to melt together into a burning expression of desire as I whirled and turned and swayed, clicking my castanets provocatively, urging the invisible lover on. I had never danced as well before, my body lithe, movement liquid, the melody a part of me. He was melting me. His mouth grew tight. His nostrils flared. I beckoned him with my body, urging him on with my eyes. He moved toward me, and I moved away, toying with him now, taunting him. I smiled, delighted with my power over him. I drew him to me and swayed, slowly, slowly, and he was mine now and I parted my lips and lifted my arms to him as the last note of music echoed into silence.

I had them. They were mine. I could feel it.

There was the slightest pause as I stood there embracing my invisible lover, and then the music began again, all fireworks and fury. The savage melody caught me and transformed me into a fiery, uninhibited creature who stamped and whirled, the black velvet corselet slipping lower, the skirt sailing higher and higher. There were gasps from some of the women as my legs were revealed from ankle to thigh, but that only spurred me on. The music grew faster, more frenzied. I abandoned myself to it. As I danced, I remembered the gypsy camp and the moors and the cliffs and the crashing waves and the man who had brought me such elation, such joy, such anguish, and that spurred me on to greater heights until the music rose to a shattering crescendo and finally stopped.

It was over. Damp with perspiration, I stood panting, waiting. There was a moment of shocked silence, and then deafening applause filled the theater. The building seemed to shake with it. Men were shouting. People were leaping to their feet. I bowed. They roared. I moved nearer the footlights and bowed again, smiling at them, and they were stamping their feet and clapping furiously and shouting their approval. I looked toward the wings. Anthony was beside himself with joy. He was clapping, too, as loudly, as enthusiastically as any of them. Men were running down the aisle with bouquets of roses. They tossed the bouquets and the ribbons broke and the air was filled with roses that fell all around me.

I had been a rose once, a rose in red tulle who had dreamed of becoming a great ballerina. I remembered the girl I had been, and I felt a touch of sadness inside even as I smiled and acknowledged my triumph. The audience continued to roar. I gathered up the roses and began to toss them to the musicians who had been so kind to me, and then I tossed them to the audience, causing an even greater furor. It was dramatic and flamboyant, exactly the sort of thing Elena would do. I was Elena now. A great success. The past was over. The future was waiting.

INTERLUDE
IN PARIS

1847

XX

It was going to be a pleasant crossing. The Channel was calm and blue and there was very little wind so the boat moved slowly. Overhead noisy gulls circled against a pearl-gray sky faintly stained with blue. I stood at the railing watching the white cliffs of Dover grow smaller and smaller, trying to still the faint unease inside me. Anthony had insisted on going on ahead, setting things up, making our hotel reservations and "smoothing the path." I would have felt much better if he had been standing beside me. He had been altogether too elusive and evasive of late, and I was beginning to wonder if our three weeks in Paris were going to be as restful and relaxing as he had promised.

There would be publicity, of course. There always was. I would be interviewed, and I would be on display, but Anthony had given his word that I would have plenty of time to shop and see the sights while he made the final arrangements for my European tour. His word, I had learned, wasn't nearly as reliable as it might have been. I had earned a rest, and I wasn't going to let him spoil it for me with more of his shenanigans. I would grant a very few interviews, but I would flatly refuse to participate in any of the clever publicity stunts he and David put such stock in. He might grumble and complain, but ultimately I would have my way.

Since we had become lovers, Anthony's manner was even more proprietary and possessive than before, and it was frequently necessary to remind him that I had a will of my own. I was content to let him handle all the business affairs and direct my career, but I was no longer willing to let him bully me. I was Elena Lopez now, not his timorous little protégée. Though I was extremely fond of Anthony, I dared not love him and knew I must keep my guard up at all times. He could push me just so far before I rebelled, and we had had some rousing fights during the past eleven months. It irritated him that I usually won.

During the past month or so I had seen very little of him. My fantastically successful tour of England had ended with two weeks in Bath. Once Millie and I were installed in the hotel and arrangements had been made with the theater, Anthony had gone to London to consult with his business associates about the railroad stocks. He hadn't returned to Bath until the end of the engagement, and then he had been preoccupied, his ordinarily exuberant manner subdued. When I had asked him about the railroad shares he had been almost belligerent, informing me that it was *his* job to manage the money, mine to dance and dazzle and keep the paying customers happy. After we returned to London, he spent most of his time away from the hotel again, dealing with business matters, he said. Then he insisted on going on to Paris ahead of us.

I couldn't shake the vague apprehension I felt, and Millie insisted that something was afoot. But she didn't trust Anthony, never had, telling me I had a soft heart where he was concerned and would ultimately be brought to grief. I realized that she was probably right, but I owed everything to him. I accepted Anthony as he was, grateful to him for all he had done, knowing he was unreliable, quixotic, an engaging rogue whose boyish charm and jaunty manner belied an essentially ruthless nature. He might be infuriating at times, might exasperate me and cause my temper to flare, but it was impossible not to forgive him. Best of all, Anthony was a superb lover, magnificent in bed, and I had come to depend on him in a whole new way.

The Dover cliffs were barely visible now, melting into a misty blue-gray horizon. The slight breeze toyed with my hair and caused my skirts to billow. I was wearing a dark blue gown with long puffed sleeves, a snug, fitted bodice, and a very full skirt adorned with rows of fine black lace. It was a dramatic garment, as indeed were all my new clothes, designed to draw attention to Elena Lopez, and I wore them with aplomb. The public expected Elena to be bold and daring in her dress, and I knew how important it was to maintain their image of me. After almost a year, it was second nature to me.

Passengers strolled up and down the deck, enjoying the salty air, the cry of the gulls, the brilliant sunshine. Most of them stared at me, for I was a celebrated figure now, immediately recognizable, a scandalous creature who caused women to exchange shocked whispers and men to entertain decidedly wicked thoughts. David Rogers had done his job well. He had accompanied us on the lengthy tour throughout England, and he had seen to it that everyone high and low knew about the legendary, tempestuous, and seductive Spanish dancer. Rarely a week had passed without at least one story in the papers. There were usually more. Tinted pictures and paintings of me had been circulated all over the country, sold in stalls and theater lobbies, and a reproduction was featured on the lid of a popular cigar box. I was constantly in the public eye, and I had grown accustomed to the stares.

Few men had stared so openly, however, as the man in the bright maroon frock coat was doing at the moment. I had been aware of him for some time. He was a large man with dark, humorous eyes, dusky skin, and crisp dark hair that covered his head in tight curls. His black boots were polished to a high gloss, his maroon breeches unusually snug. His waistcoat was silver embroidered with black and maroon silk flowers, dashing indeed, and his neckcloth was of vivid turquoise silk. Probably in his early forties, he was quite handsome in an exotic sort of way, and he seemed to crackle with vitality and health. His lips were unusually full, undeniably sensual, and a smile seemed natural on them.

He continued to stare, boldly, without real rudeness,

209

and I noticed that people were staring at him, too. It wasn't surprising. Any man who wore such outlandish clothes deserved to be stared at. He looked as if he enjoyed it, too. Aware that he had captured my attention, he gave me a friendly nod, dark eyes dancing with amusement. I put on my haughtiest manner and turned away, ignoring him. He smiled and strode briskly toward me anyway. I braced myself for another unpleasant encounter. Because of my scandalous reputation, certain men felt free to approach me, and I had learned to deal with them with an icy disdain that chilled even the most ardent.

"I think it's time we met," he said.

"I think not," I retorted, hoping my French would be adequate. I had recently had a tutor help me brush up on my schoolroom French.

"You don't know who I am?"

"No, nor do I care to."

He chuckled, clearly delighted by my rebuff. "I'm dismayed," he said, "positively dismayed. A bit deflated, too. I thought everyone knew me. Are you sure you're not just teasing?"

"I can assure you I—"

"Have you heard of *The Three Musketeers*?"

"I believe it's a novel."

"A novel! It's a phenomenon! It's taken the world by storm. Such style, such panache, such *heart*. A masterpiece, believe me. A masterpiece. Come now, you've read it. Surely you have."

I shook my head, maintaining my cold demeanor with great difficulty. There was something immediately warming about this great, exuberant man with his twinkling eyes and rumbling voice. One sensed charging red corpuscles and incredible drive, strong appetites and a terrific zest for living. He seemed larger than life, the flamboyant clothes carefully tailored to display the hefty, muscular physique. Although he spoke the language perfectly, he did not look like a typical Frenchman. The dusky skin, full lips and tight, crisp curls were faintly African.

"You *do* read French?"

"I've read everything Balzac has written."

"Balzac!" he roared.

"I read all George Sand's books, too."

"She'll be delighted to hear it," he said grumpily. "You're one of her current idols. George goes mad over colorful, independent women who defy convention and make a career for themselves—kindred souls. I'll introduce you to her."

His voice was petulant, but that was merely pretense. The dark eyes were still twinkling, and a half smile played on those sensual lips. He had an almost overwhelming presence, this great lion of a man who combined the enthusiasm of a merry child with an aura of potent sexual magnetism that was galvanizing in its effect. Women were obviously as indispensable to him as hearty meals and huge tankards of strong red wine.

"What about *The Count of Monte Cristo*?" he asked.

"What about it?"

"Surely you've read *that*."

"I'm afraid not."

"If you weren't so pretty, I'd wring your neck," he growled. "You're doing this deliberately. You know very well who I am. Everyone knows. Ask anyone on this boat. They'll tell you. See those schoolgirls over there? See them tittering and pointing? They know who I am. They know my reputation with women. They're hoping I'll scoop them up and carry them off to my cabin."

I smiled in spite of myself, melting before his jovial charm. I knew who he was now, of course, but I was enjoying the game too much to give it up just yet.

"You're not Spanish," he said accusingly. "Your accent is English."

"You think not?"

"Gorgeous, yes. Fascinating undeniably. Seductive, no question about it. Spanish, not a chance. The papers say you claim to be Lord Byron's illegitimate daughter. I doubt that, too."

"You'll admit it makes good reading."

He rumbled with laughter, drawing even more atten-

211

tion to us. I should have been uncomfortable, but I wasn't. I found Monsieur Alexandre Dumas both amusing and endearing.

"I think you're as big a fraud as I am, Elena."

"You're entitled to your opinion, Monsieur Dumas."

"Ah-ha! So you do know who I am."

"I've read about you. Your reputation is almost as bad as mine."

"Worse, *chérie*," he assured me. "We've wasted enough time in idle chitchat. The boat won't dock for at least half an hour. That'll give us ample time for a rousing bounce in bed."

"You are outrageous."

"I've the stamina of a ram. You're going to love it. They all do. Women are constantly after me; they can't leave me alone. They're always underfoot. I literally have to kick them out of the house in order to get any work done."

"So I've heard."

"Look at them staring at us. They're talking about us already, *ma petite*. By tomorrow afternoon it'll be all over Paris that Dumas went to London to see his English publishers and came back with Elena Lopez. They'll say we had a raging, lusty affair and spent the whole time on this boat making noisy love in my cabin. Come now, let us give truth to the rumors already starting."

"I'll pass, Monsieur Dumas."

"You're turning me down?"

When I nodded, his expression changed to mock dismay.

"I refuse to believe it! You're not impressed with my accomplishments? You don't find me wonderfully handsome and irresistibly virile? You're not eager to find out if all that talk about my prowess is true? Incredible!"

I smiled again. It was impossible to take offense. He took nothing seriously, himself least of all. I liked him very much.

"You're making a mistake. I really am phenomenal in bed, lusty as can be. I always leave them begging for more," he added, "I could provide references."

"You'd merely be wasting your time."

"I must be losing my touch," he complained. "You've ruined my day, you know. I'm totally crushed."

"I imagine you'll get over it."

He sighed and shook his head, and then he smiled, eyes atwinkle.

"I suppose I'll have to settle for friendship, for the time being. How long are you going to be in Paris?"

"I'll be there for three weeks. Then I begin a European tour."

"Three weeks will give us plenty of time to become *amis*. We're going to be seeing a lot of each other, I promise. Someone needs to launch you in Paris, and it might as well be me. If you're not going to come down to my cabin with me for a touch of *l'amour*, I suppose I'd better go back down alone and dash off the rest of that chapter. My publishers are screaming. They never give me a moment's peace. *À bientôt*, Elena."

"*Au revoir*," I said.

He took my hand and turned it palm upward, lifting it to his lips. After kissing my hand he gave me a merry nod and strolled off toward the stairs. The schoolgirls in white organdy tittered like a trio of nervous geese. Dumas bowed to them, growling hungrily. Their chaperone let out a horrified exclamation and herded them away. The novelist laughed boisterously, moving on down the stairs.

For a while, I strolled along the deck thinking about the encounter, and then I went down to our cabin. Millie was checking our hand luggage, counting to make sure we had it all. Our trunks had been sent on ahead to the hotel in Paris, but we still had a bewildering array of bags and hatboxes. Satisfied that nothing had been left behind, Millie sighed wearily and patted her golden ringlets; her deep blue eyes had a long-suffering look. She wore an extremely fetching pink cotton frock that accentuated her voluptuous bosom and slender waist. After almost a year as dresser-companion to the notorious Elena Lopez, Millie wasn't nearly as concerned with respectability as she had been in the beginning.

"They're all here," she informed me. "I must say I'm surprised. I felt sure that man would lose one of them. Don't know why he had to see us off, anyway."

The man was David Rogers. He had accompanied us from London to Dover and had brought all our bags on board, striving all the while to get Millie off alone for a private talk. Millie treated him with cool disdain, glaring at him when he stumbled and dropped the bags, answering him tersely when he spoke to her. The strapping, robust David who ordinarily looked as though he had just come from a rousing game of soccer had worn a pathetic, forlorn expression as he stood on the dock watching the boat pull away. Millie hadn't even bothered to wave from the railing.

"Thank goodness we've seen the last of him," she said. "He was beginning to get completely out of hand, so bossy and possessive, and all that talk about marriage! Thought he owned me, he did. A girl wants to have a bit of fun before she settles down."

She spoke with considerable emphasis, and I smiled to myself. Millie had certainly been having her share of fun during the past months, leading the enamored David on a merry chase and flirting outrageously with every lad who struck her fancy, conduct calculated to send David into bursts of jealous rage. Loving every minute of her new life, she thrived on the excitement surrounding Elena Lopez. The tour had been tedious and uncomfortable, an endless procession of dusty railway carriages, shabby hotel rooms, and drafty provincial theaters, but she had taken it all in stride. She might grumble and complain and act very put-upon, but her spirit never faltered.

"Poor David," I said. "I thought you were fond of him."

"Oh, he had his good points. He was rough and robust and ever so masterful, but he grew much too serious. Sulked a lot, too. You needn't waste any sympathy on him, Elena."

"You were rather hard on him."

"With good reason," she retorted. "It was all right for him to make eyes at those flighty little actresses and take them out on the sly, but when I happened to strike

214

up a conversation with one of the students at Oxford he had a fit. Oxford was grand, wasn't it?"

"Grand," I agreed.

"All those glorious old buildings," she mused.

"All those rowdy young men," I added.

"I didn't do anything wrong," she protested. "They wanted to show me all the pubs and give me a good time. Noisy lot, those boys, drinking and brawling and carrying on half the night, but I had the time of my life."

The boat began to slow down. We could hear gears grinding below.

"By the way," Millie said, "there's another famous person on board. One of the stewards was talking about him. Alexan-dray Du-mah, the French writer."

"I know. I met him."

"You did?"

"We had quite a long conversation."

"Humph," she sniffed. "I'd be careful, luv. I read all about him in one of the tabloids. He's supposed to be a regular devil with the ladies, positively insatiable. I read that book of his, too. *The Three Musketeers*. Can't say I cared for it, though. Too much swordplay."

As the boat lurched to a halt, there was a grating noise of wood scraping against wood. A minute later, a sharp knock sounded on the cabin door, and I opened it to admit a strapping blond steward in a gleaming white uniform. His brown eyes were decidedly roguish, and he gave Millie a conspiratorial grin. I suspected that they had entertained each other while I was up on deck. He scooped up all the bags, and we followed him out of the cabin and up the stairs.

I expected to find a swarm of reporters waiting at the bottom of the gangplank as we disembarked. There were none in sight. Anthony was nowhere in sight, either, but there was a large crowd and considerable bustle, with people hurrying toward the railway station where a train waited to transport us to Paris. Perhaps he was waiting at the station, I told myself, but somehow I doubted it. The feeling of unease rose anew, and I fought to quell it. If he hadn't come to Calais to meet us, there was probably a very good reason.

"No Anthony, I see," Millie remarked.

"He—he may be at the station. You go on to the train, Millie, and find our compartment. I'll join you there."

Millie and her handsome steward disappeared in the crowd. I lingered for a few moments, hoping against hope that Anthony would show up, but he didn't. He wasn't at the station, nor was he anywhere on the train as far as I could see. Finally, I joined Millie in our private compartment. The bags had all been stowed away and the steward's grin was even wider than before. Millie was rubbing her backside and looking very pleased with herself. The steward left, closing the door behind him.

"Cheeky lad," Millie remarked, "but nice, just the same."

"Did you tip him?"

"In a manner of speaking," she replied.

I settled back against the faded green velvet seat. At one time, the compartment had been luxurious, but now it had the frayed, worn look prevalent on heavily travelled trains. The gold fringe that hung from the green velvet curtains was tarnished, and there was the familiar smell of dust, stale smoke, and sweat. Millie and I had spent a great deal of time in such compartments, traveling from one town to the next. In three weeks it would begin all over again, and I feared that European accommodations would be no more comfortable than the English had been.

As the train pulled out of the station, I realized that I was very depressed. I missed Anthony more than I cared to admit, and I was deeply disappointed that he hadn't come to meet us. I was mystified, too, by the absence of reporters. Surely he would have informed them of my arrival. Anthony never missed a chance for publicity. That small, gnawing worry persisted. Something was wrong. I could feel it. Why had he been so adamant about coming on to Paris ahead of us? It really hadn't been necessary. I kept remembering the way he had acted when he said goodbye. His manner had been jaunty enough, but I had sensed a certain strain. He had kissed me lightly, yet his eyes had been almost sad. Or had I imagined it?

The train moved across the French countryside, passing small, desolate-looking villages and rows of slender poplar trees with vivid red poppies growing beneath them. I didn't love Anthony, but he was very important to me, just how important I was beginning to realize for the first time. He had become an integral part of my life, exasperating one moment, endearing the next. I couldn't conceive of his not being there. As I listened to the monotonous rumble of wheels, I tried to curb the apprehension inside me. Anthony would probably meet us at the station in Paris with a whole mob of reporters and a perfectly valid excuse for not being in Calais.

The train ground to a stop at a small way-station, started again a few moments later, and shortly thereafter the door to our compartment flew open as a giant of a man stumbled inside, face and shoulders hidden by the large basket he carried. Millie gave a startled cry and jumped to her feet. Alexandre Dumas plopped the basket down, straightened his maroon lapels, patted the turquoise neckcloth, and beamed at us. The beam disappeared as Millie kicked his shin. At that moment, the train lurched, and both of them tumbled onto the seat opposite mine. Millie seized a bag and began to pound him on the head with it. Dumas roared in protest, folding his arms over his head for protection.

"Help!" he cried. "Get her off me!"

"Rogue! Rapist! Thief!"

"Millie! It's all right. I know him."

Millie ceased her barrage of blows and gave Dumas a nasty look. He lowered his arms and gave her a look that was highly appreciative, taking in every detail and settling upon the splendidly full bosom encased in thin pink cotton. Millie moved away from him and brushed at her skirts, still bristling but definitely intrigued. Dumas smiled at her and growled the hungry growl he had used on the schoolgirls. She looked as though she'd like to bang him over the head again.

"*Mon Dieu*, a regular little wildcat," Dumas remarked, addressing me. "Who is she?"

"Millie is my companion."

"Thought she might be your bodyguard. An appetizing minx. I don't know when I've seen a tastier morsel."

"What did he say?" Millie snapped.

"He just paid you a compliment. Millie doesn't speak French, Monsieur Dumas."

"No? Then we'll speak her language," he replied, changing to English. "I've just finished my chapter. It's a marvelous work, charged with life. I whipped off twelve pages on the boat, and did ten more after boarding the train. So, I thought a celebration was in order. I popped off the train when it stopped back there and bought a few things to snack on."

Reaching into the basket, he pulled out a long loaf of bread, which he deposited in Millie's lap. She put it on the seat, gingerly, giving him another nasty look. A large hunk of cheese, a bunch of grapes, half a dozen apples, and three bottles of wine followed the bread. Dumas finally pulled out a whole roasted chicken and set the basket on the floor.

"Drumstick, anyone?" he inquired.

"I'm not hungry," I told him.

"Neither am I!" Millie said testily.

"No? I hope you won't mind if I indulge myself, Mademoiselles. I'm famished. I usually am. I love good food, good wine. There is nothing quite so satisfying, unless it's a saucy woman."

He tore the chicken apart and began to devour it, tossing the bones into the basket. The chicken quickly vanished. He reached for the loaf of bread, tore it in half, and uncorked one of the bottles of wine. I watched with amusement, Millie with disgust. Dumas ate with hearty relish, savoring each bite, totally unperturbed by his audience.

"So you're Alexandre Dumas?" Millie accused.

"In the flesh, *mon pigeon*."

"There's an awful *lot* of it," she observed.

"Solid muscle, not an ounce of fat on me. I've the strength of Samson. I take after my father, the General. He was one of Napoleon's men; once lifted a horse right off the ground with his bare hands. Look at this biceps. Do you want to feel it?"

"No, thank you."

218

"A charming lass, this one," Dumas told me. "I've always had a weakness for sassy blondes. Would you like to take a stroll to the next carriage and leave us alone for a while?"

"She certainly wouldn't!" Millie exclaimed.

Dumas bellowed with laughter and uncorked another bottle of wine. My depression had fled. I was enjoying myself, enchanted by this gigantic clown who was one of the most famous men in France. He finished the second bottle of wine, polished off the bread and cheese, and began to munch on an apple, keeping up an amusing patter all the while. With appealing good humor, he told us about his successes as playwright, novelist, athlete, man of action, and lover of women. He also mentioned the fabulous Chateau de Monte-Cristo the architect Durand was building for him in the forest of Saint-Germain.

All three of us were surprised when the train pulled into the station at Paris, for Dumas's monologue had made the time fly. He asked where we were staying, as he tossed empty bottles and apple cores into the basket and got to his feet, looming over us like a colossus in the confined space of the compartment. Millie eyed him slyly, clearly fascinated but maintaining her aloof pose. Dumas threw open the door and scooped up the basket.

"I'd better get back to my own compartment before some porter steals my bags and runs off with my manuscript. George is having *un petit salon* at her apartment Thursday. She usually has a number of amusing people there. I'll take you. It will be a perfect place to introduce you to our Parisian society."

"That would be lovely," I replied.

"I imagine I'll be seeing you again, *mon petit pigeon*," he told Millie.

Millie didn't deign to reply, so Dumas shambled on toward his own compartment. A porter arrived to help us with the bags, and as we followed him down the aisle I braced myself for the encounter with the reporters that Anthony would surely have waiting on the platform. Millie chattered about Dumas, affecting an outrage that was far from convincing. The porter moved through the door and down the narrow metal steps. The platform was aswarm with people, a shifting kaleido-scope of movement and color, the din incredible as trains pulled in and out. But there were no reporters, and Anthony was not waiting for me.

"He—he probably forgot we were arriving today," Millie said hurriedly, concerned at my expression. "You know how forgetful he is, Elena. He's probably at the hotel, dining in splendor and—and contemplating some new money-making scheme."

"Perhaps," I said.

"There's probably a whole fleet of chaps from the papers ready to meet the boat from England tomorrow afternoon. If I know him, he'll give us what for for arriving *early*."

I nodded, feeling lost inside.

"Look, I'll take the porter and find us a hansom. They do have cabs in France, don't they? We'll go on to the hotel, and if you don't give that man a sound scolding, I'll do it myself."

She was making a valiant effort, but I could tell from the look in her eyes that Millie suspected the worst, too. The porter spoke little English, and she had a difficult time making him understand that we wanted a cab. I didn't trust myself to speak to him, afraid that my voice would tremble, that I might actually dissolve into tears. I knew. Already I knew. I had had a premonition the day he told me goodbye. Now, standing on the platform I felt as though I were in a daze, people moving all around me, laughing, talking noisily, jostling each other. An English-speaking conductor stopped to ask me if I was all right. I smiled at him and nodded my head. He gave me a doubtful look and moved on. Another train left the station, wheels making a deafening metallic clatter, clouds of smoke filling the air and rising to the top of the vast domed enclosure. I smiled again, for no reason, and the smile was still on my lips when Millie returned.

"Come along, luv. A cab's waiting."

I moved along beside her past newspaper kiosks and stalls where candy, fruit, and all manner of tempting morsels were sold. A heavy stream of people poured out the great arched doorway ahead of us.

"I had a devil of a time making the cabbie understand me," Millie said brightly. "He just stared at me as though I were an idiot, and then he began to jabber. The porter wasn't any help at all. He began to jabber, too. I can't say I'm overly fond of the French!"

The sky was a darkening gray as we stepped outside. Millie helped me into the cab and repeated the name of our hotel to the driver. A moment later we were on our way, moving down a crowded boulevard lined with elegant shops. A soft blue haze thickened in the air as night drew nearer. Turning a corner, we drove past outdoor cafés where lights were already beginning to glow. The sky was violet-gray now, the haze thicker, and I saw that the chestnut trees were in blossom. The beauty of the city was a part of the dream, vague, unreal, a luminous illusion. Millie no longer made an effort to reassure me. She was silent and her expression was one of grim determination.

"Here we are," she said as the cab stopped.

Climbing out, she gave me her hand to help me alight. The horses stood restlessly at the curb. The cabbie leaped down and began to speak so fast that I hadn't the least idea what he was saying. The doorman came to our rescue. He paid the cabbie, collected our bags and handed them to the boy in a red jacket who rushed out to help him. The hotel was sumptuous, white and elegant in the deepening twilight. The lobby was done in shades of blue and ivory, dark mahogany gleaming with a rich luster, polished brass shining like dull gold.

At least, our trunks had arrived the day before, and our rooms were ready. Anthony wasn't registered. The boy in the red jacket led us up the grand staircase and along a hall on the second floor, opening the door to a spacious suite with lamps already glowing. I saw the letter propped up on top of the mantel almost immediately. Millie saw it, too. The boy put the bags down and told us that Millie's room was at the end of the hall.

"I'll stay here with you for a while," she said.

"No, Millie. You go on."

"You'll be all right?"

"I'll be all right," I told her.

221

She and the boy left, and I stood there for several minutes gazing at the creamy, heavily embossed envelope, delaying the pain. When I finally opened it, my hand was steady. Several pound notes fluttered to the floor as I pulled out the letter. It was written on the hotel stationery and was very short. Anthony came right to the point.

Elena,

The money in this envelope is all that's left. There's almost eighty pounds. That should take care of your immediate needs. The railroad shares were fraudulent. I was royally taken in, duped like a greenhorn fresh from the country. I've failed you. I don't know what to say except that I'm sorry.

I came to Paris hoping to arrange the tour before you arrived. That fell through, too. You'll find someone else to set things up for you. You don't need me any more, and I know that under the circumstances you won't want me hanging about, messing things up for you even more. So, I'm bowing out. I don't know where I'll go or what I'll do, but I hope someday to be able to make this up to you.

Anthony

I read the letter over again, and then I folded it up and put it back on the mantel. Moving to the window, I gazed down at the park across the way. It was brightly lighted, and couples strolled to and fro beneath trees with fragile green leaves, moving past ponds and white marble fountains. As one couple paused beside the jets of dancing water, the man took the girl into his arms and kissed her tenderly. Her dress of a pale, soft pink fluttered in the breeze. I watched, the pain sweeping over me, and at last I turned away.

He was gone. The money wasn't important. I could make more money. Anthony was gone. In a very special way, I had loved him, and now he had left me and I was alone again, just as I had been when Brence deserted me. The anguish was the same, the sense of loss almost as great. I wanted to cry, but I couldn't. The tears were locked up inside. It would have been so much easier if I could have cried, if I could have been angry, but I couldn't. There was nothing I could do but accept the facts and pray for strength. I was going to need all I could muster.

XXI

Dumas helped me out of the carriage and escorted me up the steps, holding my elbow tightly as though he expected me to break loose and flee. A servant showed us into an elegant foyer with dull red walls and a rich blue carpet. Dumas let go of my arm, whipped off his top hat, removed his cape, and handed both to the servant. He wore a suit of tobacco-brown broadcloth, the jacket with flaring tails and dark brown velvet lapels. His waistcoat was burnt orange satin embroidered with dark brown flowers, his neckcloth a vivid orange silk. His mood was decidedly playful.

"Confess now, aren't you glad you came?"

"Not at all," I said testily.

"I couldn't let you sit there in your room, pining away."

"I wasn't pining."

"Mooning, then. I've never seen such pale cheeks, such forlorn eyes. So your lover absconded, left you flat and flat broke? That's no reason to fret. You're the most beautiful woman in Paris, and Paris is eager to welcome you. George insisted I bring you. She'd have been after me with a carving knife if I had come alone."

I hadn't wanted to come, but Dumas had insisted, refusing to take no for an answer, practically abducting me. I was still very unsure of myself and not ready to face people. Four days had passed since I read Anthony's letter. They had been four of the worst days in my life. A strange lethargy had possessed me, and I had been unable to shake it, even though I knew I should be out seeing theatrical managers about an engagement. Then Dumas had come bursting into my suite like a force of nature, impossible to resist.

"Cheer up, little sparrow," he said. "You're going to have a grand time."

"I doubt it."

"A profitable one, then. Gautier will be here. He's with *La Presse*, their drama critic. He'll shout your presence in Paris from the rooftops. Once they know you're here, the theatrical managers'll storm your hotel the way the peasants stormed the Bastille."

"I'm really not in the mood to meet people."

"You'll feel better in a little while," he promised. "A few glasses of George's champagne and you'll feel marvelous. Come along, let's go set them on their ears."

"Let me check my hair first."

Stepping up to the mirror, I examined myself in the glass. My gown was a heavy, cream-colored satin with large puffed sleeves, a low, form-fitting bodice, and a skirt that belled out in lush, creamy folds. My shoulders were bare, as was a goodly portion of my bosom, and my makeup was subdued, just a touch of pink on my lips, a suggestion of blue-gray shadow on my lids. My hair was pulled back sleekly and worn in a French roll on the back of my head, my only ornament a large pink camellia fastened over my right temple. My cheeks were indeed pale, my eyes a dark, sad blue.

"You look gorgeous," Dumas informed me. "It is a pity you've decided ours must be a platonic relationship. Are you sure you won't change your mind?"

"Quite sure."

He sighed and shrugged. "That is just as well, I suppose. Overly intelligent women aren't really my style. Too much talk, too little sport. Friendship will be refreshing, for a change. Are you through primping?"

Voices and laughter could be heard coming from the end of the foyer. Dumas clamped his huge hand around my elbow again and propelled me toward the sounds. A moment later we entered a drawing room that glowed with color, rugs a warm red and blue, beige walls, elegant hangings in deep gold. At least thirty people

226

milled about, most of the men in dark formal attire, the women beautifully gowned, all of them talking with great animation. A woman in black velvet hurried over to us, a radiant smile on her lips.

"You *did* bring her!" she exclaimed in French.

"Have I ever failed you?"

"Far too many times for me to remember, you great lout. Run along now. Elena and I have things to talk about."

"Is there food?"

"Mountains of food, twice as much as I usually have. I knew you were coming. Wait until you taste the paté. It's exquisite."

Dumas bowed obligingly and made his way through the crowd toward the buffet tables, patting many a female bottom along the way. The woman in black velvet took both my hands in hers and squeezed tightly.

"I'm George Sand, my dear. I've been so eager to meet you."

I was at a loss for words. George Sand was already a legend, a notorious creature who was said to dress in male attire, smoke cigars in public, and sweep up any man who struck her fancy. Her real name was Aurore Dudevant, and she had left husband and children to live with young Jules Sandeau in a garret, in order to write novels with him. She used part of his name as her pseudonym, but eventually abandoned him, to have a short-lived but blazing affair with the arrogant and sensual Octave Merimée. She'd left him for the poet Alfred de Musset, whom she was said to have destroyed. And for the past several years she had been living with Frédéric Chopin, the ailing composer over whom she was rumored to have a demonic hold.

The woman who squeezed my hands exuded an overwhelming warmth and seemed to glow with serenity. Middle-aged, slightly plump, she had long raven-black hair, a smooth, pale complexion, and enormous brown eyes that were luminous and lovely. She looked like an amiable, kind-hearted matron, and I found it impossible to associate her with the coarse, heartless, masculine creature I had read about who preyed upon younger men and flaunted every convention with arrogant disdain.

"You seem bewildered," she said.

"You—you're not what I expected."

"You've read about me, I see."

I nodded. "You're very famous."

"So are you, *ma petite*, and you're not what I expected, either. You're much younger, for one thing, and there's a vulnerable quality that doesn't at all suit the flamboyant, mercenary Elena Lopez."

"Elena Lopez was created by the press."

"So was George Sand," she said. She gave a soft, melodic laugh and squeezed my hands again. "It's a man's world, Elena, and any woman who succeeds in it must of necessity be some kind of freak. How else explain our success?"

"I've read all your books."

"And did you like them?"

"They seemed to have been written especially for me. They expressed ideas and emotions and longings I thought were mine alone. I suppose you could say they gave me strength. I was always different, you see. I always wanted . . . something more. I could identify completely with your heroines."

"My dear, you have won my heart already! We're going to be tremendous friends. We're sisters under the skin. Come, let me get you some champagne. How on earth did you get involved with the noisy Dumas?"

"We met crossing the Channel."

"And he promptly tried to bed you," she said, leading me across the room.

"Within five minutes after we met."

She laughed again. "That's Dumas! I adore him. He has a heart of gold, you know, as well as a notorious reputation. Generous to a fault, our Alexandre, a rousing scamp who has an incredible facility for rousing fiction."

Handing me a glass of champagne, she took one herself and sipped it slowly, a pensive look in those lovely brown eyes. I sensed a vast reserve of strength in this woman, and great sadness, too. She had carved a permanent place for herself in literature, but I suspected that the cost had been extremely high in terms of personal happiness. I had heard that her affair with Chopin was going badly, that the two were on the verge of permanent separation. Was that the reason for the pensive look, the sad half smile on her lips?

Taking another sip of champagne, she sighed softly and then set her glass down. She smiled brightly again, leaving that unguarded moment behind her. I was glad it had happened, because I felt I knew her better for it.

"All these people," she said, making a futile gesture. "I adore each and every one of them, but it is impossible to have a really significant conversation in this crush. I want us to talk and talk and talk, Elena. I want us to become real friends."

"I'm sure we will."

"At the moment, I must play hostess. A bore, believe me. I don't know why I have these *soirées*. Ah, there's Lamennais. He's an unfrocked priest, and he's been telling me the most interesting things about ecclesiastical authority. He advocates the most astounding reforms. I really must go greet him."

"Please do."

A slender, impeccably dressed man with short, tightly curled hair and rather malicious eyes walked past, and George reached out and seized his arm.

"Here's Eugène. He'll keep you company. Eugène, this is Elena Lopez, the celebrated dancer. You've read about her in all the papers."

"I certainly have," he said. "I also saw her dance when I was in London last year."

"Elena, Eugène Sue. His *Mysteries of Paris* was a tremendous success, and his new novel, *The Wandering Jew*, is causing a sensation. He knows the underworld of Paris as intimately as he knows the Faubourg Saint-Germain. He'll keep you entertained."

Sue executed a deep bow, his thin lips curling in a wry smile. "I'll certainly try," he said.

"He's an incorrigible gossip," George warned, "one of the reasons I'm so fond of him. Believe only half of what he tells you. I must go speak to Lamennais. We will have to have a cozy visit soon, my dear, just the two of us."

She hurried off to greet the priest, and Eugène Sue cocked an eyebrow, the wry smile flickering again as he watched her go.

"That man will be the ruination of her, filling her head with all kinds of political nonsense. He'll have her out demonstrating in the streets before it's all over with. George is so susceptible, a revolutionary at heart. She'd like to reform the whole world." He paused and turned to me. "Have you been in Paris long?"

"Only a few days."

"You came with Dumas tonight, I notice. How like him to find you first. He's an amazing fellow. I can't say that I like his books—his plays, either, for that matter, but then thundering melodrama isn't my sort of thing. Have you met his wife?"

"I didn't know he was married."

"Dumas is extremely casual about it. Ida Ferrier was an actress with an astonishing lack of talent and no particular beauty, but her father was a broker to whom Dumas owed quite a lot of money. In order to avoid going to debtors' prison, he married the wench. I understand that soon afterwards he arrived home unexpectedly, strolled into the bedroom, and found one of his best friends making passionate love to the lady in question. He stared at the two of them for a moment and then shook his head in amazement. 'Good Heavens!' he exclaimed. 'And *he* isn't even obliged to!' "

For the next few minutes Sue continued in the same vein, pointing out guests, identifying them and relating anecdotes about each. He was amusing, malicious, and amazingly well-informed. Word had gotten around who I was, and people were beginning to stare, the men with considerable interest, the women with scarcely veiled hostility. My reputation had preceded me. Elena Lopez was almost as famous in France as she was in England, and even in this gathering of celebrated literary and artistic figures I was receiving far more attention than anyone else. I was relieved when Dumas came over to us, a glass of wine in each hand.

"You've monopolized her long enough, Sue!" he announced, handing me the wine. "I hope you haven't been telling her a raft of lies. Come along, Elena. There's someone I want you to meet."

Nodding to Eugène Sue, I followed Dumas toward the buffet tables, while everyone in the room watched. Several men smiled at me. One of them bowed. Dumas wore a broad smile, enjoying every minute of it.

"You're creating a sensation," he informed me. "I haven't seen anything like it since Rachel first took Paris by storm. They're all buzzing about you, you know. There's not a man here who isn't dying to meet you."

"Ah, yes, how tiresome."

"It's the price of fame," he said cheerfully. "*I'm* upset if they *don't* stare. By the way, how's that little companion of yours?"

"Millie? She's fine."

"I'll wager she's not mooning. No doubt half a dozen men are trailing after her already. She is a tasty little minx, deliciously put together. I just might investigate, if you have no objections."

"I don't. Millie may."

Dumas guffawed, finished his wine, set the empty glass down on a table and led me over to an artistic-looking man with long brown hair, soulful eyes and a surprisingly mischievous smile. He wore a dark gray suit, white silk neckcloth, and an exceedingly vivid crimson waistcoat.

"Théophile Gautier," Dumas said. "The man I was telling you about, my dear. The drama critic for *La Presse*. Théo is an esthete. He writes poetry and that sort of thing, but he's a fine fellow nevertheless. He has enough sense to realize he's got to make a living while he's worshipping art and beauty, and so he works for the newspaper. This is Elena Lopez, Théo. Isn't she stunning?"

"Stunning," Gautier agreed.

"Théo wants to write a piece about you," Dumas told me. "Be charming to him. Enjoy yourself. I've got some business to attend to, and must get back to it."

"I wonder what business he has to attend to?" I asked as Dumas hurried off.

"If I'm not mistaken, her name is Thérèse. She's a

231

minor actress with the Comédie Française. That young woman in yellow standing by the window. Dumas has a particular fondness for obscure young actresses."

"So I've heard."

Gautier smiled and took my empty champagne glass. I tried to relax, tried to forget the stares, the open curiosity of the others around us. Gautier noticed my uneasiness and arched an eyebrow.

"I'm honored that you want to write about me," I told him. "I'm familiar with your work."

He looked surprised. "Indeed?"

"Not your journalistic work, I'm afraid. I read your novel, *Mademoiselle de Maupin*."

"Good Lord!" he exclaimed. "I didn't know anyone had read it! That was published ten years ago and promptly banned. It was ahead of its time, I like to tell myself. How did you happen to read it? Were copies of it smuggled to Spain?"

"England," I said. "I'm English, Monsieur Gautier. All those stories you've read about me—most of them were pure invention."

Gautier nodded and smiled an understanding smile. "The public demands color, mystery, a touch of the exotic. You were smart enough to give it to them. Don't worry. Your secret's safe with me."

"You're very generous."

"Are you going to perform in Paris?"

"I may."

"You may? You must! We've all been reading about you for months. I understand that your debut in London was so successful that George Dorrance extended your engagement not once, but twice?" It was true. By the second extension the whole show featured my dancing alone. With no opera to get in the way, every performance was sold out. At least Tony had told me that much.

I smiled and nodded my affirmation, but said nothing.

"You're much too modest. I know that your tour was a sensational success, too, breaking records in theaters all over England. Tell me, did the students in Oxford really riot in the theater?"

"Let's just say they gave me an enthusiastic reception."

Gautier asked me innumerable questions, encouraging me to talk about myself. His manner was amiable, persuasive, understanding, but I was still unable to relax completely. We had conversed perhaps ten minutes, when a man came over, slapped Gautier on the back, and asked for an introduction. Another man soon followed, then another, and before long I was completely surrounded by a group of admiring males.

I tried to be gracious, but I felt trapped and wished I had never agreed to come. The men were suave, debonair, two or three of them strikingly handsome, and in their midst I found myself thinking about Anthony, wondering where he was, what he was doing. Sadness swept over me again, though I fought it. I fought it desperately. Why should I pine? I could have any man I wanted. Damn Anthony. Damn him. I didn't need him, not at all. I listened to the compliments. I laughed an unconvincing laugh. I touched the pink camellia in my hair, smoothed the folds of my creamy satin skirt, playing the role I had played so many times, but all the while I longed to flee.

Accepting another glass of champagne, I immersed myself in the role, playing it well now. While Elena charmed the men and flirted lightly, another part of me observed her and wondered why she made the effort. I wanted only to be alone. Suddenly, there was a stir of excitement in the gathering. Conversation ceased abruptly. Everyone turned toward the door. Most of the women wore a look of rapt expectation. Most of the men looked disgruntled and resentful. I wondered what had come over them. Footsteps rang loudly in the foyer. A woman in blue gasped and placed a hand over her heart.

An extremely tall man in a long brown velvet opera cape stepped into the room, pausing just inside. He surveyed the gathering with cynical eyes and sighed wearily, resigning himself to the tedious adulation that was his daily fare. The woman in blue gasped again, and several others began to murmur. Even my heart seemed to leap. I had never laid eyes on him before, but I knew him immediately. I was supposed to have had a wild affair with him, and I had seen his picture innumerable times. Those features were unmistakable. His cheeks were lean, his lips thin, his nose an aquiline beak. His eyes were dark, and his hair was a thick, tawny gold mane brushed back from his forehead and falling almost to his shoulders.

"Franz!" George Sand cried.

She hurried over to him, a smile on her lips. Giving her a curt nod, he removed his cape and tossed it across the back of a chair, a dramatic bit of business that caused even more murmurs from the women. He wore a dark tan suit, a brown silk neckcloth, and a waistcoat of brocade almost the tawny color of his hair. Well over six feet tall, with a lean, lithe build that suggested the strength and the grace of a panther, Franz Liszt was an imposing figure. The face was too lean to be really handsome, the nose too sharp, but that didn't matter at all. His effect on people was positively hypnotic; he radiated an overwhelming magnetism that seemed to crackle in the air about him.

The Hungarian pianist-composer was said to have a kind of demonic power over women. When Liszt gave a concert, women swooned in their boxes. When he dropped his handkerchief, fans tore it to shreds and divided it among themselves. Women carried his portrait in their lockets, made off with the stubs of cigarettes he had smoked, literally threw themselves at his feet when he appeared in public. His aloofness, his disdain of their worshipful adoration drove them into an even greater frenzy. Now, as I looked at him, I could believe all those stories, and I could understand them, as well. If ever a man was irresistible, this man was. His presence was that of an arrogant god.

George Sand took his hands. They spoke quietly for a moment, and then there was a fluttering noise like butterfly wings beating and half a dozen women rushed over to him, their silken skirts rustling. They all began to talk at once, and Liszt sighed again, accepting the attention as his due, bored with it already. The woman in blue seized his hand and kissed it. A young actress in pink clung to his arm. A languorous brunette turned pale when he looked into her eyes.

"Damned fellow!" one of the men grumbled. "This always happens when he shows up."

"George shouldn't have invited him," another remarked. "It's unfair to the rest of us. I say, Elena, *you* aren't going to rush over there and make a fool of yourself, are you?"

"Certainly not," I replied. "I'd adore another glass of champagne. Would one of you be an angel and fetch it?"

The party continued, but there was a new tension in the air. Liszt was surrounded by women. I was surrounded by men. Everyone seemed to be waiting to see what would happen. Ignoring the tall, magnetic Hungarian across the room, I continued to talk with the other men, but I could feel him staring at me over the heads of his admirers. I turned once. Our eyes met. He nodded at me, a curious smile playing on his thin lips. I lowered my eyes and turned to answer a question, but my pulse seemed to stop beating and I grew so weak I felt sure my knees would give way at any minute. I had never felt such panic.

He had read the stories. I was certain of it. Why had I ever let Anthony and David release them? According to the papers, Liszt and I had had a fierce, passionate affair marked by explosive quarrels and outbursts of physical violence. He had locked me out of our hotel room, and I had seized a knife and ripped his clothes to shreds in revenge. Once he had attempted to strangle me in a fit of insane jealousy, and on another occasion I had slashed him across the face with a riding crop. I had been "quoted" in the papers, calling him a coward and saying that his reputation as a lover was highly exaggerated. What were the exact words? "Zee meekest of my Cossacks could best zee great Franz Liszt when it comes to passion."

When I turned to look at him again, Liszt had started across the room toward me, brushing away his circle of admirers as though they were so many insects. The men around me tensed, and then, grumbling, moved away, realizing competition was futile. By some miracle

I was outwardly composed, betraying not the least flicker of emotion. The room, the people in it seemed to melt into a blur of colors, a hazy backdrop for the tall, godlike figure who moved toward me. He stopped in front of me and slowly lifted one brow, his eyes full of sardonic amusement.

"I think it's time we left," he said.

His manner was laconic, and there was a smile on his lips, but I knew he would not be refused. It didn't enter my mind to oppose him. I nodded meekly, and he took my hand in his and started toward the door. I felt I should speak to Dumas and thank George Sand for inviting me, but my will was no longer my own. Dumas had his young actress to amuse himself with, and George would certainly understand the lack of social niceties. Liszt's strong, sinewy fingers crushed my own, and I moved along beside him, oblivious to everything else, in a kind of daze. He picked up his cloak and slung it over his right shoulder without losing a step. A moment later we were moving through the foyer with the dull red walls, and then we were outside, the night air cool on my bare shoulders. Liszt let go of my hand.

"My apartment isn't far," he said. "We'll walk."

I took a deep breath. The cool air revived me, and I seemed to come to my senses. Liszt noticed my hesitation, and he smiled again, aloof, amused, content to let me make my own decision now. I looked at him, and in that instant I knew that although I might regret it if I succumbed to his hypnotic allure, I wasn't going to turn and flee as every instinct told me I should. The sadness was still inside, and the alternative was yet another night of grief and unbearable loneliness. I couldn't face that.

"Well?" he challenged.

"We'll walk," I replied.

Liszt smiled, and then he stepped behind me and placed the brown velvet cape over my shoulders, his long, beautifully shaped hands lingering for a moment. A light breeze caused the leaves of the plane trees to rustle overhead, and moonlight and shadow danced on the pavement before us as we started down the street.

The night was lovely, bathed in silver, rows of houses

white and gray, brushed with blue-black shadows. The air was scented with perfume from the flowering trees. Within a few minutes we were moving across an arched stone bridge, boats with small, bobbing lights passing below. The massive Cathedral of Notre Dame loomed in the distance, dark stone gargoyles crouching in the darkness. Sounds of merriment drifted from the cafés down the river, but the noise was barely audible here. We walked down a broad avenue and then turned into a labyrinth of narrow, twisting streets. Here it was still and silent; our footsteps were the only sound. This part of Paris was fast asleep.

We eventually reached an old, very beautiful building standing at the end of one of the streets, a small courtyard in front. It was all mellow elegance in the moonlight, rubbed worn with time, evoking a glamorous past. I fancied it might once have been the residence of a royal favorite, now remade into an apartment house. The foyer was unlighted, faintly aglow with moonlight that intensified the shadows, but Liszt moved with confidence, leading me up three flights of stairs. He unlocked the door to his apartment, led me inside, and closed the door. I stood in darkness while he lighted a lamp. The light blossomed slowly, pale yellow flickering, struggling to drive back the black. I realized we had hardly exchanged a dozen words since he first approached me in George Sand's drawing room.

"Home," he said.

The room was large, with very high ceilings. A grand piano dominated one corner, sleek rosewood gleaming in the lamplight. There were two oversized chairs covered in worn tapestry and a sofa in blue velvet, its nap shiny with age. Heavy blue velvet curtains covered the windows. The air was chilly, and I shivered. Liszt moved over to the soot-stained white marble fireplace and busied himself making a fire. In a few minutes the flames were devouring the logs. He put out the lamp then, so the fire provided the only light.

"Wine?" he asked.

I shook my head. He stepped into the adjoining room, leaving me alone. I removed the brown velvet cape and rubbed my arms, shivering again, but not from the chill.

It wasn't too late to leave. He was dangerous for me, dangerous for any woman, perhaps even cruel, and consumed with a genius that left little room for anything but his music. Watching the flames leap, I decided to remain. I moved over to the fireplace to warm my hands, deliberately thrusting aside reason and common sense. It was time for folly.

Liszt returned wearing a dressing robe of dark red silk brocade, the sash tied loosely at his waist. He was naked beneath it. He gazed at me, a deep frown creasing his brow, as though he wondered how I came to be here, and then he padded across the carpet on bare feet and sat down at the piano with a distracted air. I moved over to the sofa, my satin skirt rustling softly as I settled back against the cushions. Liszt scowled and flexed his fingers. His hands were lean, powerful, as strong as steel, yet when he touched the keys they were graceful, imbued with a life of their own, it seemed. He touched the keys as though in deep reverence, and then, throwing his head back, straightening his shoulders, he began to play.

The music, a soft, subtle whisper of sound at first, gradually swelled into a lovely, poignant melody that floated lightly, receded, repeated, louder than before. It was one of his own compositions, and surely it had never been played with such sensitivity, such feeling. His face was stern, his thin lips held tight, and in the light of the flames that thick, tawny mane gleamed golden-bronze. Watching him, strange emotions stirred inside me. As those strong fingers touched the keys with such tenderness, stroking gently, evoking loveliness even as his face retained that stern expression, I felt a warmth suffuse my body that had nothing to do with the leaping fireplace fire.

He continued to play, an even lovelier melody following the first, and as he raised his eyes to look at me, a sardonic smile flickered on his lips. Then I realized that he was making love to me already, making love with music. His eyes held mine, and the music changed, gentle melody giving way to a sensual throb that grew louder, thundering, a passionate barrage of sound that plunged and plundered and ravished my soul with its

238

fury. Back and forth he moved, shoulders hunched, his hands rising, falling, flailing the keys. His eyes flashed and penetrated my soul. I was breathless, besieged by the music that rose to a shattering crescendo.

The silence was abrupt, as shattering in its way as the music had been. The whole room seemed to throb with silent echoes, the fierce passion of the music vibrating still. Liszt sat at the piano, looking at me calmly, his passion pouring from him in invisible waves. I trembled when he stood up; the red silk brocade robe, covering his body loosely, swayed as he moved toward me, the cloth rustling with a provocative silken sound. He stood directly over me and looked down with dark eyes that calmly assessed me. Liszt smiled again. He caught hold of my wrists and pulled me to my feet. I felt powerless, caught up in the spell he had woven with such expert deliberation.

He led me over to the fireplace. A thick rug was spread out in front of the hearth. Placing one arm around my waist, holding me against him loosely, he looked into my eyes. I tilted my head back to meet his gaze. He cupped my chin with his free hand, and then he leaned down to kiss me. I curled my arms around his back, rubbing my palms over the smooth, slippery brocade, and as his lips grew more demanding I caught my fingers in those long, thick locks. I felt myself spinning into a void of sensation sweet and searing, and when he removed his lips from mine and raised his head I was surprised to find that I was still conscious.

Liszt turned me around, and unfastened the back of my dress, so the bodice fell loose in front, my breasts almost exposed. He planted his lips on the curve of my shoulder, and then both his hands were on my breasts, caressing, kneading the flesh, causing me to gasp. I arched back against him, and he caught the lobe of my ear in his teeth, biting it with tiny bites, not gentle, not quite painful. He turned me around and crushed my bare breast against his chest. Moments passed, each an agony, each bliss. He unfastened the pink camellia from my hair and tossed it aside, and he helped me undress, the creamy white satin falling to the floor, and when I was completely naked he removed his silk brocade robe, spread it over the rug, and pulled me onto it.

I lay on my back, looking up at him. He stood with legs apart, his hands resting on his thighs, and in the firelight his tall, lean body was superb, his manhood erect. The silk was smooth and cool beneath my buttocks and back. I could feel the warmth of the flames, the warmth inside me spreading, every fiber of my being aching for fulfillment. Liszt kneeled over me, the velvety tip of his rigid manhood touching my stomach as he leaned down to kiss my temples, my mouth, my throat, his lips burning my flesh, it seemed, yet cool, firm, pliable. He kissed each nipple, caressed my thighs, my stomach, my breasts, and then his knees slid back and he was atop me, his body heavy, hard, smooth.

Then he began to play again, a new kind of music, a new instrument employed with the same beauty, the same finesse. He entered, strong, masterful, tender, playing gently, gently stroking, and I rose to meet him, moving to the music that filled me. The tempo changed, building, building, growing fast, furious, thundering now, tearing my senses asunder. He was a master of every movement, even in his own urgency employing that magnificent finesse. We reached the crescendo together. I cried out, and Liszt grew taut, his whole body taut as a bow drawn tight, and then he shuddered convulsively, finally spent. I wrapped my arms around him, shaken, senses still in shreds. His body was dead weight now, and I cushioned it with my own, his warmth a part of me still. His head rested on my shoulder.

I stroked his damp hair, stroked the curve of his back, running my hands over the smooth, warm skin. Liszt slept, and the fire died down, a heap of rose-colored ashes, glowing brightly, growing dim, gray, and the darkness lightened as the first rays of morning sunlight streamed through the slightly parted curtains. He groaned in his sleep and shifted his body, his arms gathering me to him. Though I was deeply satisfied, warm, content for the moment, I thought about Brence and Anthony and was filled with cool determination. This time it will be different, I told myself. This time it will be on my terms. This time I won't allow myself to be hurt.

XXII

George Sand, smiling warmly, put down her pen, glanced despairingly at the messy stack of papers on her desk, and stood up. Instead of a dress, she wore a pair of beautifully tailored black velvet trousers and a white silk shirt with a loose, flowing collar. A pair of brightly embroidered Persian slippers completed her unusual outfit. I had never seen a woman in trousers before, and it must have been apparent from my expression. She laughed softly, tucking the silk shirt snugly into the waistband.

"I know it must seem shocking," she said, "but trousers are extremely comfortable. Why shouldn't I be comfortable when I work? Sitting at a desk for hours on end in taffeta and crinoline petticoats isn't at all practical."

"They're quite fetching."

"But you *are* shocked. I find that delightful. I didn't know I still had the ability to shock anyone. When I first donned male attire fifteen years ago, people were really shocked."

"Is that why you did it?"

"Well, I can't deny that I enjoyed the sensation I made, but my real reason was purely financial. All my friends were male, and we were all poor, but women weren't allowed in the inexpensive coffee shops the men frequented, nor were they allowed in the pit at the theater, the only seats we could afford. Simply because I was female, and poor, I was excluded from almost

241

any kind of social activity, and I resented it bitterly."

She pulled a bell cord to summon her servant and, taking my hand, led me over to a sofa with a fringed purple-and-black shawl draped across its back.

"Let's sit down. Mathilde will bring refreshments. Anyway, I resented being excluded, and one night when all my friends had gathered for a night of stimulating conversation at their favorite coffee house, I couldn't stand it any longer, so I borrowed one of Sandeau's suits, tucked my hair up under a top hat, and went off to join them at the coffee shop. My friends thought it a grand lark. I thought it expedient, and I continued to dress that way when I ventured out. It gave rise to the most outrageous rumors."

She reached for a cigarette from a box on the table in front of us. Lighting it, she exhaled a plume of smoke and settled back against the cushions. Her fingers were stained with ink, I noticed, and despite her gaiety, she looked extremely weary. It was just after ten o'clock in the morning, and I guessed that she had been working all night.

"Perhaps I've come at a bad time," I said.

"Nonsense. My note said Thursday morning at ten. Ordinarily I'd be coiffed and gowned and ready to greet you properly, but there was simply no stopping place. The work seemed to be flowing of its own accord, and those times are very rare. When they happen, you dare not stop. I was just making final corrections when you came in."

"You're working on a new novel?"

She nodded, and there was a rather worried look in her luminous brown eyes. "It's called *Lucrezia Floriani*. I'm afraid a lot of people aren't going to like it, Frédéric in particular. It's our story, you see. I've tried to be objective, but objectivity isn't one of my strong points. I write what I feel, and all my feelings for Frédéric are in this book, the bad feelings as well as the good."

Chopin was currently at Nohant, George's estate in the country. His refusal to accompany her to Paris had caused considerable talk. Some said he was sulking, jealous of the attention she always received in the city, while others claimed he was preparing to leave the

242

woman who had given him financial and emotional support for years. It seemed to me that if George Sand was writing a novel about their love affair, then the affair must truly be nearing its end.

"The critics will call me a literary vampire again," she continued. "They claim my books are written with the blood of my lovers. Frédéric won't understand, of course, but a writer can only write about the things she knows. Anyway," she added lightly, "I've always been more concerned with making a living than making love, despite what you may have heard."

The servant, Mathilde, bustled in with a tray, set it on the table and, making a face, opened one of the windows to let out the smoke. She cast a look around at the balls of crumpled paper littering the floor near the desk, shook her head in disgust, and marched out of the room. George poured the coffee into lovely blue-and-gold Meissen cups.

"Mathilde hates it when I work all night. She's convinced I'll write myself into an early grave. Alas, I've two grown children to support, an estate to maintain, and a lover who's grown accustomed to comfort and ease. Bills, bills, bills, and people wonder why I keep working so hard! It's impossible for me to stop."

As she handed me a cup of coffee, she said, "Well, Elena, you've certainly taken Paris by storm. I can't pick up a paper without reading about you. Gautier's piece was quite good, and so were a couple of the others. You've only been here two weeks, and already you're the darling of the press."

"They're quite inventive," I replied. "Three nights ago I was in Montmartre, dancing on top of a table in a noisy café, tossing flowers to students and artists, causing a riot. I've never been to Montmartre."

"They have columns to fill," she said.

"I suppose I should be grateful. Some of the stories may be outlandish, but at least they keep me before the public eye."

"I understand you've been offered several contracts."

"Dozens. The theatrical managers have been camping on my doorstep ever since they learned I was in Paris. The most persistent has been an American, a great bluff fellow with ginger sidewhiskers and an extraordinary flowered waistcoat. He wants me to tour America under his auspices. He claims we'll both make millions of dollars."

"Really?"

"He's thoroughly convinced of it. Perhaps you've heard of him? P. T. Barnum."

"Of course! The man who brought General Tom Thumb to Paris. It created a tremendous stir. Louis Philippe received the showman and his midget both at the Tuileries, and Barnum got almost as much attention as the General. Both of them wore knee breeches, I understand."

"Barnum told me that before Tom Thumb he sponsored a Negress who was supposed to be 161 years old and George Washington's nurse. There was also a mermaid from Fiji. After managing a midget, a mermaid, and a female Methuselah, he wants to sponsor Elena Lopez. I must say, it puts my fame in a rather unusual perspective."

George laughed and, setting down her coffee cup, lit another cigarette.

"I take it you turned him down?"

"I've turned them all down, at least for the time being. I'm not ready to go back to work just yet. I've been working so hard, for such a long time—"

I paused for a moment and thought about the past year. The London engagement had been exciting, and the success had been elating, but it had been grueling, too, particularly when the whole show featured only my dancing. Every night I left the theater exhausted, and every day I awakened to the realization that I had to do it all over again. The responsibility and strain had taken their toll, and the tour that followed had been even worse, with constant travelling, constant adjustments, nerves on edge, tempers flaring, bags lost en route, hotel rooms cold and uncomfortable. The public saw a glamorous figure on stage, dancing in a whirl of color and light. Maintaining that glamor took an enormous effort, and I was simply not up to it again, not yet.

"I'll have to take an engagement in a few weeks for

244

purely financial reasons," I said, "but at the moment, I want a little time for myself. I've earned it."

George looked at me with large brown eyes full of wisdom and understanding.

"I heard that your manager abandoned you," she said. "He was your lover as well, I gather. No matter how strong we think we are, no matter how independent we might be, we're very vulnerable creatures. Being abandoned causes terrible emotional damage that only time can heal."

How well I know, I thought.

"I've been through it, my dear. Many times."

"You know about Franz and me. You couldn't help knowing."

"I know that you've seen each other every night since my party. It's the talk of Paris."

"He's a fascinating man. I need someone like him just now."

George had been waiting for me to bring his name up, being far too tactful to be the first to do so. She and Franz had been friends for many years. I was anxious to hear what she had to say. George put out her cigarette and, picking up her empty cup, toyed with it for a moment.

"I assume you're aware of the dangers involved?" she said.

"Fully aware," I replied.

"Franz can be extremely difficult. He's a genius, you see, tormented by what's inside, consumed by the need to express it. He's selfish, spoiled, inconsiderate, far more temperamental than any prima donna. He's one of the most sensitive men I've ever known, but all that sensitivity goes into his music. In human relationships he's often icy cold, totally unfeeling."

I was silent. George poured more coffee, a slight frown creasing her brow as she sought just the right words.

"He's mercurial, sullen, frequently churlish, but if the mood strikes him, he can be gentle, persuasive, marvelously attentive. Franz is fiercely loyal to his friends, kind and helpful to other composers struggling

245

to make a name for themselves, but he's very hard on his women. A great many have been badly hurt."

"I don't intend to be. I intend to keep my head."

"I hope you can, my dear."

"I have no illusions that it will be anything permanent. In fact, I have no illusions at all."

George studied me for a moment as though weighing my words.

"When you came to my party," she said, "you were like a sad, lovely sparrow, valiantly trying to put on a brave front. That aura of sadness is missing today. I detect a new strength, a new confidence. Franz could be very good for you—as long as you don't allow yourself to expect too much from him."

"I've learned my lesson," I told her. "I don't think I'll ever expect too much from any man again."

George took a sip of coffee. "It's better that way, Elena. If we don't expect too much, we're better able to cope with the inevitable disappointments. Do you know about Marie d'Agoult?"

I nodded. Franz had lived with the beautiful and wealthy Comtesse d'Agoult for several years while her doddering, complaisant husband played endless games of solitaire. An intellectual and a bluestocking at heart, she had borne him three children, but she had borne his infidelities with an increasing lack of tolerance. His recent liaison with the ailing courtesan Marie Duplessis had cause a permanent rift between them. The Comtesse d'Agoult had settled in Paris as the hostess of a literary salon, and, under the Sand-like pseudonym of Daniel Stern, she had written a novel about her affair with Liszt. *Nelida* had been serialized in the *Revue Indépendante* and, in book form, was creating a sensation, selling in the thousands.

"Marie expected too much," George said, "even though she knew it was folly. She's putting on a very good front now, pretending to be independent and cerebral and uncaring. *Nelida* was merely an attempt to exorcise her love for Franz, but she'll never be able to exorcise it, not completely. He broke her heart."

"He won't break mine. My heart is immune."

"Oh?"

"It was broken two years ago, in Cornwall."

George didn't question me further, and I volunteered no information. I still wasn't ready to talk about Brence Stephens. We had more coffee and talked of other things until, glancing at the clock, I realized that it was almost eleven-thirty. Reluctantly, I told George that I must leave. She accompanied me to the door and stepped outside with me. The day was gorgeous, the sky a pale blue, trees ashimmer with delicate green leaves. Sunlight bathed the housefronts and sent shadows dancing on the pavements. A hired carriage awaited me; the driver was perched on his seat, top hat on his knee.

"Sunshine," George said. "It's glorious. I should get more of it. I long to return to Nohant and stroll in the fields."

"Franz is leaving for Germany next week," I remarked casually.

"Oh?"

"He has several concerts scheduled, and he wants to go to Dresden to attend an opera by his friend Wagner. He's asked me to go with him."

"Will you?" she inquired.

I hesitated a moment before replying. "I haven't made up my mind yet. I promised him I'd give him an answer tonight."

George took my hand and squeezed it. "Life is very short. For our own protection we must be cautious, but we must also have the courage to take chances. Do what's best for you, *ma chère.*"

Hugging, we touched cheeks lightly, and then I climbed into the carriage. As it drove away, I looked back to see George still standing on the front steps, hands thrust into the pockets of her trousers, a serene expression on her face. Do what's best for you, she advised. I knew what my answer should be. I knew, but I wasn't at all sure it would be the answer I'd give.

XXIII

Lunch was with Théophile Gautier in one of the lovely outdoor cafés at a table shaded by chestnut trees in full bloom. As we had our wine and cheese and fruit, we discussed the excitement of Paris on a beautiful day. Later on, we went to the Louvre, and Théo grew eloquent, as we strolled through the Grande Gallerie, explaining some of the finer points of the art we viewed. I tried to concentrate, but my mind was on Franz and the decision I must make. People stared all the while, whispering about us, and several of them approached to ask if I would sign my name for them. I should have been flattered, but it took a great effort to be gracious. Théo smiled his wry, mischievous smile and reminded me that fame had its price.

When I returned to the hotel late in the afternoon, I found the persistent Mr. Barnum lurking in the lobby, ready to pounce. His manner was even more flamboyant than his flowered waistcoat as he made a sweeping bow and launched into a paean about the wealth and glory awaiting me in America. Americans were starved for entertainment. They were ready to take me to their hearts. They would adore me. They would worship me. They would probably even erect a statue to me. The reception I'd had on this side of the Atlantic was as nothing compared to the one I'd receive on the other, and money—why, they'd shower me with gold.

He whipped out contract and pen and pretended amazement when I refused to sign immediately. Explaining, again, that I wasn't ready to return to work and that I certainly wasn't prepared to cross the ocean in any case, I suggested he find another novelty to take back to his clamoring public. Barnum grinned good-naturedly, saying you can't blame a man for trying, and told me I was making a big mistake. Handing me a card, he said I could always reach him at his address in New York if I ever changed my mind and decided to come to the land of the future. He made another sweeping bow and finally bustled away, not at all discouraged.

Amused, I hurried to my suite. I wondered idly how Millie had spent the day. I had seen very little of her since George's party. Franz had monopolized my time, and Millie was not one to sit staring out of the window. I knew that she had been seeing Dumas, and I was sure the two of them were having a rollicking good time together. Both possessed a great zest for life. Both loved fun and frolic. And Millie was more than a match for the exuberant Dumas.

I read for a while as twilight thickened outside, and then I ordered a bath, luxuriating in the hot water for a long time. Night had fallen, and lights were twinkling in the park across the way as I dressed for the evening. I selected a taffeta gown with broad black and white stripes. My hair was sleeked back and worn in the French roll I had come to favor. Taffeta crackled as I stepped over to the mirror to affix a single red velvet rose just above my right temple. As I slipped on a pair of long black velvet gloves, I heard the door to the sitting room open. Millie called out merrily, and I left the bedroom to join her. Her eyes were asparkle, her cheeks aglow, her golden hair arranged in an elaborate coiffure. She gave me her pixie smile and whirled around to show off her new gown, a gorgeous confection of salmon pink satin adorned with frothy cascades of beige lace.

"Isn't it grand!" she exclaimed. "There're seven more in my room, still in their boxes, and the undergarments are unbelievably gorgeous. Hats, too! Shoes. Everything! I thought we were going to buy the shop out!"

"It's beautiful, Millie. Exquisite."

"That's the word. That's what I said to him. I said, 'It's exquisite, Alex, but I'll have to have accessories to match.' He just kept shoveling out more money, beaming like a great big friendly bear."

"Dumas bought you the dress?"

"Who else? He bought me the clothes, and we looked at a darling little apartment with its own garden. He's signing the lease tomorrow. We also went to the bank, where he opened an account in my name and made a large deposit. I told him I didn't come cheap. 'If you want me to become your mistress, sir,' I said, 'you'd better get one thing straight right from the beginning. I expect an allowance.' I'm getting a carriage, as well."

"I don't know what to say."

"Well, luv, you might congratulate me."

Millie smiled again and skipped over to the mirror to pat her golden ringlets. "I figured I'd better make some arrangement, since you've taken up with Liszt and will probably go to Germany with him. You certainly don't want me tagging along."

"Millie—"

"I'm elated, luv. I've never met a man like Dumas, and I've never had so much fun. It won't make any difference between *us*, none whatsoever. I told him my loyalties were to you, first and foremost. If you take an engagement, if you decide to go on tour, I'll be right there at your side, same as always."

"That isn't necessary, Millie."

"Of course it is! You couldn't get along without me, and I wouldn't miss all the excitement for the world. But in the meantime—" she paused, searching for the right words. "In the meantime, both of us are entitled to a lark."

"You seem very pleased with Dumas."

She nodded, a happy glow in her eyes. "He really is a great friendly bear, and I'm terribly fond of him. Yesterday we went on a picnic, if you can believe it. We drove out to the country in his carriage and ate in a field surrounded by wildflowers, and he was so droll, so delightful. Then, he tried to have his way with me right out there in front of the birds. I put up such a fight."

251

"I'm sure you did."

"I broke a bottle over his head. He roared like a wounded bull, and that's when I told him I didn't come cheap. He's got two other mistresses that I know of, probably has half a dozen more stashed away here and there, but this one's going to be kept in style, with steady security going into that bank each month. A girl never knows when she's going to need a little cash."

"You're very practical," I teased.

"David Rogers never gave me a bloody cent, and I wound up in Paris flat broke. Your precious Anthony neglected to pay me my salary for the past four months. I never mentioned it because I didn't want to upset you. You had enough to contend with."

"I'm sorry about that, Millie. If only I had known, perhaps—"

"Things work out for the best," she interrupted. "Look at us. I've got a swashbuckling writer eating out of my hand, and you've beguiled the most famous pianist in the world. We've certainly come a long way from Mrs. Fernwood's!"

"Haven't we, though?"

"I'm having the time of my life. It's time you enjoyed yourself a bit, too, luv. I only hope—" she hesitated.

"Yes?" I prompted.

"Just be careful," she said firmly.

"I intend to be."

Millie gave me a tight hug and then scurried out in a flurry of satin and lace. I wished that she hadn't mentioned Anthony's name. It had unsettled me more than I cared to admit. I was still uncertain what I was going to tell Franz when he asked for my answer. Going to Germany with him would be exciting and stimulating, but there would be conflict, too, quite a lot of it. George had told me very little about Franz that I hadn't discovered already.

As I reached the lobby, Franz came through the door, incredibly striking in dark formal suit and white satin waistcoat, a long black velvet opera cloak sweeping from his shoulders, black silk top hat in his hand. Two women who were coming down the stairs behind me froze, awestruck by his imposing figure. I could hear

252

them whispering as Franz stopped in front of me and looked me over with those dark, hypnotic eyes, approving of what he saw. I felt a familiar weakness sweep over me, but I was determined to be cool and objective. Nodding to Franz, I put my hand on his arm and turned to raise an eyebrow to the flustered ladies behind me.

His carriage was waiting in front of the hotel, and we went to a lovely, elegant restaurant filled with lovely, elegant people, where we had a superb meal. It was a quiet dinner. I had grown accustomed to his moodiness and the long silences, for Franz detested small talk and idle chatter. He seemed preoccupied much of the time, and I had the feeling that he was often listening to inner music, hearing notes and harmonies that would eventually be given to the world. If the man who created the music seemed cool and aloof, if he wasn't a social charmer, that could be excused, for his music was magnificent.

When we left the restaurant, the night was lovely, the sky a deep blue-gray frosted with stars. Franz told his driver to wait for us. He took my hand in his, and we began to stroll, eventually crossing the street and wandering through a park. The lawns were brushed with silver and spread with blue-black shadows from the trees. Here and there a light glowed, creating a soft, golden haze. Pausing before a white marble statue, Franz gathered me into his arms and kissed me for a long time, tenderly, thoroughly.

He released me, and I shivered, and he sighed and stepped behind me and, removing the black velvet cloak, placed it over the light cape on my shoulders, as he had done the night we met. He held me against him, his arms around my waist.

"I'm writing a new piece of music," he told me. "It's been going through my mind ever since I met you. It's very controlled to begin with, like you."

"Like me?"

"Like you. The control gradually melts into a subtle melody, swelling, lovely, graceful, vibrant, like you. The melody grows, building to a crescendo, rich, sensual, alive with passion, again like you. I shall call it 'Elena's Song.'"

I was moved, too moved to speak. The feeling inside was so fragile I was afraid words would destroy it.

"I'm a very difficult man, Elena. I'm not easy to live with. I make no compromises and very few commitments."

Facing me, he placed his hands on my shoulders and looked at me with eyes that seemed to smoulder.

"I want you to come to Germany with me, Elena. There'll be strife, I make no bones about that, but there'll be splendor, too. There'll be moments of such splendor—"

I remembered George's last words to me. Life is very short, she had said. We must be cautious, but we must also have the courage to take chances. As Franz looked into my eyes, as his hands tightened their grip on my shoulders, I thought about those words.

"I want you to come with me," he said. "Will you?"

I hesitated only a moment before giving him my answer.

GERMANY

1847-1848

XXIV

They stared, but it was with adoration, with pride, as though our being in their city was a special honor. Franz' concert the night before had been an astounding success. The beautiful old theater with its glittering rococo decor had been packed to the rafters with aristocracy, with students, with stout burghers and their wives. Afterwards, we had held court in the Green Room and Franz had been in a particularly testy mood. He was testy still today as we strolled back to the hotel after a superb lunch at the sunny beer garden on the river.

The city of Bonn, dominated by the majestic old cathedral and the massive electoral palace that had been turned into the famous university favored by royalty, was glorious in the afternoon sunlight, aglow with a mellow, old-world beauty, green and gold, brown and gray. The Rhine moved placidly in its course, gray-green, spangled with sunbursts, and the sun bathed stolid stone walls and leafy treetops that spread cool blue-gray shadows over the ground. Franz and I moved past shops and stalls; he was stern and silent while I smiled at the shopkeepers and paused now and then to examine various wares. Everyone beamed, pleased to have us in their midst.

"Don't tarry!" Franz snapped.

"I was just looking at that intricate embroidery work and those clever leather vests. Why is your stride so brisk, Franz? We've the whole afternoon to ourselves."

"I've got work to do. You can idle about all you please, charming the good citizens with your beauty and wit, but I have a sonata to finish."

"An afternoon off would do you good," I told him. "You've been working much too hard."

"Please don't tell me how to spend my time, Elena," he said coldly. "You might be able to exist on a diet of frivolity, but I have certain responsibilities."

I did not bother to reply. I knew all too well the reason for his testiness. It was as surprising as it was childish, as petty as it was unworthy of a man of his stature. Franz was jealous. He was jealous of me, of the attention I had been receiving. The Germans had always treated him like a golden being, a radiant young deity, and he loved every minute of it. He reveled in the glory, the rapt adoration, and he didn't care to share it with anyone. But I had received almost as much attention as he ever since we first arrived in Germany two months ago. He had performed "Elena's Song" at his first concert and it caused a furor. Unfortunately, the papers had devoted as much or more space to the woman who inspired it than to the composition itself, and that had not set at all well with Franz.

Put out, he had at first adamantly refused to play the piece again, but the audiences demanded it, shouting, stamping, insisting, and, against his will, he'd had to include it in his repertoire ever since. People packed the theaters and concert halls to hear Franz Liszt play, but they also came to see Elena Lopez, sumptuously gowned, sitting in a prominent box, on display as it were, and if I did not attend people felt cheated. I had deliberately stayed away once or twice, and the audiences had been so disappointed and restless that Franz himself had grimly informed me that I must be present at every concert. I had no desire to steal the limelight from him, would have been glad to remain in the background, but that was impossible. We moved in a constant glare of publicity, and I was expected to be at his side.

And then last night, when "Elena's Song" inspired a standing ovation. Franz had to take bow after bow, but that didn't satisfy the audience. They turned en masse toward the box where I was sitting, and I had to bow, too, while Franz stood on stage with nostrils flaring and eyes ablaze. University students tossed flowers to me, and afterwards, at the reception in the Green Room, I was surrounded by an adoring mob of young men who paid no attention to Franz. The newspapers this morning carried a full account of the evening, devoting an inordinate amount of space to my appearance, my gown, my gracious acknowledgment of the crowd's applause. Franz hurled the papers into the fire.

I was particularly sorry that there was such a fuss right now, for I had a favor to ask Franz, and in his present mood it would be a touchy matter indeed. As we strolled down the narrow cobblestone street through the arcade of shops, the impressive cathedral looming up ahead, I wondered how best I might approach him with my request. I would have to wait until he cooled down, of course, but time was of the essence, since we would be leaving Bonn for Dresden in eight days. As we passed one stall, Franz halted abruptly, glaring at a rack of cards.

"Damn!" he exclaimed.

"What's wrong?"

"That!" he thundered, pointing at the cards.

Colored reproductions of my portrait had been on sale in England ever since my first success in London, and I had no idea that they had reached Germany. But there they were. The rack was filled with cards depicting an unusually seductive Elena wearing a low-cut black velvet gown and a black lace mantilla, a crimson rose behind her ear. Franz' cheeks were ashen as he stared at the offending cards, his dark eyes flashing dangerously. The stout, smiling vendor hurried to greet us, enthralled that his humble stall had attracted our attention. Franz dug into his pocket, took out a bill and handed it to the man in icy silence, then seized the cards, all of them, almost knocking over the rack in his fury.

The stall keeper beamed, nodding his head vigorously. "Is Elena," he said thickly. "Is lovely. No?"

"Lovely!" Franz said through his teeth.

As the bewildered man watched, Franz ripped the

259

cards apart one by one, scattering the brightly colored pieces over the cobblestones. Finished with his destruction, Franz asked the trembling vendor if there were more cards inside. The man shook his head, backing away slowly as though he feared personal assault.

"There's a tobacconist across the way," I said, trying not to give in to the anger I felt.

"And?"

"He sells cigars. Perhaps you'd better buy all the cigar boxes and tear them up, too. My picture is featured on the inside lid of the most popular brand."

"I suppose you're proud of that!"

"Pleased," I replied. "You may be a sensitive artist, my dear Franz, above such things, but I happen to be a performer who makes her living from the sale of tickets. Those reproductions stimulate interest, make people want to see me dance."

"It isn't your *danc*ing they're interested in," he said savagely.

"No?"

"You're a freak, a nine day's wonder. They don't come to see a dancer. They come to see a brazen creature who's supposedly slept her way through every royal court in Europe."

"Of course," I agreed.

Franz hated it when I refused to argue with him, but I had learned in the beginning that a calm facade was my best weapon when he was in one of his moods. I lifted my skirts slightly for emphasis, stepped over the scattered bits of cards and continued on down the arcade. A sullen Franz followed me, not chastened but fully aware that he had made a childish spectacle of himself. He wouldn't apologize. He never did. His pride wouldn't permit it, but later on he would make amends in his own special way, with a small gift casually bestowed, an intimate evening of music played especially for me, a tender caress.

Leaving the arcade, we passed the cathedral and walked on toward the hotel, reaching it a few minutes later. The hotel was immense and imposing, built of stone, ornately carved, and it had wide verandahs crowded with potted plants. Without speaking, we moved up the steps, into the vast lobby that reminded me of a railroad terminal, and on up the grand staircase. A flustered chambermaid bowed to us as we walked down the hall.

Our suite was large, five spacious rooms occupying a choice corner, and lavish in the German sense with gloomy wallpaper, dark engravings in heavily ornate gold frames, ponderous fumed oak furniture and an abundance of dusty green and brown velvet hangings. A large, dull gold piano dominated the sitting room. The sheets of foolscap scattered atop the piano were covered with musical notations in black ink. Franz had been working on the new composition for the past month and was determined to finish it before we left for Dresden. He wanted it to be ready for his friend Richard Wagner to hear.

I had promised Madame Schroeder, our official "hostess" in Bonn, that I would let her show me the university that afternoon, and we arranged to meet in the lobby at three. I had a couple of hours and thought I would write letters to Millie and George. Franz looked at the piano and frowned. Then he looked at me and, still frowning, pulled me into his arms. I stiffened, resisting him, but he sighed and tightened his arms around me.

"I need to work," he said.

"Work then," I retorted. "I'm not stopping you."

"You're much too beautiful."

"Let go of me, Franz. I'm not in the mood."

"We'll have to do something about that."

"I have letters to write, and I'm going out at three."

"You can write your letters some other time."

"Please let go of me."

"Are you going to get angry? I've yet to see the famous Lopez temper. They say your eyes are like blue fire. Is that true? Do you really scratch and kick and throw things? I can't believe that. My gentle, patient Elena."

"My patience is wearing thin."

He laughed softly, holding me, his eyes full of sardonic amusement. "I've certainly given you provocation."

"You have indeed."

"I'm difficult, demanding, impossible. I know. Do you know why? Because, my love, you're a damnable distraction. I should work right now. I should lock you out of the room and sit at the piano, but I won't. Not just yet, my beautiful distraction."

I tried to pull away, but he held me firmly. "I told you I'm not in the mood, Franz!"

"You *are* angry with me. Why do you put up with me?"

"That's a question I often ask myself."

He smiled and kissed my bare shoulder. "You put up with me, my love, because I'm an addiction, an opiate you can't give up, just as I can't give you up. We're very bad for each other. We both knew that from the beginning. These two months have been exasperating."

"Exasperating," I agreed.

"And splendid," he murmured.

He sought my mouth with his own, kissed me repeatedly, breaking through my resistance with practiced skill. He could be so tender, so gentle and persuasive, and he was persuasive now, terribly so, his mouth caressing mine, his arms holding me close, his body firm, strong—an opiate, just as Franz had said, in my blood, a dangerous addiction that I was foolishly indulging in and not yet strong enough to relinquish. Lifting me up, he carried me into the bedroom, where he undressed me and made love to me slowly, superbly, carrying us both into realms of splendor.

Much later, as I sat at the dressing table, I wondered how long it would be before both of us became immune to the effects of the opiate. Applying a touch of pink lip rouge to my lips and smoothing a suggestion of violet-gray shadow on my lids, I thought about the past two months. Traveling through Germany had been exciting and stimulating and, for the most part, marvelous fun, but Franz had grown increasingly jealous of the attention I was receiving. He could be enchanting, exhilarating, but he could also be infuriating. Such outbursts as that at the card stall had become more frequent, and I was finding it difficult to keep the "famous Lopez

262

temper" under control. When it finally flared, there would be fireworks indeed.

I dressed slowly, still thinking about our weeks together. Delightful as it was to be treated as royalty, to be lavished with attention, I knew it was only a matter of time before Franz and I parted. Our bond was purely physical, and such things burned out quickly. I was not at all in love with him, nor he with me, and that, at least, was a blessing.

Taking my hat from its box, I stepped over to the mirror to put it on. My afternoon dress of maroon-and-black-checked taffeta had long, tight sleeves, a square neckline and a skirt that flared out over half a dozen full petticoats. A wide black velvet belt emphasized my narrow waist. The hat, a wide-brimmed black velvet creation with a tall crown, had frothy maroon and white plumes spilling over one side. I pinned it on and adjusted the tilt of the brim, and then I stepped back. The total effect was quite spectacular, I knew. It might be lost on Madame Schroeder, but the students at the university would be most appreciative.

Franz had been very good for me, I decided. I felt stronger, much better able to cope, no longer the emotionally vulnerable creature that I was when Anthony deserted me. Elena Lopez had finally come into her own. The fanciful girl had grown up at last, with just the right amount of light cynicism to enable her to survive. I no longer expected too much, and that was an achievement. When the affair with Franz ended—and the signs were already present—I would suffer no pain, no remorse.

He was at the piano when I entered the sitting room, his tawny gold mane a long, gleaming cap on the head bent forward, in concentration as he studied a sheet of foolscap, pen poised to make a correction. He was a beautiful male creature, and he was the most gifted man I was ever likely to know. Our affair would end, but "Elena's Song" would live forever, immortalizing our months together. To have inspired that piece of music was something of which I would always be proud. Franz made a notation and then looked up. He slowly arched one brow.

"You look stunning, my love."

"Thank you, Franz."

"If I didn't know you better I'd think you were on your way to an assignation."

"Madame Schroeder is meeting me downstairs in the lobby. She's taking me on a tour of the university."

Franz grimaced. "You have my sympathy. She's a thoroughly detestable type."

"She's been very kind and helpful."

"She's fussy, foolish, talks incessantly, and is inordinately obsessed with *culture*. Why are these matrons always the ones who arrange the receptions and set things up? Why must they always be plump, have girlish ringlets and stuff themselves into outlandish satin gowns?"

"You do her an injustice. She's very dedicated."

"God spare me from her like," he said wearily. "I'm surprised you'd give her the time of day, my love."

"She's arranging a benefit," I told him.

Franz grew wary. "Oh?"

"It's to be held next Friday. Several local musicians are going to perform and—it's for a very good cause. They're trying to raise money to build a new orphanage, and—"

"She hoped I'd volunteer my services," he interrupted.

"Tickets go on sale tomorrow afternoon. Your appearance would insure a sell-out, Franz, and they could ask twice as much for the tickets. You would only have to play one piece. I promised Madame Schroeder I'd ask you."

"The answer is no. I have work to finish."

"It wouldn't take that much time, Franz, and, as I said, it's for a very good cause."

"My music is more important than any number of orphans. Madame Schroeder will have to make do without me."

He turned back to the sheet of foolscap. I stared at him, fighting to control my anger.

"Sometimes," I said, "you really are a bastard."

"There's never been any question about that," he said amiably. "Have a nice afternoon, my love."

I was seething as I went downstairs, and I found it difficult to hide my anger as Madame Schroeder hurried over to me. Fussy and foolish she was, and she did talk incessantly about *culture*. Girlish blonde ringlets bounced about her exceedingly plump shoulders, and her body was stuffed not into satin this afternoon but into a tight black bombazine asparkle with jet bead embroidery. But her blue eyes were warm and friendly, her small pink mouth forming a merry smile. Though Franz might despise her kind, she was well-meaning, and it was the Madame Schroeders of the world who helped keep culture alive and flourishing.

She chatted constantly, in heavily accented French, as we drove to the university and as we strolled over the grounds. Realizing that she was nervous and a little in awe of me, I doubled my efforts to be gracious and charming, showing far more interest than I felt as she pointed out architectural features and elaborated on them. Word spread quickly among the students that Elena Lopez was visiting the university, and soon we had an audience of strapping, robust young men following us about.

Inside the former palace we paused in the great hall before a huge painting in an ornate gold frame. It was a life-sized full-length portrait of a youngish man in a striking white and gold military uniform holding his plumed golden helmet under one arm and standing against a dramatic background of mountains. He was slightly overweight with long, sensitive hands and a melancholy expression. His light brown hair was clipped short, and his deep blue eyes seemed to reflect on a lifetime of sadness. He smiled the pensive smile of a man resigned to perpetual loneliness. Although he was by no means handsome, he had a compelling quality that was immediately touching. One wanted to comfort him as one might a lost child   to take his hand and speak quiet words. Rarely had I been so moved by a painting.

"King Karl of Barivna," Madame Schroeder informed me. "He attended the university twenty years ago, then went back to Barivna to found a university of his own, second only to Heidelberg."

"What expressive eyes he has," I remarked.

"He's much older now, in his mid-forties. A gentle man, dedicated to the arts and, alas, caught up in a touchy political situation. Barivna is a tiny kingdom, unfortunately hemmed in on either side by large states, each of which wants to annex Karl's country."

"I've heard of him," I said. "Barivna is supposed to be the Athens of Germany."

"King Karl has devoted his life to art and beauty. He's spent several fortunes turning Barivna into a wonderland of palaces, gardens, museums. The neighboring states are quite alarmed by his expenditures. He's never married, you know."

I gazed up at those sad blue eyes that were so full of silent yearning. Madame Schroeder glanced at the students standing a discreet distance away and lowered her voice.

"He's been in Italy buying marble," she confided, "and rumor has it that he'll stop in Bonn next Friday on his way back to Barivna. He might even attend our benefit! He'd never miss an opportunity to hear the celebrated Liszt play."

We had not yet discussed the benefit, and I dreaded telling her the bad news. Madame Schroeder looked at me, a little alarmed by my silence.

"You did speak to him?" she inquired.

I nodded. "I—I'm afraid Franz won't be able to perform," I said hesitantly.

Madame Schroeder's face seemed to collapse, her eyes filling with disbelief. I thought she might actually burst into tears, and I damned Franz for putting me in such an awkward position. The corners of her lips quivered in a brave smile as she sought to conceal her disappointment. She might be a silly woman with silly ringlets, but the benefit was of paramount importance to her, and I knew what hopes she must have cherished.

"He's terribly busy, you see," I explained. "He's working on a new composition, and he desperately needs to finish it before we leave for Dresden."

Madame Schroeder managed a tremulous smile. "I understand, of course," she said. Her voice quavered. "It was foolish of me to think I could get someone of his stature for my benefit. It's just a local thing, very unimportant. Of course he's too busy. Dear me, and I went ahead and rented the theater for Friday night, thinking there'd be a vast crowd. Oh well, that can be mended. I feel sure I can—"

She broke off, unable to go on, actively fighting the tears now. I took her hand and squeezed it.

"I'm so sorry," I said quietly. "I—I wish there were something I could—" I paused. "Madame Schroeder, would it help if *I* performed? I haven't been on stage in over three months, and I have no costumes here, but—" Again I paused. "I'd be glad to help in any I could."

Madame Schroeder looked at me as though unable to believe what she had just heard. "Would you?" she asked.

"I'd be happy to."

"But—that's marvelous!" she exclaimed. "You'd be an even greater attraction. Half of Bonn heard Liszt play last night, but no one's seen *you* perform! We'll sell out immediately. Oh, Miss Lopez, you're an angel. An angel! This will be my greatest triumph. I just know it!"

Several of the students had overheard our exchange. They began to talk excitedly in German. "Elena's going to dance!" I heard. "Elena's going to dance!" Three of the youths rushed over to ask Madame Schroeder about tickets, and at once she became very dignified, very efficient. Soon we were surrounded, and the previously reserved youths, smiling and laughing, made a merry racket as they followed us out to the carriage. They cheered noisily as we drove away. I waved. Madame Schroeder did, too, dignity deserting her in her excitement.

I said nothing to Franz about my decision to perform. He was immersed in his music, and if he saw the announcement in the newspapers the next morning, he made no mention of it. I left the hotel early, for there was much to do. Madame Schroeder was in her element arranging for rehearsals and musicians and music. We were able to use the theater to rehearse in, and though she could only locate one copy of my Spanish music, she had several young men make copies for each of the musicians. After rehearsal schedules were set up, she bustled me off to a dressmaker she knew and I sketched a costume for her. The dressmaker said it would be impossible to have such a costume ready in time, but Madame Schroeder threw her hands in the air and said that was nonsense, sheer nonsense, we must all accomplish miracles, think of those poor little orphans. Finally, the dressmaker said she would try, and Madame Schroeder hugged her and whirled me away in search of castanets.

As Madame Schroeder had predicted, tickets for the benefit sold out immediately, and for double the price that she had originally set. The newspapers were filled with stories. In order to keep the journalists away from the hotel, I gave an interview at the theater after one of the rehearsals. Madame Schroeder took charge, acting as translator for those journalists who spoke no French. With rehearsals, costume fittings and conferences, I spent very little time at the hotel during the days that followed, but Franz appeared not to notice. At least he did not comment on my frequent and lengthy absences. Caught up in the throes of creation, he wanted only to work. His meals were sent up to the suite and, generally, he worked late into the night, retiring to his own bedroom when he finished.

The dress rehearsal lasted until four on Friday afternoon, and I was apprehensive as I returned to the hotel. I knew Franz wouldn't approve of my performing, and I had been expecting a scene ever since the announcement first appeared. Even though he might be too busy to squander time on anything as mundane as newspapers while in the midst of composing, he knew full well that something was afoot. During the past week, though I had been away from the hotel a great deal, it was never in the evening, and I wondered what his reaction would be when I told him I was going out again and wouldn't be in until very late. He might merely have shrugged his shoulders. We hadn't slept together since the afternoon I toured the university, and had exchanged hardly a dozen words.

Madame Schroeder would be waiting for me in the

lobby at six thirty, ready to whisk me off to the theater, and I knew I should try to get some rest, but I was much too tense. Finally, I sat down at the gilt rosewood secretary and wrote the long overdue letters to Millie and George Sand, and when I finished it was time to dress. Franz was still in the study at six fifteen, sitting at the piano and staring gloomily at the sheets of music on the music rack in front of him. He looked up as I entered, raising his eyebrows as he noted my formal gown.

"Going out?" he inquired.

I nodded. "I won't be in until—quite late."

"I see," he said.

He knew. I could tell that.

"It's just as well, Franz. You'll probably spend the evening at the piano, as you've done every evening this past week."

"As a matter of fact, I won't. I've just finished the sonata. I thought I'd play it for you tonight, after we'd gone out to dine. I thought we might celebrate."

"I'm sorry, Franz."

My voice was cool. I knew he was playing a game with me, but I refused to be put on the defensive. There was absolutely no reason for me to feel guilty. I was going to dance, and if he was unhappy about it, that was just too bad.

"I've missed you, my love," he said tenderly. "Now that this piece is finished, I promise to be more attentive. Starting tonight," he added.

"I have other plans tonight," I told him.

He watched me, one brow arched caustically, as I pulled on a glove, flexed my fingers to get a proper fit, and calmly told him goodbye, pulling on the other glove as I left. He could sulk and brood all he liked, I told myself. At least there hadn't been an angry scene. That might well come later, but I intended to waste no more time thinking about it. I had to devote all my energy and concentration to my performance.

Madame Schroeder was wearing a pale blue satin gown and a glittering diamond necklace. She was a bundle of nerves as we drove to the theater. There were thousands of things to do before the curtain went up at eight, literally thousands, she informed me. A solo violinist had taken ill, at the last moment, of course, it always happened that way, and she would have to put someone in his place—who, she had no earthly idea— and the programs had already been printed up and the audience would be confused and thank God the dressmaker had delivered my costume that afternoon and she only hoped it would fit properly. No woman in her right mind would take on all this responsibility, she declared. This was her last benefit, positively the last, and it would take her a good two months in bed to recuperate.

Backstage was in chaos, everyone rushing to and fro, it seemed, and nothing going the way it should. There was trouble with the lamp, trouble with the pulleys, and an overweight soprano was threatening to walk out because she was scheduled to appear *after* the choir when it had been firmly understood that she would appear *before*. Little girls from the ballet school, prancing about in their tutus, giggled noisily, having the time of their lives. The programs hadn't been delivered yet. One of the ushers had sprained an ankle. Three of the men in the choir, having spent the afternoon in a beer garden, were decidedly tipsy. Madame Schroeder shouted for attention and turned into a harsh drill sergeant, barking orders left and right. If anyone could make order out of this wild confusion, it was she.

I retired to my dressing room, the same one Franz had used the week before, when he gave his concert. Located in the rear of the building, it was removed from all the noise and confusion. I closed the door and tried to compose myself. I was tense and nervous, worried about my performance. I hadn't been on stage since Bath, where I ended my English tour. Three months without dancing was a long time, and there hadn't been sufficient rehearsals. Could I still achieve that fluid movement and sinuous grace? Madame Schroeder's benefit might be a "local" affair, but every seat in the theater had been sold, and I owed it to the audience and to myself to do my very best.

I undressed and slipped into a thin silk robe, tying the sash at my waist. I had well over an hour to get ready, but as I had to make up and do my own hair, that was none too long. At the dressing table, I sat reveling in the smells of grease paint and dust and damp that seemed to permeate every dressing room. Although nervous, I was pleased to be back in a theater, excited at the prospect of performing again. I opened various pots and jars, took out brushes and hair pins, feeling peculiarly at home. I spent almost half an hour doing my hair, trying to perfect the curls that curved over each temple. How I missed Millie! I applied my make-up next, darkening brows and lashes, shadowing lids a smoky blue-gray, painting my lips the desired shade of scarlet, creating the exotic, seductive Elena the public paid to see.

I felt anything but exotic and seductive until I slipped into my costume. A bright red silk, it was entirely covered with glittering red spangles that shimmered like crimson fire as I moved. The low bodice was trimmed with red ostrich feather, which also adorned the off-the-shoulder sleeves. It was a bit snug at the waist, but I was pleased with the way the skirt fell over the underskirts of ruffled red gauze. The costume was bold and dramatic, certain to dazzle the eye. If my dancing wasn't all it should be, at least they could enjoy the dress, I thought ruefully, turning around and looking over my shoulder to check the back in the mirror. As I did, there was a knock on the door.

Madame Schroeder entered breathlessly. Her satin gown was slightly rumpled, her blonde ringlets askew, but she wore a look of radiant triumph.

"At last, it's all under control!" she informed me. "Everything's running smoothly. The theater is packed to the rafters, my dear, and people are standing in back! You couldn't squeeze another soul inside if your life depended on it, and they all paid a fortune to come tonight!"

"I'm so pleased."

"My dear, you haven't heard the most exciting part yet. He's here!"

"Who?"

"King Karl! He slipped into the Royal Box just as the lights began to dim. He doesn't like fuss and didn't want anyone to know. He's sitting well back, half concealed by the curtains. Just think, tonight you'll be dancing for a king!"

Madame Schroeder paused to catch her breath, hand clutched to her bosom. Fastening a curl of red ostrich feather over my right temple, I thought about the man in the painting, remembering those sad, expressive eyes. Knowing he would be out front was strangely disconcerting. Suddenly, I wished that I had had more time to rehearse.

"Are you ready?" Madame Schroeder asked. "The show's already begun, of course, but you're scheduled to appear last. Who could follow Elena Lopez? Nedda's singing her aria right now. The audience is being *most* patient. I thought you'd like to watch from the wings until it's time for you to go on."

I was not terribly enthusiastic about the idea, but I smiled nevertheless and followed her out of the dressing room and down the long, dimly lit hall. Nedda, whose voice was less than lilting, was indeed singing. She hit her last note as Madame Schroeder and I found a place to stand in the shadows. The audience applauded tepidly, and then the choir marched onstage in gold and green uniforms, three of its members sadly out of step. Nedda stalked past us in a fury as the choir began to sing a rousing number which, mercifully, I was able to tune out.

Standing in the wings, smelling the familiar musty smells, brought memories I could have done without. How many times had I stood in the shadows waiting to go on, while Anthony stood beside me, jaunty, possessive, mentally tallying up the box office receipts? Where was he now? Why couldn't I hate him as I had every right to do? The little girls from the ballet school went on, dancing to a piece by Chopin, and that caused even more memories. I hardened myself against them, forced them out of my mind. Edgy, nervous, impatient, I endured the rest of the local performers, and then an expectant hush fell over the audience and I realized it was time for me to go on.

"This is what they've all been waiting for," Madame Schroeder whispered excitedly. "You're going to be marvelous!"

272

I had my usual moment of panic, but as the Spanish music began, filling the theater with the sultry, scorching evocation of the Spanish plains, swelling and ringing, I fastened on my castanets and closed my eyes . . . letting the music become part of me, letting it carry me onstage. Panic vanished, as it always did with my movements. Castanets clicking, heels stamping, I ignored the audience, the lights, keeping time to the music as it grew torrid and tempestuous, my spangled red skirt whirling as I whirled, swaying as I swayed. . . . The music grew louder, rising to a passionate crescendo that vibrated with violent emotion, commanding me to obey each urgent beat until finally, climatically, the music came to an abrupt end and I stood still, arms outstretched, head thrown back.

The cheers and applause lasted for several minutes, and I had to step to the footlights and bow and smile as the cheers continued, the applause thundered on. Looking up toward the Royal Box, I saw the man sitting far back, his face a pale blur in the shadows, and I could feel his eyes on me. King Karl nodded, and I acknowledged the nod with one of my own. The musicians began to play the second piece, as slow and sinuous as the first had been fierce, a seductive love song that lifted and lilted in swirls of melody.

I danced for the King, and I knew that I had never danced so well. Every movement sent a message, graceful, fluid, filled with meaning. The dance was seductive, sensual, but as I danced it now it took on a new color, conveyed a new message. I did not lure a lover into the warm moonlit night, I led him gently into the dawn and showed him the beauty unfolding. I did not beguile and implore, but comforted and soothed. I gathered the music to me and gave it to him as a shimmering gift. Even though the audience wasn't aware of anything unusual, he understood because I willed it, and when the last note melted into silence and the dance was done, he nodded once more.

When the curtain fell, the audience went wild. I walked into the wings, depleted physically and emotionally, wanting only to rest, but they wouldn't let me. I had to take curtain call after curtain call, twelve in all.

273

The curtain fell for the last time and the lights came on backstage. Before I could escape to my dressing room I was surrounded by people, all of them congratulating me, thanking me, Madame Schroeder beside me, hugging me, and then the crowd parted and Franz strolled casually across the stage toward me. Resplendent in formal black suit and white satin waistcoat, his tawny mane gleaming, his expression inscrutable, he took my hand.

Silently, he led me away from the people and down the hall to the dressing room. There, he gathered up my things and gave them to his driver and then took me out the back exit to the carriage that stood waiting. Allowing him to assist me, I climbed into the carriage, arranged my spangled red skirt and adjusted one of the red ostrich feather sleeves. He climbed in beside me and closed the door—still silent, his face still inscrutable. As we drove away he pulled me into his arms and kissed me savagely, furiously, hurting me, and there was no need for words.

XXV

A glorious day dawned, with dazzling sunlight, and a delicious silence that was broken only by the sound of distant cowbells. Climbing out of bed, I slipped on my dressing gown and stepped out onto the balcony to look at the spectacular view. Viridian trees covered the hills, and light green slopes leading into the small valley were slashed with patches of blood-red wildflowers. A stream wound through the valley like a sparkling silver-blue ribbon, while the pale tan road curled around the hills upward to end in a circular drive in front of the inn.

Franz and I had driven up that road late the previous afternoon to this charming inn, perched on the side of a hill. A gigantic Swiss chalet of yellow and tan and white, it had all sloping roofs, spacious verandahs and gingerbread woodwork. I had been enchanted with it immediately, but was even more enchanted when I discovered that we had the inn all to ourselves, not even one other guest was in residence. It was going to be a peaceful, idyllic week, a week of rest, relaxation and intimacy. I visualized long walks over the hills, picnics by the stream and cozy dinners in front of the fire in the sitting room downstairs, where we would be served by the silent, efficient staff.

Leaning over the bannister, I breathed in the marvelous air and let the sunlight bathe my cheeks. I was in an optimistic mood. Franz had been thoughtful and attentive the night before. Although we had taken

275

separate suites, he had spent most of the night in mine, making love to me with the same passion and excitement he had shown the first time we were together. My greatest hope was that this week of seclusion would enable us to mend the rift that had grown between us.

Dresden had been a disaster from first to last, and I still fumed when I thought about the man who had spoiled it for us. I was ready to concede that Herr Richard Wagner might well be the greatest composer of the century, as Franz claimed, but he was one of the most detestable men I had ever encountered.

On our first night in Dresden, Franz and I had attended a performance of *Rienzi* in the gorgeous Court Theater. We had watched the opera from the private box of Joseph Tichatschek, the Bohemian tenor who had created the title role when the opera had had its premiere five years before. I was overwhelmed by the dramatic sweep of the story, the powerful melodies, even though six full hours of political protest set to music was difficult to take at one sitting. Wagner had come to our box during the entr'acte. He was a striking figure with his sharp features and fierce hazel brown eyes flecked with gray and green. When Franz introduced us, Wagner stared at me with open hostility. After giving me a curt nod he ignored me completely.

I sensed immediately that he despised women, considered them inferior creatures to be used when necessary and then brutally dismissed. His marriage to the actress Minna Platte had been tempestuous, to say the least—that much was public knowledge. She had run away from him on two or three occasions, and he had instituted divorce proceedings only a few months after their marriage, later withdrawing them. Finally subdued, Minna Wagner was kept so securely in the background that most people were surprised to discover that Wagner actually had a wife.

Wagner monopolized Franz during the midnight supper party that followed the opera and throughout the following week as well. The two men spent all their time together, immersed in deep conversation about music, Wagner's music. They ate together, drank together, and

276

I had the feeling that had it suited Wagner's purposes, they would have slept together as well.

I knew that Franz had first met Wagner in 1840. He had immediately taken the German composer under his wing, using his power and influence on Wagner's behalf, helping him in every way possible. Franz was a towering giant in the musical world, Wagner still relatively unknown, but Wagner was the one man to whom Franz was willing to take second place. It was almost as though their positions were reversed. Franz wanted to please Wagner, wanted to impress him and win his approval, while Wagner treated Franz with a patronizing superiority that was infuriating to behold.

Wagner exploited their friendship even to the point of imitating Franz. He wore his bronze hair brushed back in a lion's mane like Franz. He dressed like him. He imitated Franz' detached, sardonic manner, but where Franz was ready to help his fellow composers with unstinting generosity, Wagner considered them all his rivals and deeply resented their successes. I saw that he resented Franz, too, although he was careful not to show it openly. Franz was much too useful to him. Wagner was exceedingly vain, exceedingly arrogant, thoroughly convinced of his own superiority. A number of women evidently found him irresistible, but I was not one of them. I found him cold, hard, callous, totally unscrupulous.

Wagner disliked me as much as I disliked him. He had known Franz much longer than I, of course, and he considered me an intruder, a threat to his friendship with Franz. Each time he looked at me I had the feeling he would happily have strangled me. He called Franz a fool for traveling with a whore in tow, and he had informed all their friends in Dresden that I was wrecking Franz' career.

Sighing, I brushed a lock of hair from my cheek and left the balcony to return to my bedroom. That week in Dresden had almost destroyed our relationship. On more than one occasion I had been tempted to pack my bags and return to Paris, leaving the two of them to continue their chummy talks without the irritant of my

277

presence, but Wagner would have loved that. I was glad now that I hadn't let my anger and frustration get the better of me. A week in this lovely inn, surrounded by the magnificent countryside, would be just the tonic we needed.

As I stepped back inside, a plump, rose-cheeked maid with thick blonde braids came into the room carrying my breakfast. There was a silver pot of coffee, a blue cup and saucer, a plate of rolls, butter, honey, and a vase of red wildflowers on the tray. Setting the tray down, the maid gave me a broad smile and then hurried out in a fit of giggles. The coffee tasted rich and tangy, and the rolls were flaky and delicious. When I finished eating, I selected a dress to wear—a dark pink cotton with a snug waist and a very full skirt—and went about completing my toilette. I hummed as I brushed my hair.

Feeling marvelous, my hair spilling in loose waves over my shoulders, I floated downstairs to find Franz. He was in the sitting room, at the grand piano, a sheaf of music in front of him. He looked up as I entered, a preoccupied look in his eyes.

"Working already?" I inquired.

"I hope to make some headway on a new arrangement this week."

"It's a glorious morning, Franz, much too glorious for you to be at the piano. We're on a holiday."

"I need to work."

"You can work this afternoon," I protested, "all afternoon long. I promise not to bother you. Let's take a walk this morning. The fresh air will do you good, and so will the exercise."

He scowled and straightened the sheets of music and then, sighing heavily, stood up.

"You really are a distraction, my dear."

"Am I?"

"A damnable distraction. I should have thrown you out a long time ago. You've no idea how many times I've longed to be done with you, to send you packing."

I smiled. "But you haven't."

"I shall eventually," he promised.

"Perhaps not," I teased. "Perhaps I'll leave you."

"I doubt that."

"You're insufferable, Franz. I don't know why *I* put up with *you*, but I refuse to let your grumpiness spoil our holiday." I took his hand and gave it a tug. "Come, we'll have our walk, and then you can sulk for the rest of the day."

Franz lifted his thin lips at one corner, but he followed me docilely enough. We left the inn and climbed down one of the gentle slopes. I paused to gather some of the wildflowers as Franz watched wearily. The air was scented with pine, and the sky was a pale, pure blue-white, cloudless. We continued on our way, and Franz maintained his disgruntled expression, obviously bored by the beauty of the countryside, the fresh air, the serenity.

"Isn't this marvelous?" I said.

"Marvelous."

"I feel so free, so lighthearted."

"That, my dear, is obvious."

"You're such a grump, Franz."

"I've never pretended to be otherwise. If you wanted a charming, attentive companion, you should have taken up with someone else. I'm quite fond of you, Elena, in my way, but I've never been gallant, nor am I likely to be."

Though his manner was cool and matter-of-fact, I was finding it more and more difficult to maintain my own good mood. Franz was a splendid creature, handsome, magnetic, exuding fierce sexual allure. Just to be with him was exciting and stimulating, and he was unquestionably a magnificent lover, but I was beginning to realize that I really didn't like him at all.

I fell silent, pensive as we continued our stroll, moving under the trees now. Dry pine needles crunched underfoot. The sky was almost obliterated by heavy boughs that cast soft purple-blue shadows on the ground. How much longer did we have together? How much longer before it dissolved into active hostility? I thought of Marie d'Agoult, the countess who had shared so many years of her life with Franz, bearing him three children. Marie had endured much grief, much heartbreak, suffering terribly before she was finally free of her Demon Lover. I was not as patient as the stoic countess, nor was I in love with Franz. Thank God for that, I told myself.

We started up another slope back toward the inn, which appeared an ornate doll's house in the distance. The bright optimism I had felt earlier in the morning had vanished, a wry resignation taking its place. Perhaps we would have another month, perhaps six weeks, perhaps less, but I knew separation was inevitable. Franz needed a meek, worshipful woman who would sit silently at his feet, speak only when spoken to and cater to his every whim. He would despise her, of course, but then I was beginning to suspect that, like Wagner, he secretly despised all women.

Just as we were crossing the drive in front of the inn, a dashing open carriage wheeled around a curve in the road. The driver sat on his high perch, urging the pair of grays on, and a single passenger lolled in the plushly upholstered seat, his bags beside him. As the carriage came nearer, I recognized the bronze mane, the sharp features, and I felt myself turn white. Richard Wagner raised his arm in salute, and Franz raised his in return, totally unsurprised to see his friend.

"You—you knew he was coming," I accused.

"But of course," he replied.

"You *invited* him."

"How perceptive of you."

"This was to be our week, our holiday, and you—you asked that man to join us, knowing how I feel about him. I can't believe it. I simply can't believe you could be so—so—"

I cut myself short, striving to control my anger. Franz lifted his lips in a wry smile, amused by my outrage.

"Jealousy becomes you, my dear," he remarked, "but do try to keep it under control. Richard's sensitive about such things."

"Richard can go straight to hell," I snapped.

Franz chuckled to himself and then stepped forward as the carriage drew up in front of the inn. Wagner alighted briskly, and the two men fell upon each other, embracing heartily, pounding each other on the back. Franz' face was aglow with pleasure, and I realized bitterly that I had never evoked such a look of elation in his eyes. Disengaging himself from Franz' embrace, Wagner ordered the driver to carry his bags inside, and then he looked at me. I returned his look with pure loathing. He smiled and turned back to Franz, dismissing me.

"I've finished it," he announced. "I finished it last night."

"Finished what?" Franz asked.

"The wedding march, of course, the wedding march. I have finally worked it out to my satisfaction. Remember that passage I played for you in Dresden? I threw out everything but the basic melody, and I've strengthened that, given it a new power. It's nothing short of majestic."

"You must play it for me."

"I've every intention of doing just that."

Wagner was undeniably attractive with those eyes glowing dramatically beneath low, stern brows. His nose was too large, his lips too thin, but these flaws somehow only enhanced his ruthless good looks. He wore tall brown boots and a dark tan suit, the breeches snug, the jacket with long tails. His satin waistcoat was brown and white striped, his neckcloth a vivid green that picked up the green in his eyes. Arrogant, cold, seething with ambition, he tossed his long bronze mane and followed Franz up the steps and into the inn.

I stood there in the sunlight, fuming, as angry as I had ever been in my life. The driver came back out to take the carriage around to the carriage house in back of the inn. It was several minutes before I felt composed enough to join the men in the sitting room. Wagner stood in front of the mantle, a glass of red wine in his hand, and Franz was examining a musical score. Wagner had been working on *Lohengrin* for months. They had talked of nothing else in Dresden.

"Magnificent," Franz remarked.

"A masterpiece, no question about it," Wagner told him. "Verdi and Bellini will be pronounced passé."

Neither man so much as glanced at me. I might have been invisible.

281

"Shall I order lunch?" I inquired.

Wagner looked at me as though I were carrying the plague. Franz lifted his eyes from the score.

"We're busy, Elena."

"Too busy to eat?"

"We'll eat if we get hungry. I'm sure you can find something to occupy yourself with this afternoon."

"I feel sure I can," I retorted.

"Good," he said, dismissing me.

I left without a word, my cheeks flaming. When I reached my room, my first impulse was to pack my bags, but I managed to restrain myself. I wasn't going to give up so easily. Oh no, I wasn't going to let Herr Richard Wagner drive me away. I had never run from a fight before, and I didn't intend to start now. The anger boiled inside for several more minutes, and then a determined calm came over me. We'd just see who left first.

After a while I heard Wagner at the piano, playing his march. It was stately and solemn and quite lovely, and I hated it. He played it repeatedly as the afternoon wore on. Not once did Franz play his own new composition. It was that bloody march over and over again until I wanted to scream. It was nearly seven before I heard them come upstairs, laughing heartily at some private joke, like two noisy schoolboys. A few minutes later Franz strolled into my room.

"Still sulking?" he inquired.

"Whatever gave you the idea I've been sulking?"

He ignored the question. "We'll be dining at eight thirty. I thought I'd let you know."

"How very considerate."

"I'll see you downstairs, my dear."

It was five minutes after nine when I entered the sitting room. Both men were waiting. They had been waiting for some time. I smiled graciously and apologized for being late, explaining that it had taken me longer to dress than I had expected.

"I hope the result is satisfactory," I added.

Wagner scowled, but Franz' look was one of considerable appreciation. My gown of deep, rich, royal blue satin was a gorgeous garment, basically simple and exceedingly provocative. My ebony hair was pulled back sleekly and worn in a French roll on the back of my head, and my lids were brushed with soft blue-gray shadow, the natural pink of my lips heightened with deep pink lip rouge.

"You look lovely, my dear," Franz remarked.

"Thank you, Franz."

He had changed into a black suit with white-on-white waistcoat and white silk neckcloth. Wagner wore a dark maroon suit, his white satin waistcoat embroidered with black floral patterns, his neckcloth maroon silk. Both men looked handsome and distinguished. Wagner's imitation of Franz' manner, his similar style of dress and the identical hair style made the resemblance between them remarkable. They might have been taken for brothers.

"Shall we adjourn to the dining room?" I said.

A table had been set for three. Everywhere tall candles burned. The tablecloth was snowy white. China, crystal and silver gleamed. Franz helped me into my seat. I smiled and thanked him. Wagner scowled again, not at all happy with the way things were going. A waiter brought our first course, a thick, creamy turtle soup. Franz' dark eyes were filled with amusement as his friend grew more and more sullen.

"Did you have an interesting afternoon, my dear?" Franz inquired.

"As a matter of fact, I did," I replied. "I've been reading George's new novel, *Lucrezia Floriana*. It's just been published and she forwarded a copy to our hotel in Dresden. It's all about an actress approaching middle age and her twenty-four-year-old lover, a frail, clinging, self-centered intellectual who arouses her maternal instincts. I can easily see why she was so concerned about Chopin's reaction to it. It's their story, thinly disguised. Very thinly."

"Chopin," Wagner said. "A minor talent. All sweet melody, no power. He'll be forgotten in a decade or so."

"I disagree," I told him.

Wagner curled his lips in a deprecatory smirk, shaking his head as though amused at my temerity in expressing an opinion.

"I'm afraid I do, too, Richard," Franz said. "Frederic has his own kind of genius."

"He's let that woman ruin him."

"On the contrary," I said. "Everyone says that George has devoted herself to him, nursing him like a baby, indulging his every whim, giving him the financial security and peace of mind he desperately needed. Had it not been for her, he would probably have succumbed to consumption years ago. He'd certainly have given up composing."

"I can see you admire her," Wagner observed. "I'm not surprised."

"What Elena says is true, Richard. George has sacrificed a great deal for Frederic. I fear he's never fully appreciated just how much."

"Sometimes, Franz, I wonder about your taste in friends."

"Sometimes I do, too," I said sweetly, looking directly at Wagner.

He glared at me with fierce eyes. I smiled. Franz' eyes danced with amusement. Wagner maintained a stony silence throughout the rest of the meal while Franz and I made small talk. But after the waiter had cleared away the dishes and set a bowl of fruit on the table, Franz brought up the subject of music—*Lohengrin*, of course.

"I still maintain that it's going to be almost impossible to produce, Richard," he remarked. "All those scenes, all that spectacle. It'll cost a fortune to mount. No opera house in Europe could afford it without a wealthy patron."

"I'm well aware of that," Wagner replied. "I just might be able to arrange that."

"Oh?"

"Karl of Barivna is a great patron of the arts. He came to Dresden to attend the first performance of *Tannhäuser* two years ago, and I understand he was quite impressed, both with the opera and with my conducting."

Bored by Wagner's egotism, bored by his talk, I had been less than attentive, but at the mention of King Karl my interest was aroused immediately. I remembered that gentle face and those sad eyes and the curious compassion I had felt for the man who sat half-hidden in his box as I danced for him.

Wagner continued: "He's a notoriously easy mark when it comes to any kind of artistic endeavor. Half the painters and sculptors and composers in Germany would be starving were it not for good King Karl. He rarely refuses a request for aid."

There was disdain in his voice, as though the King were a pitiful weakling to be used by superior men like Wagner who might condescend to accept his largess. Wagner took a sip of wine, thin lips smiling as he contemplated a huge donation.

"I understand that's one of the reasons Barivna's in such a turmoil," Franz said. "The recipients are delighted with Karl's generosity, but Sturnburg is extremely displeased and wants to curtail his spending."

"Sturnburg?" I said. "Who's he?"

"Sturnburg is a state, not a person," Wagner informed me.

"I thought Barivna was an independent kingdom. Why should Sturnburg be concerned with his expenditures?"

"It's an extremely complex political situation," Franz said, "but perhaps I can explain it."

He reached into the bowl of fruit and, taking out a small red plum, set it on the table.

"Barivna is a plum," he explained, "very rich, very juicy, highly appetizing. Unfortunately, it's also very small and, as you can see, completely unprotected."

Reaching into the bowl once more, he removed two large apples, one red, one green. He set the green apple on the left side of the plum, the red on the right. The plum looked small and extremely vulnerable, overpowered by the apples.

"This," he said, pointing to the green apple, "is Sachendorf, which borders Barivna on the left. Sachendorf is an aggressive, war-like state which would like nothing better than to snatch up Barivna and annex it. It would undoubtedly have happened a long time ago had it not been for Sturnburg—" He indicated the red apple on the other side of the plum.

"For years Sturnburg has provided 'protection' for Barivna. Karl has devoted his life to building palaces and parks, art museums and theaters and to making the university he established one of the finest in Germany."

Madame Schroeder had used similar words when telling me about Karl and Barivna. Franz poured more wine into his glass and sipped it before continuing.

"He has no army, no police force of his own. The leaders of Sturnburg have supplied them, gradually increasing their numbers over the years. The population of Barivna is primarily made up of students and artists who have migrated to Karl's Mecca of culture. At the moment there is an almost equal number of Sturnburgian soldiers in residence. The barracks will soon outnumber the dormitories."

"That must cause a great deal of tension."

"The students idolize Karl and are wildly loyal to him. They resent the presence of 'foreign' soldiers in Barivna, and the militia, in turn, despise the students. There've been frequent clashes, some of them quite fierce."

"The King can do nothing about them?"

"Karl rules Barivna, yes, but everything he does is closely 'supervised' by Sturnburg. The Sturnburgian leaders act as if every cent Karl spends is coming directly from their own treasury. In protecting Karl from Sachendorf, Sturnburg has become an even greater menace."

"Have they threatened him?"

"Not yet, but any day now they're likely to lose patience, annex Barivna and send Karl packing."

Franz paused, gazing at the plum and the apples.

"It's more complex than that, of course. There are international ramifications much too complicated to explain. All Europe is in a state of political turmoil, and any move against Barivna would be apt to set off a chain of explosions that would rock the whole continent."

"Sturnburg must know that."

"Their fear of repercussions is Karl's greatest protection, but, as I said, they're likely to lose patience. The situation is growing tenser by the month."

"Karl's a fool," Wagner said. "He's a weakling who's

286

brought all these problems down on his own head. I've no sympathy for him."

"Yet you'd let him finance your opera," I remarked.

"Gladly," he replied. "I only hope I can get to him before he's pushed off his throne."

"I find your attitude despicable."

Wagner gave me a condescending smile. "My dear Elena, the end justifies the means. People will be applauding *Lohengrin* long after Karl of Barivna has become an obscure footnote in history books."

"It must be wonderful to have such confidence."

"Those of us who are genuinely gifted have reason to be confident," he retorted. "We rely on our gifts, not shabby journalism."

I was finding it more and more difficult to maintain my poise, but I managed to ignore the remark. I toyed with the stem of my wine glass for a moment and then stood up, smoothing the folds of my skirt.

"It's such a lovely evening, I think I'll stroll in the gardens for a while. Care to join me, Franz?"

"Later on perhaps."

Both men watched me as I left the room. I was pleased with the way things had gone. Franz had sided with me about George and Chopin, and he had ignored Wagner long enough to explain the political situation in Barivna. He had also complimented me on my appearance. Herr Wagner had definitely come in a poor second that night.

The gardens at the side of the inn were bathed in moonlight, everything dark blue-black and ashy gray and silver. I moved slowly down the path, enjoying the loveliness of the night, the fragrance of flowers. I could hear the horses moving about restlessly in the stable behind the inn, and a bird was warbling sleepily in one of the trees. Would Franz join me? I remained in the gardens twenty minutes or so, and I was beginning to despair when I saw him coming down the verandah steps.

"It's a gorgeous evening," I said as he joined me. "I've never seen such moonlight."

"What a romantic you are, my dear."

"I can't help it."

"You were rather hard on Richard tonight."

"I find him unbearable."

"He tells me I should get rid of you."

"Does he indeed?"

"He claims you're a bad influence, claims you're keeping me from doing important work."

"And?"

"I'm inclined to agree with him."

He smiled a crooked smile, his eyes dark with amusement. He was in a peculiar mood, teasing, ironic, unusually sardonic. I turned to gaze at the valley below, a patchwork of moonlight and shadow. I could feel him watching me.

"You're so damnably beautiful, my dear. Particularly tonight. I suspect it was no accident."

"It wasn't. I chose this dress with care."

"You had something in mind?"

"Perhaps."

The bird warbled again, and a gentle breeze caused leaves to rustle. I sighed and turned. The smile still played on his lips, and I had a feeling he was planning some kind of mischief.

"The dress, the subtle manner, that sigh—one would think you were in an amorous mood."

"Last night was nice, Franz."

"You *are* in an amorous mood. Perhaps I should do something about it."

"Perhaps you should," I replied.

I gazed at him for a moment with challenge in my eyes, and then I left, moving toward the verandah. Franz didn't follow me, but I felt confident he would come to my room later on.

Out of politeness, he would have to spend a little more time with Wagner, talking, having a final brandy, and it would probably be after midnight before he came up. I decided to write a letter to George, thanking her for the book and telling her how much I had enjoyed it. I heard loud, hearty laughter coming from below as I sealed the envelope. Glancing at the clock, I saw that it was already well past midnight.

I turned the lamps out, and moonlight spread across the balcony and into the room through the opened

French windows. I undressed and my nightgown rustled silkily as I stretched out on the brocaded chaise to wait for Franz. There was another burst of laughter, louder, heartier than before. The clock ticked. One. One thirty. Silver shimmered. Shadows grew hazier. I closed my eyes.

Footsteps in the hall awakened me. I sat up, and in the moonlight I checked the clock and saw that it was after four. The door opened. As he came into the room and closed the door, I smiled, moving across the room to meet him.

"I hear you're in an amorous mood," he said.

It wasn't Franz. It was Wagner.

XXVI

For a moment I was absolutely paralyzed. Finally I managed to stumble over and light one of the lamps, and when I turned around to face him my heart was pounding. Still elegantly attired in his maroon suit and satin waistcoat, he stood there smiling smugly. I was angry, so angry I couldn't speak, and I was frightened, too. His eyes glittered, and there could be no doubt about his intentions.

"Everything they say about your beauty is quite true," he remarked. "I'll grant that. You're gorgeous. A whore, of course, but a gorgeous whore. I can see why Franz has been so bewitched."

"Get out of my room," I said.

"You seem upset, Elena. Why should you be upset? Isn't this what you wanted?"

"Get out."

"Franz assured me you were in an amorous mood. He said you required attention and that he was a bit tired himself. He went on up to his room to get a little sleep. I told him I'd be glad to fill in."

"I don't believe—"

"He sent me to you. Franz and I are very close, you see, like brothers. We share everything."

"Leave my room this minute!"

Wagner laughed a dry laugh and moved closer. I backed against the dressing table, my hand closing around the silver handle of my hair brush. His eyes were dark, gleaming with malicious intent. His bronze hair was burnished by the lamp light, a rich red-brown, and his face was all sharp planes.

"You should be flattered," he said. "One day you'll boast about this. You'll brag about the night you slept with Richard Wagner." He moved closer.

Gripping the hair brush tightly, I swung it out, intending to slam it across his temple. His hand flew up and his fingers closed about my wrist, squeezing, twisting. I winced and dropped the hair brush. Bringing my wrist down, he gave it an extra twist. Pain shot through my arm. He smiled, and his eyes were filled with satisfaction. He enjoyed giving pain.

"Franz—Franz will kill you," I whispered.

"I told you, he sent me. He didn't want you to pine."

"I don't believe you!"

"Ask him yourself—in the morning. You'll have to do it promptly, though. We're leaving at ten, Franz and I, going back to Dresden for a day or so, and then we're taking a walking tour together."

"You're lying."

"Afraid not, Elena. Franz has finally decided to leave you, something he should have done weeks ago."

"Let go of my wrist!"

"Frightened?" he inquired. "I should think you'd be elated. I'm much better in bed than Franz could ever hope to be."

He was tall and lean and lithe, with the wiry strength of most slender men. The fingers tightened around my wrist were like steel. There was no way I could pull free. I knew I had to keep calm, but the anger and panic continued to mount, and I began to tremble inside.

"I'm going to enjoy this," he informed me. "That first night I saw you, I wanted you. I wanted to drag you out of the opera box and take you on the floor, use you the way I'd use any other whore."

"You're despicable!"

"And you would have loved it. You would have left Franz in a minute if I'd crooked my little finger. I told him so, but he laughed. If I had wanted to take you away from him—"

I kicked his shin viciously. He cried out then, releasing my wrist. I tried to dart past him, but he was too

292

quick, too agile. He seized me and pulled me into his arms. I struggled violently, but it only encouraged him. His arm tightened about my waist as he tilted me back and pressed his lips to mine. Pounding on his back with my fists, I turned and writhed, but his arms only tightened. He forced my mouth open and thrust his tongue inside. I shuddered, fighting still.

Bringing my hands up I caught hold of his hair and pulled at it with all my might. He released me abruptly and slapped me across the face with such force that I reeled backward and stumbled, falling against the bed. As I struggled into a sitting position, Wagner undid his breeches, then shoved me back down and whipped my nightgown. up. I fought. For several moments I fought, until Wagner laughed and slapped me again, and I realized that further struggle was futile, that I was only making it worse for myself. He was too strong, much too strong for me to keep him from raping me.

"That's more like it," he growled as I stopped twisting.

He squeezed my breasts brutally, his teeth bared, his eyes flashing green fire. He spread my legs and entered me, moving deep with a powerful thrust. I endured without struggle, refusing to be caught up in the rhythm, and that angered him and he sought all the harder to awaken a response, driving his manhood into me like a spear, plunging with passion, the weight of his body crushing me.

His expression was determined, his eyes fierce, and he continued to thrust. I imagined him conducting one of his overtures—in my mind I could hear the drums roll and the cymbals crash as his music grew louder, harsher, until finally he grew taut, his body rigid in that instant of suspension, and then he shuddered as the life force jetted out of him and he came down atop me, limp and spent and heavy. I cringed, enduring, and after a while he withdrew and got to his feet and fastened his breeches.

I did not move from the bed, but watched as Wagner stepped over to the mirror to tug at the hem of his satin waistcoat and smooth the lapels of the elegant maroon jacket. He fooled with his neckcloth for a moment and then, satisfied with his appearance, turned to face me. Lips curling in that ever present sarcastic smile, he took a handful of bills from his pocket and tossed them onto the bed.

"I've had better from tawdry whores who stroll the backstreets at midnight," he informed me. "Your lack of talent in bed is exceeded only by your lack of talent on stage. I suggest you find a new trade."

He left then, and I closed my eyes and tried to compose myself. A few minutes later I summoned enough strength to put on my robe and go downstairs. Waking Hilde, the plump blonde maid, I told her I must have a hot bath immediately and she nodded groggily. Fifteen minutes later I was sitting in a tub of steaming hot water, scrubbing, scrubbing. The sun was shining when I returned to the bedroom. I dried my hair with a towel and then sat down to brush it, brushing vigorously until it crackled, releasing my anger with every stroke.

Pulling my hair back I fastened it in a loose French roll, then began to dress. When Hilde brought in my breakfast tray, I thanked her and, taking the tray, forced myself to drink several cups of the scalding hot coffee. I looked at the clock and saw that it was almost nine.

I moved briskly down the hall to Franz' suite and opened the door without bothering to knock. He wasn't in the sitting room, but his bedroom door was open and I saw him leaning over to fasten the clasp of one of his bags. He looked up. He didn't seem at all surprised to see me. Lifting the bag off the bed, he set it on the floor, then sauntered on into the sitting room.

"All packed?" I inquired.

"Almost."

"Then it's true?"

"I'm leaving, yes."

"With Wagner."

Franz nodded; his face was expressionless. Sunlight streamed in through the windows. The room was done in shades of white and gray and blue. A row of lovely blue and white Wedgewood plates stood on a rack above the mantle, and a Wedgewood box was on the

294

table in front of the gray velvet sofa. The carpet was dark blue, the walls gleaming white. I observed these details with strange objectivity as I tried not to believe what was happening.

"It was inevitable, Elena," he said. "We should have parted a long time ago."

"Yes."

"You seem very calm, my dear."

"I've never been calmer in my life."

"I'm glad to see you taking it so well."

There was a moment of silence as we looked at each other, and then I stepped over to him and drew my hand back and slapped him across the face so hard that I almost sprained my wrist. Franz didn't so much as wince. I stepped back, my palm stinging.

"Satisfied?" he inquired.

"Not entirely."

"Oh?"

"You sent him to my room, didn't you?"

"I thought it might amuse you."

I slapped him again, even harder this time. He grimaced, but he made no move to restrain me. I stepped back, rubbing my wrist. The right side of his face burned a bright pink. Moving over to the table, I picked up the Wedgewood box and hurled it against the wall. It shattered with an explosion of sound.

"Feel better?" he asked.

I whirled around and, taking down one of the plates from the mantle, I hurled it against the wall, too. It made even more noise. I took down another and shattered it. I was on the fifth plate when the door burst open and the proprietor rushed in with a horrified expression, throwing up his hands and babbling excitedly in German. I threw a plate at him. He covered his head with his arms and ducked, but Franz smiled his wry smile and told the man he would pay for the damage. The proprietor babbled something else and ran out of the room. I demolished the remaining plates and then, for good measure, tore the rack off the wall and heaved it across the room.

295

"An admirable performance," Franz said. "Are you quite finished?"

"Not quite," I fumed.

My bosom was heaving. I took a deep breath, trying to compose myself. Franz watched me with that damnable amusement in his eyes. I pushed a strand of hair from my temple, went over to him and picked up a delicate vase. Planting my feet firmly on the carpet, I smashed it over his head with all the might I could muster. He made a gasping noise and almost lost his balance.

"Now I'm finished," I said.

I turned and left the room, feeling sure that if I hadn't knocked the breath out of him he would have burst into laughter. In my room, I sat and seethed and drank another cup of coffee, hoping to calm down. My conduct appalled me, but it had been satisfying, marvelously satisfying. I only wished I had been able to hit him twice as hard. About half an hour later, I heard horse hooves on the drive in front of the inn. I went out onto the balcony and looked down to see Wagner's driver piling luggage into the open carriage.

A moment later, Franz and Wagner strolled out toward the carriage, in a jolly mood, both of them. Franz said something I couldn't make out and Wagner slapped him on the back and laughed heartily. I began to seethe again, the anger as good as new. As the men took their seats in the carriage, the driver climbed up on his perch in front and took up the reins. The grays stamped impatiently, eager to be off.

As if he could feel the intensity of my stare, Wagner turned and looked up. When he saw me standing at the bannister, he gave Franz a nudge and then lifted his hand and waved merrily. A heavy pot of red geraniums rested on top of one of the bannister posts. I picked it up and smiled to see Wagner's expression change from sarcastic mockery to stark horror. He threw his arms up over his head as I hurled the pot. It landed directly on top of him and broke into many little pieces. Had it not been for the protection of his arms, it would probably have cracked his skull. Startled by the noise, the horses reared and took off, almost pulling the driver from his perch. As the carriage bowled down the drive, Wagner frantically brushed clumps of dirt and shreds of geranium from his head and shoulders.

I went back inside and spent the rest of the morning packing my things. It was a time-consuming job. Why did I always travel with so many clothes? I fervently wished Millie had been there to help and to provide an audience. How I longed to launch into a tirade against Franz and Wagner, for the anger was still raging inside. I prayed that their carriage would turn over on one of the mountain passes. I prayed that they would both catch some dreadful disease. I hoped they would be very, very happy together. They deserved each other!

As I packed a final bag, there was a timid knock on the door and plump Hilde came into the room, her blue eyes wide with nervous curiosity.

"You want de lunch?" she asked in halting English.

"No thank you, Hilde. I'm not hungry."

"Jou are leavink, too?"

I nodded. "I—Hilde, I wonder if you'd check and see if—if Mr. Liszt paid for my room, and could you have someone arrange for a carriage to take me to the nearest railway station?"

"Ja," she said.

Hilde left and I sighed, and then a terrible realization came over me. I had almost no money. I had never taken a penny from Franz, but he had paid all our expenses. What little money I had was in a bank in Paris, and even that wouldn't be enough to hire a carriage and pay for my ticket to Paris. I was stranded. And after my exhibition in Franz' suite the proprietor wasn't likely to be in any mood to extend credit. Cheeks ashen, I sank into a chair, and then, seeing the humor of the situation, I laughed to myself.

Well, Elena, you've really gotten yourself into it this time, I thought, and you've only yourself to blame. Wait till the newspapers get hold of it . . . and they will!

I sat there for a long time, feeling remarkably good-humored about it all. Remembering the horrified expression on Wagner's face, I laughed again. I found myself thinking of Anthony. He would have appreciated

297

the situation, would have had some jaunty, outrageous remark to make, and then he would have started bossing me around. Men. I had chosen some real treasures. Here I sat, the most celebrated temptress of two continents, a tempestuous, mercenary adventuress who was supposed to drive men mad, without a sou, stranded in an isolated German inn on the edge of the Black Forest, and there wasn't a savior in sight. I wondered what would happen next.

I hadn't long to wait.

I spent the day feeling alternately relieved and desperate. In the late afternoon I heard a carriage driving up the road, and I stepped out onto my balcony just in time to see a young man climbing out of the carriage and walking toward the entrance. The carriage was closed, a gorgeous mahogany vehicle pulled by four snowy white horses with red plumes affixed to their heads. On the side of the door facing me there was an elegant gold and white crest, and I could see red velvet curtains hanging inside the windows. The driver sitting on the seat in front wore spotless white livery adorned with an abundance of gold braid. I was extremely impressed.

A few minutes later Hilde tapped on my door again, and when she came in her cheeks were flushed with excitement. She began to speak rapidly in German, making sweeping gestures. It was some time before I could calm her down enough to learn that a young Frenchman was downstairs in the sitting room and wished to see me. He was very beautiful and he had given her the warmest smile and had driven up in a magnificent carriage that was just like something out of a fairy tale. She'd never *seen* such a carriage in her life and she didn't know who he was but he must be someone very important and very rich, too.

"He wants to see me?"

She nodded vigorously, blonde braids flopping.

"Ja, Ja," she exclaimed, and then she launched into another excited tirade in German as I gently eased her out of the room.

I had no idea who he might be, but he would have to wait a while. My face and hair needed repairs. Fortunately, I hadn't yet packed my cosmetics, and I sat down at the dressing table and spent twenty minutes redoing my hair and applying make-up. Finished, I stood up and adjusted the hang of my skirt, glad I had chosen this particular frock—a fetching pale lavender with black stripes—which was not as flamboyant as most of my things.

Curious but composed, I descended the stairs. The young man was standing at the mantel as I entered the sitting room, his back to me. He was very tall and slender, and his thick, abundant hair was a very light brown, silvery brown, rich and wavy. Hearing my skirt rustle, he turned and smiled. I could see why Hilde had been so overwhelmed. He was indeed beautiful. Perhaps twenty-four years old, with clear blue eyes, a perfect Roman nose and full, curving lips. There was a deep cleft in his chin, and he had high, aristocratic cheekbones with slight hollows beneath them. His eyelids were heavy, his silver-brown brows beautifully curved.

"Miss Lopez?"

I nodded. He smiled. It was such a lovely smile. He was immediately engaging, a polite, friendly young man who, I suspected, was essentially shy and quite oblivious to his own beauty. He wore tall black boots, a dark blue suit and a waistcoat of sky blue satin embroidered with black and royal blue floral patterns. His neckcloth was black silk. Strong and virile, he had an innate gentility that was most refreshing.

"Phillipe Du Gard, Madamoiselle," he said, bowing. "I've come all the way from Barivna to abduct you."

"Oh?"

"My orders are to bring you back with me by fair means or foul. I'm prepared to clamp my hand over your mouth and drag you out by force if necessary. Although"—Phillipe Du Gard smiled once more, a mischievous twinkle in his eyes—"I must confess I've never abducted anyone before."

"I'm sure you'd be very good at it."

There was a shining quality about him, a youthful glow that was both touching and sad. He radiated an air of innocence and idealism. Though he appeared to be only a year or two older than I, he made me feel terribly worldly and experienced.

"Perhaps I'd better explain," he continued. "His royal highness, King Karl of Barivna, has just completed a magnificent new theater, all white and gold and red velvet within. He's very proud of it, and his desire is that you be the first to perform there."

"I'm very flattered."

"When he saw you dance in Bonn, he said he knew he must have you to open his theater. He promised to send me packing if I failed to return with you."

"How did you know where to find me?" I asked.

"The King himself told me to come here," he replied, as though that explained everything. "He gave me explicit directions."

"I see."

"He said you were with Liszt and that you might not want to come with me. . . ."

"Liszt and I are no longer—together."

Phillipe smiled. "Good," he said. "Perhaps I won't have to abduct you after all. Perhaps you'll come willingly."

"Perhaps."

"I'd hate to have to use force. I would, though. I used to beat up my younger brother at least once a week. He was a terrible pest, chasing after me like a gnat."

"Surely you didn't really beat him?"

"Really. Thoroughly. At least once a week."

He was such a charming young man—so sweet, so handsome, his nature as yet unmarred by the ugliness of the world. He aroused a tender feeling inside of me, making me wish I were still that innocent young girl who had roamed over the moors of Cornwall with a heart full of dreams and illusions.

"It's a long journey to Barivna," he informed me. "If we leave immediately we will have to drive until dark, spend the night at an inn and drive most of tomorrow. But there's some lovely scenery and I'm sure you won't be bored."

300

"I'm sure I won't."

"Will you come peacefully, or shall I have to use force?"

I smiled, absolutely enchanted by Monsieur Phillipe Du Gard, the most delightful savior imaginable.

"I don't think force will be necessary," I replied.

XXVII

The sky, a pale blue canopy, stretched above spectacular mountain vistas as the carriage moved up yet another perilously steep road. Peering out the window, I saw gorgeous peaks in the distance covered with green and studded with white and gray boulders, while two feet from the road there was a sheer drop. The carriage shook, bouncing on its springs, and I couldn't help being a bit nervous. Phillipe watched me, a teasing smile on his lips.

"We're not going to fall," he assured me.

"What if one of the wheels came off right now? We'd go careening over the edge and tumble down thousands of feet. It's fortunate that you didn't tell me about the mountain passes yesterday, Phillipe. I'd never have come with you."

"Yes you would have. Bound and gagged."

"And kicking furiously," I added. "Look, there's a cloud. I could almost reach out and *touch* it. I shan't try. I don't dare lean out the window. It might throw us off balance."

Phillipe laughed, enjoying himself almost as much as I was. He was a marvelous traveling companion, amiable, attentive and wonderful to look at. We had spent the night in a comfortable inn, and he had arranged everything in advance, clean, cozy rooms for both of us and one for the driver as well. Phillipe and I had dined in splendor. There had been caviar, pâté, champagne chilling in a silver bucket.

We had stayed up talking until after midnight, and he told me how he, a young Frenchman, happened to have a position at Barivna's Court. Phillipe had attended the university there and had fallen in love with the country. Through various friends, word had gotten back to the king of Phillipe's feelings for Barivna, and the king immediately sent for him and offered him a minor role at Court upon his graduation. Which Phillipe accepted with great pleasure.

The carriage hit another deep rut and I said, "I hope there is not much more of this."

"The road will level off in a little while, and there'll be no more dizzying drops, no more narrow curves. Barivna is situated in a large, lovely valley nestled right on top of the mountains. It's completely surrounded by peaks, and there are half a dozen sparkling lakes."

"You really are fond of Barivna, aren't you?"

"I hate the thought of leaving it."

"Must you?"

"I've no doubt Father will win eventually. He usually does."

Phillipe had grown up in Touraine where his father, Marquis Du Gard, maintained a large, ancient chateau surrounded by woodland. As a child Phillipe had swum naked in the Loire, scurried up trees to rob birds' nests and had been the leader of a rowdy gang made up of children of the tenant farmers. When he reached his teens, he gave up pretending to be a pirate or a red Indian and developed an interest in poetry and music, disappointing his father who wanted him to stop wasting his time and learn to manage the estate. Marquis Du Gard had opposed Phillipe's attending the university at Barivna from the start and was now demanding that he return to Touraine.

"Have you a sweetheart in Barivna?" I inquired.

A faint pink blush tinted his cheeks. "There's no sweetheart," he informed me.

"Not even a rosy-cheeked barmaid?" I teased. "I understand the girls who work in the beer gardens are terribly fetching."

"I spend very little time in the beer gardens."

I smiled as Phillipe brushed a wave of silvery brown

304

hair from his forehead. My first impression had been correct. Despite his personable manner and his adeptness at light banter, Phillipe was essentially shy and far more sensitive than one might expect.

"You can look out the window again," he told me. "The sheer drop is behind us. We're moving toward the valley. In half an hour you'll have a stunning view of Barivna."

"Is—is the political situation really as tense as I've heard?"

Phillipe frowned, reluctant to discuss it. "There've been a few clashes between the students and the Sturnburg militia," he conceded. "Sturnburg is making unreasonable demands on the King and trying to impose restrictions, but there's nothing for you to be concerned about. Let me tell you about your palace."

"I'm to have a palace?"

"A rather small one," he hastened to add, almost apologetically, "that His Majesty has allocated for your use. But it's white marble, two stories high, with lovely gardens. And the interior is all white and gilding, with crystal chandeliers and exquisite French furniture and blue and violet and silver-gray velvet hangings. The King had it redecorated especially for you."

"I—I'm amazed."

"He put the decorators to work as soon as he returned from Bonn. He's renamed the palace 'Chez Elena.' You'll have a complete staff, chef, butler, footmen, maids. His Majesty wants you to be very comfortable."

I was silent, thinking about the sad-eyed king and all the preparations he had made for my arrival. Phillipe fell silent, too, and a short while later the carriage rounded a curve on the mountain road and I had my first glimpse of the tiny kingdom of Barivna, incredibly lovely in the distance, its capital iridescent in the late afternoon sun. Sumptuous palaces cast shimmering reflections in lakes and lagoons, surrounded by a landscape lush with trees and gardens. The university was a vast complex, the buildings almost as ornate as the palaces. A glittering stream, spanned by several bridges, wound through the streets of the town proper.

"It's beautiful," I said.

"Much larger than it looks from here," Phillipe informed me. "There are outlying villages and rich farmland throughout the valley. Barivna is extremely wealthy and commands a very strategic position."

"I didn't see the barracks," I said as the carriage rounded another curve and the view of Barivna was cut off.

"They're behind the town, blessedly hidden by groves of trees. The King refused to let Sturnburg build barracks within the town itself. They're not very pretty."

"I can imagine."

We fell silent again as the carriage began to descend into the valley, passing lush fields where cattle grazed and small, quaint villages where healthy, robust men and their stocky, pink-cheeked wives paused to wave at the royal carriage, thinking, perhaps, that the King was inside. On the floor of the valley now, there were fields and farms on either side; the town lay three miles ahead. The road broadened and became a wide avenue lined with tall, graceful elms, and soon we were riding through the capital, bowling past the shops and cafes, moving over stone bridges.

A loud, roaring noise startled me. Phillipe smiled, and I looked out the window to see a mob of young men deserting their tables at a beer garden to rush toward the carriage. They yelled and waved and pursued the carriage in a merry pack, their number constantly increasing. Had it not been for their obvious good humor I would have been terrified.

"What—what's that they're yelling?" I asked.

" 'Elena,' " Phillipe said. " 'Bravo Elena.' "

"But how did they know I—"

"All of Barivna knows I went to fetch you. The students have been expecting you, and when they saw the carriage they knew you were inside. When tickets to your performance go on sale they'll probably tear the theater down in their scramble for seats."

"They're certainly exuberant."

"Students must have an idol. You're theirs. You represent freedom, liberation from dull convention. You've dared to defy the bourgeois world, to live with

306

color and boldness, breaking all the rules, making your own choices. They adore you for it."

Phillipe opened the window for me to lean out. As I did so, the roar was deafening. The students swarmed around the carriage like a pack of puppies, running to keep up with the horses, cheering lustily. I felt a glorious exultation as I saw those handsome, glowing young faces and heard the students crying my name. I wished that I had flowers to toss, but I blew kisses instead, and they cheered all the louder. Finally, the carriage rumbled over a narrow bridge and the students fell back, unable to keep apace. Phillipe shook his head as I settled back against the cushions.

"You're going to love Barivna," he promised.

"I've never had such a rousing welcome. They make the students in Oxford and Cambridge seem positively demure."

As we drove on through the town I noticed stern-looking soldiers in white and green uniforms, their helmets adorned with stiff red crests. The soldiers strolled about arrogantly, and several lounged at outdoor cafes, staring at the carriage with sullen eyes. We went by parks and museums and circled one of the small, sparkling blue lakes, then passed a parade ground where more soldiers rode in formation on splendid chestnut horses. Still elated by the students' reception, I paid little heed to the large, brutish men in uniform. We entered sumptuous formal gardens, near the largest lake. A few minutes later the carriage slowed down and turned up a circular drive before coming to a stop in front of Chez Elena.

As Phillipe helped me out of the carriage, I gazed in wonderment at the small, ornate palace. It was even more beautiful than I had imagined; its white marble polished by sunlight, fountains splashing, gardens abloom with roses. The palace stood on the edge of the lake, and I could see the royal castle on the other side, across the water, an immense, majestic edifice that sprawled in splendor, white and gold, with elegant staircases and graceful wings and galleries that extended on either side of the main structure.

"How do you like your new home?" Phillipe inquired.

"I—I'm overcome."

"There are only twenty rooms," he apologized, leading me up the front steps.

"Only twenty?" I teased.

"The drawing room is huge, perfect for receptions, and the ballroom is grand."

"I've always wanted my own ballroom."

The household staff was assembled in the front hall to greet me, the chef beaming broadly in his white mushroom hat, the butler severe in black, the six footmen stalwart and sober in dark blue livery. Five of the maids wore black dresses with crisp white aprons. The sixth, a slender girl with dreamy blue eyes and long copper hair, wore violet-gray silk. Phillipe introduced each servant, and I learned that the blue-eyed girl, Minne, spoke perfect French and was to be my lady's maid.

The butler dismissed the servants, and Phillipe showed me through the house, as pleased as a child showing off a new toy. Each room was more spectacular than the next, the ceilings exquisitely molded with patterns picked out in gold leaf, the white walls with gold leaf panels. Magnificent chandeliers dripped with sparkling crystal pendants, and more pendants dangled from golden wall sconces. The rich velvet drapes and the upholstery of the elegant white and gold French furniture were further distinguished by the blue and violet and silver-gray motif that ran through the entire palace. A gracious spiral staircase curved up to the second floor, the bannisters white, the carpet a deep blue. Phillipe led me upstairs and took me to the door of my bedroom.

"I imagine you're tired," he said, "and I must present myself at the palace and report to His Majesty."

"When will I meet him?"

Phillipe hesitated a moment before replying. "The King is—rather shy, particularly with beautiful women. Don't be too disappointed if you don't see him right away. It may be several days before he sends for you. I'll return this evening to discuss arrangements for your performance."

"Perhaps you'll dine with me."

"I'd be honored."

He smiled that lovely smile again, bowed politely, and left. I went on into the bedroom. Royal blue drapes hung at the windows. The carpet a pale, pale blue was deep and rich. The graceful white bed had a canopy of pale blue silk and royal blue satin, the counterpane of matching royal blue. Tall French doors stood open, leading out to a semi-circular balcony with a white marble railing. Stepping out onto it, I looked down at the gardens and across the lake to the royal castle.

I found it hard to believe that only yesterday I had been sitting in a chair at the inn, wondering how I was going to pay for a train ticket. It seemed weeks ago, somehow, and Franz and Wagner were already a part of the past. So much had happened so quickly. Was I really in this small, incredible kingdom, standing on the balcony of my own palace? I felt a curious disorientation, as though I were in the middle of a lovely dream and would awaken at any moment to reality. Sighing, I went back inside and looked around the room as though to determine if it were real or part of the dream.

I was still in a daze when Klaus, one of the footmen, came in with the first of my bags, and Minne appeared a few minutes later to help me unpack. Seventeen years old, shy, demure, Minne was as efficient as she was pretty, a dreamy-eyed charmer who blushed and lowered her eyes when the strapping and sternly attractive Klaus returned with the rest of the bags. I suspected a downstairs romance was blooming, a suspicion that was confirmed when Klaus left the room and Minne sighed wistfully.

After I unpacked, I explored the palace more thoroughly, took a leisurely bath and selected my gown for the evening. Although it was still too early to expect Phillipe, I began to dress, putting on a deep rose silk with a provocatively low bodice and off-the-shoulder sleeves. Minne proved herself extremely gifted with hair, arranging my ebony locks in a sculptured roll and affixing a pale white rose above my temple.

I stood up to examine myself in the mirror.

"Thank you, Minne," I said. "You've done a marvelous job. You're a treasure. And I've a feeling Klaus thinks so, too."

She blushed prettily, lowering her eyes again. I smiled and told her I was going to stroll in the gardens for a while and wouldn't be needing her any more that evening. Minne curtsied and left, perhaps to search for her handsome footman, and I went downstairs into the gardens. The setting sun spangled the lake with shimmering silvergold sunbursts, and the pale blue sky was gradually darkening. I strolled down the formal paths, inhaling the fragrance of roses, serenaded by the soft splashing of the fountains.

It was so beautiful, so serene. Shadows began to lengthen like bolts of dark blue-gray velvet, and a cool breeze drifted over the water, causing leaves to rustle quietly. Across the lake, the sprawling palace was bathed in dark gold for a few moments, and then the sun vanished and it was shrouded in shadows that deepened from gray to hazy purple. Strolling down another path, I thought about the students who had given me such a rousing welcome earlier, and I thought about Phillipe, so young, so polite. But most of all I thought about the shy, enigmatic king who had turned Barivna into such a wonderland of beauty and culture.

King Karl was forty-six years old, a very private person who eschewed all pomp and ceremony and rarely showed himself in public. He devoted his life to art and architecture and to the university. Although his love for beautiful women was well known, he had never married, not even to produce an heir. I wondered why, and so did most of Europe. His failure to marry was a mystery to all, and there had been a great deal of speculation. Karl's gentility and generosity were well known, but the man himself remained a mystery.

As I started back toward the palace I heard a horse cantering up the drive. I wondered who could be calling. It was still early for Phillipe, who in any event would have come by carriage. The horse stopped. I heard a curt, harsh order, then the sound of boots on the steps. As I stepped into the front hall, Otto, the butler, was just coming out of the small front parlor. He seemed disturbed, but when he caught sight of me he straightened his shoulders and resumed his customary, unperturbed manner to inform me that a Captain Heinrich Schroder wished to see me and was waiting in the parlor.

"Thank you, Otto. Wait a moment and then show him into the drawing room. You may bring brandy a little later on."

Otto nodded, and I went on into the sumptuously appointed drawing room. Captain Heinrich Schroder. Why would a military man be calling on me? I had the feeling it was not merely a friendly visit to welcome me to Barivna. Stepping over to one of the windows and pulling back the rich silver-gray drape, I struck a deliberately casual pose, slowly turning around as Otto brought Captain Schroder into the room and announced him.

"Captain Schroder," I said politely, giving him a brief nod.

Schroder clicked his heels together and bowed curtly. Otto left the room, and the captain stood erect, his white helmet with its stiff red crest held under one arm. He stared at me with blue-gray eyes that seemed to smolder with hostility. His light brown hair was clipped very short, his skull visible beneath the fuzz. His nose was large, his mouth wide and full, a cruel mouth designed to curl thinly at the corners. A jagged scar ran from the edge of his right cheekbone down to his jaw—apparently a saber scar, famous as a symbol of Prussian virility.

"Won't you be seated, Captain Schroder?" I said in French.

"I prefer to stand." He answered in German.

His voice was deep, a harsh, gutteral rumble that seemed to grate as it rose from his chest. Six feet tall and heavy-set without being stocky, he exuded an aura of coarseness and brutal strength. His black knee boots were highly glossed, and his white breeches fit like a second skin, tightly stretched over long, muscular legs and left no doubt as to his generous physical endowments. His long-sleeved forest green tunic had a tight collar trimmed with gold braid. Gold epaulettes rested on his broad shoulders.

"I assume this is not a social call," I remarked, still speaking French.

"No, it is not a social call," he said, this time in French. "I am Captain of the Royal Guard. I have come to order you to leave Barivna at once."

"Indeed?"

I looked at him with cool, level eyes, refusing to be intimidated.

"I don't like your manner, Captain Schroder, and I certainly don't like your choice of words. No one orders me to do anything. I was invited to Barivna by King Karl. I rather doubt that he sent you here."

Schroder smiled, the wide mouth spreading, curling up at the corners as I knew it would. It was the cruelest smile I had ever seen, calculated to make the blood run cold. No doubt he smiled just such a smile when he ran an enemy through with his saber; or when he raped a young, helpless maiden—activities I felt sure he had indulged in frequently. Schroder was clearly sadistic, a brute who thrived on cruelty.

"No, Karl did not send me," he said. "He knows nothing of this call."

"I didn't think so."

"It is my job to look after his safety."

"And I present a threat?"

"Your presence here is an agitation, a dangerous agitation. The students are already unruly and rebellious. We have had to put them down several times already, using harsher measures each time. Your presence in Barivna can only cause more unrest."

"I fail to see your reasoning, Captain Schroder."

"There was a disturbance in town only this afternoon, a near riot caused by your arrival. The students went wild, shouting, charging your carriage like a band of ruffians, disturbing the peace."

"It was a harmless display."

"It could have turned into a riot. There could have been serious injuries. We cannot risk another such outbreak."

"We?"

"The Royal Guard. I told you, I am in charge of all

312

military personnel in Barivna. I receive my orders directly from Sturnburg."

"And you were ordered to send me away," I said.

"Precisely."

"I'm afraid you've wasted your time, Captain Schroder. I came here to open King Karl's new theater, and I've no intention of leaving until the King himself asks me to leave."

"You are making a mistake, Elena Lopez."

"Am I?"

"A mistake that could be quite costly."

There was menace in his manner and his voice. Those blue-gray eyes looked at me with smoldering hostility so intense that I couldn't help but feel a tremor of alarm. I could understand his wanting to force me to leave Barivna, but I couldn't understand that active hostility. Heinrich Schroder was a dangerous man, vicious, sadistic, and he hated me. That had been apparent from the moment he swaggered into the room. But why?

Otto chose that moment to enter with a crystal decanter of brandy and two glasses on a tray. He set the tray down, straightened up and looked at me for instructions.

"Thank you, Otto," I said. "That will be all."

Otto left, and I indicated the brandy. Placing his helmet on the table, Schroder took hold of the decanter, uncapped it and poured a glassful. The brandy glass was large, but it looked extremely fragile with those large, brutal fingers curled around it. He lifted it to his lips, tilted his head back and tossed the brandy down in one gulp. He filled the glass again, looking at me with cold calculation now, the smile flickering.

"You are very obstinate, Madamoiselle."

"I don't like bullies."

"You are a fool. I could crush you."

"I rather doubt that."

"Sturnburg won't tolerate another of Karl's whores at this point. He has already spent a fortune redecorating this palace, and we have no doubt that he is prepared to pay lavishly for your services."

"I'm afraid I'm going to have to ask you to leave, Captain Schroder."

Schroder tossed down another glass of brandy and set the glass on the tray. Folding his arms across his chest, he looked at me as though I were an insect he contemplated squashing.

"You are very beautiful," he remarked. "I can see why Karl is so enamored. If I had the price, I would not mind having you myself, but I am sure I could not afford you."

"There's not enough money in the world," I assured him. "I suggest you leave now, Captain, before I'm forced to call the footmen and have them throw you out."

"No need. I should not want them injured in the attempt."

Schroder picked up his helmet and held it stiffly in his arm. It made the picture of the brutal Hun complete.

"You intend to stay?" he asked.

"I intend to stay."

Schroder's mouth curled once more in that sadistic smile, and his gray-blue eyes were filled with savage amusement, as though he were contemplating some especially delightful cruelty.

"You are going to regret your decision, Elena Lopez. I personally shall see that you regret it."

I pointed toward the door. Schroder hesitated.

"One thing more: I would advise you not to mention our little discussion to anyone, particularly young Du Gard. It would only make things all the more unpleasant for you."

"In other words, you don't want the King to find out about it."

"Karl is a fool, too. Sturnburg will tolerate fools just so long."

"Goodbye, Captain Schroder."

Schroder clicked his heels together again, executed another stiff bow and left the room, the fringe on his epaulettes shimmering. I could hear his boots stamping on the marble tiles, and a few moments later I heard his horse galloping away down the drive. What a dreadful person he was. If the other guardsmen were anything like Schroder, it was no wonder there was so much unrest in Barivna. He had come to menace, to threaten, to try and frighten me into leaving, but I knew full well that his power was limited. As long as Karl remained on the throne, neither Schroder nor any of his men would dare harm me. Common sense told me that it had all been a grand bluff.

Nevertheless, a feeling of uneasiness remained. I was shaken by his visit, far more shaken than I cared to admit.

XXVIII

I was always nervous before a performance, but on this night the tension was worse than usual. I had created a new dance in King Karl's honor, a lively, graceful waltz with a touch of fandango, and I had had only a week of rehearsals. The musicians were marvelous, but I was still unsure of myself. The curtain was to go up in half an hour, and when I looked through the peek hole I could see that the sumptuous new theater was almost filled—with the exception of two rows near the front, reserved, no doubt, for a group who would arrive later on.

I went back to my dressing room and tried to calm down. I kept telling myself that the performance would go well. Once the house lights were dimmed and the music began and I started to dance, the nervous tension would dissolve as it always did. It was the interminable waiting that caused apprehension. Try as I might, I couldn't shake the feeling that something disastrous was going to happen tonight. I had felt it ever since I arrived at the theater. How I wished Millie had been there to cheer me up with her bright chatter.

Standing before the mirror, I examined myself with a critical eye. I had done my hair in the customary French roll, fastening a purple velvet flower above my temple. My make-up—pale mauve shadow on the lids, a faint pink rouge on my cheeks, a soft pink on my lips—was more subtle than the usual stage make-up. The seamstress had done a marvelous job on my costume, a shimmering creation of vivid purple silk aglitter with shiny black spangles. The low bodice was trimmed with purple ostrich feather, as were the sleeves, and there was a row of ostrich feather around the hem of the full, swirling skirt as well.

Picking up the exquisite black lace fan I would use in lieu of castanets, I toyed with it nervously. I had been in Barivna for ten days, and I had yet to meet the King. He hadn't sent for me, and Phillipe wasn't even certain that King Karl would attend the performance. If he did come, he would slip into the Royal Box unobtrusively. The King had sent warm messages through Phillipe, telling me how pleased he was that I had come to Barivna, saying he hoped I found Chez Elena satisfactory. But ever since my arrival he had remained closed up in his palace, available only to a few intimates. Was something wrong? Was he sorry that he had sent for me? Was he worried that my presence might indeed prove "a dangerous agitation" to the students?

The students. I smiled to myself. I had seen no more of Captain Schroder, and I had seen his soldiers only when I went for my afternoon drives in the magnificent carriage the King had provided, but the students were very much in evidence. Almost every night a group of them assembled under my balcony to serenade me, and, of course, I asked them in for refreshments each time. They were a boisterous group, filling the elegant drawing room with hearty laughter, and several of them had become my friends, calling on me whenever they could. Chez Elena was already more popular than any of the beer gardens, and I found myself conducting a salon for budding young poets and painters and philosophers.

A resounding knock on the door brought me out of my revery. Before I could respond, the door burst open and a pack of young men spilled into the dressing room. There were only three, actually, but Eric, Hans and Wilhelm *en masse* managed to seem like a pack. Wilhelm grabbed me and gave me a mighty hug. Eric handed me a bouquet of roses. Hans grinned and began to recite a poem he had written about my beauty, but Wilhelm gave a groan and, stepping behind the exuberant poet, slammed a palm over his mouth, stopping him mid-verse.

318

"She doesn't want to hear that nonsense now! You can recite it to her some other time."

Hans pulled Wilhelm's hand from his mouth and whirled around to glare murderously. "Some people just don't appreciate art!" he exclaimed.

Wilhelm gave him a friendly shove. Eric shook his head, disassociating himself from his rowdy companions.

"The roses are from all three of us," he told me.

"We combined our resources," Wilhelm added. "We wanted you to know we cared."

"Thank you very much. They're lovely," I said, suspecting that they had totally depleted their resources.

"Lovely flowers for a lovely lady," Hans said gallantly.

Wilhelm made a face. Eric sighed. I smiled and put the roses in a vase as the boys watched, all three beaming, all three handsome and glowing with youth and vitality. These young men had taken it upon themselves to make me feel welcome in Barivna, a trio of lively gallants who showered me with attention.

Eric was tall and slender with dark brown hair and soulful brown eyes. He painted nudes and longed to go to Paris and use real models. Hans was a plump youth with floppy blond hair, merry blue eyes and a sunny disposition not at all in keeping with the epic tragedies he churned out at an alarming rate. He loved to recite them and, alas, knew each by heart. Wilhelm was a robust, muscular redhead with roguish brown eyes, humped nose and a lopsided grin. The university's champion wrestler, Wilhelm lived to grapple on the mats with a groaning opponent thrashing beneath him.

"Do you have good seats?" I inquired.

"Ten rows back," Eric said. "We had to fight to get them. Wilhelm barreled through for us, knocking the mob aside. Someone jumped Hans just as we reached the ticket window, but I managed to plop down our money and get the seats before someone shoved me out of the way."

"I hope I don't disappoint you."

"Not a chance," Wilhelm assured me. "You're going to be sensational!"

"All Barivna's been waiting for this night," Hans said. "I just hope there isn't any trou—"

319

He cut himself short, glancing nervously at his companions. Both Eric and Wilhelm glared at him. Hans sighed and looked down at his feet, painfully aware that he'd made a faux pas.

"Are you expecting some kind of trouble?" I asked.

"Of course not!" Wilhelm exclaimed.

"Certainly not!" Eric added.

"Something is afoot," I said. "You might as well tell me about it. I'm used to trouble, you know. I'm not likely to fall to pieces."

"As a matter of fact, there was a group of soldiers in front of the theater," Hans said. "Not a large group, no more than thirty at the most. They glared at us as we came in and looked as though they were planning a demonstration of some kind. It's nothing to worry about. There are over five hundred students here tonight, and we're not about to let any rotten soldiers spoil your performance."

"I—I see."

Wilhelm scowled and yanked Hans' head back against his shoulder. "Now you've upset her!" he snarled.

"I almost expected something of this sort," I said calmly. "I've had a strange feeling ever since I arrived at the theater. You see, Captain Schroder is very unhappy about my being in Barivna."

Hans struggled, trying to say something more, but Eric spoke first.

"Schroder's all bluff and bluster," Eric told me. "He likes to strut about and look fierce, but he hasn't nearly as much authority as he'd like to think he has. Sturnburg is very cautious. They're not about to disturb the status quo."

"I don't quite understand just what the status quo is."

"It's simple enough to explain," Wilhelm said. "Sturnburg has a military stranglehold on Barivna—" He looped a muscular arm around Hans' throat in demonstration. "They could tighten their grip and crush the life out of it—"

He yanked his arm back, forcing Hans up on his tiptoes. Hans made a series of gurgling, gasping noises, blue eyes wide with alarm, mouth working like a fish's as he struggled for breath. Wilhelm chuckled and loosened his hold.

"But actually they maintain a very loose grip," he continued, "giving the King and Barivna plenty of room to breathe, knowing full well there'd be terrible repercussions if they really were to squeeze too tightly."

He flexed the muscles of his arm, causing Hans to splutter, and then he released his victim and gave him an amiable shove. Hans coughed and gasped, plump cheeks still a bright pink from Wilhelm's demonstration.

"You damn near choked me!" he protested noisily.

"I should have broken your neck while I had it in the crook of my arm," Wilhelm told him. "The situation is both vexing and uncomfortable, Elena, but there's no real danger. Half a dozen states would invade Sturnburg if they made a serious move against Barivna."

"Don't worry about the soldiers," Eric said. "They're not likely to try anything tonight."

Wilhelm nodded in agreement. "If they do, we'll take care of 'em."

"We'd better go take our seats," Hans said, adjusting his neckcloth. "Good luck, Elena. We'll all be cheering for you."

"Thank you for coming back. I'll see you all later."

"You certainly will!" Wilhelm exclaimed. "Come on, you two. It's almost time for Elena to go on."

Their exit was as noisy and boisterous as their arrival had been, and shortly after they left, the stage manager came to inform me that the curtain would go up in five minutes. I made another quick inspection in the mirror, touching the side of my hair, adjusting one of the feathered purple sleeves. As I left the dressing room and walked down the hall toward the spacious backstage area, I could smell new paint and varnish. The traditional smells of dust and flaking plaster were missing, as was the clutter of flats and ropes and boxes.

The silver backdrop curtain gleamed brightly, and a stagehand stood ready to pull the ropes that would lift the heavy purple velvet front curtain. I moved quietly across the stage to peer through the peek hole once more. The theater was a gleaming jewel box, white and gold and red, crystal pendants glittering on the chandeliers. The musicians were in the pit, instruments at the ready, and the house lights were beginning to dim. The students were talking excitedly and waving their programs, their faces young and bright and eager. The two rows of seats near the front were still empty. I had a good idea who would be sitting in them, and I was ready. I took my place in the wings, not at all nervous now, thankful that Hans' slip of the tongue had given me time to prepare for what I suspected would be an ordeal.

The house lights went out. A hush fell over the audience. The music began, softly at first, gradually swelling into a melodic waltz, and the stagehand tugged on the rope. The purple curtain parted, rising in scalloped folds to reveal the shimmering silver backdrop with shadows dancing across it as the footlights flickered. I took a deep breath and began to sway with the music, letting it sweep over me, and then, as the strains of the waltz merged into sumptuous melody, I smiled radiantly and sailed onstage, fluttering the black lace fan, black spangles all aglitter as my purple skirt swirled. The applause was thundering, and there were hundreds of cheers. Still smiling, I acknowledged the reception with a slight nod, waltzing, whirling, using the fan skillfully.

The music was rich and romantic, and I was a vibrant young girl aglow with the joy of first love, dancing joyously in an empty ballroom to celebrate the love that filled me with such splendid bliss. The dance was a drama, as were all my dances, but I was no longer Elena. I was the young girl in Cornwall, remembering, conveying what I had felt when the blossoms of emotion had first unfurled. I thought of Brence, dancing for him, remembering only the joy, blocking out the grief. I sailed on the wings of love, time dropping away as I danced.

There was a disturbance in the audience. As I turned, skirts lifting and belling, I noticed that the two rows in front were still empty. The Royal Box was in shadow, curtains half closed. Was that a pale face peering down at me, or was it my imagination? The waltz music flowed, and I flowed with it, dancing, smiling, and a clicking undercurrent stole into the melody, a subtle change taking

322

place as the Spanish melody gradually rose to replace the waltz. I adapted my movements as waltz faded and the fandango took over. I swayed. I clicked my heels, a Spanish maiden now, in love as before but far more sensual in nature, dancing in the hot sun for my sullen, dark-eyed caballero.

I heard loud voices, murmurs of alarm. Soldiers were parading down the aisle, talking loudly, deliberately making as much noise as possible. It had begun. I ignored them and continued to dance for my invisible Spanish youth as they filled up the two empty rows and began to exchange crude comments about me in rough, strident voices. The students immediately behind them tried to shut them up, but that only spurred them on. The musicians played nervously, concentration broken, discordant notes stealing into the music. I pretended not to notice anything, and then the first rotten tomato sailed across the stage, splattering against the backdrop.

"Whore! You call that dancing!"

"Go back to the streets!"

"Strumpet! Corrupting our young men!"

"Get out of Barivna!"

"Did you hear what they called her!" I recognized Wilhelm's voice over the din. "Look, they threw another tomato! Are we going to stand for this outrage?"

"No!" the students roared.

"Come on! Let's get 'em!"

The music stopped. The musicians put down their instruments and huddled in the pit as more tomatoes flew over their heads. The whole audience was standing now, all shouting. One of the soldiers raced down the aisle, hoping to reach the stage. A husky student flew in the air behind him and brought him down roughly. The other students cheered. I ducked as another tomato flew across the stage, almost hitting my shoulder. I saw Schroder in the aisle watching with an evil smile on his face. When the next tomato came, I didn't duck—I caught it in my hand. Pulpy red seeds spurted out, but most of the tomato remained intact. I took careful aim and let fly. The tomato splattered magnificently as it hit Schroder's jaw. The students roared, cheered, and at least a hundred of them poured over the seats to launch their attack on the soldiers, yelling lustily as they fell upon the troublemakers.

The melee began in earnest, then, and it was spectacular, spilling out into the lobby. The soldiers fought viciously, but they were hopelessly outnumbered. More and more students leaped into the fray, fists flying, and soldier after soldier went down, three or four students on top. Hans and Eric had one of them in the aisle, Hans sitting astride him as Eric seized his hair and pounded his head on the floor, and Wilhelm was doing his best to strangle another. I stepped to the edge of the stage and watched with a feeling of savage satisfaction as I saw Schroder stumble to his knees and disappear beneath a tangle of bodies.

"Out with 'em!" Wilhelm yelled. "Let's throw 'em out!"

Arm still hooked around the throat of his soldier, Wilhelm twisted the man's arm and shoved it brutally up between his shoulder blades, goose-stepping him up the aisle as his companions cheered. Uniforms torn, faces battered, other soldiers were forced up the aisle, still struggling violently. The roars of delight were so loud that the elegant chandeliers trembled. When the final soldier had been evicted, the young combatants came back inside to take their seats. Wilhelm clasped his hands over his head and shook them victoriously. There was a deafening round of applause as he sank into his seat, and after a few moments the audience settled down, waiting for me to say something.

I smiled. They smiled back. I spread my skirts and bowed.

"I'm pleased to see that chivalry isn't dead," I called. "Thank you, my gallants."

Again they cheered. I nodded to the flustered, still frightened musicians as the cheering died down.

"Gentlemen? Shall we start at the beginning?"

They began to shuffle their music, as stagehands rushed to clean the stage of tomatoes. With cool poise that belied the elation inside me, I stepped back to the wing. I felt gloriously vindicated, and when the music began again I danced as I had never danced before, sailing through the waltz, performing the fandango with new verve. After

324

the dance was over I performed one encore and then another, doing yet a third before I stopped. When, exhausted but aglow, I stepped to the footlights to take my bows, the audience leaped to their feet to yell and stamp and applaud, giving me a standing ovation that went on and on. Ushers began to parade down the aisle with bouquets of flowers, red, orange, yellow, blue, a rainbow of bouquets from my student admirers.

I bowed again and again. I waved. I blew kisses. Finally, I gave a signal to a stagehand and stepped back with an armload of bouquets as the curtain fell. The lusty cheering continued. Backstage, I was surrounded by a jubilant crew who congratulated me noisily, faces split with wide grins. I was eventually able to return to my dressing room, the theater still filled with jubilant yells. Setting down the bouquets, I looked at myself in the mirror, a smile on my lips. Tonight had been a triumph, my greatest triumph, perhaps. I wondered what the press would make of it. Newspapers all over Europe would doubtlessly carry accounts of the riot, each more exaggerated than the next.

I removed my costume and stepped behind the tall screen to slip into my rich maroon taffeta gown. I touched up my make-up and was straightening my hair when once again the door flew open and Eric, Hans and Wilhelm rushed in, accompanied this time by six or seven other youths.

"You were magnificent!" Hans cried. "Magnificent!"

"And what a marksman!" Wilhelm exclaimed. "I saw you catch that tomato, saw you hit Schroder sploosh in the face with it! Those sodding soldiers will think twice before messing with us again, I can tell you for sure! Did you see me? Did you see what I did to that brute?"

"I saw. You were wonderful, all of you."

They continued to carry on, and I wondered where Phillipe was, wondered why he hadn't come backstage. Had he been here tonight? Had King Karl been in the Royal Box? I couldn't be certain. Perhaps Phillipe was waiting out in the hall for the boys to leave before he came in. They were making so much noise I couldn't even think properly. When I finished with my hair, Eric handed me my reticule and Hans scooped up the bouquets as Wilhelm seized my elbow and hurried me out of the dressing room, the others following on our heels.

"I—I really—I should wait for—"

"No arguments! We've got a surprise!"

I let them lead me down the hall. Surrounded by the merry pack, caught up in their excitement, I realized that any further protest would be futile. Hans flung open the side door and Wilhelm rushed me outside onto the steps. The cheering was deafening, a thundering earthquake of noise that seemed to make the ground tremble. At least two hundred students crowded around the steps and spilled out onto the street beyond, several of them holding torches that blazed with leaping orange flames. My carriage was in their midst, the horses stamping and neighing, terrified by the uproar and the leaping flames that drove away the darkness.

"Elena! Elena! Bravo Elena!"

Wilhelm released me and pushed forward with four other youths to unharness the horses. My driver protested vehemently. Wilhelm shoved him aside. I stood there on the steps, slightly dazed. Hans plunged through the mob with the bouquets, placing them inside the carriage, and Eric took my hand and led me forward.

"Make way, lads! Make way for Elena! Ready, Wilhelm?"

"Ready!"

"Go on, Elena! Climb in!"

Two of the students led the horses to one side. Six strapping youths lifted the shafts of the carriage, three on either side. I climbed inside surrounded by flowers, and with gleeful yells the boys began to run, pulling the carriage down the street. It bounced dreadfully. I was knocked from side to side until I had the sense to catch hold of the window frame for support. The mob of students ran along on either side, waving their torches, yelling my name with lusty glee.

"Elena! Elena! Elena!"

"Out of the way up ahead! Out of the way!"

"Watch that damn bridge! Don't stumble on the cobbles!"

They carried me past the lighted cafes and beer gardens, past the stately museums. I leaned out the window

326

and waved, and the students roared all the louder. Torch flames leaped. The carriage rocked and swayed. We were moving along the side of the lake, and now that we were outside the main part of town the uproar seemed even greater. Eric grabbed a torch and ran beside one of the windows, smiling at me, and Hans was right behind him, blond hair flopping over his brow, cheeks bright pink with excitement. I continued to wave until we pulled up in the drive.

The carriage stopped in front of Chez Elena, tilting precariously as the boys let go of the shafts. Wilhelm hurried around to help me alight, holding my hand in a bone-crushing grip. His red hair was damp with perspiration, his roguish brown eyes dancing with delight as he smiled a lopsided smile and led me toward the steps. Hans and Eric scrambled into the carriage to gather up the bouquets. Behind the mob of students, the driver came trudging wearily up the drive, leading the two horses by the reins and looking thoroughly disgruntled. I smiled and gave my attention to the rapt young mob that filled the front yard, torches held aloft.

"Say something, Elena!" Wilhelm urged.

"Thank you!" I called. "Thank you! I love you all!"

They roared their appreciation, and they helped the driver take horses and carriage around to the stables, and then they left, torches flaming, voices raised in song. As I turned to go inside I was startled to see Phillipe standing in the shadows beside the door. He moved forward, elegant in formal attire, dark lapels gleaming, neckcloth snowy white.

"Phillipe! I—I didn't see you."

"You've had quite a night."

"You were at the theater?"

He nodded, smiling. "I was there."

"You didn't come backstage. I thought—"

"I expected the students might do something like this. That's why I came on ahead. His Majesty was at the theater tonight, too, Elena."

"He was?" I asked nervously.

"He thought you were marvelous," Phillipe said. "He asked me to come fetch you and bring you to the palace. It's very late, and he knows you must be tired, but he thought you might like to have a midnight supper with him."

"I—I'll have to change."

"There's no hurry. The King is an extremely patient man."

XXIX

I had changed into my loveliest gown, a pale oyster gray
satin completely overlaid with dark, delicate black lace
in floral designs, lace as fine as cobwebs. The long, tight
sleeves left my shoulders bare, and the bodice was low,
exposing a great deal of bosom. The full skirt belled out
at the waist to cascade over half a dozen pale pink underskirts. I had fastened a pink velvet rose above my
temple, another at the side of my waist. As Phillipe
helped me out of the royal carriage, I felt sure that I
had never looked more glamorous.

The lake shimmered in the moonlight, silvery threads
dancing on the surface, and a gentle breeze drifted
through the formal gardens. I heard a solitary bird
warbling quietly from his perch in one of the trees. It was
well after midnight as Phillipe led me up a long flight of
white marble steps awash with moonlight. The palace
was truly imposing, a vast, sprawling structure shrouded
in shadow. My skirts made a silken rustle as we climbed.

"The King does not sleep well," Phillipe explained.
"He rarely goes to bed before dawn. He roams the
palace, examining his paintings, his statues, his various
collections. Sometimes he plays solitaire in front of the
fire, and sometimes he just strolls in the gardens."

"He must be very lonely."

"He has a great many problems," Phillipe said quietly,
"and there are very few people in whom he can confide."

"He's lucky to have you, Phillipe."

"I'm only a minor aide," he protested, "not important

at all. His Highness entrusted me with looking after you because—well, because I requested it. I was very eager to meet you."

"Oh?"

"I'd seen you dance, you see. In London. While I was still attending the university, I went to England on holiday with one of my friends, and we managed to get tickets for your performance. It was—it was one of the most exciting nights in my life."

"You have never mentioned it before."

"You were the most beautiful creature I'd ever seen, incandescent with beauty, aglow with fire and passion. I was very nervous that day I came to the inn. I expected a mercenary creature who would be rude and sullen and perhaps even throw things."

"I had been throwing things earlier on," I confessed.

A footman opened the heavy door, and we entered the palace. We were in a long, sumptuous hall with pale ivory walls. Chandeliers hung from the exquisitely gilt ceiling, crystal pendants aglitter. A dark gold carpet covered the floor, and it seemed to extend for miles. Phillipe nodded to the footman, and led me down the hall.

"I fancied myself an authority on Elena Lopez. I'd read all the stories about you, everything I could find, and then I met you and discovered a completely different person."

"Disappointed?" I asked.

"On the contrary. We turn here."

He led me down a smaller hall, this one not as brightly lit, all done in pale blue and white and gold, magnificent paintings on the walls, mostly French. I recognized several Watteaus, a Boucher, a stunning group of small Meissoniers framed in ornate gold. We moved down a flight of stairs and into yet another part of the palace. It was drafty here, the air chilly, and there was a distinct musty smell.

"This is my last official duty," Phillipe said casually. "I'm leaving Barivna tomorrow."

"Phillipe! I—I'm sorry to hear that."

He sighed and smiled sadly. "I received another letter from my father. He wants me to return to Touraine. He

330

insists, as a matter of fact. He claims he is no longer able to manage the estate on his own."

"I thought you had a brother."

"He's away at the Sorbonne and will be for the next two years. The estate is very large, you see. There are over fifty tenant farms, and the chateau is in need of repairs and—Father used words like duty and responsibility and so on, all calculated to make me feel guilty. I suppose I should have returned to Touraine a long time ago."

"You hate the idea so much?"

"Especially now," he said.

We stopped before an ornate white door with lovely tapestries hanging on either side. Phillipe looked at me with those clear blue eyes, so sad now, despite the gentle smile on his lips, and I suddenly realized that he was in love with me. He was much too polite, much too genteel to declare himself, but there was no need for words.

"I wonder if I might write to you?" he asked.

"Of course you may, Phillipe."

"And when you return to Paris—well, I'll be coming up to Paris, and I thought perhaps I might call on you."

"I'll expect you to."

He gazed at me for a moment longer, leaving so much unsaid, and then he sighed again and indicated the door.

"The King maintains an elaborate set of rooms for show," he told me, "but this is his private apartment, where he comes when he wants to get away from all the pressures. He's expecting you, Elena. There's no need for me to announce you. The King doesn't believe in formality except on state occasions."

"Will I see you tomorrow?"

Phillipe shook his head. "I'll be leaving first thing in the morning. My bags are already packed."

"I shall miss you, Phillipe."

"And I you."

"Have a safe journey. I won't say goodbye. I'll simply look forward to your letters and count on seeing you again in Paris."

"You shall," he promised.

He opened the door for me, and, after a moment's hesitation, I went inside. Phillipe closed the door behind me, and I found myself in a surprisingly small room filled with comfortable clutter. Unframed paintings leaned against the wall. Tables were piled high with books and journals, and there were several rolls of paper that looked like blueprints. The furniture was elegant but unimposing, the atmosphere snug and welcoming. A fire crackled in the lovely white marble fireplace, spreading warmth throughout the room, and only two lamps burned, making hazy pools of light and creating nests of shadow in the rest of the room.

For a moment I thought I was alone, but when I stepped further into the room, King Karl arose from a wing-backed chair in the shadows. Moving into the light, he smiled a warm, timid smile.

"Elena," he said. "We meet at last."

I made a deep curtsy. "Your Majesty."

"Please, I'm 'Your Majesty' when I'm dressed in splendid attire and entertaining dull, pompous statesmen. Here I'm simply Karl, a lonely man who's grateful you've accepted his invitation."

"It was kind of you to invite me."

The King took my hand and lifted it to his lips.

"I had wanted to ask you earlier, but there were—problems, distractions. I trust you've been comfortable?"

"Very."

"You're extremely lovely, my dear, incredibly so, even more so in this light than behind the footlights. I can quite honestly say that I've never seen a more beautiful woman."

"You're very gallant."

The King kissed my hand and held it a moment longer before releasing it, and then he stepped back. Not much taller than I, he was solidly built, a bit too fleshy, although his stoutness was not unattractive. His hands were long and sensitive, and his expression was as melancholy as I remembered it being in the portrait I had seen in Bonn. His light brown hair was turning silver at the temples. Over dark trousers and a white cambric shirt he wore a quilted dressing robe of rich blue brocade, the lapels heavy black satin, as was the sash tied at his waist. His slippers of soft black kid were obviously well worn.

Middle-aged, weary, Karl of Barivna was not a hand-

332

some man, but there was a compelling quality about him, much warmth and a curious compassion that I sensed immediately. He was neither grand nor imposing, yet he was undeniably regal, the authority unmistakable even though veiled by his timid, unassuming manner. One sensed great kindness and an even greater vulnerability. His loneliness was immediately apparent, something he had lived with for a very long time.

"I'm so pleased you could come," he said. "I enjoyed your performance tonight very much."

"I'm sorry about the fracas at the beginning. I hope you don't think that I deliberately instigated it."

"Of course not. Truth to tell, I rather enjoyed that, too. Schroder and his soldiers went altogether too far. Don't give it another thought, my dear. Come, sit by the fire."

He took my hand and led me to a chair. Then he pulled a silk bell cord and took the chair opposite mine. The small table between us was set with gold-rimmed delicate china and glittering, ornate silverware, napkins of the finest linen, crystal glasses on fragile stems. A minute or so later the heavy velvet curtains concealing an archway parted, and a footman in palace livery appeared with a cart. Silent, efficient, he set ornate silver covered dishes on the table as well as a tall bottle of champagne in a silver bucket filled with crushed ice. He removed the covers from the dishes, twirled the bottle of champagne once or twice, uncorked it and then left as unobtrusively as he had come, rolling the cart in front of him.

"Hungry?" Karl inquired.

"Actually, I'm famished. I never eat before a performance."

Smiling, Karl poured champagne into our glasses, then took my plate and filled it with food, waiting on me as though it were the natural thing to do. I found myself completely at ease with him, not the least bit of strain between us. Karl was utterly charming, still rather shy, asking me questions about myself and listening with total absorption as I told him about my girlhood in Cornwall and the early days with Madame Olga. I gave him a brief account of my career as Elena Lopez, and he laughed quietly when I described the deception Anthony had so successfully put over on the paying public.

"Of course, everyone knows I'm English now," I continued. "It was in all the papers—the shocking truth revealed at last. The public found it delightful, and somehow it only enhanced the legend."

"And your love affairs?" he inquired.

"Vastly exaggerated. They're already making up stories about us, you know. The Paris papers arrived yesterday, and were full of highly colorful accounts of how Elena Lopez conquered the King of Barivna. You have set me up in my own palace and we're shamelessly flaunting our affair."

"Would that the stories were true," he said quietly.

He looked up at me with a sad, lost longing in his eyes. Something about Karl had puzzled me ever since I arrived, and I suddenly realized what it was—a total lack of sexuality. He was warm, charming, attentive, clearly interested in me and pleased to have me with him, yet there was not the least glimmer of active desire as he gazed at me. I was beginning to suspect the reason for that haunted look.

"More pheasant?" he inquired.

"I couldn't eat another bite. It—it's very late."

"Must you go?"

He was clearly distressed at the thought of my leaving so soon. Those sad eyes were filled with concern. I felt a great empathy for him, pitying him without really knowing the full reason. I wanted to take his hand and smile a reassuring smile and speak soft, consoling words. There was a moment of silence, and Karl seemed tense, almost on the verge of panic. This man needed me tonight, and his need was great even though there was nothing at all physical about it.

"I would love to stay, if I'm not intruding," I said. "I'm always stimulated after a performance. I won't be able to sleep for hours."

The look of distress vanished. Karl poured more champagne for us and relaxed, looking as though the weight of the world had been lifted from his shoulders. He plainly dreaded being alone tonight. I suspected that there were nights when his melancholia became almost unbearable, that tonight was one of them. I asked him questions about himself, and he talked freely and a bit wistfully about his childhood, his early manhood, his student days in Bonn. He had been an enthusiastic horseman, inordinately proud of his stables, and at seventeen he had owned a fine line of pure-blooded Arabians as beautiful as fresh snow, as fast as lightning.

"I wasn't aware of your interest in horses," I said.

"I had to give it up. After the accident I—there were a great many things I had to give up."

"Accident?"

"I was riding one of the Arabians. We leaped a fence, and I miscalculated. The horse fell—on top of me. Two of its legs were broken and it had to be shot. My own injuries were—" Karl paused, gazing into the fire. "I've often thought it would have been better if they had shot me, too. I was engaged to a Romanian princess. The engagement was—tactfully broken off."

"I—I see."

"Very few people knew the reason for the broken engagement. All Europe wonders why I have never married, why I have no heir. I'm a great connoisseur of beautiful women—my Gallery of Beauties is quite famous —but I have never shown an interest in marriage. I'm an enigma, they say. Fortunately my companions have been both loyal and discreet."

Karl fell silent, eyes dark as he remembered the tragic events of his life. I understood now. I understood the haunted look in his eyes, the melancholia, that curious lack of sexuality. He continued to gaze at the fire, and then he sighed and looked up at me and smiled a pensive smile.

"I cultivated an interest in art and architecture, and when I became King I devoted myself to turning Barivna into the Athens of Germany. I had a vision, and I endeavored to bring art and beauty and culture to my people. Instead of factories I built theaters and museums. Instead of manufacturing cannon and guns and establishing an army, I established the university and filled Barivna with bright, vital young men who cared nothing for war. Many people believe I've been very foolish."

Karl set his champagne glass aside. "You must find this all extremely boring, my dear."

"Not at all. I was just wondering if it would be presumptuous of me to ask a favor."

"Anything you like."

"Your Gallery of Beauties—I've heard so much about it. I wonder if you might show it to me?"

He looked pleased. "But of course," he said, "although I feel sure you'll find it quite disappointing. You see far greater beauty each morning when you gaze into your mirror."

"You're being gallant again."

"Merely honest, my dear."

Taking my hand, he led me out of the room. The palace was still, the silence broken only by our voices and the rustle of my skirt and his brocade robe as we moved down the carpeted corridors with their sparkling chandeliers and exquisite pieces of furniture. All the candles were burning brightly in the dead of night, an indication that Karl's nocturnal habits were well established. Over a hundred people dwelled here, but with the exception of the footmen who kept watch over the candles no one else was visible. I found the atmosphere rather eerie as we moved from corridor to corridor. It must have been ten minutes before we finally reached the gallery.

"Here are my beauties," Karl said quietly.

The gallery was long and brilliantly lit, and there were thirty-six paintings. Each sumptuously framed portrait was of an exceptionally beautiful woman. Karl worshipped beauty in all its forms, and each time he saw a strikingly lovely woman, be she the butcher's daughter or an elegant aristocrat, he had her immortalized on canvas. I recognized several of the women, one a very famous French actress, one a cool English beauty notorious for her sexual liaisons. The English woman had stayed in Barivna for several weeks, and Karl had given her many expensive gifts. Their "affair" had been the talk of Europe a few years back. Karl was silent as we moved from canvas to canvas, a dreamy look in his eyes.

"They're quite impressive," I remarked. "You've known a great many beautiful women."

"None so lovely as you, my dear. I'd like very much to add your portrait to the collection."

"I'd be quite honored."

"I already have an artist in mind," Karl confessed shyly. "Only Joseph Stieler could do justice to you. I'll let him know my wishes and have him arrange with you for your time." He turned to me, "It's almost dawn. Would you like to see the gardens?"

I nodded, and Karl took my hand once more, leading me down yet another corridor and out onto an open passageway, its roof supported by slender white marble columns. We went down a flight of steps and into the spacious gardens. Shrubs rustled quietly. The breeze caused my black lace overskirt to lift and billow over the oyster gray satin. The moonlight had faded to a milky white, and the sky was the color of pale ashes, faint pink stains beginning to spread in the east.

We strolled slowly toward the low white marble bannister that stood at the edge of the lake. Beyond the rippling blue-gray water we could see the town's majestic white buildings a pale violet in this light, rooftops beginning to catch the first pink stains. I wondered how frequently these periods of acute melancholia came over the King. Was that the reason he had made no effort to see me sooner? I suspected so, but he seemed far more at ease now, as the breeze rippled the water and the sky lightened.

While we watched, the lake turned pink, shimmering as though covered with pink spangles. The spangles changed to gold, becoming brighter still as the first real rays of sunlight touched the water. The buildings beyond lost their violet hue, white and gold now, gleaming as the sun grew stronger and shadows melted away in the morning light. The King was silent, gazing at the town he had created, the vision he had transformed into solid reality. He would leave no heir, but he would be leaving a legacy of beauty and culture far more durable than flesh. Few men had achieved as much.

"I thank you for tonight," he said. "You've performed a great kindness, my dear, greater far than you suspect."

"It's been my pleasure," I replied.

"Have you immediate plans?" he inquired.

"Not really. I thought of returning to Paris, but I have no engagements. Eventually, I'll have to go on another tour. I am a dancer and must dance for my living."

"Perhaps you'd consent to be my guest for a while? It will take Stieler some time to paint your portrait. You seem pleased with Chez Elena, and I know you've made friends among the students. I would make very few demands on you, my dear. Occasional companionship, nothing more."

He looked at me with those sad eyes, eyes filled with silent pleading. I was deeply moved. Karl of Barivna needed me as no man had ever needed me before, and there could be only one answer.

XXX

The studio was bright and sunny, and through the bank
of windows to my right I could see the small, lovely
garden with lush purple bougainvillea spilling over the
wall and vivid blue larkspurs in neat beds. I had grown
very fond of the garden as the weeks went by. The
birds that splashed in the white marble bird bath were
almost old friends. The chair used for my sitting stood
on a low wooden dais and was covered with worn
maroon brocade. It wasn't very comfortable, but it
suited Stieler's purpose. He wanted me sitting very
straight, resting my left elbow casually on the arm of the
chair, my head turned slightly to the right.

Stieler had been working on the painting for over six
weeks. For two hours each day during the best afternoon
light, I posed, wearing a black velvet gown with long,
tight sleeves and a form fitting bodice, the skirt spread
out in lustrous folds. My ebony hair was pulled back
sleekly, and just above my temple was a spray of three
vivid red carnations. A drift of fine, flowered black lace
floated around my face to create the Spanish mantilla
effect Stieler wanted. These sessions provided serene in-
terludes, and I had come to enjoy them despite Stieler's
fawning, ingratiating manner. The final sitting came at
last.

"Are you growing tired, Countess?" he asked.

"I can manage for a while longer."

"Half an hour more and I'll be finished."

"Completely?"

He nodded, stepping back from the canvas to gaze critically at his work.

"I'll want to do some work on the background, but today will be your last sitting. I must say, I'll miss working with you. I've never had a more cooperative model."

"Indeed?"

"Most of the ladies can't sit still. Either they want to chatter away with a flock of friends who come to keep them company, or they sit and eat chocolates or play with their lap dogs. Most trying. You've been a joy, Countess."

Stieler dipped his brush into the paint on his palette and moved back to the canvas, the tip of his tongue caught between his teeth, a look of intense concentration in his cool gray eyes. Tall, slender, older than he cared to admit, he sported a neat ginger goatee and long sideburns, looking far more like a diplomat than an artist. The long frock coat he wore in lieu of the traditional artist's smock was always spotless. Stieler had painted so many aristocratic ladies that it had gone to his head. Rarely had I encountered a greater snob, yet he was unquestionably a superb artist. Each painting he did glowed with life.

"This shall be my masterpiece," he declared. "It's going to eclipse everything else in the Gallery."

"Do you think so?"

"There's no question about it."

Karl's decision to include my portrait in the Gallery of Beauties had caused a great stir at Court. Count Arco-Valley had adamantly declared that if a painting of "that whore" was to be included, Stieler's portrait of his wife would promptly be removed from the gallery. A surprising number of Karl's courtiers and advisors had Sturnburgian connections. They resented my presence in Barivna, and their resentment had flamed even more when, two months earlier, Karl decided to bestow citizenship on me and make me Countess of Landsfeld, granting me an annuity of twenty thousand florins a year and the Landsfeld estates. He had done so against my wishes. Insisting that he wanted to show his appreciation, that he wanted me to have security, he explained that, as King, he had the power to do anything he pleased and it pleased him to do this for me.

"I'll wager your blood is as blue as the blood of most of those parasites and hangers-on who surround me," he claimed. "I'll brook no further argument, Elena. You're going to be a citizen of Barivna, and you're going to become a countess whether you like it or not."

My elevation to the aristocracy had been a great boon for the press, providing even more material for the sensational stories that had appeared in every paper in Europe. It was the most delicious scandal in months, making my affair with Franz seem a trifle in comparison, and the writers outdid themselves. I was a scheming, mercenary temptress taking advantage of the poor, deluded King. I was ruling Barivna from behind the throne, advising Karl on every move. The papers reported that I was brazenly carrying on affairs with a number of students as well, a new one each night, and that I had already caused numerous riots because of my outrageous, immoral conduct.

Smiling a rueful smile, I gazed out at the garden again. If only they knew, I thought. If only they knew how many nights I had done nothing but sit with Karl in his private apartment, amusing him with bright chatter and the gossip that he adored, playing cards with him, discussing painting and literature and music, doing my best to keep away those dark demons that so often threatened to take hold of him. The title he had bestowed upon me, the gifts he insisted on giving me were tokens of appreciation, yes, but not for favors granted in the bedroom. The sensation-seeking newspaper writers would never have understood our platonic relationship, a relationship I could never discuss wtih anyone.

The stories they wrote about my friendship with the students were just as preposterous, but then who would believe that Elena Lopez could entertain rowdy groups of young men without sex entering the picture? How surprised the journalists would have been to see me serving ale and cheese in the elegant drawing room, patiently listening as my young admirers engaged in

341

heated discussion about painting and poetry. Encouraging them in their ambitions, pleading with them to be temperate when they railed against the influx of even more soldiers from Sturnburg, I tried to be a wise and gracious hostess. But despite my good intentions, the newspapers apparently chose to believe only what they wanted to believe. And when a particularly bitter clash erupted one day between soldiers and students— a clash provoked by too much ale and too many hot words—I was the one the newspapers blamed.

The stories didn't bother me in the least. I had long since grown immune to sensational journalism. The increasingly grave political scene did disturb me. I knew my presence in Barivna had added further tension to an already tense situation, but I also knew how much Karl needed sympathetic companionship during his dark periods of melancholia. It wouldn't have helped the political situation one jot if I had left, and my presence gave comfort and support to a man who needed it desperately. I had received anonymous letters filled with threats, and once, late at night, my carriage had been pelted with stones by a group of men in uniform, but I wasn't about to let such things frighten me away.

Growing weary, muscles stiff from sitting so long in the same position, I sighed. Stieler stepped back from the canvas again and, frowning, came over to the dais to rearrange a fold of my black velvet skirt. Returning to the canvas, he picked up his brush, stared at me and resumed his work. Trying to relax my neck muscles, I touched the spray of red carnations and thought about my relationship with Karl, so different from my relationships with Brence or Anthony or Franz and, in some ways, more fulfilling than any of the others had been.

I needed to give of myself, and with Karl I was able to do that without reservation, without fear of rejection. I gave warmth and understanding and concern, and it was received freely, appreciated fully. He listened to my opinions with respect, and our conversations were spirited. The bond between us was not physical, and for that reason there was none of the stress or friction, none of the contention and subtle rivalry that marked my relationships with other men. When I was with Karl

342

there was no need for guile, no need to keep up my guard.

I knew full well that I was living in a fool's paradise which would soon come to an end, but after so much pain I was content to live from day to day, to deny those other needs that had brought about the disastrous relationship with Franz. My devotion to Karl and, to a lesser degree, my friendship with the students helped me to forget. If, occasionally, there were restless nights when memories plagued me and I was filled with a terrible ache inside, they always passed.

"There," Stieler said, applying a final daub of paint. "You can relax now, Countess. It's finished except for the background work I mentioned earlier."

I stood up and stretched, the folds of my black velvet skirt rustling softly. Stieler wiped his hands with a cloth and then opened a bottle of champagne that had been chilling in a bucket of ice. The cork popped loudly. The champagne fizzed. Stieler filled two glasses and handed one to me as I stepped down from the dais.

"I thought a bit of celebration might be in order," he said. "Care to see my masterpiece?"

Smiling his ingratiating smile, he led me over to the canvas that he had refused to let me look at until now. I felt a strange sensation as I gazed at it. Stieler had surpassed himself. The woman in the painting was the essence of feminine allure and loveliness. I couldn't associate her with myself at all. The ebony hair was rich with blue-black highlights, the spray of red carnations standing out in sharp relief, the lace mantilla a fragile drift of lighter black. The skin glowed, cheeks delicately flushed, and the sapphire blue eyes were sad and wise and full of longing.

"It's glorious," I said. "I—I can hardly believe I sat for it."

"I like what I've done with the texture of the velvet," Stieler remarked. "The dark black nap seems to shine with a silvery haze, and the maroon brocade of the chair provides just the right contrast, very subtle and quiet."

Finishing his champagne, he surveyed the canvas with a look of great satisfaction. "I'll fill in the background with pale gray hazy with mauve and gold shadow and deliver it to the King tomorrow. I've a feeling he's going to be pleased."

"Undoubtedly. You've done a magnificent job."

"I had a magnificent subject to work with."

A loud ruckus in the adjoining room prevented him from paying me further excessive compliments. I was relieved when the door flew open and my escort spilled in with noisy abandon. Ever since the incident in which my carriage had been pelted with stones, Eric, Hans and Wilhelm had insisted on accompanying me to and from the studio each day, a totally unnecessary precaution which was really merely an excuse for them to spend more time with me. They filled the studio with youth and noise, exclaiming over the portrait, pounding a highly disconcerted Stieler on the back, and finally whisking me out of the studio and into the waiting carriage.

Hans plopped down beside me, Eric and Wilhelm onto the opposite seat, and the carriage started down the street. As we settled back, I noticed a nasty purple-blue bruise on Wilhelm's right cheekbone. It hadn't been there the day before, nor had the cuts on his knuckles. When I asked him about them, Wilhelm scowled, angrily shoving a lock of dark red hair from his forehead.

"Sodding soldiers!" he snarled.

"There was another incident?"

"You mean you haven't heard?" Hans exclaimed. "It was a regular free-for-all, the biggest brawl yet! Several wounded—mostly military. It happened at the university, right outside the dormitories!"

"All because of the curfew," Eric added.

"Curfew?"

"Schroder's idea," Wilhelm said. "He has decreed that all students must be off the streets by nine o'clock each evening. *He* decreed, just as though he had the authority to do so! When the announcement was made we went crazy, I can tell you! Schroder had to call in a troop of his men."

"We gave 'em a run for their money!" Hans bragged. "The brawl lasted at least an hour before the soldiers

344

had the sense to retreat, dragging their wounded after them."

"Several students were injured, too," Eric said quietly. "One isn't expected to live. This wasn't merely another clash, Elena. It was an act of outright aggression."

"We're not taking this sitting down!" Wilhelm vowed hotly. "No sodding Captain is going to impose a curfew on us!"

Hans and Wilhelm continued to rail against the military as we drove through town. There were far more soldiers in evidence than usual. The cafes and beer gardens seemed to be full of arrogant brutes in tight white breeches and green tunics who acted as though they owned the town. Eric informed me that a fresh detachment had arrived from Sturnburg that morning. So many new men had come that the barracks wouldn't hold them and tents were being pitched on the parade ground.

"Everyone's outraged," he said, "not just the students. The shopkeepers are complaining, the farmers as well. They're expected to provide food for the new men, without reimbursement, mind you. Bad feelings are running high."

"We're not going to stand for it!" Wilhelm declared. "This time the citizens of Barivna are fully behind us. Either the soldiers go, or there's going to be hell to pay!"

I couldn't really become too alarmed. I had heard such fiery declarations all too often to take them seriously. The students would rail against the injustice of it all, but eventually they would return to their books and concern over really pressing matters such as exams and passing marks. Schroder had not dared order his men to fire on the students. But even though the military regime was still maintained loosely, the arrival of the new men was certainly discomforting.

We drove on past the lake, and within minutes the carriage drew up in front of Chez Elena. My three young gallants helped me out and escorted me to the door, their good mood restored. Hans was babbling about his new epic, and Wilhelm was asking Eric if he'd taken notes during that morning's history lecture.

"I'm not giving you my notes," Eric said firmly. "If you expect to pass, you'll have to attend an occasional lecture instead of spending all your time in the gymasium."

"Thanks," Wilhelm retorted. "You're a great help. Wait till I get *you* on a wrestling mat!"

"May we call on you tonight, Elena?" Hans asked.

"I'm afraid not. I'm expected at the palace. The King and I are going to dine with Franz von Klenze, the architect responsible for so many of the magnificent buildings in Barivna."

"Has von Klenze finished his designs for the new Greek Gallery?" Eric asked.

"We're going to see the blueprints tonight," I replied. "I understand it's his most impressive achievement yet."

"And the most expensive," Wilhelm added. "Sturnburg is going to love that. They're going to scream like stuck pigs when the King starts dipping into the coffers to finance it."

"Tomorrow night?" Hans persisted. "I want to recite my new epic for you. It concerns a Norwegian nobleman during the Middle Ages who falls in love with a peasant maid and—"

Wilhelm grabbed him by the arm and pulled him back. "Come along!" he growled. "We've heard enough about your sodding epic! I don't suppose *you* took notes this morning?"

"Skipped the lecture myself. Had to finish my epic."

"We'll see you later, Elena," Eric said.

"Thank you for escorting me."

After they departed, I spent the rest of the afternoon writing letters. I had owed Millie one for some time, and two more from Phillipe had arrived only yesterday. Both of his had been rather grim in tone. He was very unhappy in Touraine. Most of his time was spent riding about on horseback supervising tenant farmers and examining livestock. Repairs had begun on the ancestral chateau; scaffolds surrounded the place; workmen swarmed about every day. Phillipe told me quite a bit about the chateau and the history of his family which, it seemed, could be traced all the way back to Charlemagne.

346

As I read his letters over, I recognized his loneliness and his longing. He missed me a great deal, he wrote, and he wished I could visit the chateau. I would find it very beautiful, very spacious. He never used the word love, but his letters were love letters just the same, subtle, understated, written by a shy, sensitive young man who had developed a hopeless infatuation for a worldly woman. I knew I shouldn't encourage it by answering his letters, yet I hadn't the heart to deny him that consolation. I was extremely fond of Phillipe, and I missed him, too, but our worlds were far too separate for there to be anything but friendship between us.

My letter to him was bright and chatty and friendly, with nothing he could possibly misinterpret. He would stop writing to me before long, I fancied. He would meet someone in Touraine, and he would fall in love with her, genuinely in love, forgetting all about his infatuation for the exotic creature who had bedazzled him. Sighing, I sealed the envelope and began my letter to Millie. By the time I had finished, it was time to bathe and dress.

I always took special care to make myself as glamorous as possible for Karl. After I had bathed, I slipped into a sapphire blue petticoat, the bodice very low, half a dozen skirts spreading out in rustling layers. Minne helped me with my hair. Pulling the ebony waves back sleekly, she arranged them in an elegant French roll. Her eyes were even dreamier than usual, for the stalwart Klaus had given up his energetic wooing of all the other maids and was devoting full time to Minne. She was holding out for marriage, and I expected an announcement any day.

I brushed a pale blue-gray shadow on my lids and used a touch of faint pink rouge to emphasize my high cheekbones, applying a richer pink rouge to my lips. Satisfied with the results, I stood up to don the gown Minne had taken from the wardrobe. Of shimmering silver cloth, it was perhaps the most exquisite gown I had ever worn, certainly the most expensive. The dress belled out over the sapphire underskirts in gleaming silver folds. When she had finished fastening up the gown, Minne opened my jewel box and took out the diamond and sapphire necklace that had been a gift from Karl.

Fastening it around my neck, I stepped back to examine myself in the mirror. The diamonds glittered with dazzling prisms of light, ashimmer with silver and violet fires, four scalloped strands with twenty large sapphire drops. The sapphires blazed with deep blue flames that danced and darted. The woman in the mirror might have been a queen, but why were her eyes so sad? Why did I keep thinking of that girl who had roamed over the moors of Cornwall, wild and free and full of dreams? I was a countess, with my own small palace. I wore a silver gown and a necklace that Marie Antoinette would have envied. I had come a long, long way, yet my heart was full of longing for the one thing that had been denied me.

"You are a vision," Minne said. "I've never seen you look so beautiful."

"Thank you, Minne. Is that a carriage coming up the drive?"

"It sounds like one. Yes, it's stopped. Someone's getting out."

"I wonder who it could possibly be? The students know I'm going to the palace tonight."

"Want me to go down and see?" Minne asked.

"Would you, Minne? I'd appreciate it."

She hurried out of the room, and I gazed into the mirror again and wondered why, amidst all this splendor, I should feel such discontent. It was foolish. It was self-indulgent. Why should I expect happiness? Happiness was a bright illusion, shimmering in the air, always out of reach. The girl in Cornwall had believed in it, had tried to grasp it, but I was no longer a naive young girl. I was older and wiser, and this longing inside was something I had learned to live with. Happiness? I had fame and riches, everything the world valued most. That should be enough for any woman.

This mood will pass, I told myself, straightening a fold of the silver skirt. I sighed and turned away from the mirror as Minne came back into the room.

"A gentleman from Sturnburg," she said. There was a worried look in her eyes. "Otto told him you were going out tonight and wouldn't be able to see him, but the gentleman insisted. He said it was urgent."

"I see."

"He's an Englishman," she added. "He told Otto he was from the English embassy in Sturnburg, and he wouldn't be put off. Otto showed him into the drawing room."

"Thank you, Minne."

"I hope it isn't some kind of trouble," she said nervously.

"It's nothing I can't handle," I assured her.

My skirt made a crisp, rustling noise like dry leaves as I moved down the gracious curving staircase. The crystal chandeliers shed brilliant light over the foyer. In my present mood, I almost welcomed the confrontation I knew awaited me. Because I was English, the embassy in Sturnburg would naturally be concerned about my presence in Barivna, would undoubtedly try everything possible to get me to leave. I was surprised they hadn't sent someone to call on me long before now. But I had no intention of yielding to any kind of pressure, and as I stepped into the drawing room I was prepared to be as hard as steel.

The Englishman was standing with his back to me, examining one of the small Bologna bronzes that stood on the mantle. He was very tall and obviously young, his hair a rich jet black. At least they hadn't sent a doddering old diplomat to do their work for them. He was still wearing his long travel cloak, and as he turned it swirled from his shoulders. He observed me with dark brown eyes full of cool self-possession. "Ah, the Countess of Landsfeld," he said, with a correct bow.

I was unable to speak. My heart seemed to have stopped beating.

"Brence Stephens," he said. "I'm Chief Aide to the English Ambassador in Sturnburg.

Once, long ago, he had told me that he was going to be aide to the English ambassador of a tiny state I had probably never heard of. I remembered that now. I remembered so much more as well. The years seemed to evaporate, all the years between, and a flood of memories swept over me. I could feel my knees grow

349

weak as I fought desperately to stem the surge of emotions that welled up inside, and it took every ounce of strength I had to keep from fainting.

I had dreamed of this moment. I had dreamed of confronting him in all of my splendor, and in my dreams I had been haughty and aloof, treating him with disdain. Now that the moment had actually arrived I felt sheer panic. I mustn't let him see it. I mustn't let him know. I was trembling inside, and I knew that my cheeks must have paled.

I stared at him, and he slowly arched one brow as I had seen him do so many times in the past.

"Is something wrong?" he inquired.

"Nothing at all," I said.

My voice was calm, but it seemed to come from someone else. I managed to control the trembling inside. With superhuman effort, I maintained a rigid composure that I feared might crumble at any moment. I looked at him with a level gaze, silently praying for strength.

"I suppose you know why I'm here," he said.

"I have a fair idea."

"I've just arrived in Barivna. I came here immediately after taking a room at the hotel. This is an urgent matter, Countess. That's why I'm calling on you at such a late hour. Your butler told me that you were going out, but I insisted on seeing you."

His voice was deep and melodious, as I remembered, with the same husky catch. He had lost the dark tan he had acquired in India, and the new pallor somehow enhanced his good looks. There was a cynical curl to his mouth that hadn't been there before, an aura of disenchantment that made him seem more vulnerable. Brence Stephens was plainly discontented with his lot. The success that had meant so much to him had eluded him thus far. He was still only an aide after all this time, and I could tell that he was dissatisfied. The old moodiness was immediately apparent.

"Won't you take off your cloak, Mr. Stephens."

He shook his head. His manner was cold and remote, hostility barely veiled. He hadn't recognized me, hadn't associated the resplendent creature in silver gown with

350

the innocent young girl from Cornwall whose virginity he had taken and whose heart he had broken. To him I was a notorious courtesan, a mercenary adventuress, immoral and unscrupulous.

"I've come to take you away from Barivna," he said. "My instructions are to get you out of the country as soon as possible."

"Indeed?"

"My instructions came from the ambassador. He received his from London. Your presence here is a dangerous irritant, as you surely must realize. You're an English citizen, and England wants you out of Barivna before the situation grows even worse."

When I did not reply, his frown deepened.

"How long will it take you to pack your things?" he inquired.

"I have no intention of packing, Mr. Stephens. I have no intention of leaving. I'm a citizen of Barivna now, proclaimed such by the King himself. I fear you've made your trip for nothing."

"I can see you don't realize the seriousness of the situation, my dear Countess. It's imperative that you leave at once."

"Imperative to Sturnburg," I retorted.

"I don't represent Sturnburg. I represent England. The Embassy isn't at all pleased with the recent developments in Sturnburg, nor do we condone their military policies. Citizen or not, you're an Englishwoman and as such under our jurisdiction."

"I disagree."

"I didn't come here to argue with you, Countess. I came here to get you out of the country before you're caught up in the middle of a full scale military takeover."

"Military takeover? Sturnburg wouldn't dare attempt such a coup. You needn't think you can frighten me with such statements, Mr. Stephens. I'm fully aware of the political situation."

He scowled. "You haven't an inkling of what's going on," he informed me. "No one in Barivna does. I reside in Sturnburg. I know what's happening, what's about to happen. That's why I'm here."

"To rescue me?"

"You might put it that way."

"I'm afraid I must refuse your offer."

"You're a stubborn woman, Countess."

"You're quite right," I replied.

Stepping over to the window, I pulled the long silken bell cord to summon Otto. Brence stared at me, as I turned around to face him again, my manner icy cold, belying the turmoil inside. He started to say something more, and then his eyes grew dark with puzzlement. Moving nearer, a deep frown creased his brow. I stood very still. He continued to stare at me, recognition slowly dawning, and then he shook his head, refusing to believe what his eyes told him was true.

"No," he said. "No, I—I'm imagining things. It can't be." His cheeks seemed to grow paler. He passed a hand across his brow, completely taken aback.

"You—you danced. One night at the gypsy camp you danced. Elena Lopez is—she performs Spanish dances like—like the one you did with that gypsy boy. Mary Ellen?"

"Mary Ellen no longer exists," I said coldly. "The girl you seduced and deserted ceased to exist a long time ago."

His cheeks were ashen, and he started toward me, just as Otto stepped into the room.

"Please show Mr. Stephens out," I said. "If he tries to see me again I will not be in. Do you understand? I never want to see him again. He is not to be allowed inside under any circumstances."

"Mary Ellen!" Brence cried.

"Summon the footmen if necessary, Otto."

With perfect composure, I left the drawing room and moved across the foyer and up the stairs. It was the most difficult journey I had ever made in my life.

XXXI

It was a lovely night, cool and serene. Three days had passed since Brence had come to Barivna, three long days and three long nights. It was shortly after midnight as I rode in the carriage back to Chez Elena after a visit with Karl. He had been in a very good mood, excited about the new Greek Gallery. Material had already been ordered, and the actual construction would begin just as soon as it arrived, von Klenze himself supervising every step. Observing that I looked a bit weary, Karl had smiled and suggested I return to Chez Elena early. His dark demons were far away tonight. They hadn't plagued him in over a week.

I was thankful, for that, having my own demons to contend with.

Peering out the carriage window, I could see the lights of the town in the distance, and as we moved around the curve of the lake I saw the flickering orange blossoms of light where the newly arrived soldiers had lighted their campfires on the parade ground. Karl was unhappy about their presence and had issued a formal complaint to Sturnburg, but he was not unduly concerned. He had severely reprimanded Schroder for trying to impose the curfew on the students, and there had been no more trouble. The status quo had been resumed. The students were busily preparing for upcoming examinations, and the soldiers seemed to spend most of their time performing tactical exercises on the fields outside of town.

Sturnburg wanted me to leave Barivna, and they had

sent Brence to call on me because they thought an Englishman would have a better chance of convincing me of "imminent danger." The English embassy was undoubtedly working hand in glove with Sturnburg. Schroder had tried to frighten me into leaving the day I arrived. I had refused to be intimidated then, and I refused to be alarmed now. Brence Stephens' mission was to get me to leave Barivna, and he would use any means in order to accomplish his goal. His talk about a military takeover was merely part of his tactics.

The carriage moved slowly around the lake. The flickering orange campfires were no longer visible. I was tired, but I knew that I wouldn't be able to sleep. I hadn't been able to sleep properly for the past three nights. Each night, after I went to bed, I was plagued by memories, vibrant memories of incredible joy and unbearable grief. I had never stopped loving Brence Stephens. Never. I had buried that love deep inside, had shut it away in darkness, denying its existence, but it had always been a part of me. The moment I saw him again it had broken free of its prison, as strong, as vital as it had been in the beginning.

When we arrived at Chez Elena, I didn't go inside at once. As the carriage moved away, I paused on the steps, dreading the hours ahead, dreading the memories. I wished now that I had remained at the palace, even though Karl hadn't needed me. I decided to stroll in the gardens for a while to delay that moment when I climbed into bed and closed my eyes and the past came to life in such vivid detail. Leaving the steps, I moved around the house toward the gardens, my skirts billowing in the soft breeze.

My pale pink silk gown had narrow sleeves that left my shoulders bare and the skirt was aglitter with hundreds of clear, transparent spangles, thin, tiny spangles like slivers of crystal. In my hair, I wore a large, creamy white camellia. Elena Lopez in all her finery strolled in the gardens after midnight, alone. There was splendid irony there. I wished I were able to appreciate it more.

The cool night air stroked my bare shoulders as I moved down the pathway between beds of flowers.

Long blue-black shadows moved and shifted at my feet, making patterns over the silvered path. Shrubs rustled, and fountains made a soft, splashing patter as water spilled over marble brims. The moonlight created a world of black and silver, blue-black and pewter gray, lovely and peaceful. I walked slowly, inhaling the fragrance of flowers and listening to the quiet night noises. A bird warbled sleepily. A crunching sound, like footsteps, caused me to pause, vaguely alarmed, and then I decided that it had merely been an echo of my own footsteps.

Brence was still in Barivna, staying at the hotel. He had attempted to see me two more times, and both times he had been turned away. I knew that I couldn't risk seeing him again. I was still in love with him, and that love must be forced back into its prison, contained, controlled, ignored. Once it had almost destroyed me, and I couldn't afford to let that happen again. I had to be strong. I had to be very strong. Seeing Brence again would be a disastrous mistake. Eventually, he would admit defeat and go back to Sturnburg, and then I could relax.

I paused beside one of the fountains, but as I stood there a feeling of uneasiness gradually stole over me. I was uncomfortable without knowing why. I sensed that something was not as it should be. Moonlight spilled over the white marble tiles, tinting them silver, and the tall shrubs near the edge of the lake swayed gently, a mass of dark shadows. I could feel someone watching me. That was it. That was what caused the uneasiness. The sensation was so strong it was almost physical.

"Who—who's there?" I called.

I recalled the hatred in Schroder's eyes when I defied him the day I arrived. He had promised me I would be sorry. What if he had come to take his revenge? What if he had sent one of his men to get rid of Elena Lopez once and for all? It was wildly improbable, but my mind conjured up all sorts of terrifying images. Staring at the shrubs, I thought I could discern a darker form standing in front of them, a tall black form outlined

355

against the grayness behind. I tried to tell myself I was imagining things, but then the form moved, detaching itself from the shadows.

For a moment, I felt stark terror. I was at the very foot of the gardens, far away from the house. If I were to call out, it was unlikely anyone inside would hear me. Cold with fear, I watched as the man moved across the dark patch of lawn and stepped into the moonlight. I could see his features clearly as he moved toward me, and terror gave way to a new kind of alarm, quickly followed by anger. I stared at him coldly, one hand curled into a tight fist. He stopped a few feet away, an amused smile spread across his face as he saw the fist.

"Are you going to hit me?"

"I should!"

"I've read that you have a fierce temper."

"How dare you frighten me like that."

"I can imagine what you thought. You have a great many enemies in Barivna. You had no business coming out here alone, at this hour. What if I had been someone else?"

"What are you doing here?"

"I was waiting for you to return. I've been out here in these gardens for at least three hours, and I was prepared to wait all night if necessary. When the carriage pulled up, I planned to intercept you before you went inside, but then you paused on the steps and started toward the gardens."

"And you've been watching me."

He nodded slowly. "Watching you," he said, "trying to convince myself that the moonlight wasn't playing tricks on me, that such overwhelming loveliness wasn't an illusion."

His voice was like music, a low, husky caress of sound. I steeled myself against it, thankful for the anger that kept other emotions at bay. I gazed at him with a hard, stony expression.

"You were a beautiful girl," he continued. "You're an even more beautiful woman."

"I'm going inside, Brence."

"No you're not. You're going to listen to me."

"You shan't stop me. I'll call the footmen."

"Call them," he said.

"We have nothing to discuss, Brence. I told you the other night that I had no intention of leaving Barivna. I should think that after being turned away from the door twice you'd realize your mission was futile."

"I don't give up easily, Mary Ellen."

"Don't call me that. No one has called me that in years."

"You'll always be Mary Ellen to me. You'll always be that lovely, vulnerable girl with windblown hair and lightly flushed cheeks and eyes full of secret longing."

"The girl you abandoned," I said coldly.

He nodded again. "I've never been able to forgive myself for leaving you behind. I tried to forget you—tried desperately. I knew it was foolish to let myself be haunted by you, but that didn't help. Nothing helped. I couldn't get you out of my mind."

"I'm touched."

He ignored the sarcasm. "I fell in love with you, Mary Ellen. I had never been in love before, and it—disoriented me. It seemed a kind of weakness. I had bold plans for a major career in diplomacy, and—"

"And I didn't fit into them," I said. "I wasn't rich or aristocratic. I couldn't help further your precious career. I was the bastard daughter of a gypsy, and that wouldn't do at all."

"I won't deny that," he said quietly.

He was standing very close, looking at me with dark, grave eyes, his cheekbones taut, his full, smooth lips parted. He was so very handsome. I sensed again his disenchantment, the new vulnerable quality not at all disguised by the cynical curl at the corner of the mouth. Once I had run my finger over that mouth. Once I had reached up to rest my palm on that lean cheek. I remembered the feel of his arms closing about me, remembered those lips covering mine, firm, moist, demanding response. I tried to stem the flow of memories, hardening myself against them.

"And so you left," I said. My voice was hard. "You gave me money in order to ease your conscience, and you left, knowing I was alone, knowing I had no one to turn to."

"I'm not proud of it."

"John Chapman came to visit me that night, the night after you left. He no longer wanted to make me his mistress. As far as he was concerned, I was damaged goods. He raped me."

Brence looked stunned.

"I survived," I continued in that same hard voice. "I put it out of my mind. I put you out of my mind, too, Brence. I grew up, you see. I grew up, and I had no time to weep over the past."

"I came back for you," he said.

He moved nearer. I felt a tremulous feeling stirring inside.

"For three months I tried to forget you, but I realized the attempt was futile. I was in love with you, Mary Ellen, and I knew that life without you would be meaningless. So, I took leave from the embassy and returned to Cornwall, praying you hadn't already found a husband."

"You expect me to believe that?"

"You had vanished. Your house had been sold, and no one knew where you'd gone. I remembered that you spoke of wanting to become a dancer, but I never took that seriously. I never dreamed you'd take off to London on your own. I assumed you'd moved to another village. I spent two weeks searching for you, going from village to village, traveling all over Cornwall, and finally I had to give up and return to Sturnburg."

I was silent. A deep frown creased his brow.

"It's true," he said. "Don't you realize what I'm telling you? I'm telling you that I'm in love with you."

"And I'm supposed to melt into your arms and sigh and grieve over all the years we've lost? Is that what you expected? I'm sorry, Brence. I'm no longer that naïve. You're wasting your time—and mine."

He looked at me with eyes full of puzzlement and pain. Though I wanted to believe what he said with all my heart, I dared not trust him. Nor myself. There was a long silence. The fountain pattered softly behind me, and I shivered as a fresh breeze blew in across the lake. I felt a familiar weakness, and I fought it valiantly,

358

knowing I couldn't maintain my icy composure much longer.

"You have every reason to hate me," he said quietly.

"I don't hate you, Brence. I feel nothing at all."

"I don't believe you. The other day, when I finally realized who you were, it all came rushing back to me. It was as though there had been no interval, as though all the time between had been a kind of sleep. I know it was that way for you, too, Mary Ellen."

"No."

"You recognized me immediately. You were stunned, and you were frightened, but you still loved me."

"No."

"You're lying."

"Please go."

Shaking his head, he placed his hands on my shoulders. I trembled and tried to pull away. His hands tightened, fingers digging into my flesh, and as I closed my eyes, he pulled me into his arms and covered my lips with his own. I stood very still, refusing to bend, refusing to respond even though every fibre of my being seemed to vibrate with sweet sensation. His lips caressed mine, gently, and his arms tightened about me, drawing me against him. Inside me there was nothing but sweet languor that melted into an aching need. His lips grew more insistent. I held myself rigid, resisting still, clinging to a hard core of resolve.

He lifted his head and peered down at me, his face inches from my own. He looked into my eyes for a long time, and then he kissed my cheek, my shoulder, the curve of my throat, his hands caressing me. I shivered again, feeling my resolve shredding, as he tightened his arms once more, once more lowered his head, kissing me with fervent urgency.

For one more moment I clung to that scrap of resolve, and then my body went limp and I wrapped my arms around his shoulders as his lips parted mine. Reality dissolved and blossoms burst in explosions of splendor inside of me. That kiss seemed to last for an eternity, an eternity of splendid torment, and when finally his lips left mine I looked up into his eyes with a strange composure despite the sensations shimmering within me. A part of me seemed to be standing back calmly observing the scene. When I spoke my voice was level.

"Will you leave now?"

"You want me. You can't deny that."

"I'm human. You've proved that."

"You love me."

"It was an automatic response—"

"No, Mary Ellen."

"Nothing else."

"You lie. You're afraid."

"Yes."

"You've nothing to fear."

"Everything."

"I love you, Mary Ellen."

If only I could have believed it. If only I hadn't known why he had come to Barivna.

He touched my cheek. His eyelids grew heavy. He parted his lips and tilted his head and he held me close, kissing me a third time, and I told him silently, with my lips, my body, what I had refused to say aloud. Conflicting emotions surged through me. I was sad because I had lost the battle, elated because I would share in his victory, and yet part of me still remained aloof, observing calmly. He removed his lips from mine and smiled, leading me toward the shadows, the soft grass. I drew back, shaking my head. He gave me an inquisitive look.

"The house," I said. "My bedroom."

"The servants?"

"My maid never waits up for me. I've instructed her not to. And the footmen will remain at their posts. We'll use the side entrance."

He nodded and let go of my hand, and I moved as though in a trance, through moonlight and shadow, the transparent spangles on my pink silk skirt glittering. He walked beside me, stern and silent, his cloak lifting in the breeze like dark wings. We passed tall shrubs and neat, formal flowerbeds, finally crossing the drive that led around to the carriage house and stables. We stepped into the dim side hallway and a moment later started up the servants' stairs.

360

A lamp was burning in my bedroom. As I closed the door and looked at Brence, I felt a sense of unreality. I seemed to be in the middle of a dream. Reaching up to brush the errant jet locks from his forehead, I rested my palm on his cheek. He smiled and turned his head to kiss my fingers. I pulled my hand away, and he laughed softly and removed his cloak, flinging it over a chair. He was wearing an elegantly cut dark blue suit and a white satin waistcoat embroidered with tiny blue flowers. A black silk neckcloth nestled under his chin. He stood with legs apart, his hands resting at his sides, tall and handsome, dazzling really.

I recalled that afternoon in Cornwall when I had seen him for the first time. He had been dazzling then, too, and I had gazed at him with a kind of wonderment. But there had been something else—a vague, disturbing feeling, like a premonition of danger, telling me that I had come face to face with my fate, warning me to flee. I felt that same premonition now. I paid it no heed. My other feelings were much too strong. I stepped over to turn off the lamp. The doors to the balcony were open. Hazy rays of moonlight streamed into the room, growing stronger, penetrating the darkness.

"I've waited so long for this," he said huskily. "Now that I've found you I'll never let you go."

Drawing me to him, he kissed my brow, my nose, my cheek, let his lips slide down to my throat. They seemed to burn my skin. He kissed the swell of my bosom, and I caught my fingers in his hair, trembling. Moments passed, and then he straightened up and held my arms and smiled, eyes dark with hunger. He was in no hurry, deliberately delaying the ultimate ecstasy. He squeezed my arms and then pulled me against him and held me tight, kissing my ear lobe, catching it between his teeth. Moonlight polished the floor and caused shadows to dance on the wall.

"I can't believe I'm holding you in my arms," he said.

"Nor I. It—it's like a dream."

"It's real, Mary Ellen."

He pulled the camellia from my temple and threw it aside. His fingers toyed with my hair, undoing the French roll. Pins scattered and long ebony waves tumbled down over my shoulders. Turning me around so that my back was to him, he lifted my hair and kissed the nape of my neck. Cool night air filled the room. I felt it on my skin.

"You're lovely," he murmured and held me close.

"I feel lovely now."

"How could I have deserted you?"

"Enough," I whispered. "We've talked enough."

"Right," he said.

"Now is the time to feel."

He released me and stepped across the room to remove his jacket and waistcoat, placing them on a chair. He pulled the neckcloth away from his throat and dropped it on top of the other garments, and then he sat down on the bed to take off his boots. I recalled those afternoons long ago when we had come into the house after strolling on the beach. It seemed like yesterday. His boots clattered to the floor and he stood up to pull off his shirt. I watched him, feeling love that was new and vibrant and glorious, as heady as fine champagne, as elating, filling me with a delicious dizziness that made me want to weep with joy. I allowed myself to feel it, allowed myself to believe it wasn't merely part of the dream.

He removed his breeches, and stood naked in the moonlight, a superb statue transformed into flesh and blood. His manhood throbbed, erect, eager. Taking hold of my shoulders, he turned me around to unfasten my gown in back. I felt his hands sliding my bodice down. I freed my arms from the sleeves. Pink silk rustled. Spangles gleamed and flashed. His hands moved over my hips, and the gown fell to the floor. Stepping out of the silken circle, I kicked off my shoes and removed my undergarments. Now, I was naked, too, shivering with cold, shivering with desire.

He lifted me up in his arms and carried me to the bed, easing me down onto the silken counterpane. I raised my arms, and he caught my wrists and smiled a savage smile, kneeling over me. I waited, lips parted, looking up at that face sculptured in moonlight as he leaned down to kiss me. Caressing me gently, he made his entry. It was galvanizing, sending shock waves throughout my body. I moaned, closing my eyes, whirling into a delirium of sensation as he thrust deeper, filling me with hard, fierce warmth. I put my arms around his shoulders, holding tightly as the breathless descent continued, faster now, both of us caught up in a wild abandon. Together we spiralled into an ecstatic void, and for one shattering instant we hung suspended. I sank my teeth into his shoulder as the instant ended and we plunged into completion, life force jetting out of him in a fountain of fulfillment.

He fell limp, the weight of his body pressing, crushing. I held him to me, cushioning his body with my own, my senses still reeling, the glowing aftermath warm and tingling inside. He groaned and nestled his head on my breasts, and I stroked his back, his skin silken smooth, damp with perspiration. This was right. This was the way it was meant to be, this love, this lover, the two of us with limbs closely entwined. I closed my eyes, holding him, loving him, smelling his flesh, his hair, the wonderful masculine musk of his body. I drifted into a blissful sleep, and when I opened my eyes sometime later the moonlight was brighter and Brence was leaning over me, his full, sensual mouth curving in a teasing smile.

"I—I fell asleep," I murmured.

"So did I. I'm glad I woke up."

He lowered his head until his lips touched mine, lightly brushing them at first, then pressing gently and parting my own. He filled my mouth with his tongue, and I wove my fingers into his hair, twining the dark jet locks around them as his lips and tongue continued to tease. Finally, he raised his head. I let my hands slip to his shoulders, and he smiled again and touched his hand to my breasts, caressing. He leaned down to kiss each nipple, and then he made love to me again, slowly this time, lazily, urgent abandon replaced by a tantalizing lethargy, each stroke tender, carefully prolonged to insure the greatest pleasure for each of us. I seemed to be stretched on a rack, and the divine torment went on and on, finally demolishing me in an explosion of delight that seemed to shred my senses.

When I woke up again the room was filled with a hazy pink light that gradually melted into gold. Brence was sleeping next to me on his side, one arm curled around my waist, his right leg resting heavily over both my own. I carefully disengaged myself and slipped out of bed. Brence groaned and stirred and opened his eyes. He struggled into a sitting position, his back against the headboard, a mass of jet locks covering his brow. His eyelids drooped sleepily.

"There's water in the white porcelain ewer," I said, "a fresh cloth beside it."

"What time is it?"

"I'm not sure. Early."

Gathering up all my clothes, I went into the dressing room and closed the door quietly behind me. I washed, put on a fresh white petticoat, then sat down at the dressing table to brush my hair. The night was over. The dream had ended. Common sense had returned with the dawn. But I was undecided about what I was going to do. A great deal would depend on Brence.

I could hear him moving around in the bedroom. The porcelain ewer rattled. I put down the brush to arrange my hair in a loose roll. My eyes in the mirror were calm, as I thought about why he had come to Barivna. Last night had been magical, a lovely sojourn from reality created by mood and moonlight, memory and physical need joining forces to overthrow reason. That part of me that had remained aloof and objective last night was in complete command today.

Leaving the dressing table, I buttoned on a rich blue dress. Brence had finished dressing when I entered the bedroom. He was standing at the mirror, adjusting his black silk neckcloth. I could hear the servants moving about downstairs. Brence had smoothed down the counterpane. The room was neat, the wilting camellia on the floor the only sign that remained of last night's passionate encounter.

Brence turned. He too, was composed, his manner remote and slightly official.

"Good morning," I said.

He gave me a curt nod, his lips set in a thin line. Had

364

those lips spoken words of endearment? Had those grim, determined eyes gazed into my own with love?

"Would you like some breakfast?" I asked.

"I'll eat at the hotel. I have to pack my bags. You'll need to start packing, too." He picked up his cloak and fastened it around his shoulders. "We'll leave as soon as possible," he informed me. "Around eleven. Can you be ready by then?"

"You seem to be in quite a hurry."

Brence frowned. "I've spent too much time in Barivna already. Time is of the essence, Mary Ellen. Things could start happening here any moment."

"I suppose you're talking about the military take-over."

He nodded again. "Schroder's men have been practising tactical maneuvers all week long. That doesn't bode well. I want to get you out of the country immediately. Your departure might well forestall things, at least for a while, but a military coup is inevitable."

"I see. And when you get me out of the country?"

"I'll report back to the embassy in Sturnburg. My success with this mission will lead to an advancement, just as failure would have meant dismissal from the corps. Things haven't been going well with my career. The Ambassador made it clear that this was my last chance to redeem myself."

"I—I wish you hadn't told me that."

"There's no danger now. I'm sure to get a advancement."

Moving across the room, I stepped out onto the balcony to look down at the garden, which was bathed in dazzling yellow-white sunlight. Moonlight and magic had vanished. There was a tight, hard feeling inside me. I had only myself to blame. I smiled ruefully and rested my hands on the marble bannister, refusing to feel pain. When Brence joined me on the balcony, I didn't turn around.

"I'll ask for a new post," he said. "You can join me there. Things will be different from now on, Mary Ellen. With you at my side, there'll be nothing I can't achieve."

"At your side? Are you asking me to marry you?"

He hesitated. "I'll marry you, if that's what you want."

"How generous of you."

"No one need ever know about your past. Elena Lopez can quietly disappear. I'll say you're from an old, aristocratic family in Cornwall. We needn't provide details. As Mrs. Brence Stephens you'll dress differently, act differently. You'll be a diplomat's wife, and it's unlikely you'd ever run into any of your old associates."

"Most unlikely," I said.

I turned to face him, my decision made.

"You need to get back to the hotel, Brence. I'll have one of the carriages brought around front for you."

I moved across the room to pull the silken bell cord that hung beside the bed. Klaus appeared a few minutes later. If he was surprised to find Brence in my bedroom, he didn't show it. His face was expressionless as I gave him instructions. He left, and after a short while we heard the carriage moving around the side of the house. We went downstairs and out to the carriage.

"I'll be back for you at eleven," Brence said.

"No," I replied.

"What do you mean?"

"I'm afraid your mission has been a failure."

"Mary Ellen—"

"I'm sorry, Brence."

"You—you think I—you think it was all—" He was incredulous, unable to articulate properly.

"You'd better go," I said.

"Everything I told you last night—it was true! I love you, and you love me, too."

"Yes, Brence, I love you."

"Then—"

"Once, a long time ago, I told myself I must dare to love. I ignored all my instincts. I loved, without reservation, and then you left me. It almost destroyed me. I'm not going to let myself go through anything like that again."

"You're talking nonsense!"

"I don't expect you to understand."

"You can't do this!"

"I'm afraid I can."

"Mary Ellen!"

"Go back to Sturnburg. Tell them Elena Lopez refuses to bow to their authority. Tell them nothing worked, not even seduction. Tell them—" I cut myself short. "Goodbye, Brence," I said, and hurried inside.

I locked the door. He pounded on it, calling my name. Klaus looked at me, his face still expressionless. I went upstairs and fought the tears and fought the pain, and it was a long time before the carriage finally drove away.

XXXII

The pearl gray sky took on a soft violet hue as the last
rays of the sun began to stain the horizon. It had been
cloudy all day, thunder rumbling in the distance. As I
stood on the balcony, looking out over the gardens to
the lake beyond, the water shimmered with reflections of
the sunset, orange and scarlet lights dancing on the
surface. The great palace on the other side of the lake
was slowly being wrapped in shadows. It would soon
be time for me to go to the palace, for Karl was expecting me at eight.

I looked forward to seeing him. Although he had
asked no questions and made no effort to find out what
had happened, Karl knew that I had been upset all
week. Seeing him each evening had been a comfort.
He had made a distinct effort to distract me in his kind,
subtle, warmly attentive manner. Seven days had passed
since Brence left Barivna, seven of the longest days in
my life. Even though it had been an agonizing one, I
knew in my heart that I had made the right decision. I
had gotten over Brence once before, and I would get
over him again.

There seemed to be a great deal of activity going on
across the lake. Several soldiers on horesback rode
up, dismounted in front of the palace and hurried up the
front steps. Almost simultaneously, a carriage appeared
from behind the palace, moving rapidly down the road
that led away from Barivna. Was it Karl's private carriage? The horses were white, and I thought I caught a

glimpse of the Royal Crest, but I couldn't be certain from such a distance. Why would Karl be leaving the palace? No doubt I was mistaken. More soldiers arrived, at least twenty men, and they, too, hurried into the palace. Perhaps the Royal Guard were returning from some kind of maneuver, I thought, stepping back into the bedroom.

Another rumble of thunder sounded, a strange, distant crackling noise unlike the previous rumbles. It was going to storm. In my present mood, I would welcome thunder and lightning and sheets of driving rain. The lovely blue skies and radiant sunshine of the past week had merely played against my mood. I refused to grieve, sternly repressing the impulse to sink into a state of abject self-pity. Instead, I became irritable. I longed to throw something, longed to indulge myself in one of the fiery tantrums for which Elena Lopez was famous. Perhaps that would have helped.

In my dressing room, I slipped off my robe and, wearing only my petticoat, sat down to do my make-up. I had bathed earlier, soaking for a long time in the hot, perfumed water, and I had washed my hair as well. It fell in gleaming blue-black waves about my shoulders as I brushed a touch of shadow on my lids. Minne wasn't there to help with my hair. I had given her the day off, Klaus as well, and they were undoubtedly strolling hand-in-hand through one of the parks or shopping for wedding bands. Klaus had finally asked Minne to marry him. Her eyes glowing with triumph, she had related the news to me that morning. I brushed my hair away from my face and let it fall down my shoulders, fastening it in back with the gorgeous clasp Karl had given me, a silver filigree bar aglitter with more than twenty diamonds.

Leaving the dressing table, I put on the gown I had selected earlier. It was a creamy rose-pink satin. As I dressed, I found myself thinking of Anthony Duke, wondering where he was, what he was doing. Why should I be thinking of Anthony now? Was it because I associated him with temperamental outbursts I had been tempted to indulge myself in? What fun would a fit of temper be without him to appreciate it?

Anthony had helped me get over Brence the first time. He was an outrageous rogue, thoroughly impossible, but what fun it had been to fight with him. I wished he were back now. He would shake me and bully me, and I would yell at him and he would make some audacious remark and I would pick up some breakable object and hurl it at him and it would be such blessed relief. Had he found some new protégée to aggravate and intimidate and transform into a glamorous success? Was he knocking about without money, living off his wits? I felt a great fondness for him still, even though the scoundrel had lost all my money and left me to fend for myself in Paris. I wondered if I would ever see him again.

My skirt made a soft rustling noise as I moved back into the bedroom. Night had fallen now, and the lights burned brightly inside. Glancing at the clock, I saw that it was almost time to summon the carriage. I would dine with Karl, who would be charming and attentive, and for a few hours I would forget. Immersed as he was in plans for the new Greek Gallery, spending hours and hours each day in happy conferences with von Klenze, Karl seemed a different person of late, his dark moods temporarily banished. Although we dined together every evening, I usually left the palace shortly after midnight. There hadn't been one of those midnight till dawn watches for a long time.

The strange, crackling thunder sounded again, louder this time, nearer, it seemed, accompanied by a curious din like . . . like distant shouting. Beginning to feel vaguely alarmed, I was about to go out when I heard running footsteps on the stairs. Minne burst into the room, her long copper hair in wild disarray, her cheeks flushed a bright pink, her eyes full of agitation and excitement. Her dress was torn at one shoulder, the sleeve hanging down limply, and there was a dark smudge on her chin.

"Minne! What on earth—"

"It's happened!" she cried. "The soldiers are taking over!"

"What—"

"They've been massing all day. Klaus and I didn't

371

pay much attention at first. We saw them gathering, but we didn't think anything about it until—they're fighting with the townsmen and the students! It started about an hour ago. They're using guns. Shooting! Klaus and I had a terrible time trying get back—they're fighting in the streets. We could hardly get through."

"Karl?"

Klaus stepped into the room, a bad gash streaking his cheek. He was in street clothes, and his jacket was torn. Black stains on his right trouser leg looked as though they'd been made by gunpowder.

"The soldiers headed for the palace first," he told me. "Someone said the King got away in his private carriage. They'll be coming here soon. I'm surprised they haven't arrived already."

"They fired at us!" Minne exclaimed. "They were firing at everyone! They were breaking into shops, rounding people up! People were running in every direction, and at the university—the students—"

Minne cut herself short, wringing her hands. Klaus touched her shoulder and gave her a stern look, which seemed to calm her. Tears spilled down her cheeks. Karl had gotten away. The carriage I had seen leaving the palace had been his after all. I prayed that he had made it to sanctuary. Soon the soldiers would be coming to Chez Elena, and I knew Schroeder would be with them. I would be placed under arrest . . . if I weren't murdered first. Suddenly, I heard horses approaching, a great many horses. Klaus looked at me, waiting for instructions.

"Bolt the doors," I told him. "You and Otto and the other footmen keep them out as long as possible, but if —when they break in, I want no fighting. Don't try to resist them."

"You intend to give yourself up to them?"

"I have no other choice."

"I shouldn't advise it," Klaus said sternly. "We have guns. We can hold them off until you get away. I'll get a carriage ready at once. If we hurry—"

The horses stopped in front of Chez Elena. Loud, raucous voices called out and soldiers pounded furiously on the doors. Otto had obviously already bolted the doors, but it wouldn't take the soldiers long to break in.

"No guns," I said. "Go downstairs and see that the rest of the doors and windows are secure. Minne, you gather up the rest of the maids and take them down into the wine cellar. Bolt the door. Don't open it under any circumstances."

"But—"

"Do as I say!" I snapped.

Minne sobbed and rushed out of the room. Klaus followed her. Going into the dressing room, I took down two of my bags and began to pack, ignoring the shouts, the furious pounding. I folded gowns and placed them in one of the bags, filling it, closing it, fastening the lock. I had no idea why I was packing. I wouldn't get away. It was just something to keep me busy. They would break in any moment now and come rushing up the stairs and . . . I folded another gown, neatly, took down another. There was a loud splintering sound as they used the butts of their guns on the door, the tinkle of glass as they shattered windows.

I finished filling the second bag with undergarments and placed my jewel box on top. I closed the bag and fastened it. At least two dozen gowns still hung in the wardrobe, but I would have to leave them. I was sure to be placed under arrest, and I imagined the consequences. I might be roughed up a bit, but they would have to be careful—I was an international celebrity, and Sturnburg wouldn't dare allow any real harm to come to me. I would no doubt be officially exiled from the country, taken to the border under military escort. Still . . . I tried to maintain a semblance of calm. Panic wouldn't help at all.

The din downstairs was deafening. More glass shattering, wood splintering. The raucous shouts grew louder, more vicious. I took a deep breath, stepped out of the bedroom and moved to the top of the staircase, my pink satin skirt rustling softly.

I paused at the head of the stairs, bracing myself. Otto and all six of the footmen stood in a huddle below, watching the rifle butts tear through the door. There was a mighty groaning noise as the hinges gave way, and then the door fell with a loud crash, splitting apart, pieces of wood scattering. The soldiers poured into the foyer, at least twenty of them, stomping, shouting, waving bayonets. The menservants were surrounded immediately and backed against the wall. One of the footmen panicked and tried to flee. A soldier raised his rifle and fired. There was a puff of smoke and a blazing red streak. The footman seemed to fly into the air with arms and legs akimbo, and then he crumpled to the floor. Half his face was missing. Blood gushed from his head, making a vivid red pool.

Otto tried to move. A soldier, his bayonet at Otto's stomach, lunged forward. Otto screamed, made a gurgling noise and fell forward, his blood spurting in crimson jets. The soldier stepped aside to let the body topple to the floor, then wiped his dripping bayonet on the back of Otto's jacket. His colleagues hooted with glee. I stood at the top of the stairs, in plain sight.

"Where is she! Where is the whore!"

"She's gone," Klaus said. "She left an hour ago."

"You lie!"

The soldier swung his rifle around so that the butt was turned toward Klaus. Rearing back, he drove it into Klaus' stomach with vicious force. Klaus gasped and sagged against the wall, almost losing consciousness. His face was stark white with pain, and it was a moment before he could speak.

"She left," he said hoarsely. "You're too late."

"Let's wreck the place!" one of the soldiers cried. "Let's burn it down!"

They seemed to go wild. They began to break furniture and tear down curtains and hurl vases against the wall, yelling lustily. I stood very still, watching the scene of horror with a curious detachment. It wasn't real. It wasn't happening. I seemed to be far, far away, and everything blurred together like a crazy kaleidoscope of movement and color, soldiers in green and white uniforms and helmets with red crests darting about in a frenzy of destruction, blue velvet curtains tearing, furniture falling, shattering, two red pools spreading on the floor. One of the soldiers climbed up on a table, caught hold of a chandelier and swung himself out on it. It came crashing down, crystal pendants scattering in every direction, and then a man stepped through the doorway and barked a sharp command and everything grew still.

Heinrich Schroder glanced at the bodies and the debris with cool indifference. His men stood at attention, plainly intimidated. His boots were glossy, gleaming black, and his white breeches were like a second skin, outlining muscular legs. His short forest green tunic was spotless, aglitter with gold braids, the epaulettes on his broad shoulders shimmering. He wore no helmet, and his skull gleamed baldly under the short, stiff fuzz of light brown hair. There was a moment of tense silence as he surveyed the scene with icy gray-blue eyes. Then he tensed his mouth, which exaggerated the jagged scar on the right side of his face.

"Where is she?" he demanded.

"She's gone," one of his men replied. He pointed to Klaus. "That one says she left an hour ago."

Schroder glanced at Klaus. "Kill him," he said. "Run him through. Then perhaps one of the others will tell us the truth."

"No!" I cried.

They all turned to look up at me. The soldiers were startled. Klaus made a face. Schroder curled his lips in a sadistic smile, eyes glittering with anticipation. His men were silent, afraid to speak. Schroder took a deep breath, and a long moment passed.

"Amuse yourselves, men," he said. "Carry on with your fun. I'll see to Miss Lopez. We'll leave in half an hour or so."

The men cheered and gleefully continued their destruction of the palace, some of them rushing into the other rooms seeking more furniture to smash, and others to rip down drapery cords to tie up the servants. I felt a terrible chill as Schroder laughed gruffly and started up the stairs toward me, moving slowly, smiling that terrible smile. I seemed to be frozen in place, unable to move.

"I'm placing you under arrest," he said, still climbing the stairs. "My orders are to escort you to the border."

He moved up another step, and another. I could see

375

the murderous hatred and the naked lust in his eyes, and I knew what he planned to do. I would "resist arrest" and he would be called upon to take strong measures and there would be an "unfortunate accident" and even if the officials disbelieved his report it would be too late. Schroder planned to murder me, but he intended to rape me first.

"I've been looking forward to this," he told me.

"I'll go peacefully," I said.

"No. You're going to try to escape."

"Keep away."

He paused on the steps and laughed. It was a horrible sound, chilling. I moved back, trembling inside. Smiling evilly, he continued up the steps. I backed away from him, my heart pounding. I was against the wall now, unable to move another step. He stopped, toying with me, savoring the cat and mouse game to the fullest. There was a table beside me, a heavy silver candlestick within reach and I seized it. Schroder leaped forward and took hold of my wrist and twisted it savagely sending the candletsick clattering to the floor. He chuckled, twisting my wrist again, and whirled me around, forcing my arm up between my shoulder blades.

"I'm going to enjoy this," he crooned.

He wrenched my arm up higher. The pain was excruciating, sharp, hot stabbing needles. He laughed. His free arm went around my throat, his forearm pressing viciously against it. Darkness and bright orange and blue lights whirled in front of me as my breath was cut off and his arm tightened as if to crush the life out of me. My head spun faster and faster—blinding pain was the only reality, coupled with his sadistic laugh. I prayed for oblivion, for quick release into unconsciousness.

Schroder loosened his grip on my throat, relaxed it just enough so that I could breathe. The orange and blue lights vanished and my vision was blurred as he forced me along the hall toward the door of my bedroom. Taking his arm from my throat, he shoved the door open, then pressed his palm in the small of my back and with a mighty shove propelled me into the room. I stumbled forward, falling to the floor in a heap of pink satin, hair spilling over my eyes. Jolting pain shot through my body. Schroder stepped inside and closed the door behind him. Striding over to where I lay, he stood over me with legs spread wide, hands resting on his hips.

My arm felt limp; hot needles still stabbed at my throat, hurting even more as I gasped for breath. My heart was pounding . . . pounding somewhere else. Was I hallucinating? The noise grew louder until the whole house seemed to reverberate with it. There were hoarse shouts and tromping footsteps and terrible explosions like the one that had sounded just before the footman flew into the air and fell. Gunfire. Shouting. More shouting. Someone was shouting my name. Pounding, louder, louder, shaking the walls. . . .

Still dazed, I looked up and saw the glossy boots, the clinging white breeches, the green tunic. I saw the roll of flesh beneath his jaw, saw his lips, his large nose, his eyes, half shrouded now with heavy lids, saw his brow and the fuzz of hair covering his skull, all from a crazy angle, looming there above me. He seemed to rock back and forth, seemed about to topple, but I knew it was my own blurred vision that caused the illusion. The room began to spin slowly, the air filled with a bright, burning haze that shimmered. I tried to sit up, but I hadn't the strength.

"You have a balcony, I see," he remarked. "That's convenient. It's perfect."

"What—"

"You'll try to escape. You'll fall off the balcony. You'll break your neck."

He chuckled and reached down to take hold of my hair. Grabbing a handful he pulled me to my feet, tugging brutally. I cried out. I couldn't help it. I felt sure my hair would come out by its roots. Schroder continued to chuckle, releasing my hair, curling an arm around my waist, holding me against him in a loose grip.

"I'll break your neck first, before I hurl you over," he said casually, "just to make certain. I wouldn't want there to be any slipups."

His voice seemed to come from a long way off. He tightened his arm around my waist, crushing me against

377

him. His body was solid muscle. He smelled of sweat and leather and lust. As I tilted my head back, looking up into those glittering gray-blue eyes, he ran the tip of his tongue across his lower lip and lowered his heavy eyelids as he bent over to kiss me. A surge of anger stronger than the pain, stronger than my fear, shot through me. Drawing back, I kicked him and clawed his face. He let out a shout and almost lost his grip on my waist, when I kicked again, aiming for his groin with all the force I could muster.

Schroder doubled over and fell back. His eyes were glazed. His mouth was wide open. He made horrible gutteral noises. Seizing a vase, I cracked it over his head. He stumbled and almost fell. He reeled and tottered for a moment, and then he gave a mighty bellow and clenched his fists. I saw his arm swing back. . . . There was an explosion of pain and a burst of bright lights. I fell backwards, landing on the bed with such impact that the springs squealed. My jaw was on fire. My head was whirling. Black wings rushed toward me.

As I managed to struggle into a sitting position, Schroder started toward the bed. Outside the pounding was louder than ever, thundering, deafening. The door flew open, crashing back against the wall. Two men rushed into the room, one of them in a long black cloak. Schroder turned and bellowed again. He leaped toward the men. The man in the cloak raised a pistol and fired. There was an explosion, an orange streak, a puff of smoke. Schroder's forehead sprouted a wet red blossom and he crashed to the floor like a felled oak. Getting to my feet, I staggered and almost collapsed again, but Brence gathered me into his arms and held me close.

"You—" I whispered.

"I knew what was going to happen. I found out early this morning. I rode all day."

"But—"

"I couldn't just ride off and leave you here, knowing what was going to happen. It seems I got here just in time."

"The soldiers—downstairs—"

"Your student friends are taking care of them. They

378

were pouring into the house just as I arrived, at least thirty of them."

"They—"

"There'll be time for talk later!" he said sternly. "Now I've got to try and get you out of this bloody country in one piece."

Half carrying me, he guided me toward the door. I tottered, still dazed, my jaw still burning. We moved down the hall and to the top of the stairs, and Brence saw that I wouldn't be able to make it down on my own. Glaring at me with dark, angry eyes, he swung me up into his arms and carried me down through the bedlam of thrashing, slamming bodies. The students had almost overpowered the soldiers, but the struggle was still fierce. There was blood everywhere, and three students lay in a heap, covered with scarlet banners that streamed and stained the floor.

As Brence set me down, one of the soldiers broke free and raced toward us with his bayonet raised. Eric tripped him. The soldier fell. Four students jumped on top of him. Wilhelm flung another soldier against the wall, wrestled his rifle away from him and smashed his head with the butt. Hans was merrily kicking a soldier who was already writhing on the floor. As Brence led me toward the doorway, my three gallants formed a guard around us, all three flushed and elated, having the time of their lives.

A plain closed carriage was waiting, a driver I had never seen perched on the seat in front, reins in hand. Klaus had already stowed my bags inside and stood holding the door open. Brence thrust me inside and climbed in after me. Leaning out the window, I looked at the trio who had led the charge on Chez Elena, brash musketeers without plumes or sabres who grinned broadly, eager to get back to the fray.

"Will—will you be all right?" I asked shakily.

"Don't worry about us!" Wilhelm exclaimed. "We plan to leave Barivna ourselves as soon as we finish up here."

"We're going to Paris!" Hans cried. "We're going to rent a garret and Eric is going to become a great painter

379

and I'm going to write great epic poems and Wilhelm is going to beg on the streets or pick pockets for a living or—"

Wilhelm scowled and gave his friend an amiable shove. I signalled them to come closer to the window and then kissed each of them on the cheek. The driver clicked the reins. The students cheered as the carriage began to move down the drive. I looked at Brence and started to say something but couldn't speak. . . . Layers of darkness descended, dark gray, gray-black, pitch black . . . and a strong arm curled around me as I drifted into unconsciousness.

The carriage was jouncing and people were shouting. I opened my eyes and saw that we were in the middle of town and soldiers were rushing the carriage, but we were still moving. A soldier leaped and caught hold of the window frame and held on. Brence raised his pistol and fired; the soldier fell away and I sank into oblivion again. I woke again later on and realized we were moving up a mountain road and there was only the sound of hoofbeats and whirling wheels and creaking springs. Through the window I saw Barivna in the distance, in the moonlight, several fires burning bright orange, flames licking the sky.

"We—we made it—" I murmured.

"Not yet. There's still danger of pursuit. We have a long way to go before I'll feel safe."

"You came back for me."

"Yes, Mary Ellen, I came back."

"You love me," I said groggily.

"Yes, I love you."

"I love you, too, Brence."

I smiled and rested against the soft cushions. Glorious waves of happiness swept over me making the pain recede. I loved him and he loved me and the nightmare was over and we were going to be together and happy at last. He loved me. He really loved me. I had been dreadful to him. I had doubted him. I had sent him away, but he had come back, because he loved me, because he couldn't live without me just as I couldn't live without him. He had saved my life and for the rest of my life I would be his and he would be mine and nothing would come between us. The carriage rocked and bumped but I was drifting on a lovely smooth cloud, smiling through my exhaustion and sinking into a deep and beautiful slumber.

XXXIII

Silvery-white sunlight, spilled over gorgeous country-side. There were trees and rolling green hills with cattle grazing peacefully, the sky a pale, pure blue-white. We had crossed over the mountains. I could see them in the distance, a purple-blue haze. Sitting up, I pulled off the cloak Brence had put around me sometime during the night. The carriage was moving at a smooth, steady pace, no longer rushing furiously. I sighed and shaded my eyes against the sunlight, feeling stiff and sore. My jaw ached terribly but it no longer burned.

Brence sat across from me, looking remote, his dark eyes expressionless. There were four bags on the seat beside him, only two of them mine.

"Are you all right?" he asked coldly.

"I—I think so, a little stiff. I must look dreadful."

He made no reply. He gazed out the window, his profile stony.

"What time is it?"

"Well after twelve, I should think. There's an inn a few miles up the road. We'll stop there."

"Last night was—"

"It's over now, Mary Ellen. We're safe. You can forget about it."

"I remember—we passed through town. There were soldiers. One of them—"

"It was touch-and-go for a while, but we made it. Fortunately they were too busy fighting to pay too much attention to a plain carriage. There was no pursuit."

"It was a nightmare."

"Forget about it," he said tersely.

Why was he so cold, so remote, so untouchable? Last night he had said he loved me. I hadn't dreamed that. *Yes, I love you*, he had said just before I went to sleep, yet now he acted as though I were his sworn enemy. We were together again at last and the nightmare was over and he had never been so icy and detached.

"I see your bags," I said. "You—you've given up your post?"

"I'm no longer with the diplomatic corps," he said frigidly. "I was sacked. Two days ago the Ambassador called me in to give me the news. He had been waiting for official word to come down. I failed in my mission, you see, when I returned to Sturnburg leaving you in Barivna."

"Brence—"

"My diplomatic career is over. Early yesterday morning, as I was packing, one of the junior aides happened to come in. He mentioned that the military takeover had begun. Another aide had left to warn Karl and try to help him escape. I threw the rest of my things in the bags and hired this carriage. When I explained to the driver what would be required of him, he insisted on a huge fee in advance."

"You—"

"I knew what Schroder would do, that he would go looking for you himself. I got there in time, thank God. I had planned to blast my way in with my pistol, but the students arrived at the same time and I went in with them."

"You—you were willing to take the risk."

"It was something I had to do."

"You do love me."

"I told you so that night in the gardens. I said a lot of things that night. All of them were true."

"I thought—"

"I don't care to discuss it, Mary Ellen."

He turned once more to stare out the window. He was angry, rightfully so, and he was still tense after last night's ordeal. But I felt sure that everything would be all right. Brence loved me. He had been willing to risk his life to rescue me. I had caused him to lose his post, but I would make it up to him somehow. I would give up my career. I would remain at his side, helping him, encouraging him. He would forgive me in time, and we would make a new start, together.

We rode on in silence, and after a while the carriage stopped in front of a small, pale yellow inn with brown shutters at the windows. Tall shade trees grew on either side, their leafy boughs touching the roof. Geese honked noisily in front of the stables, and a plump black and white cow was grazing near the vegetable garden. Brence opened the carriage door and, climbing out, helped me to alight. Though he was gripping my hand firmly, I stumbled. He frowned and, when I had steadied myself, let go of my hand. He took my bags out of the carriage and silently led me inside the inn.

The proprietor was fat and jolly and wore a black leather apron to cover his considerable girth. The sleeves of his white shirt were rolled up, and he held a sharp knife. He had obviously been chopping onions— he reeked of them. Brence told him we would need a room, and the proprietor nodded vigorously. When Brence asked him if he could provide lunch, he nodded again, his blue eyes twinkling, his double chin bobbing. Chattering on in German, he darted behind the counter to take down a key. I heard the carriage moving around to the stables as we started upstairs, following the proprietor who continued to talk enthusiastically, though neither of us answered him.

Leading us down a narrow hall, he opened a door and showed us the room. Brence nodded tersely and set the bags down. The proprietor handed him the key, beamed happily and hurried back down the hall. We heard his footsteps clomping noisily down the stairs. Brence glanced around at the small, cozy room. A brightly colored patchwork quilt was spread over the golden oak four-poster. A wide mirror hung over the dressing table, and fresh white curtains billowed at the opened window that looked over the cobbled yard in front of the stables. I heard the geese honking, heard our driver talking with one of the stable boys as they fed the horses.

"This seems to be satisfactory," Brence said. "I'm going back downstairs. Lunch should be ready soon."

"Something with onions, no doubt."

Brench looked at me for a moment, hesitating. I had the impression there was something important he wanted to add, something he couldn't quite bring himself to say. He frowned, his eyes dark and moody, a spray of jet locks tumbling over his brow. I waited for him to speak, meeting his gaze with level eyes. His frown deepened and then, abruptly, he turned and left the room. I shrugged. There would be plenty of time to patch things up later on.

Catching sight of myself in the mirror, I was aghast. The skirt of my gown was torn and crumpled, the sleeves limp, and the bodice had slipped perilously low. My hair was in shambles, my face wan, a bruise on my jaw. I opened my bag, took out a brush and some theatrical make-up and set them on the dressing table beside the pitcher of water. I scrubbed my face, removed the diamond studded bar from the back of my hair and, sitting down, began to restore my appearance. Twenty minutes later my hair was gleaming, and I had managed to cover the bruise with make-up. I added a touch of pink lip rouge for good measure.

Adjusting the bodice of my gown, I puffed up the sleeves and was able to smooth out most of the creases in the skirt. As I did so, I thought about Karl and prayed that he had made it to safety. He had gotten a good head start, and there had been no immediate pursuit of his carriage. Hans, Eric and Wilhelm were undoubtedly already on their way out of the country, and Klaus would probably leave, too, taking Minne to the small farming community where his parents still dwelled. My German sojourn was almost over, but for Brence and me there was a new beginning.

As I left the room, I heard a carriage turning around in the cobbled yard. I moved slowly down the stairs, creamy pink satin rustling, eager to find Brence and charm him out of his dark mood. The proprietor stood

386

behind the counter, wearing a confused expression, and looked at me as though he couldn't quite make out whether I was fish or fowl.

I asked him where Brence was. He muttered something I couldn't understand. I tried to explain that we were lunching together and asked if Brence was in the dining room. He began to speak German again, throwing his hands up, looking distressed. I was beginning to grow impatient when he finally turned and took down an envelope from the shelf behind him. He gave it to me, and I felt my heart stop beating. I opened it with trembling hands. There was a sheaf of German currency inside, no note. I dropped the envelope on the counter and rushed outside. The driver, reins in hand, was ready to depart. Brence had the carriage door open and one foot on the step.

"Brence!"

He turned, stepping back from the open door.

"Damn!" he exclaimed. "I hoped there wouldn't be a scene. I hoped I could get away before—"

"You—you're not leaving!"

"I left money for you at the desk. There's enough to pay your bill and get you back to Paris. The nearest train station is only three miles away, and you can hire a carriage from the innkeeper."

"Brence—"

"I don't want a scene, Mary Ellen."

He stood there beside the carriage with a grim expression on his face. Distraught, I stared at the full bell sleeves of his silky white shirt billowing in the breeze. My heart was bursting. I could actually feel it expanding, swelling, bursting. I caught my breath, shook my head, tears spilled down my cheeks. I took a step toward him. But he scowled and I stopped. I felt I was going to faint. I was dizzy, and my vision was beginning to blur.

"No," I whispered.

"This is the only way."

"I love you. You love me."

"That's my misfortune. You've wrecked my career. You would surely ruin my life. I love you, Mary Ellen,

387

yes, and someday, God willing, I'll be able to get over it. I don't know where I'll go or what I'll do, but I'll do it alone."

"Don't. Please don't do this."

"I have to," he said tersely.

"Brence!"

"Goodbye, Mary Ellen."

And he climbed into the carriage. As he closed the door, the driver clicked the reins and the carriage started down the road. My heart finally exploded. Pain swept over me and the tears spilled wetly down my cheeks. My life was over; it had no meaning for me anymore. I stood very still, whispering his name over and over again. The carriage disappeared around a curve in the road. Brence was gone.

INTERLUDE
IN PARIS

1850

XXXIV

The house on the Champs-Élysées was small and elegant. Chestnut trees grew in front, behind the wrought iron fence, and a small garden flourished in back. I had leased it, furnished, for three months only, for I was uncertain about the future. I had only been back in Paris for two weeks, and Millie was one of my first visitors. She had just returned herself from a long trip with Dumas. He was an inexhaustible and incorrigible traveler, exuberantly exploring every cave, every cathedral, every museum, taking voluminous notes and, according to Millie, devouring every crumb of food available.

"And then, mind you," she declared as I showed her into the sitting room, "when we finally got back to the hotel or wherever, he'd stay up half the night writing, writing, writing. Travel books! And a book on food! And working on another novel as well, and expecting me to entertain him in between chapters when all I wanted to do was soak my feet in a tub of hot water and get some sleep!"

"You've certainly traveled a great deal," I observed.

"Climbing all over the Pyrenees, *me*, climbing mountains and getting rocks in my slippers and tearing my skirts on wild shrubs and staying in country inns with donkeys braying outside my window all night long! And then *Italy*—you can't believe how many churches they have, how many ruins, how many smelly restaurants! All those Italians eating garlic and chattering away a mile a minute, waving their hands and trying to bully you into buying garishly colored picture cards or hand woven baskets! I tell you, it's enough to drive one berserk!"

"It seems to have agreed with you."

Millie smiled her pixie smile and admired herself in the mirror across the room. She was as bright and irrepressible as ever, but there was a new sophistication, in both manner and speech, as well as a wry detachment that hadn't been there before. The gorgeous yellow brocade gown she wore embroidered with gold and silver flowers had an extremely low-cut bodice. Her golden hair, arranged in waves with half a dozen ringlets dangling down in back, was very stylish, and her make-up was subdued: lips a pale rose pink, eyelids softly shadowed with mauve gray. The capricious minx had been transformed into an elegant coquette, but the minx still lurked beneath the surface, pert, merry, refusing to take her new affluence too seriously.

"I shouldn't complain about the traveling," she sighed. "Now that we're back in France it'll be even worse. Paris will be a constant round of parties and theaters and there'll be fights with publishers and collaborators and Alexandre will churn out a couple of more books and then we'll go down to the chateau for a little peace and quiet and it'll be twice as bad!"

"Is the Chateau de Monte Cristo as fabulous as they say?"

"It's incredible. It's like something out of the Arabian nights, showy, ornate, three storeys topped with mansard attics, and has an oriental minaret rising from the facade. A frieze runs around the first storey adorned with the busts of all the great dramatists, including a bust of Alexandre in prominent position. There's a Louis XV salon and an Arab room decorated with stucco arabesques and verses from the Koran painted in gold and bright colors, and—"

Millie shook her head. "You'd have to see it to believe it. The place is a madhouse, swarming with barking dogs and unpaid secretaries and unexpected guests every time you turn around! Alexandre prowls about with a drumstick in one hand and a flagon of wine in the other, dictating to one or another of the poor secretaries who stumbles along after him, and I'm supposed to keep the guests occupied and fight off all the bill collectors! It's absolutely frantic."

"You seem to thrive on it."

"Alexandre has been very good to me," Millie confessed. "I never thought we'd stay together all this time. He's noisy and boisterous and always blustering about, and he's been shockingly unfaithful, and he's kind and lovable and *most* generous."

"I'm happy for you, Millie."

"Truth to tell, Elena, I fear we'll come to a parting of the ways any day now. He's got his eye on a tasty little brunette of the Comédie Française, and I think he'd like to move her in. I'll share him with his wife, but I'll be hanged if I'll share him with Mademoiselle Arlette!"

I smiled, and Millie smiled, too, blue eyes atwinkle.

"But I'll have no regrets. Actually, I'm rather tired of all these literary chaps who prattle about novels and newspapers and royalties and sales. I'm in the mood for someone rough and rugged who'll sweep me off my feet and not waste time talking! But I rather doubt I'll find him in Paris."

"So do I."

We were sitting on a pale ivory satin sofa. Sweeping pale blue drapes hung at the opened French windows, and sunlight streamed into the room, making silvery flecks on the ivory and blue carpet with its fading pink cabbage roses. I poured tea for us and handed Millie a cup. It was the first time we had seen each other since my return to Paris from Barivna a year and a half ago. I had stayed in the city then just long enough to arrange a dancing tour that had kept me on the move for the past eighteen months.

"It's good to see you again, Millie," I remarked. "I've missed you dreadfully."

"I've missed you, too. You've been gone so long! The tour must have been exhausting—England again, half of Europe, and you finally made it to Russia! Was it really as exciting as you claimed in your letters?"

"Very bizarre," I replied. "Travel by sleds, fur lap

robes, gorgeous palaces with colored domes, starving peasants and cossacks, cossacks, cossacks, following me about like bands of wolves, drinking vodka, riding their horses up the stairs and through the halls of my hotel."

"And the Grand Prince?" she inquired.

"He was a dear—sweet and attentive and very married. The stories you read in the papers were pure invention. He did escort me to several court functions, but there was no romance, not even a mild flirtation. He is in his mid-fifties, not at all the dashing figure the journalists presented in their stories."

"Shades of Anthony Duke," Millie quipped. "From all reports, though, it was a wildly successful tour."

"Wildly. There were fantastic crowds everywhere I appeared. I'd like to believe they came to see my dancing, but I've no such illusions. They were attracted by my reputation, not my art. They clamored to see the notorious woman who started a revolution and caused a king to lose his throne."

"At least it must have been financially rewarding."

Smiling, I shook my head. "I only wish that were true. Most of the money was eaten up by expenses— traveling, hotel bills, food. Elena Lopez has an image to maintain. She must travel first class, stay at the grandest hotels, eat in the best restaurants. On this tour I paid my own way, and—I'm afraid it was a disaster."

"You don't mean you're *flat?*"

"Not quite. I was able to lease this house, and there's enough left to live on for a couple of months. But I really have no idea what I'm going to do next. There've been dozens of offers, but I'm not up to another engagement just yet. I still have the jewels Karl gave me. I suppose I could always sell them."

Millie took a final sip of tea and set her cup down. "Do you ever hear from Karl?" she asked.

I shook my head again. "We—we no longer exchange letters. I saw him once, very briefly, when I was in Nice. He's living there, you know, since his exile. We decided it would be best to—sever all ties. There was such notoriety, and Karl hopes to be restored to the throne one day."

I paused, and explained, "He has some—very bad

spells—he's not very well—but on the whole he's content. He lives in a spacious apartment, surrounded by books and papers and paintings. Several loyal members of his court went into exile with him, and they see that he is comfortable."

Looking out at the garden, I thought of the poor, defeated man I had seen in Nice, a gentle soul living in the past and clinging to futile hopes for the future. I put my cup down, sighed and smoothed a fold of my pale violet watered silk skirt.

"Strangely enough, I'm still a countess," I continued. "After the revolution, the new regime acknowledged the validity of my title, although they naturally appropriated my estates and the annual revenue. Legally I'm still the Countess of Landsfeld, for what it's worth. Not much, I fear. I never use the title myself, but the journalists adore it."

During the momentary silence, Millie took my hand and gave it a tight squeeze.

"It really *is* wonderful to see you again," she said. "The tour did you good. You look much better than you did the last time I saw you—after Barivna."

"Older," I said.

"At peace with yourself, a bit weary, but—healed. You're over it, and that's the important thing."

"I suppose so."

"Have you heard from Brence?"

"Not a word. The last time I saw him he was climbing into a carriage in front of the inn. I have no idea where he is or what he's doing."

"It's just as well."

"I know. Life goes on."

"True, and something thrilling is always just around the corner," Millie said brightly. "Just think, both of us could still be at Mrs. Fernwood's!"

"God forbid."

"Do you remember that ghastly wallpaper?"

I nodded. "And those endless stairs."

"*I* remember her wretched cat. It always hissed at me."

"We were so young—"

We began to reminisce, and I found myself smiling

395

as Millie dredged up half-forgotten episodes, recalling them with high humor as only she could. Time seemed to fly, and suddenly, glancing at the clock, she let out a shriek and leaped to her feet, yellow brocade skirt crackling.

"Lord! I was supposed to meet Alexandre at his publisher's office at six, and it's ten past already! I told the driver to pick me up in front of your house at five-thirty. He'll have been waiting all this time, and Alexandre will be having a fit! If I don't hurry he'll sign another contract just to kill time."

"You must come back soon, Millie," I said, walking her to the door.

"I will, Elena. Very soon. I may bring my bags and move in."

"I'd love that."

"I've a feeling Alexandre would, too," she said wryly. "Don't be surprised if I actually do show up with a mound of luggage."

"It would be like old times."

"The two of us against the world," Millie said.

We hugged each other in the doorway, and Millie dashed out to the waiting carriage, waving blithely as it pulled away. I waved back and then went upstairs to bathe and dress. Phillipe was to pick me up at eight to take me to the theater and for dinner afterwards. We had exchanged letters over the past two years, and as soon as I returned to Paris Phillipe had come up from Touraine. I had seen him almost every night since. He was very dissatisfied with his lot as a gentleman farmer, very lonely as well, and I hadn't the heart to deny him companionship.

For the evening, I wore a lovely gown of deep blue velvet and my hair, falling in long, lustrous waves, was held back by diamond clips.

Phillipe, who arrived at the stroke of eight, was resplendent in a dark plum-colored suit and a white satin waistcoat embroidered with flowers in black and maroon silk, his white silk neckcloth neatly arranged. He was thinner than he had been in Barivna, which made him seem even taller, and there was a wistful look in his clear blue eyes. With his cleft chin, his virile, aristocratic features and rich, wavy silvery-brown hair, he was strikingly handsome, an admirable escort.

"Punctual as usual," I remarked.

"One of my failings, I fear," Phillipe replied.

"Failings?"

"I'm always punctual, always polite, always considerate. In a word, frightfully dull."

"Nonsense."

"I'd like to be rakish and bold, arrive two hours late, snarling and making masterful noises. I'd like to be mysterious and mercurial and fascinating."

"I've had my share of fascinating men," I informed him.

"So now you're content to be squired about by a dull young man from Touraine who spends most of his time supervising tenant farmers, keeping track of livestock and investigating fertilizers to determine which will insure the best results."

"Nonsense. I consider myself fortunate to have an escort who is so attentive and charming and—quite the nicest young man I know."

" 'Nice,' " Phillipe said. "That's almost the same as dull."

"Phillipe—"

"Sorry," he said. "Just teasing."

Phillipe smiled his warm, engaging smile that I had found so winning the first time I met him and, taking my arm, escorted me down to the waiting carriage.

The warm night air was fragrant with the scent of chestnut blossoms. As we drove through the streets of Paris we talked lightly of inconsequential things, but I could see that Phillipe was preoccupied, though striving valiantly to conceal it. I realized that his discontent went much deeper than I had suspected and had been growing steadily ever since his father insisted he return to Touraine to manage the family estate.

The theater was ablaze with lights, and elegantly attired couples poured into it. After helping me out of the carriage, Phillipe paid the driver and took my arm again. People stared as we passed under the marquee and into the plush blue and gold lobby. Because of the episode in Barivna and the tour that followed, Elena

Lopez was even more famous than ever, and according to the newspapers Phillipe Du Gard, wealthy young aristocrat, was only the latest in a long line of lovers. Phillipe had been rather embarrassed by the stares and the newspaper stories at first, but after a few days he stopped paying attention to them.

Dozens of pairs of opera glasses were turned on us as we took our seats in the box. I was relieved when the house lights dimmed and the blue velvet curtain rose with a soft rumbling noise. The play was a revival of Hugo's *Hernani*, the thundering melodrama that had been a *cause célèbre* when first performed two decades earlier, revolutionizing French drama. This production was performed to the hilt, flamboyantly done with high color and excessive verve. I found the raging histrionics a bit tiresome, and Phillipe sat with elbow on bannister, chin in hand, immersed in thought, paying not the least attention to the tumultuous drama being enacted beyond the footlights.

As we were making our way down the grand staircase after the final curtain, I heard boisterous cries of "Elena! Elena! Wait!" The staircase was crowded, the chandeliers dazzling, and at first I couldn't tell where the noise was coming from. Then I saw the three young men pushing their way down the staircase from the upper balcony. I could hardly believe my eyes. Hans waved. Eric smiled broadly. Wilhelm cheered, shoving past a group of humbly dressed young people who blocked his way. I felt a great rush of elation as they hurried toward us like a tribe of American Indians.

Phillipe and I moved on down the grand staircase to the lobby, and the boys joined us a moment later, after almost knocking down a plump matron in white satin. Hans threw his arms around me. I kissed his cheek. I kissed Eric and Wilhelm as well, ignoring the stares of people moving past us. Poorly but neatly dressed in dark suits, flowing white collars and colorful neck scarves, wearing their hair much longer than they had in Barivna, they looked properly Bohemian. Hans' fingers were ink-stained. Eric's sleeve had colored chalk marks on it, and Wilhelm looked as though he were suffocating in his too-tight suit.

"We've been reading about you!" Hans exclaimed. "I told these two we should look you up, find out where you were staying and pop in for a visit, but Eric here, he said you wouldn't remember us."

"Shame on you, Eric," I scolded. "You all know Phillipe Du Gard, don't you?"

"We've been reading about him, too," Wilhelm said gruffly, as they acknowledged Phillipe.

"We saw you in the box," Hans continued. "I nudged these two and told 'em, 'the one with the long dark hair, it's her!' Eric said no, but then we were so high *up*, right under the rafters, and he's half blind anyway."

"It's marvelous to see you three again. Did you find your garret?"

"We found it," Eric said. "It's freezing cold in winter and warm as Hades in summer, and sharing it with this pair isn't a joy, believe me. If I'm not tripping over Wilhelm's barbells I'm stumbling over Hans' piles of newspapers. Every time one of his articles appears he buys five copies of the papers."

"You've given up poetry?" I asked Hans.

He grinned. "I'm writing for the newspapers now, short, gossipy articles about theatrical folk, longer articles about local sights and scenes—'human interest' stories, they call 'em. It helps pay the rent while I toil away on my novel."

"Damned novel," Wilhelm grumbled. "He reads each chapter aloud to us as soon as it's finished. I thought his epics were bad, but this novel—six hundred pages—and he hasn't even introduced all the main characters. Chap thinks he's a genius."

"*He* works in a gymnasium," Hans informed me, "pushing and prodding flabby aristocrats into shape and teaching 'em to wrestle. Makes a fortune in tips. The patrons are afraid if they don't tip him he'll tear off an arm next time he has 'em on the mat."

"And you, Eric?" I inquired.

"I discovered quite soon that I'd never be another Rembrandt," he explained. "I'm doing illustrations for the journals, pen and ink drawings, pastels in chalk. It doesn't pay much, but they like what I do, and I enjoy it immensely."

We chatted for a few minutes in the crowded lobby, attracting considerable attention. Despite their long, flowing locks and Bohemian affectations, the three of them were the same exuberant youths I had known in Barivna, bright, merry, delighted with life and living it with gusto. I gave them my address, insisted they call on me and hugged each one before they charged on out of the theater arm-in-arm, three jolly musketeers who found Paris an enchanting playground.

In front of the theater, the street was jammed with private carriages and cabs. Since the restaurant was only a few streets away, we decided to walk. Although his manner was amiable, Phillipe was silent and withdrawn, still immersed in thought. The usual stares greeted us as we entered the restaurant and the headwaiter showed us to our table. Throughout the meal, Phillipe made an effort to keep conversation alive. He smiled frequently, but his clear blue eyes retained their sad, wistful look.

It was after one o'clock when the carriage pulled up in front of the house on the Champs-Élysées again. Phillipe walked me to the front door. Moonlight polished the steps, and the trees cast soft black shadows that brushed the walls. A thread of music drifted through the night from a distant cafe, and the horse moved restlessly on the cobblestones, hooves making a quiet clatter. Phillipe stood on the steps with his hands thrust into the pockets of his breeches, his head tilted slightly to one side. A tender smile played on his lips.

"I haven't been very good company tonight," he remarked.

"You've been delightful, as always."

"Polite, undemanding—"

"Don't start that again, Phillipe. You mustn't deprecate yourself that way. You're everything a woman could hope for."

"Truly?"

"Truly," I said.

He looked so very young, so beautiful, so vulnerable. I was touched. Tender feelings stirred inside me. I was reminded of the gentle squire who pined silently for his lady fair during the Middle Ages. Smiling at him I brushed the wave back from his forehead, and then I rested my fingers on his cheek. Phillipe took my hand and held it tightly, nervous now, an uncustomary frown creasing his brow.

"Do you mean that, Elena?"

"Of course I mean it. These past two weeks have been wonderful. I'm very fond of you, Phillipe."

"I only wish you had used a stronger word."

"I—"

"I love you, Elena," he said. "I've loved you ever since that first day in Germany when I came to abduct you. I fell in love with you immediately. I'll never be able to love anyone else."

"You—you don't mean that."

"I do. I know. I haven't declared myself before because —well, I suppose I was afraid. I was afraid that any kind of declaration would drive you away, and being near you meant too much for me to risk that. I know you don't love me, not the way I love you, but—"

He paused, groping for words. The frown deepened. I was silent, sad inside, dreading what would come next.

"I hope you might come to love me," he continued. His voice was low, filled with emotion. "I want to marry you, Elena. I guess I—it probably seems unthinkable to you at the moment, but I want you to consider it."

Moonlight shimmered at our feet, and shadows brushed the walls. When I did not reply Phillipe let go of my hand. He had been squeezing it so tightly that my fingers felt numb.

"My father has already turned the management of the estate over to me and I will inherit everything someday. I'll be a wealthy man, Elena. We could live in Touraine for part of the year and take a house here in Paris for the rest of the time. We could travel. We could do anything you wanted to do. If you wanted to, you could continue with your dancing. I wouldn't stand in your way."

"Phillipe, I—I don't know what to say."

"I don't want you to say anything now. I want you to consider it. I have to return to Touraine tomorrow. I'll be there a week. When I return to Paris perhaps—perhaps you'll give me an answer."

I nodded. Phillipe smiled, the most beautiful smile I had ever seen. It went straight to my heart, and I had to fight the tears.

"I—I know I'm not like the other men you've known," he said, "but I could make you happy, Elena. I'd like to have the opportunity. I want to devote the rest of my life to you."

He leaned forward to brush my lips with his, gently, so gently, and then he stepped back and smiled again, young, beautiful, a suitor any woman in her right mind would hold fast. Shaken, I watched him move back down the walk and through the gate. As his carriage drove away, I stood in front of the door with the cool night air stroking my shoulders, feeling touched, torn, hoping with all my heart I would have the strength to make the right decision.

XXXV

Although we had kept in touch through letters, it had been over two years since I had seen George Sand. I didn't know she was back in Paris, and her invitation came as a surprise. After her break with Chopin, she went through a period of zealous political involvement, but recently she had begun to spend more and more time at Nohant, her lovely country estate. The flamboyant, outrageous George of earlier days had become something of a recluse, seeing few of her friends and completely avoiding the limelight to spend more of her time writing.

As the carriage drove over the bright, sun-splattered streets, I wondered how I would find her. She was, I knew, still grieving over Chopin. His death in October had affected her deeply. He had been the great love of her life, and many claimed that their final separation had broken her spirit as well as her heart. Would I find a sad, pitiful creature who was a shadow of her former self? I doubted it. The fires of old might have burned themselves out, but the George I knew glowed with a serene flame of compassion eternally bright.

The carriage shook as we crossed over one of the great stone bridges that spanned the Seine. The river was gray-green, sparkling with shimmering sunbursts, small boats bobbing along briskly, a great barge slowly making its way downstream. In the distance I could see Notre Dame looming majestically above the feathery green treetops. We passed book stalls and lively cafes and eventually turned down the street lined with plane trees. I remembered walking down that street in the moonlight, Franz' heavy brown velvet cape wrapped around my shoulders. That seemed a lifetime ago.

As I paid the driver, I gave him a winning smile and asked if it would be possible for him to return for me in two hours. The smile worked beautifully. He agreed and, pocketing his fare, drove on off. I stood in front of the house for a moment. I had stood on this identical spot after leaving the party with Franz. I'd had a very difficult decision to make that night. I had an even more difficult one to make now.

Phillipe was returning to Paris this afternoon. I would see him tonight. I had weighed his proposal carefully, hardly thinking of anything else, and I still hadn't reached a decision.

Sighing, I moved on up the steps and rang the bell. George opened the door herself, a gentle smile on her lips, her large, luminous eyes full of warmth. She wore a lovely wine-colored afternoon gown, and her raven hair was in a long pageboy, several soft gray strands among the dark. She took my hands in hers and squeezed them. She had indeed aged during these past two-and-a-half years and was slightly plumper than before, more matronly looking, but the glow was still there, suffusing her with a beauty that had nothing to do with physical appearance.

"Elena, my dear," she said. "It's been much too long."

"Far too long," I agreed.

We hugged briefly, and then she led me into the drawing room. It was as snug and welcoming as I remembered it with its aura of rubbed, slightly shabby elegance. The plush blue sofa was still draped with the fringed purple and black shawl, and the desk was cluttered with books and papers, the floor around it littered with wadded balls of discarded pages. The only new touch were the plants, a profusion of them in varying shades of green, some with delicate blossoms, growing in pots all over the room. A brass sprinkler sat on the desk atop a stack of books.

"I'm afraid the place is a bit dusty," she apologized. "I keep it closed while I'm at Nohant, and I didn't give Mathilde much advance warning."

"What lovely plants."

"I was just watering them as you rang. You don't mind if I continue? They're quite demanding. I brought them up with me from Nohant. They would have perished otherwise. One can't depend on servants to care for them properly."

"I didn't know you loved plants so much."

"Plants, flowers, all things green and growing—the gardens at Nohant are splendid. I like nothing better than puttering around in an old dress and a pair of heavy gloves as I dig in the flower beds."

George smiled and took up the sprinkler. I sat down on the sofa to watch as she watered a delicate fern. The smile lingered on her lips, soft, tender, and I saw at once that the things I'd heard about her weren't at all true. George Sand was not a broken woman. There was sadness in her eyes, but her manner was wonderfully serene. She had clearly found peace, inside herself, and that was something the gossips would never be able to understand.

"It's been months since I've been in Paris," she said. "The noise, the odors, the pace—I ask myself how I was ever able to live here. After the fresh air and open spaces and heavenly smells of the country the city seems uninhabitable."

"Will you be here long?"

"For another week at least. My play *Claudie* is to be produced, and I must discuss arrangements. It's tiresome, but it's absolutely necessary if I'm not to be robbed blind. Contracts! And theatrical producers aren't the most trustworthy breed around."

"How well I know."

George touched the fern lightly and then moved on to water a frail African violet.

"I've brought my work with me, as you can see. That's my one consolation. After I've haggled for hours in a stuffy, smoke-filled office and yelled myself hoarse over unethical clauses, I can retreat to my desk and the book in progress. I prefer to work on the lawn at Nohant," she added, "curled up on a chaise longue with a shawl wrapped around my shoulders, writing pad on my knees, a bird singing on a nearby limb."

"You love the place, don't you?"

405

"I've always loved it," she replied. "It was never my intention to leave. I could have spent my whole life in that house but my husband made that impossible. When I was living there with him, Nohant was a prison. I had to leave for self-preservation. Now it's become a haven."

"You seem—very content, George."

"Content?" She examined the word thoughtfully. "I suppose I am. Contentment—in the long run it's much nicer than happiness. Happiness makes far too many demands on us, depends all too frequently on—on other people, but contentment—" She paused, idly sprinkling the violet. "It's something altogether different."

George set the sprinkler down and brushed a soft raven lock from her temple.

"It's ironic, isn't it? After so many years spent in frantic pursuit of happiness I've found something far more satisfying, something no one will ever be able to wrest away from me."

There was a moment of silence. George gazed across the room, eyes seeing only the memories that haunted her.

"George," I said. "I—I was sorry to hear about Frederic."

She didn't reply at first. She stepped over to the window to peer out at the patch of pale Parisian sky visible above the tangle of rooves and chimney pots. When finally she turned to smile at me, her dark eyes reflected the sadness inside.

"He didn't ask for me," she said quietly. "At the end, he—he made no mention of my name, but my love for him was still there. I know he felt that. Pride alone kept him from sending for me. Frederic was always so very proud—"

"His music will live forever. You're responsible for much of it."

George nodded, but as she stepped across the room to rearrange the flowers that stood in a lovely white porcelain vase, I wished that I hadn't mentioned Chopin. His death was too recent, her memories of him still too fresh, too painful. George gave the flowers a final touch, then came to sit beside me on the sofa.

"Tell me all about yourself, my dear. I hear you've been seeing quite a lot of a young aristocrat from Touraine. I may have turned into a rustic country lady, but I still keep up with all the gossip. You and Du Gard are the talk of Paris. They say you're robbing the cradle."

"Phillipe is actually a year older than I. He—he's a very fine young man, George. I met him in Barivna. He was one of Karl's aides. His father called him back from Barivna to manage the family estate. We kept in touch, and when I returned to Paris—" I hesitated, thinking of Phillipe, thinking of the decision I must make.

"He's in love with you?" George asked.

"Yes. But Phillipe is the first man I've known who hasn't tried to sleep with me. He wants to marry me."

"I see. And do you love him?"

"Not the way I'd like to love him. I'm very fond of him, and I think in time I could grow to love him. He's tender and kind, attentive, always thoughtful. He's handsome and wealthy and—and there's not a girl in Paris who wouldn't jump at the chance to marry him."

"You're not any girl," George said in a gentle voice. "You're Elena Lopez."

"I know. I've become the creature Anthony Duke created. Sometimes I wish none of this had ever happened. If only I had met Phillipe before Anthony, before Franz, before—"

I paused, gazing at the hazy white rays of sunlight streaming through the windows.

"We would live in the country most of the time," I continued. "The chateau is lovely, and it would be— very peaceful. Phillipe would always be there. I could always depend on him. The men I've loved—they always leave, George. Brence, Anthony, Franz—each one abandoned me. I could feel secure with Phillipe."

"I've no doubt you could."

"He loves me so much, and—for the first time in my life I would have stability. I've lived the life of a gypsy, moving from place to place. Oh, it's been glamorous, and heady and exciting, but—" Again I paused, turning to look into those dark, lovely eyes. "I no longer have any illusions about happiness, George. I'd like to find the kind of contentment you've found."

George took my hand and held it lightly, hesitating a moment while she considered her reply.

"I can understand your desire, my dear," she said, "but you're very young. I'm forty-six years old. I have gray hair. I can afford to settle for contentment, but you—you, my dear, have a great many years of living to do before you can make any kind of compromise."

I was silent. George continued, "You're an extraordinary woman, Elena. You've had fame and glory and glittering success. You could give it all up for love—real love, eternal and consuming—but mild affection isn't enough. I've no doubt you could be content for a while with this young man, but ultimately—"

She let the sentence dangle. She didn't need to finish it.

"It wouldn't be fair to Phillipe," I said.

"Nor to yourself. You've been hurt, my dear, and you want to retreat. That might be satisfying for a few months, a year, but the music would still be playing, the flags still waving, and you would long to take your rightful place in the parade."

"You're right, of course."

George had said nothing I hadn't already said to myself, but it was good to hear it confirmed. Marrying Phillipe would be a compromise, a retreat, an easy out for me at this particular time in my life, but ultimately a disastrous mistake. During the past week I had toyed with the idea of marrying him, for it was a very attractive idea, but I realized now that I had never seriously considered it. I was far too fond of Phillipe to use him, and I would be doing just that if I accepted his proposal.

George and I talked of other things then, in that warm, comfortable room with its plants, its littered desk, its glowing colors. She told me more of life at Nohant and about Alexandre Manceau, the young engraver, a friend of her son's who had come to stay with them. Manceau was very attentive, she confided, and very efficient as well. He helped out in so many ways. He was like a second son to her, she confessed, but as she spoke of him there was a tender smile on her lips, a warm glow in her eyes, and I suspected that her relationship with Manceau was part of the contentment she spoke of so eloquently. The passionate fireworks might be over, she might be plump and have strands of gray in her hair, but George was far too womanly a woman to be able to exist without some kind of love. Manceau was clearly a comfort to her, and I was pleased to hear about him.

"I think I hear my carriage," I said a while later. "I really must be going and let you get back to your work."

"Revisions, revisions!" she said. "Act One is adequate, Act Two needs a great deal of work, and they tell me Act Three is utterly impossible. Why did I ever undertake this project?"

As George walked me to the door, the skirt of her gown made a quiet rustle. She took both my hands in hers and held them for a moment, her dark, glorious eyes full of affection.

"It's been wonderful seeing you again, my dear. You must come visit me at Nohant one day soon."

"I'd like that."

She held on to my hands, reluctant to let them go, and I could see that there was something else she wanted to say. She finally gave me a quick hug and kissed me lightly on the cheek.

"Take care, dear," she said gently, "and—don't give up on happiness just yet. Hold on to the dream a while longer. Perhaps—perhaps you'll be one of the fortunate ones."

XXXVI

Phillipe arrived at the house on the Champs-Élysées shortly after six. He had come directly from the hotel, stopping only long enough to change clothes. His hair was gleaming, boyishly unruly as usual, and his eyes were filled with expectancy. Young and splendid and wonderfully handsome, he was in wonderful spirits. He pulled me to him and kissed me exuberantly, confident my answer would be the one he wanted to hear.

"Sorry I'm so early," he exclaimed. "You look marvelous with your hair like that, and that light blue dress —it's so good to see you! I've missed you dreadfully."

"I've missed you, too, Phillipe."

"I suppose you'll want to change before we go to dinner. We're going to the grandest, plushest restaurant in Paris."

"I—I'd rather not."

"Oh?"

"I thought we might just go to one of the cafes and have a—a glass of wine."

"That'll be fine. Shall we leave now?"

"Let's," I said.

Phillipe kept up a bright, engaging chatter as we drove to an outdoor cafe with its tables scattered beneath gaily striped red-and-white umbrellas. Humble clerks in neatly brushed suits dined early with their girlfriends, vivacious shopgirls whose gloves and befeathered hats were a pathetic attempt at elegance. Carriages passed to and fro. Couples strolled in the park

411

across the way. Shadows lengthened on the pavement as daylight began to fade. An old woman in a tattered gray shawl attended a pushcart filled with brightly colored flowers.

"This is nice," Phillipe said. "I'm glad you suggested it. Who needs red plush and fancy chandeliers when you can have Paris itself? Are you sure you'll have nothing to eat?"

"Just a glass of wine. I—I'm really not hungry."

"Wine it shall be. The best."

He signaled a waiter and ordered the most expensive wine with an endearing flourish, and then he sat with chin propped in hand, looking at me with that marvelous half-smile playing on his lips. He was so happy, so full of hope, so certain of future happiness. He was one of the truly good people of this world, and he deserved a woman who would love him without reservation. I fervently wished I could be that woman.

"I never knew a week could be so long," he said. "I thought about you night and day, Elena, as I made my rounds on horseback, as I supervised the construction of a new barn for one of the tenants, even as I cleaned and oiled my gun."

"Your gun?"

"We're having a plague of rabbits in Touraine. They're destroying the crops. As soon as I get back I'll have to take a shooting party out to discourage the pests."

"Somehow I can't see you doing that sort of thing."

"I'm very efficient," he told me. "If a job needs to be done, I do it promptly, without fuss. That's something you don't know about me. You see me as—as a dreamy-eyed youth. I'm not, you know. Perhaps when you see me in boots and old brown breeches and sweat-stained white shirt with sleeves rolled up to my elbows you'll get a different impression."

The waiter brought our wine. Phillipe handed me my glass and toyed with his own, the smile still playing on his lips. Around us glass tinkled and merry laughter sounded. Paris wore a festive air as the evening sky became a dark, dull silver.

"I turn brown as a savage in summer," Phillipe continued. "I ride. I shoot. I even get into an occasional fight. One of the tenant farmers was trying to cheat us last summer. I blackened his eye, kicked him off the farm. In Touraine I'm a different person altogether."

"Phillipe—"

"You'll love it there," he said hurriedly. "I—I talked with my father about you. He's eager to meet you, to welcome you. The chateau is lovely, and you could redecorate some of the rooms if you liked. I'm really quite wealthy, you know. I—"

"Don't," I said quietly.

"I can be the man you want me to be, Elena."

"I don't want you to be—anything but what you are."

"And that isn't enough, is it?"

His voice was pleasant, almost playful, and the half-smile curved on his lips, but his eyes were filled with desperation. I felt terrible, for I did love him. I loved the cleft in his chin, the heavy, errant wave that continually tumbled over his brow. I loved his vitality and charm and that aura of innocence. But I loved him as I might love a dear younger brother, and that wouldn't suffice.

"I love you, Elena. I love you with all my heart and soul."

"I'm sorry."

"The answer is 'no,' isn't it? I saw it in your eyes when you opened the front door. I saw the sadness, the reluctance. I—I tried to fool myself, tried to convince myself I was mistaken, but—"

He cut himself short. He sighed quietly and shook his head and took a sip of wine, and then he stared down into the glass. The couple at the table next to us got up to leave. Two of the waiters began to argue amiably. Smells of cooking came from inside the cafe. The old woman in the gray shawl brightened up and smiled a crooked smile as a gentleman paused to buy a bouquet of flowers and present them to the demure brunette beside him.

"Perhaps I was too precipitate," Phillipe said quietly. "I should have waited to declare myself. I should have given you more time to get to know me, really know me."

413

"I do know you, Phillipe. I know you're one of the finest young men I've ever met, and—"

"The answer is 'no,'" he said.

"I wish it could be different. I wish I could be the woman you deserve. There is so much you don't understand, so much I—couldn't explain. I'm not right for you, but the loss is mine. If I thought I could make you happy, if I didn't know I'd eventually disappoint you, hurt you—"

"I'm willing to take that risk."

"It wouldn't work, Phillipe. I wish it could. I wish I could use you to solve my own problems, but I'm much too fond of you for that. Marrying you would be an easy solution, but it wouldn't be fair to either of us. The problems would still be there, only temporarily assuaged."

Silently he set his glass of wine down. A small band began to play in the park across the street. Carriages continued to rumble gaily over the cobblestone street, and a little girl shrieked with laughter. As he gazed at me, smiling a brave smile, I felt that he had never looked more beautiful, and my heart ached miserably.

"I guess that's that," he said.

"Go home, Phillipe. Go back to Touraine and—and meet a nice young girl who will live for you alone, who will bring you the kind of happiness I could never bring you."

I spoke quietly, trying to keep the emotion out of my voice. Phillipe did not reply. The music from the park across the way was light and airy, a lilting waltz. Phillipe finally sighed and pushed his glass aside.

"I suppose I'd better take you home now," he said.

"I think I'll finish my wine. You—you go on, Phillipe. I'll take a cab when I'm ready."

"If that's what you want."

He stood up, tall, elegant, beautifully controlled despite the anguish in his eyes. He seemed older at that moment—lost, defeated.

"There'll never be anyone but you, Elena," he said.

"You may believe that now, but you'll feel differently soon. You'll meet the right girl, and you'll marry her and this—this will all be forgotten."

414

"I'm afraid not."

"It has to be this way, Phillipe. Please understand."

"I understand."

"Forget me. Forget me and—please forgive me."

"I'll never forget you," he said, "and there is nothing to forgive."

He smiled that lovely, tender smile, gallant, trying to make it easier for me, polite and charming even in this moment of despair. In a rush of emotion, I longed to take back everything I had said, longed to make it right for him and undo all the pain I had caused. Phillipe hesitated for a moment, then stepped around the table and took my hand. Lifting it to his lips, he kissed it.

"Goodbye, Elena," he said, looking into my eyes and smiling once more.

He turned and left the cluster of tables. Hurrying past the pushcart full of flowers, he moved on down the street in a brisk stride and merged into the crowd to disappear from sight. I remained at the table, fighting to maintain my composure. It was over. I had sent him away. The others had abandoned me, brutally, and I had rejected the one man who loved me completely, selflessly, the one man who loved me the way every woman dreams of being loved. Still, I had done the right thing, I knew that, but the knowledge was little consolation. I sat quietly, filled with grief as I thought of what might have been.

XXXVII

"It's just as well," Millie announced blithely as we strolled under the arcades of the Palais Royale. "I was getting a mite tired of it all, to tell you the truth, all those bill collectors, all those harried secretaries underfoot, and he was always writing! Literary life's not for me, definitely not. It was a very amiable parting," she continued. "Alexandre gave me a kiss on the cheek and a smack on the behind and stuffed an enormous roll of bills down the front of my dress. I'll always adore the man, even if he is an outrageous scamp."

A week had gone by since Phillipe had left me sitting at the outdoor cafe. Millie and I were out early shopping. She had moved in with me the day before, bringing an inordinate amount of luggage and filling the house with her merriment. I was very thankful. It had been a bad week. I was still trying to forgive myself for what I had done to Phillipe, and his brave, tender smile seemed to haunt me. He was back in Touraine now, and I prayed he would meet a beguiling young girl who would make him forget me.

"I love this place," Millie announced, gazing around at the masses of ancient gray stone that surrounded the gardens. "Just think, royalty used to cavort here. Now the arcades are lined with shops, gambling halls up above. Want to sample some perfume? I understand this shop is one of the best."

"Not really. I'm afraid I'm not very good company today."

"Nonsense. You're just preoccupied. You did the only thing you could do."

"I know that, but I still can't help blaming myself."

"You mustn't, Elena. He'll suffer a bit, yes, but I daresay he'll thank you one day for what you did."

The arcades were cool and shadowy, the tiles uneven beneath our feet, and there were smells of damp stone and sweat and ancient dust. Dozens of shoppers moved about, examining the wares in the windows, and children played noisily amidst the flowers in the untidy gardens. A dog barked, leaping after a stick thrown by a chubby little girl in pink. Millie and I stepped into one of the dim, narrow shops to look at some outlandishly priced hats, and then we paused a moment to look through the window of a pet shop where brilliantly feathered birds perched in bamboo cages. Soon we found ourselves going through the narrow passageway and out the gate, leaving the Palais Royale behind.

Millie and I strolled aimlessly through a labyrinth of shadowy, twisting streets, enjoying the walk, in no hurry to fetch a cab. A streetcleaner swept the cobblestones listlessly. Dingy gray pigeons fluttered about the buildings, cooing serenely. Paris wore an air of mellow beauty and elegance, slightly shopworn and rubbed at the edges. The seductive charm of the city seemed to have paled, but I knew that was because of my own state of mind.

"Have you thought about what you're going to do next?" Millie asked.

I shook my head. "I suppose I'll take another engagement. Not in Paris. I may even go on another tour."

"That would be smashing! I'd adore it."

"You mean you'd go with me?"

"Of course! Truth to tell, I've missed the old excitement—all that discomfort, all those frayed nerves and shouting matches and opening nights in drafty theaters without proper lighting. I loved every minute of it."

Millie began to chatter merrily about the past, recalling some of our adventures—the time Anthony forgot our tickets and we were stranded in a chilly train station all night long, the night we stepped into the dressing room to find a trained seal act occupying it, the hotel in Bath we shared with dozens of haughty, arthritic old women who were outraged by our presence and watched our comings and goings through a sea of lorgnettes. I began to feel much better, smiling as I remembered. Incidents that had been infuriating at the time seemed vastly amusing now.

"And all those *men*," Millie continued. "I made ever so many friends! At least one in every town. I guess you could say I was shopping around for the right one. Maybe I'll find him yet."

"And then?" I inquired.

"I'll latch on to him and he'll *never* get away. I'm not going to find him in France, that's for sure. These Frenchmen! They're charming and lusty and ever so gallant, but I want someone big and strong and stable, someone who'd rather get out and work than sit around discussing books and paying compliments."

We turned the corner and started down a broad avenue lined with elegant shops. The people strolling there wore much more splendid attire, and the carriages bowling up and down the street seemed shinier. Mellow beauty gave way to glittering newness and swank glamor. Exquisite jewelry and fine plate sparkled behind clear, polished glass, gold awnings above the windows, and gleaming white marble steps tempted one to enter plush dress shops and perfumeries. The contrast was startling, but that was Paris.

Millie continued describing her ideal man: "Virile, of course, someone who can be rough if necessary, stern and forbidding, but tender, too, gentle and soft-spoken. He needn't be too highly educated. I want someone more interested in me than in politics and plays and the latest novel, someone honest and unspoiled and—"

Millie cut herself short with alarming abruptness. Wearing an expression of thorough amazement, pink lips parted, blue eyes wide with surprise, she pointed. I turned to peer at the window of a chic, expensive bookstore, and I could feel the color leaving my cheeks. I stared in stunned belief at the pyramids of books and the poster behind them. It featured a vivid painting of me in spangled Spanish costume, and the words in French read: AT LAST! THE TRUE STORY OF

ELENA LOPEZ IN HER OWN WORDS! THE AUTOBIOGRAPHY ALL PARIS HAS BEEN WAITING FOR! The books were bound in bright red, with the title, *ELENA LOPEZ: Ma Vie et Mes Amours,* in gold leaf on the spines.

"You didn't tell me you'd written a book," Millie exclaimed.

"I haven't," I retorted.

"But—"

"Fetch a cab, Millie," I said. My voice was like ice. "Wait for me. I'll be right out."

I swept into the store. A prissy, self-satisfied clerk in a tailored tan suit hurried over to me, ingratiating smile fixed in place. He didn't recognize me at first. I was wearing a modest pale violet frock and no make-up. I pointed to the table laden with copies of the book, so new that they still smelled of printer's ink and glue.

"Ma Vie et Mes Amours," I snapped.

My cheeks were flushed with anger and my eyes must have flashed. The clerk was taken aback, supercilious manner giving way to awe as he recognized me. Flustered, excited, he was momentarily at a loss for words. I tapped my foot impatiently, and he scurried over to fetch a copy for me.

"How much?" I demanded.

"Oh, Miss Lopez, we wouldn't dream of charging you. I wonder—I wonder if you might sign a few copies for us. I'm sure our customers would be thrilled if—"

I stormed out of the store before he could finish the sentence. A cab was waiting at the curb, the door standing open, Millie already inside. I climbed in, closed the door and opened the book. I began to read as the cab moved down the street. I skimmed, turning the pages at a rapid rate, pausing now and then to take a deep breath as I spotted a particularly outrageous passage. When the carriage stopped in front of the house, Millie paid the driver, and we went inside. I sat down in the drawing room to read for another half hour, and then I slammed the book shut and hurled it across the room.

"Is—is it that bad?" Millie asked nervously.

"It's abominable!"

"I wonder who wrote it?"

"There's only one person who *could* have written it! I intend to find him, and when I *do*—"

I marched upstairs, sat down at the dressing table and put my hair up in the old style. I applied stage make-up: dark mascara, blue-gray shadow, rouge, vivid red lip rouge, and then I took down one of my boldest gowns, a vivid crimson brocade. Elena Lopez was going to make a call, and no one was going to doubt my identity. I only wished I had a horse whip to carry with me.

"Elena!" Millie exclaimed as I came downstairs. "Surely you're not going out like that? It's not even noon!"

"I don't know when I'll be back!" I informed her. "I may not even *be* back. Before the day is over I may be behind bars, waiting sentence for cold-blooded murder!"

Millie looked aghast, but there was a twinkle of amusement in her eyes just the same.

"Do take care," she cautioned gaily.

I hurried out of the house, hailed a passing cab and gave the driver the address of the publishing house that I had carefully noted earlier. I couldn't remember ever having been so angry in my whole life. I was absolutely consumed with rage, and it seemed to grow as the cab made its way across the city, finally reaching a dingy, run-down district of gray brick buildings. The driver stopped in front of a tall, narrow building festooned with ornate plaster work crumbling sadly under the grime. The front door was painted blue. I asked the driver to wait.

The office I wanted was on the third floor. My heels rang loudly as I climbed the stairs. The door to the office was closed, but I didn't bother to knock. Monsieur Hulot was sitting behind his desk, eating his lunch from a brown paper bag. There were bundles of books all over the floor, piles of manuscript all over the battered desk. He looked up in dismay as I entered and scrambled hastily to his feet, knocking over a stack of papers as he did so.

"Miss Lopez!" he exclaimed. "What—what a surprise!"

"Who?" I demanded, holding up the book.

"Uh—I don't know what—Miss Lopez, I—uh—I trust there's been no misunderstanding. He told me he'd written the book with your full approval. He said—"

"I want a name. I want an address. I want them now!"

Hulot supplied them promptly, and twenty minutes later I found myself in an even dingier district on the other side of the Seine. This was the Paris of struggling painters and writers, the true Bohemia, a labyrinth of narrow, twisting streets with tall, crowded buildings and cheap cafes. No trees and flowers relieved the gloom. Windows were unwashed. Very little sunlight found its way there, yet a curious atmosphere of hope prevailed. The young people I saw on the streets seemed unusually carefree, immersed in dreams of a glorious future.

Dismissing the driver, I looked up at the building. It certainly wasn't what he had been accustomed to. I frowned, trying to hold on to my anger, but it was ebbing—much too rapidly. There was no concierge inside, and although the lobby was thankfully dim, I still caught glimpses of the hideous wallpaper and dusty potted plants. I climbed more stairs, six steep flights this time, the last two bare of carpet. I could smell dust and flaking plaster and cheap wine as I reached the top floor and banged on the bare wooden door.

"Just a minute!" he called.

I could hear him moving around inside, and then he threw the door open with jaunty aplomb and smiled. The smile vanished immediately. He had obviously been expecting someone else, someone female judging from the enthusiastic way he had opened the door. Anthony stepped back, at a loss for words for perhaps the first time in his life. I swept past him into the cluttered garret apartment, gazing around with cool disdain. Stacks of newspapers and magazines covered the floor. A table littered with empty wine bottles stood in front of a lumpy sofa that clearly served as a bed.

"You've come down in the world," I observed.

"Oh, these are just temporary lodgings," he assured me. "I'll be moving out any day now, as soon as Hulot sends the first check. You—uh—you look smashing, luv. Always did have a sense of style. That dress is certainly *red*, but then red *is* your color."

He had overcome his surprise and seemed quite at ease now. He wore snug blue and gray checked breeches and a white linen shirt open at the throat, the sleeves rolled up. His rich, wavy brown hair was as unruly as ever, and the merry blue eyes sparkled with mischief. With his slightly twisted nose and wide, engaging grin he was as devilishly handsome as I remembered. I steeled myself against the flood of memories.

"I guess you've read the book?" he said.

"I read it."

"Terrific, isn't it? I thought I did a super job."

"There is an awful lot about *you* in it."

"Best part of the book," he said brightly. "I wrote it in English, of course. A friend of mine translated it into French chapter by chapter. The English version will come out in London next month, and there's going to be an American edition as well."

"Don't count on it."

Anthony arched a brow, tilting his head to one side. "Hey, you're not angry, are you?"

"Angry? *Angry!* The whole book is a pack of lies! It's outrageously sensational. Pure fabrication from first page to last! Those chapters about my affair with Franz! That section about my stay in Barivna! How dare you? How *dare* you!"

"Guess you are a bit miffed after all," he observed.

"I intend to have every copy recalled from the stores! I intend to sue you for libel! I intend to—to—"

Too angry to continue, I glared at him with blazing eyes. He sighed and shook his head, and then he grinned again. That was the last straw. I raised the book I was still holding and hurled it at him. Ducking nimbly, he flung his arms up to protect his face. I then reached for one of the empty wine bottles and let it fly. Then another . . . and another . . . Anthony leaping out of the way of each burst and pleading with me to listen to reason. I continued my barrage, blind with fury, until I finally ran out of bottles. As I searched for something else to throw, he dashed across the room and grabbed me.

423

"Get your hands off me!"

"Easy, Elena. Easy. Ouch!"

"Let go of me!"

"Still a wildcat, I see. Still full of spirit."

"I said let go!"

"Can't, luv. Afraid to."

I kicked his shin and pounded on his chest with my fists. As he tried to restrain me, grinning broadly, I saw that he was enjoying himself immensely, and that merely spurred me on. I fought viciously. Anthony chuckled and finally managed to get his arms around my waist, holding me in a tight grip with my arms trapped at my sides. I struggled for several more minutes, and then, energy spent, I finally stopped resisting. Cautiously, he loosened his grip, afraid to let go entirely.

"Feel better now?" he asked.

"I detest you, Anthony."

"I seriously doubt that, luv."

His arms held me loosely, ready to tighten again at the least sign of struggle. I could feel his strength, the power in his tall, hard body. I could smell his skin, his hair, the tangy shaving lotion he still used. I remembered other times, other fights and the rowdy, passionate reconciliations that invariably followed. I tried to put those rousing bouts out of my mind, but the memories were too strong. Anthony Duke was a rogue through and through, but he had been a magnificent lover.

He seemed to be reading my mind.

"Missed me?" he inquired.

"The day you walked out on me was the happiest day of my life."

"The saddest day in mine, luv. I didn't want to do it, you know. I hated myself for losing all your money to those swindlers with their phony bonds. I couldn't face you, couldn't bear to tell you what happened."

"So you skipped."

"I left a letter," he protested. "Surely you got it?"

"I got it."

"Hardest letter I ever had to write."

"I'm sure."

"You did all right for yourself."

424

"Indeed I did. I proved to myself I didn't need you."

"You need me, Elena. You still need me. I've got plans."

"Let go of me, Anthony."

"I've got big plans. We're going to——"

There was a knock on the door. Anthony hesitated a moment and then released me. He frowned and glanced at the door. There was another knock and another, much louder. Sighing, he looked at me with indecision but still reluctant to open the door. I gazed at him coolly. Finally, he shrugged and stepped over to open the door. The girl was blonde and voluptuous, a gaudy coquette with a friendly smile and far too much make-up. Anthony said something I couldn't hear, and the girl peered over his shoulder. When she saw me she bristled and opened her mouth to protest, but he quickly gagged her with his hand and shoved her out onto the landing, closing the door behind them. I heard shrill, angry cries and then the sound of high heels clattering down the stairs. Anthony wore a sheepish grin as he came back in.

"Sorry, luv. Business."

"One of your protégées, no doubt. You shouldn't have sent her away. I'm leaving."

He pretended to look crestfallen. "Leaving?"

"You haven't changed a bit!" I snapped. "You're still the most outrageous, the——the most infuriating man I've had the misfortune to meet!"

"You still care. I knew it."

"Get out of my way!"

"You're really leaving? So soon? I thought we might have lunch together and then have a real reunion. Hey, wait a minute! Let me get my vest and jacket. I'll take you home."

"No, thank you!"

"Hold on! You don't know the neighborhood. There's never any cabs. You'll get lost. Can't have you wandering about the streets in an outfit like that."

I started toward the door, but he grabbed my wrist and yanked me back and down into a chair. When I tried to get up he raised his hand back as though to slap me, a gesture that was only half playful. I didn't want another fight, so I sat there resigned and maintained an icy, aloof silence while he scrambled into his dark blue vest and blue-and-gray checked jacket. His manner was jaunty as he stepped to the badly cracked mirror to adjust his gray silk neckcloth.

"There!" he announced. "Dashing as ever."

I continued my silence as we went downstairs and outside, but Anthony was not at all perturbed. His old charm was working full force, and I was furious with myself for letting it get to me. He was so damnably engaging. It was impossible to stay angry with him, impossible not to forgive him. I wasn't going to do anything about the spurious autobiography. I knew that already. He clearly needed the money. His suit was beginning to look threadbare, and I suspected it was the best he owned. The garret apartment was frightful, probably freezing cold in winter.

Damn him, I thought ruefully. I came here intending to inflict mortal wounds, and now I'm actually beginning to feel sorry for him.

"We'll have to walk a spell," he said chattily. "There's sure to be a cab down near the river. Lovely weather, isn't it? You really look sensational, Elena. The past three years have been good to you. Glad you came to see me. Would you believe I was planning to call on you any day now? I have a terrific proposition—"

"I'm not interested in any of your propositions."

"America, luv. I spent two years in America after you and I separated, and the country's fabulous—rough and rowdy and exuberant and wealthy beyond your wildest imagination. There are towns out West you wouldn't believe—endless plains with real live Indians—I saw 'em with my own eyes. And California! They've discovered gold out there, you know. It's the most incredible spot on earth, and they're starving for entertainment—"

"Here's the river. I don't see a cab."

"I made connections while I was over there, Elena. I was in charge of a theatrical troupe. We traveled all over. I met a lot of people, and all of them asked me about you. You're famous over there, too, and when the book comes out—"

"I told you I'm not interested."

"I've already started making arrangements," he continued. "When you hear what I've got in mind you'll jump at the chance."

"You don't give up, do you?"

"We'll make a bloody fortune," he assured me.

"Dream on," I said dryly.

"Oh, I know you're put out with me," he admitted, "but you're not one to hold a grudge. It's going to be you and me, luv, just like it used to be."

I gave him a look. He ignored it, thrusting his hands into his pockets and sauntering along as though he owned the world. We passed a weathered gray bookstall heaped with yellowing pamphlets and tattered prints and hundreds of used books. Students browsed leisurely, searching for treasures. A young man in splattered blue smock sat at his easel, painting one of the arching stone bridges, and two weary prostitutes strolled by, their make-up and garish attire somehow pathetic in the bright daylight. Spotting a cab in the distance, I stepped to the edge of the pavement and waved.

"We need to get together," Anthony said. "We need to talk."

"I don't think so."

"Don't be that way, luv."

"We have nothing to discuss, Anthony."

"I've never been able to forgive myself for what I did to you. I want to make amends. I mean that. I want to—"

The cab pulled over. The driver tipped his hat, and I opened the door and climbed inside. Anthony, looking genuinely worried, reminded me of a forlorn little boy whose sand castles were about to be destroyed. The old feelings rose up inside me, and there was a moment of dangerous weakness as I looked into his eyes. He stood there in front of the bookstall in his near-threadbare suit, valiantly striving to maintain an air of confidence, and my heart went out to him. It took great effort to resist the impulse to reach out to him.

"Be reasonable, luv," he pleaded.

Giving the driver instructions, I closed the door of the cab and said, "Goodbye, Anthony."

He looked crestfallen. As the cab drove back through the city I was filled with remorse. I thought about the past, reminding myself of Anthony's bullying manner, his outbursts of temper, the infuriating way he had taken me for granted. But as I listed all his faults, I kept remembering his faith in me, his engaging grin, his enthusiasm and high spirits and that incredible charm. In some ways those days when we were together seemed to be the happiest days of my life.

I steeled myself against the memories, and by the time the cab finally stopped in front of the house I had them under control and was irritated at myself for being so vulnerable where Anthony Duke was concerned. Millie was waiting for me inside, wearing a deeply concerned expression in place of the lively curiosity I expected.

"You needn't look so grave," I said wryly. "It was Anthony, of course. I got his address from the publisher. I threw a few things, but there was no actual bloodshed. He hasn't changed at all! He had the temerity to suggest a tour of America. Can you believe it? He spent two years over there and—"

I cut myself short. Something was wrong. Something was very wrong. I could sense it. Millie wasn't herself at all, and she hadn't paid the least bit of attention to what I was saying.

"What is it?" I asked.

"A messenger came while you were gone, Elena. He —he brought a letter from Touraine, from—Phillipe's father. I didn't open it, of course, but the messenger was a Du Gard servant and he told me—"

She took both my hands in hers and squeezed them tightly.

"There—there's been an accident. . . . Phillipe went out with his shotgun to hunt rabbits and apparently he tripped over a log and—I'm sure the letter will provide all the—"

I heard the words, but none of them registered because none of it was real.

"It was an accident. . . . One of those crazy freak accidents—"

Millie's voice seemed to grow fainter and fainter and

then I saw her lips moving but there was no sound, only the buzzing noise inside my head. We were in the sitting room and it began to revolve and colors blurred together, the blue sofa a smear of blue, the violet drapes shimmering violet that melted into the ivory walls, blurring, the room spinning now.

"No," I whispered. "No—"

Millie took hold of my arms, gripping them tightly, and gradually the room stopped spinning and the colors grew still, took shape and texture and became sofa, drapes, wall, but a terrible hollow feeling inside of me seemed to expand, emptying me of all thought, all emotion, annihilating me. I looked at Millie and I could no longer see her.

"It—it happened three days ago," she said. Her voice seemed to come from out of a void. "His father wanted you to know. He knew how much Phillipe loved you and—"

"He isn't dead. He isn't. It's not true."

"Elena—"

"It's not true."

She gripped my arms, holding me firmly. "Elena, you've got to be strong—"

XXXVIII

Paris had lost all its charm for me. The majestic old buildings, the elegant parks, the gardens, the festive cafes—all of them reminded me of Phillipe. As long as I remained the grief and the guilt would be constant. It was three weeks since I had received Monsieur Du Gard's letter, but the feeling of emptiness was as strong as it had been when Millie first broke the news. I had gone through day after day in a kind of trance, and Millie had stayed by me constantly, fending off the journalists, screening my callers, being as protective as a feisty mother hen.

I had seen no one but George and Theophile Gautier and my three young cavaliers who had come to call to express their sympathy quietly, their manner touchingly subdued. Today was the first day I had dared venture out alone. Ever since they had learned of Phillipe's death, the journalists had been like a pack of blood-hounds. Millie literally had to fight them away from the door, and dozens of them had camped out in front of the house, hoping to get an interview. They had managed to get to Phillipe's father, and even though he had insisted that his son's death was an accident, it hadn't stopped them from printing wildly sensational stories of his suicide.

Young Du Gard was an expert with guns, the stories claimed, who had been going out into the woods to hunt ever since he was ten years old. But crushed by Elena Lopez' refusal to become his wife, unable to endure life any longer without the woman he loved, he had fetched his shotgun, bid his father farewell and wandered off into the woods to die. He had made his death seem "accidental" to spare pain to those he loved, they wrote. The stories were extremely convincing, and there were dark moments when I believed them myself.

I walked slowly through the park. Millie had wanted to come with me, still worried about the state I was in, but I had insisted she stay home. I had a lot of thinking to do.

I wanted to believe Phillipe's death had been an accident, but grave doubts assailed me. I kept remembering that final goodbye, that final smile, and deep inside I realized that suicide was a very real possibility. Phillipe had been so very sensitive, and he had been very unhappy. Always considerate of others, he would have left no note, and he would indeed have made his death look like an accident. Suicide or not, I knew in my heart that if I had agreed to marry him he would still be alive. He would still be smiling that boyish smile, radiating youth and innocence and goodness.

I paused beside one of the plane trees, and the lawn stretching before me became a hazy jade green blur. I hadn't intended to cry, but the tears came of their own accord, spilling down my cheeks in tiny streams. I let them flow, giving way to my grief this one last time. I allowed myself to think of him as he had been when I first knew him, and for several minutes the pain was almost unbearable. It swept over me in waves, but time passed and finally I drew myself up, wiped the tears away and took control.

I had to make some kind of plans for my own future. I could always take another engagement. The theatrical managers had been almost as persistent as the journalists during those empty weeks. The new "scandal" made Elena Lopez an even greater attraction, and I knew I could name my price. I didn't relish the idea. I was weary of glamorous engagements and plush surroundings and sophisticated friends and newspaper headlines and all that went with it. I wanted something new and different, something fresh and exciting, something that would present a challenge. I wouldn't find it in Paris. I doubted that I would find it anywhere in Europe.

I wanted to forget, and in order to forget there would have to be a complete change. America was the answer, of course. I had been thinking about it quite a lot. It was probably insane even to consider Anthony's proposition, but nevertheless I *had* considered it, and under the circumstances it seemed the perfect solution. It would certainly be a challenge. I would never have dreamed of undertaking such a venture before, not with Anthony Duke, but now . . . Millie would leap at the chance to go, I knew. We would probably end up stranded in some wretched frontier town swarming with gunslingers, but it would be a grand adventure.

I moved on down the walkway, lost in thought, and then I looked up and saw him sauntering across the lawn toward me. At first I couldn't believe my eyes. I thought I was imagining things, but even in the distance that tall, slender figure and that jaunty walk were unmistakable. He wore a dapper new tobacco brown suit and a dashing brown-and-cream striped satin waistcoat, his neckcloth dark, dull orange. He was spruce and neat and shining, the picture of success. M. Hulot's first check had obviously arrived. As I watched him approach I assumed a cool, haughty composure that belied the elation stirring within me.

"*Here* you are," he said. "I've been looking all over. Do you realize how bloody *big* this park is?"

His manner was extremely casual, as though our encounter had all been arranged. So I, too, maintained a distant demeanor, refusing to give way to his abundant charm so dangerously seductive.

"Surprised to see me?" he inquired.

"How did you know where to find me?"

He grinned that familiar grin that was so irritating and so enchanting. "Millie told me. I had to choke the information out of her. Enjoyed it thoroughly. Just as her face was about to turn purple she spluttered and gasped and confessed you'd come for a walk in the park."

It was a preposterous exaggeration, but that was Anthony.

"Minx has been trying to keep me from seeing you for the past two-and-a-half weeks, and I'd had enough."

"You—you've been trying to see me?"

"I've come to the house at least a dozen times. The little hussy refused to let me in."

"She never mentioned it."

"Should have finished the job while I had my hands around her throat," he muttered. "Don't know why you want to take up with *her* again, luv. She thinks she's your mother!"

"Millie loves you, too."

Anthony smiled, and then he looked grave.

"Look—uh—I—" He paused, clearly embarrassed. "I was sorry to hear about young Du Gard, Elena. Rotten thing to happen. I know it must have hit you pretty hard. Those wretched stories in the papers and all. I'm truly sorry. . . ."

There was sincerity in his voice. I could tell he meant it.

"It's been—pretty dreadful," I confessed.

"I'd like to murder some of those chaps," he said darkly. "No respect for your feelings at all. I'm taking you away from all this, luv. We're going to leave Paris as soon as possible."

"Oh?"

"We're going to America. I've made all the arrangements. The book's a smash, and by the time our ship docks in New York it will have come out over there, too. Everyone in America will be clamoring to see you."

"I thought I told you I wasn't—"

"We'll tour the Eastern Seaboard," he continued, "and then we'll sail around the Horn and go to California. It's going to be terrific! Just like old times."

"Just like old times," I said dryly.

"They weren't so bad, you know."

"I can just see it. You'll play the tyrant, bossing everyone around. You'll handle all the money and lose it in some improbable investment—a gold mine with no gold, a cattle ranch with no cattle."

"You don't have much confidence in me, do you?"

"None at all," I replied.

"I'm hurt," he said, "deeply hurt, but I'm going to

434

rise above it. Come on, let's go back to the house. We've got a lot to discuss. I know you're going to argue, but you might as well save your breath. I've been working on this for weeks."

"Have you? What a shame. I have no intention of going to America with you—or anywhere else for that matter."

"You don't mean that, luv."

I didn't, but he'd have to work to discover it. He took hold of my elbow and guided me toward the boulevard, confident of his ability to make me do his bidding. I felt that marvelous stimulation he always inspired, and it was like a glorious tonic. Anthony was right. I was going to argue. I was going to put up a grand fight. In the end he would have his way, of course, but the victory would be all mine.

CALIFORNIA

1853

XXXIX

The gunfire no longer disturbed me. I had grown used to it. From my window, I peered down at the sea of mud that passed for a street. There were no bodies lying there, but a drunken miner stood in front of the Chinese laundry firing his pistol into the air while the pigtailed proprietor and his wife huddled in the doorway. Three tough-looking, bearded men in boots, faded blue breeches and plaid shirts rushed out of the saloon, then scurried back through the swinging doors as the miner yelled and pointed his gun at them. After a moment he burst into laughter, took an unsteady step forward and tumbled face first into the mud.

I sighed and moved away from the window. Such scenes were not at all unusual in the rugged mining towns we had been touring for the past eight weeks. Gunfire, fist fights, saloon brawls that spilled out into the street were common fare. Thank goodness this was the last town on our tour and we were leaving for San Francisco this morning. I had given my final performance the night before on a tiny stage in a saloon packed full of rowdy men who stomped, yelled, fired at the ceiling, guzzled bottles of whiskey and, as I took my bows, showered the stage with gold and silver coins. The rain of coins occurred in every mining town I played, an added bonus that brought joy to the heart of my manager and filled me with terror. I was delighted to receive the extra revenue—often the amount thrown

439

on stage was almost as much as that taken in at the box office—but dodging the flying coins was hazardous.

Moving to the wardrobe, I took down the last dress, folded it and placed it in the large leather traveling bag that stood open on the bed. I wondered where Millie could possibly be. It was almost eight thirty, and the coach was due to pick us up in front of the hotel at nine. She hadn't shown up for breakfast, and I hadn't seen her since she helped me dress for last night's performance. I wasn't worried, not really. Though the mining towns were dangerous, filled with riffraff from all over the world and virtually lawless, Millie invariably had a personal bodyguard of ardent suitors. In a territory where women were still scarce and even the plainest was avidly courted, she was having the time of her life.

Millie adored California. She adored the excitement, the noise, the raw pioneer atmosphere that prevailed throughout most of the state. I, too, found it fascinating, but a little disconcerting. It certainly provided a contrast to the rest of the country we had visited. New York, Philadelphia, Boston and the other eastern cities were surprisingly sophisticated, and the southern cities had a special charm that won me over immediately. But California was unlike anything I had ever seen. There was incredible vitality, a sense of newness in the air, a feeling that anything at all was possible.

Closing the suitcase and fastening it, I glanced around the room to see if I had forgotten anything. The hotel, which had been hastily thrown up four years ago, was already run down and decrepit. My "suite" consisted of a sitting room with a bare wooden floor and lumpy sofa, and a bedroom with tarnished brass bed, battered wardrobe and unsteady dressing table with a spotty mirror hanging over it. In Europe, such a hotel would have been avoided as a slum. Here it was sheer luxury, and its rates were higher than those charged by the grandest hotels in Paris. Still, it was better than sleeping in a pitched tent, and we had done that on more than one occasion on this tour.

I heaved the bag onto the floor and, pulling a small black leather jewel case from under the bed, set it on the dressing table. Although we had left most of our trunks in storage in San Francisco, I had refused to travel without my jewelry. Not that I wore any of it—not in these lawless mining towns—but I wanted to have it with me just in case. The past two-and-a-half years of touring had been very successful financially, but a great deal of the money had been eaten up by expenses. I had managed to put money in banks in both New York and New Orleans, it was true, but the amounts weren't all that large, and the jewelry Karl had given me remained a form of insurance. I wasn't about to leave it with any storage company.

There was more gunfire outside, more yelling and the sound of horses galloping through the mud. I didn't even bother going to the window but, instead, examined myself in the dull silver mirror with its murky bluish-gray spots. I had pulled my hair back sleekly and fastened it in a French roll, leaving a large fishhook curl over each temple. I wore a gown of deep maroon satin, which was hardly a suitable garment for traveling by coach over thirty miles of rugged terrain, but Anthony had cautioned me to look my best when we arrived in San Francisco. I was eager to get back to the city of hills, for I had seen precious little of it the first time I was there.

Our ship, the *Northener*, had entered the harbor on the twenty-first of May, and Anthony had smuggled Millie and me to the hotel. My presence in the city was to be kept secret while he arranged a future engagement at the American Theater, set up the tour of the mining towns and made valuable contacts with the press. The tour would provide just the right "build up" for the San Francisco debut, he informed me. Thanks to his showmanship and knack for publicity, I had created a sensation in each town we played. Journalists following me from town to town supplied the San Francisco papers with dozens of sensational stories about the celebrated Elena Lopez. When I was ready to perform in San Francisco, the whole town would be clamoring to see me, Anthony claimed. He had planned everything carefully, working hand-in-hand with the gentlemen of the press.

And so, Anthony had left for San Francisco immediately after the final saloon performance—that is, immediately after the last coin was collected, counted and added to the box office take. Because of the large amount of cash he would be carrying to place in a San Francisco bank, he had decided to travel by night, on horseback, an armed guard riding at his side. Since the countryside was swarming with bandits, Anthony felt Millie and I would be much safer traveling by coach in broad daylight. A rifleman would be perched up on the seat next to the driver, ready to blast away at the first sign of trouble. I wasn't too worried about bandits—so far, we had traveled all over this part of the state without being robbed—but I was thankful for the precaution nevertheless.

Stepping back from the mirror, I pulled on one of my long black lace gloves. I didn't like being separated from Anthony even for a day, but I was confident that he knew best. He planned to deposit the money in the bank, first, and then make arrangements for my "welcome" to the city later in the day. There would undoubtedly be huge crowds to greet my coach, dozens of dignitaries, perhaps even a brass band. Anthony knew his job, and during the past two-and-a-half years he had proved himself a shrewd and brilliantly capable manager. I had played extended engagements in all the major cities and most of the large towns on the Eastern seaboard, and then the tour had continued on through the South. The show, which was an enormous success everywhere, played a three-month engagement in New Orleans to packed houses. After that ended, we boarded the ship that brought us around the Cape to California.

I pulled on the other glove and smoothed it over my elbow. I had very few complaints about the way Anthony had handled things. He still tried to bully me on occasion, but for the most part his manner was considerate and extremely protective. I had come to depend on the rogue, and he was the most important person in my life at the moment, even though I wasn't in love with him. I loved him in a way, I couldn't deny that, but there was no deep emotional attachment. I knew him far too well for that. I had gone out with other men during the tour, and Anthony had dazzled countless women along the way, but none of this affected our basic relationship. We fought, we made love now and then, and we enjoyed each other's company. I nevertheless kept my guard up with him, and he maintained an attitude of casual fondness with me.

A knock on the sitting room door announced the hotel clerk who came to take my bag downstairs. He started to take the jewel case as well, but I told him I would attend to that myself. With a nod, he carried the bag out, exiting just as Millie burst into the room, bright and lively and full of enthusiasm which, this morning, I could definitely do without. Looking fetching in a sky blue muslin frock printed with small black polka dots, and her blue eyes sparkling, Millie had a soft pink flush on her cheeks, suggesting that she, at least, had not spent the night alone.

"All ready to go?" she asked.

"As ready as I'll ever be."

"Oh dear, you're in a bad mood."

"Getting up at seven o'clock in the morning isn't my idea of bliss. I didn't sleep well last night. All that noise."

"I think there was a fire. Someone said a storehouse burned down. Have you had breakfast?"

I nodded. "The bacon tasted like strips of broiled leather, the coffee like muddy water. And had they been dropped on the floor, the scrambled eggs would've bounced like yellow rubber balls. I didn't see *you* downstairs."

"I skipped breakfast this morning."

Millie smiled her pixie smile and stretched languorously, looking as if she were a sleek, tawny cat that had just lapped up a bowl of cream. Millie had decided that it was time to find herself a husband, and she had been shopping for just the right one ever since our arrival in California. Apparently, she felt it was a delightful occupation, for it kept her in splendid spirits, and Millie definitely believed in the value of comparison. Fancy free, capricious, she had left a string of rejected suitors in her wake, enchanting each briefly and then moving on in pursuit of some ideal.

"You needn't look so pleased with yourself," I snapped.

"His name was Frank," she informed me. "Such shoulders, and a smile you couldn't resist. He begged me to marry him."

"And?"

"Another reject," she sighed. "No ambition, poor dear. He'd be content to work as a ranch foreman for the rest of his life. Sometimes I think I'll *never* find the right man," she added. "It's so frustrating."

I was unable to resist a smile. Millie smiled back and sauntered over to the window to look down at the street. I heard horses and splattering mud, and a whip cracking as a husky voice cried "Whoa!" Millie, pushing a tumble of curls from her temple, told me that the coach had just pulled up. I picked up my jewel case, and we left the room to descend the wooden staircase into the lobby. As I glanced around at the shabby flowered carpet, dusty plants and peeling mahogany desk, I breathed a sigh, thankful to be leaving.

Four stout horses stamped impatiently in the mud as the hotel clerk helped the driver secure our bags on top of the coach. The worn brown cumbersome vehicle was liberally caked with mud. A crusty-looking old-timer with beard and fringed leather jacket sat up on the seat in front, rifle across his knees. Millie and I exchanged glances. Anthony had told us we would have our own private coach. I should have known he would hire the cheapest he could find.

"Charming," she said.

"Economical," I remarked.

"I don't know why you put up with that man, Elena."

"Sometimes I wonder myself. Well, at least it will get us to San Francisco. I suppose that's really all that matters."

Millie looked up at the guard. "Sixty if he's a day," she observed. "Do you suppose he knows how to use that rifle?"

"Let's hope he won't have to."

"They say the Black Hood bandit and his gang are somewhere in this area. I must confess, I'm a tiny bit worried."

"About bandits?"

"The Black Hood in particular. I—I didn't plan to tell you this, but Frank said the bandit was in town last night. He came to see you dance. Frank said the man sat in one of the balconies that overlook the stage."

"That's absurd. He wouldn't dare show himself."

"Frank swears it's true. He says Black Hood and four of his men came in the rear entrance just as the lights were going down and slipped up the back stairs to a box. They were armed with guns. The box was already occupied, but the bandits held the occupants at gunpoint throughout the performance, while their leader sat and watched you dance."

"I—I did notice that one of the boxes was curtained off last night. I thought it was—rather unusual."

"They slipped out the way they'd come just as you were taking your final bows," Millie continued. "No one knew anything about it until an hour or so later when the men who'd paid for the box finally managed to kick and stomp enough to attract attention. They were found squirming around up there on the floor, tied up and gagged. Frank knows one of them. That's how he got his information."

"How did they know it was the Black Hood gang?"

"The leader didn't make any effort to conceal his identity. He was dressed all in black and wore a heavy silk hood over his head, just like in those posters we've seen tacked up. The men said he spoke in a soft, raspy whisper to disguise his voice. They were terrified. It was them, all right, no doubt about it."

"I wonder why they'd take such a risk?"

"To see you, luv. Why else?"

"Well, now that they've seen me," I said, "I doubt that we have anything to worry about. Our money's safely in San Francisco by this time."

"But they don't know that," she pointed out. "Besides, you've still got your jewel case. I can't help wishing that guard were a little *younger*."

Millie thrived on drama and excitement, but I could tell that she was genuinely concerned. Black Hood was a notorious figure, already a legend in these parts. He had been marauding this section of California for over two years, eluding the law with diabolical skill. Many claimed he was a prominent citizen who took to the road in order to maintain his high standard of living. Others claimed he was a Russian whose lands had been confiscated. He had staged over seventy successful hold-ups, and there was a fifty-thousand-dollar reward for his capture. His coming to see me perform had been risky indeed, but he was celebrated for his boldness. He was also known for his gallantry toward the ladies, and he didn't prey on defenseless women. I decided not to give it any more thought.

The driver and the hotel clerk had finished fastening our bags on top of the coach. The guard sat on his perch, idly stroking his rifle. Three men on horseback galloped down the street, slinging mud in every direction. A great commotion broke out in the saloon across the street. Guns were fired. A man came sailing backwards through the swinging doors and toppled onto the wooden walkway. A blond giant in shirtsleeves and apron stepped out to observe his handiwork, scowling fiercely down at the man he had knocked unconscious. The Chinese laundryman and his wife were having a violent argument. Pots and pans clattered. It was only nine o'clock in the morning.

"It's not Paris," Millie observed.

"Or New York or Boston, for that matter. San Francisco will be better."

Millie didn't reply. She was too busy staring at the man who strolled lazily toward us carrying a battered leather bag. He was very tall, very lean, with a loose, lanky build that somehow suggested wiry strength. His sandy brown hair was sun-streaked, and his amiable brown eyes were half-concealed by heavy lids that gave him a sleepy look. His nose was sharp, his cheeks lean and taut, and his mouth was a wide pink slash, crooked at one corner. He wore scuffed brown boots, tight tan breeches and a faded beige cotton shirt printed with brown flowers. A lethal-looking pistol rested on his right hip in a leather holster as scuffed as his boots. It had obviously seen years of service.

"Pardon me," he said, addressing the driver. "You wanna tie this up there, too?"

As the tall man hoisted the bag on top of the coach, the driver looked hesitant. The stranger smiled. He was probably in his early thirties, and he wasn't at all good looking, but there was a casual self-confidence and an aura of indolent sensuality about him that many women would find extremely appealing. Millie was giving him a careful inspection, hands on hips, a defiant look in her eyes.

"This is a private coach," she said.

"Goin' to San Francisco, isn't it?"

"As a matter of fact it is."

"Then it's the right coach," he informed her.

His voice was soft and lazy, slightly slurred, with that distinct, enchanting flavor indicating he came from the Deep South. I loved the sound of it, but Millie wasn't at all pleased with this tall intruder with his floppy, sun-streaked hair and sleepy demeanor.

"You can just take that bag right back down!" she told him.

"Wouldn't dream of it. You got it fastened up good?"

The driver looked at the stranger, then eyed his gun and scrambled onto the front seat beside the guard. The guard hadn't so much as glanced at any of us. He continued to stroke his rifle and stare fixedly into space.

"Reckon we might as well climb in, ladies," the stranger said.

"Now you just wait a minute!" Millie snapped. "I told you this was a private coach."

"Reckon you did," he drawled.

"In case you don't *know* it, this is Elena Lopez, and I—"

"And you're Millie," the man said. "Fella told me about you. Said you'd probably give me some lip. Said I should bust you one if you got too uppity. Might do it, too."

Millie gasped, but there was a certain gleam in her eye as she sized up the man. I suspected that she just might have met her match. The stranger smiled his crooked smile and turned his attention to me, ignoring her completely.

"Saw you dance last night," he remarked. "I'm mighty proud to be accompanyin' you to San Francisco.

Fella offered to pay me—wanted an extra guard along —but when he told me who I'd be ridin' with, I wouldn't take his money. I was plannin' to go to Frisco anyway."

"I assume you're referring to Mr. Duke?"

"Cocky English fella. Dressed like a dude. I didn't catch his name. He acted like I shoulda known it already."

"That's Anthony, all right."

"Do you have a name?" Millie snapped.

"Bradford, Ma'am. James Bradford. My friends call me Brad."

"Well, Mister Bradford, I suggest you climb up there with the driver and the other guard. You certainly aren't going to ride inside with us."

"That's exactly what I'm plannin' to do," he replied, ignoring her hostility.

He opened the door of the coach for Millie, who gave him a furious look and climbed inside, swishing her skirts defiantly. Bradford grinned and, taking my hand, helped me inside with great gallantry. I sat beside Millie and placed the jewel case at my feet, and Bradford took the seat facing us, pulling the door shut behind him. I was beginning to like him. But he was the first man we'd met in California who hadn't been immediately captivated by my audacious companion, and Millie didn't like that at all. She was prepared to sulk. I found it amusing. Bradford stretched his long legs out and folded his arms across his chest, his eyelids drooping, his wide mouth curling in that amiable, crooked smile.

The driver yelled and cracked his whip, and the coach lurched forward as the wheels pulled out of the mud. Millie toppled sideways, revealing another two inches of bosom as her bodice slipped down. Bradford appeared not to notice. She gave an exasperated sigh and straightened back up, brushing her skirt as though to erase the small black polka dots, determined to draw attention to herself. Bradford's lids drooped lower, leaving only a slit of eye visible as he rested his head against the tattered green velvet padding. Indolent, sensual, indifferent, Bradford presented a definite challenge to the minx at my side.

Jostled along, we made our way down the muddy street, wheels sinking and slipping, sloshing the thick brown mire as the horses strained forward. Before long the town was behind us, and we were passing the gold fields. The mining sites were depressingly ugly, a blight on the gorgeous countryside, but it was gold that had made California, bringing countless thousands to what had been primarily a Spanish territory with a few trappers, explorers and White Russians mixed in. California had become part of the Union less than three years before and was still an infant as far as statehood was concerned.

Soon the road grew firm and hardpacked, and the horses moved along at a faster clip, the wheels skimming noisily, the ancient coach shaking from side to side. It was terribly uncomfortable at first, but I soon got used to the motion and paid no attention to it. Bradford seemed to be asleep, resting head and torso against the padded seat, legs sprawled out in front of him. Millie was simmering, planning a new tactic, no doubt. I gazed out at the countryside, so unlike any I had ever seen before. There was coarse gray-green grass with patches of brown, slender trees whose twisted limbs spread hazy shadows and, in the distance, bare redddish-brown mountains that took on a gold hue in the sunlight. Beyond the mountains was the vast Pacific Ocean. California and its stark beauty was somehow magical and invigorating to me.

The carriage rolled over a particularly nasty rut and bounced heavily. Millie let out a cry and grabbed the window sill for support, golden curls falling across her cheek. Bradford lifted his heavy lids part way, gazed at her with pointed lack of interest and then shifted position, burrowing his broad, bony shoulders deeper into the cushion, his arms still folded across his chest. Millie pursed her lips, sat back angrily and shoved the curls back into place.

"I wonder how long we'll be in this thing?" she asked querulously.

"Should get to San Francisco late afternoon, early evening," Bradford said, not bothering to open his eyes.

449

"I'm hungry," she complained. "I don't suppose any arrangements have been made for lunch."

"We'll come to a way station around noon," he drawled. "There'll be food there."

"I must say, he's certainly stimulating company." Millie turned to me, and announced, "If there's anything I hate, it's a shiftless, dim-witted male, particularly one who looks like a scarecrow!"

"Millie!" I scolded.

Bradford's lips curled with the faintest suggestion of a smile, but he gave no other indication that he had heard her insulting remarks. For once at a loss with a male, Millie pouted in silence, and as the coach continued to shake and sway I found myself thinking of Anthony. I was provoked with him for hiring such an ancient coach in order to save a few dollars, but at the same time I was touched and pleased that he had been willing to hire an extra guard. It must have done his heart good when Bradford refused to take his money. Knowing Anthony, I doubted that he had insisted too strongly.

Anthony was probably arranging my welcome to San Francisco at that very moment, setting things up, placing placards all over the city, recruiting the newspapermen. There would be crowds, music, fanfare, the inevitable little girl in white frock who would hand me a bouquet of roses. I wouldn't have been at all surprised if the Governor of California appeared as well. I was lucky to have such an efficient manager, I reflected. How right I had been to let him bring me to America. In many ways the past two-and-a-half years had been the most exciting in my life, at least professionally. In Europe I had been a celebrity, true, but here in America I had been treated like visiting royalty, welcomed with exuberant gusto wherever I appeared. Good-humored and easygoing, the Americans had been prepared to love me, and my notoriety seemed to delight them.

An hour passed, an hour-and-a-half, and Bradford still hadn't opened his eyes. The coach rattled over a bridge spanning a small, shallow stream and moved laboriously up a slope. Millie looked at me, then glanced out the window. Suddenly she placed a hand over her heart and let out a very effective shriek, causing Bradford to leap up and crack his head on the roof.

"Oh!" she exclaimed. "Oh dear! I thought I saw some men in masks riding toward us, but," she added sweetly, "I see now that it was only a group of trees."

Bradford, who had whipped his pistol out of its holster, replaced it and sat back down, his expression exceedingly grim. Millie glowed with triumph as he rubbed the top of his head. She smiled a smile that should have earned her a resounding smack across the mouth. Bradford looked as though he were contemplating one.

"I really *did* think I saw some men," she purred.

"I'm not amused."

"I hope you didn't hurt yourself," she taunted. "But I'm relieved to see you have good reflexes. I guess I'm just on edge," she continued. "I've heard so many stories about the Black Hood gang, you see, and I'm absolutely terrified."

Bradford smoothed his hair back, eyeing her with considerable displeasure.

"This *is* their territory, isn't it?"

"They are supposed to have a hideout around here, yes," Bradford said, "but I don't think you have anything to worry about, not from them at least. Black Hood and his crew only rob the exploiters."

"You sound as though you *admire* him."

"Reckon I do in a way. He's something of a hero to a great many people. He strikes back, you see, hits the big money men where it hurts 'em the most."

"What do you mean?" I inquired.

Bradford looked at me and frowned, trying to find just the right words to express himself. "Poor folks, dreamers, workers, they came to California in search of gold. Most of 'em didn't find it, of course. They put down roots and dug in and settled the place, buyin' up land for next to nothin', and then the big money men moved in. They began stealin' the land through legal shenanigans, stealin' the gold mines, too."

He paused and brushed a floppy wave from his brow, still searching for the right words. "Most of the gold was discovered by independent prospectors, poor, uneducated men who had nothin' but strong backs and determination. They found the gold and staked their claims, and then the men with the power came in with their teams of lawyers, cheatin' the miners who were too ignorant to protect themselves. There's a lot of money in California. Most of it belongs to twenty or so men who've never touched a pick, never worked a piece of land in their lives. Those're the ones Black Hood robs."

"Next you'll be telling us he robs the rich to give to the poor," Millie declared.

"He's helped a lot of people," Bradford admitted. "He's given money to families who were about to have their homesteads sold out from under 'em by the exploiters. He's no saint. He's a vicious outlaw who's going to be caught and hung one day, but a great many folks're cheerin' him on."

"I'm still terrified," Millie claimed. "I'd just as soon talk about something else."

But Bradford had said his piece and wasn't inclined to talk any more. He folded his arms across his chest again, burrowed his shoulders back into the cushion and let his eyelids droop again. Bradford, I suspected, was playing his own little game, deliberately trying to provoke Millie, and she sensed what he was doing. Smiling to herself, she settled back, perfectly willing to bide her time. When we finally stopped to eat an hour later, she carefully ignored him.

The way station was a small, primitive building that looked as though it had been built to withstand Indian attacks many years ago. A plump Mexican woman in white peasant blouse and soiled red skirt served food at two battered wooden tables. Millie and I sat at one, while Bradford joined the driver and the guard at the other. The three of them talked together in low voices, eating their beans and tortillas while a dark-eyed Mexican lad took care of the horses. After we finished eating, Millie and I strolled under the trees surrounding the building, grateful to be free of the jostling motion of the coach, if only temporarily.

Millie was exceptionally cheerful as we resumed our journey. She had, to all appearances, lost interest in

James Bradford and addressed all her remarks to me. After a while she lapsed into a pensive silence that was most becoming, if hardly typical. Bradford studied her through narrowed eyes, definitely intrigued but stubbornly determined not to show it. Millie was going to give him a hard time in San Francisco, I feared, for I had no doubt that the two of them were destined to see a great deal of each other in weeks to come. Bradford looked as though he could discourage any competition with ease.

Another two hours passed as the horses moved along at an unhurried pace. The coach rocked with monotonous creaks and groans. The road wound through an area studded with huge golden-tan boulders, some as large as houses, vivid red wildflowers glowing in scattered clumps beneath them. Thin, sparsely leaved trees traced pale shadows over the rocks. The sun was high, a bright silver ball in the blue-white sky. It was very warm and dusty. My maroon satin gown with its rows of fragile black lace ruffles was going to be in a sad state by the time we reached San Francisco.

Bradford had the best idea. He seemed to be fast asleep, and Millie was gazing thoughtfully out the window. As the coach crossed a dry, rocky riverbed I leaned back against the cushion and closed my eyes. I must have fallen asleep, for when the coach lurched to an abrupt halt I sat up with a start. There was a loud yell, then a deafening explosion as a gun went off. Bradford leaped up, pistol in hand. Millie gasped and seized my arm. Bradford started to open the door. A long, slender rifle barrel, thrust savagely through the open window, jabbed him in the stomach.

"I wouldn't try anything," a rough voice announced. "If I were you I'd drop that gun and step out of the coach. You women, too. Everyone out! Pronto!"

XL

Bradford tossed his pistol out the window. With the barrel of a rifle jammed against his stomach there was little else he could do. The man holding the rifle slowly withdrew it and opened the door of the coach. Bradford climbed out, his hands over his head. Millie looked at me, her cheeks pale, and then she pressed her lips together and followed Bradford, eyes flashing defiantly. The rifleman took her elbow. She pulled it away. I shoved the jewel case under the seat with my foot and, gathering up my skirts, climbed out with a composure that belied the nervous trembling inside.

Bradford was standing to one side with the driver and the guard. Millie stood with hands on hips, ignoring the man with the rifle and glaring at the three men who sat on horseback, pistols leveled at us. One of them was dressed entirely in black, black boots, tight black pants, black shirt, black leather gloves. A silky black hood covered his head, leaving only his eyes visible through two round holes. The other two men wore faded cotton shirts and pants, red bandanas hiding the lower part of their faces, wide-brimmed hats on their heads.

The man with the rifle was dressed in Spanish style, tight leafbrown pants that flared at the bottom. The hem and lapels of his short, square jacket were faced with bands of black and green embroidery. Both jacket and pants had seen better days. His dark brown hat with low crown and wide, round brim was fastened under his chin with thin leather thongs. He had pulled his neck scarf up over his nose and cheeks. Coal black eyes glowed belligerently as he studied us. I felt sure his mouth was curled in a scornful sneer.

The Spaniard walked over to his horse and thrust his rifle into a long, narrow sheath hanging across the saddle. He moved arrogantly, his shoulders rolling, the spurs on his boots jangling noisily. He exuded an air of fierceness. Even though they held pistols on us, the other three men weren't nearly as frightening, not even the man in black. I sensed instinctively that the man in brown was both vicious and highly dangerous. He glared savagely at Bradford and the two men beside him. All three had their arms raised above their heads. Bradford's face was expressionless. The guard seemed ready to yawn. The driver was clearly terrified.

"Where ees the other man?" the Spaniard demanded.

"What other man?" Bradford inquired. "You think someone else was travelin' with us?"

"The Englishman who wears the fancy clothes and handles the gold. He ees supposed to be with you."

" 'Fraid he isn't, partner."

"They think we're carrying gold," Millie exclaimed. "They think we have all the money from your performances. Well," she said, addressing the Spaniard, "you're wasting your time. That money is already in a bank in San Francisco."

He wheeled around to stare at her and clearly liked what he saw. His coal black eyes glowed with naked lust. Millie kept her hands on her hips, her stance deliberately audacious. Her cheeks had regained their soft pink hue, and her eyes were even more defiant. I knew that she was as frightened as I was, but she wasn't about to show it.

"Thees one ees cocky," the Spaniard growled, devouring her with his eyes.

"I hope you like what you see!" she snapped. "Seeing is all you're going to do. You lay one hand on me and I'll bite it off!"

The Spaniard took a step toward her. "I think maybe I teach her to be respectful."

"Easy, Rico," Black Hood warned.

Rico jerked his head around to glare at his leader,

456

Black Hood, who sat on his horse like some bizarre medieval prince. The leader shook his head. Rico made a disgusted noise in his throat, but he moved away from Millie. She turned to Bradford with an exasperated look.

"What kind of coward are you?" she wanted to know. "Aren't you going to do something?"

"I'm no coward, Ma'am," he drawled. "Neither am I a fool. I'm not going to do anything with three pistols pointin' at me."

"A wise man," Black Hood rasped.

The hooded man slipped his pistol into its holster and swung lightly out of the saddle, strolling toward us. He was tall, very tall, with the lean, muscular build of an athlete, and he carried himself with supple grace. He waved Rico aside and, ignoring Bradford and the others, stopped a few feet in front of me, dark brown eyes observing me through the holes in the hood.

"It seems we've made an error," he remarked.

His voice was a soft, husky rasp, not really a whisper but closely akin to it. He seemed to caress each word fondly, and the result was unusually seductive—that was the only way to describe it. I wondered what he sounded like when he wasn't disguising his voice. I wondered what he looked like behind the hood. Now that he had subdued Rico, I wasn't at all afraid. The nervous trembling had vanished.

Millie was no longer afraid either. She was fighting mad.

"We've got no gold!" she said. "Why don't you and your men just ride off and leave us alone!"

Black Hood didn't seem to hear her. His luminous brown eyes held mine. The man had a strange, compelling magnetism that seemed to vibrate in the air around him. I had the feeling he would have commanding presence even without the disguise. One sensed great strength and ruthlessness as well, despite the genteel manner and caressing voice.

"You're even more beautiful than they claim," he said. "The reports don't do you justice."

"You've seen me before."

"Oh?"

"You saw me dance last night."

"So you know about that?"

"Everyone does. It was an unusual risk to take."

"But worth it, Elena."

My name was a low, seductive caress, soft and silken and husky, spoken with incredible tenderness. I realized with a start that the man was wooing me, wooing me with gentle gallantry that would have been far more appropriate in a moonlit garden.

"What about the gold?" Rico protested. "You told us the Englishman would be with them! You said he would be carrying twenty thousand dollars!"

"So I did."

Anthony had had only a few dollars more than that amount in his saddlebags when he departed with the guard the night before. I wondered how Black Hood had reached a figure so nearly exact. It represented what we had taken in during the past two weeks at three different mining towns. I suspected that he had a whole network of people spying for him, providing information about gold shipments and such. One of them had obviously been keeping an eye on us for at least two weeks.

"The money is already safely in the bank," I said calmly. "My manager left with it last night."

"That presents a problem," Black Hood replied. His voice was full of regret. "You see, I need that money."

"Then I suppose you'll have to rob the bank."

"Not necessarily," he said.

Rico climbed angrily inside the coach and began tearing it up. A moment later he gave a loud exclamation and jumped out with the jewel case. Millie gasped and started forward. Bradford restrained her with a sharp command, his hands still in the air. I stood very quietly as Rico broke the clasp on the case, opened it and took out a handful of jewelry. Diamonds and sapphires glittered with shimmering blue and silver-blue flames as they dripped from his rough tan fingers.

"Holy Virgin Mary," he said thickly. "Look what ees here."

"Let me see them," Black Hood ordered.

Rico shook his head in awe, dropped the jewels back

458

into the case and held it out with both hands. Black Hood examined them thoughtfully for a moment, then reached in to extract a narrow silver filigree hair clasp set with over twenty superbly cut diamonds. I had worn it the night revolution broke out in Barivna, the night Brence had killed Heinrich Schroder and carried me away to safety. Black Hood studied it closely, turning it this way and that, the diamonds throwing off dazzling spokes of light in the sun.

"Lovely," he remarked. "A gift, I assume."

"It was given to me by the King of Barivna."

He nodded slowly. "Yes, I read about him. He lost his throne because of you. Isn't that right?"

"Some people chose to think so," I answered coolly.

He chuckled softly and gazed at the clasp again, then dropped it back into the case.

"I don't think we're interested in jewelry," he said. "Put the case back in the coach, Rico."

"You're out of your mind! They're worth a fortune!"

"Put the case back in the coach."

Rico stood there defiantly, clutching the case to his chest. His eyes flashed dangerously, and I knew his cheeks must be flushed bright red with anger. Black Hood didn't repeat his command again. He waited, tapping his fingers on his thighs, and suddenly the genteel manner was gone. Though he didn't speak, though he made no menacing gesture, he had become as hard as steel and chillingly lethal. Rico still hesitated, clearly contemplating rebellion. But finally, muttering a curse in Spanish, Rico slammed the case shut and hurled it into the coach. Black Hood turned to Millie.

"I want you to deliver a message," he said.

"A message?"

"I am releasing you and the men. I want you to go to San Francisco and locate Miss Lopez' manager. I want you to tell him that she will be returned to him safe and sound as soon as he brings me twenty thousand dollars."

"What?" she cried.

"Now hold on!" Bradford yelled.

"I'm taking Miss Lopez with me. I assure you she won't be harmed, not if my instructions are followed.

459

Her manager is to come to this spot tomorrow afternoon at four o'clock, with the money and without the law. I'll meet him, and as soon as I have the money, she'll be returned."

"You can't do this!" Millie exclaimed. "It's—it's *kidnapping!* If you think—"

"I think you'd better follow instructions," he interrupted, speaking in that soft, raspy voice. "Duke must be unarmed, of course, and there must be no lawmen with him, nor any lurking behind rocks. For Miss Lopez' sake, I suggest the law know nothing about this."

"So this is Black Hood?" Millie snapped, turning to Bradford. "You told us he robbed only the exploiters! You told us he helped poor people!"

"Yeah, this isn't your style," Bradford said to the tall bandit. "You've never abducted a woman before."

"I have my reasons," the outlaw replied.

"And I know what they are!" Millie exploded. "Well, I can tell you one thing, if you're going to abduct Elena, you're going to abduct me, too! We go everywhere together."

"Hush, Millie," I said.

"I'm not leaving you alone with these villains, not for a minute!"

Bradford had regained his indolent, laconic manner, holding his arms in the air as though in an idle stretch. His brown eyes surveyed the ground casually, and I saw them rest on the pistol he had tossed out of the window. The gun lay about five yards away, near the foot of one of the large rocks.

"I reckon there's not much we can do," he drawled. "This isn't going to endear you to folks though, Hood. Robbin' the money dealers is one thing. Abductin' women is another."

"Miss Lopez won't be harmed."

"I have your word on that?"

I sensed the outlaw's smile. The dark brown eyes were amused, as he said, "You have my word."

Bradford nodded, apparently satisfied, and then he seemed to fly forward, lunging into space, skidding across the ground, his hand reaching for the pistol. But

460

Black Hood's arm moved with even greater speed. He whipped his gun out and fired. There was a puff of smoke and a blazing streak of orange. Millie shrieked. Bradford fell to the ground as the pistol flew out of Bradford's fingers and clattered against the face of the rock. He looked up in amazement. His cheekbone was badly skinned, but otherwise he appeared to be unharmed. It had all happened in less than five seconds.

Black Hood kept his gun leveled on the man on the ground.

"Can't blame a man for tryin'," Bradford observed.

"I could have killed you."

"Mighty glad you didn't, I must say."

"Get up."

Bradford climbed to his feet, brushing dust from his tan breeches. The tail of his worn cotton shirt had pulled loose from his waistband. He calmly tucked it back in, brushed a smudge of dirt from one of the sleeves and ran his fingers through his mop of sunstreaked hair. Millie looked at him with new appreciation. The incident had shaken her considerably, but she made a quick recovery, rushing over to examine the skinned place on his cheekbone.

"You've hurt yourself," she said testily. "That needs to be washed and tended to. There's a canteen of water in the coach, and I've got some ointment in my carry bag."

"Get back," he ordered. His voice was stern.

"No one's going to do any more shooting," she informed him. "There'll be no more foolish heroics. Come on over to the coach. I'll fetch the canteen."

"I said get back!"

"Go on over to the coach with her," Black Hood said. "Climb inside, both of you." Then, pointing his gun at the driver and the guard, he said, "You two, get back up on the seat."

The terrified driver wasted no time. He scurried over to the coach and scrambled up onto the seat as though pursued by demons, then seized the reins with trembling hands. One of the horses reared its head irritably. The guard lowered his arms and swiped at the fringe on his soiled leather jacket, completely unperturbed.

"What about our guns?" he inquired. "I've had that rifle for nigh on to twenty years."

"Empty the rifle, Rico," Black Hood ordered. "Empty the pistol, too, then return them to these gentlemen."

Rico obeyed, muttering angrily to himself as he picked up the battered old rifle and emptied it of shells. He snapped it shut and thrust it into the guard's hand. The guard sauntered over to the coach and climbed up beside the driver, resting the rifle across his knees again and gazing indifferently into space. Bradford slipped his emptied pistol into its holster and continued to stand where he was. Millie stood close beside him.

"Get in the coach!" Rico snarled. "Move!"

"You're going to regret this, Hood," Bradford said. "If you harm so much as a hair on her head, I'll personally track you down and put a bullet in your gut. That's a promise."

He took Millie by the wrist and started toward the coach. She protested vehemently, planting her heels firmly in the dirt, trying to pull free, declaring at the top of her lungs that she wasn't about to go off and leave me. Bradford sighed and scooped her up into his arms and carried her to the coach. She kicked. She shrieked. She pounded on his chest with her fists. He didn't seem to notice. He tossed her bodily into the coach and climbed in beside her, calmly looping an arm around her throat when she attempted to jump back out.

"All *right!*" she snapped.

"You goin' to behave?"

Millie flung his arm aside and flounced angrily onto the opposite seat, tears splashing down her cheeks. She wiped them away and stared out the window at me, looking absolutely wretched. I managed to smile. I told her I'd be all right, told her not to worry.

"I can't help but worry," she said irritably. "Anthony's so tight with a dollar he'll probably let them keep you!"

The driver clicked the reins. As the horses took off, the coach bounced vigorously, spraying loose gravel in all directions. The luggage on top shifted and slipped, but the ropes kept it from toppling off. There was a cloud of dust, and by the time it lifted the coach was disappearing around a mass of boulders in the distance. I told myself I wasn't afraid, but there was a hollow feeling in the pit of my stomach, and my hands were shaking. I hid them in my skirts and tilted my chin defiantly.

"Well?" I said.

"You're very brave," Black Hood told me.

"Not nearly as brave as my friend. Millie would have shot you herself if she could have gotten hold of a gun."

"There was no need for anyone to shoot anyone. I could have put that bullet between your man's eyes if I'd wanted to. I admire a man with courage, and he was courageous indeed."

"Now I suppose you're going to carry me off."

"That's right. You'll come peacefully? I've read a great deal about the famous Lopez temper."

"I promise not to scratch," I said acidly.

Black Hood chuckled again, and then, taking hold of my arm, led me over to his horse, a beautiful chestnut. Rico was already mounted and was watching us with hostile black eyes. The other two men had put away their pistols and waited patiently. Neither of them had spoken a word, unlike the volatile Rico. Black Hood released my arm, placed the toe of his boot in the stirrup and swung lightly into the saddle. Leaning down, he circled my waist with his hands and swept me off the ground, settling me in front of him.

"Comfortable?" he inquired.

"Not very."

"You're going to be less so, I fear. This is necessary."

He whipped out a black silk scarf, folded it neatly and, before I could protest, tied it over my eyes. The blindfold immediately disoriented me. I tried to turn around but felt myself slipping. A strong, muscular arm wrapped around my waist, drawing me back against him. I grew dizzy, and the dizziness increased as the horse started to move. The arm tightened, holding me securely.

"It's a very long ride," he murmured. "We'll stop to rest in an hour or so."

"How considerate of you."

"I wouldn't want you to get too tired. I plan to take very good care of you."

I tried to relax. The world was a black void full of movement and noise and sensation. The dizziness vanished as soon as I grew accustomed to the motion. I wondered if we were heading east, or west. Perhaps it was south. Yes, we were going south. Then, the horse turned and headed in another direction. North? I sat rigidly, holding my back stiff, refusing to lean against him, but that was foolish. My spine hurt dreadfully. I forgot my pride and leaned back, resting my weight against his chest. His arm loosened, tightened again as he adjusted his hold to accommodate me.

"Better?" he inquired.

I didn't deign to reply, and Black Hood didn't press, content to maintain the silence I clearly preferred. We were riding fast now, the horse racing along on powerful legs, undeterred by its double burden. The wind tore at my hair and stung my cheeks, and my skirts flapped, billowing up over my calves. I folded my arms over his arm and leaned against his chest, almost comfortable. The joggling motion was beginning to make me drowsy. The black silk was soft against my eyelids. The man who held me so close smelled of silk and leather and sweat and skin, and I could feel the warmth of his body, the strength of his arm around my waist.

I wondered what kind of man he was; why he had resorted to a life of crime. His air of good breeding wasn't something that could be simulated. He was ruthless, too, I had sensed that, and he had been absolutely chilling when Rico attempted to defy him over the jewelry. He had returned the jewelry. Why? A fortune had been right there in his grasp. I was puzzled and, I had to admit, intrigued. The man was a fascinating enigma.

A long time passed, perhaps an hour, perhaps two, before Black Hood called out and tugged at the reins, bringing his horse to a sudden halt. I was startled by the abrupt cessation of movement. I had been drowsing off and on, spinning in darkness. He removed the blindfold. The sunlight almost blinded me at first, even though it wasn't strong. I blinked and rubbed my eyes. We had stopped in a lightly wooded area. Trees spread soft mauve-gray shadows over the pale green grass. I could hear water rushing nearby and guessed there must be a small river behind the boulders that rose on our left, a short distance beyond the trees.

Rico and the other two men had already dismounted and turned their horses loose to graze. All three still had their bandanas in place. They didn't want me to see their faces, I realized, for I might be able to identify them later on. Black Hood swung down out of the saddle and then reached up to encircle my waist, lifting me down as though I weighed nothing at all. I was a bit unsteady on my feet at first, and he held onto me until I gained my balance. A light breeze stirred the grass. His loose silk hood fluttered, flattening against his face. For a moment I could see the shape of his nose and cheeks and mouth outlined in black, dark brown eyes peering at me through the holes.

"How do you feel?" he inquired.

"Hot and tired and dusty."

"Frightened?"

"Not a bit," I lied. "That black outfit might intimidate some people, but I find it—ridiculous. You can't be much of a man or you wouldn't have to hide behind a hood."

His eyes were amused. "You do have spirit," he observed. "Here you are, in the hands of a vicious outlaw, and you brazenly insult him."

"Are you vicious?"

"Only when I have to be. Ordinarily I'm the best natured of men."

"Robbing banks, holding up coaches, abducting women."

"But politely," he said.

"You just sit back and let your man Rico do the bullying. I'd hardly call him polite."

"Rico has a tendency to get out of hand," he admitted. "I believe I may have made a mistake letting him join us, but then he's only been with me for a few weeks. I'll soon have him under control."

"I wish you luck," I said. "How long are we going to stop here?"

"Twenty minutes or so, long enough for you to stretch your legs. The horses need a rest, too. It's still a long way to the hacienda."

"Is that a river I hear?"

He nodded. "There's a small stream behind those rocks."

"I wonder if you'd allow me to go wash my hands and face and have a few moments of privacy? I promise not to run away."

"You wouldn't get very far if you did," he told me. "Go ahead. I'll trust you."

I turned and started toward the low gray boulders. The two men with the red bandanas over their faces were sitting under a tree. One of them had taken out his knife and was whittling at a stick. Rico leaned against a tree trunk, watching me with those smoldering black eyes as I moved past. Muttering something in Spanish, he bristled with hostility. I suspected that he blamed me for Black Hood's returning the jewels. He was clearly still unhappy about that. I ignored him and moved on across the short, stiff grass, across the small clearing in front of the boulders.

I was hot, tired, and I felt as though I were covered with a layer of dust. My maroon skirt belled out in the wind, black lace ruffles fluttering. The gown was probably ruined, and the black lace gloves felt sticky. My hair had come loose, the French roll threatening to topple at any moment. I wondered why I wasn't more frightened. I should have been on the verge of hysteria —that would have been perfectly natural under the circumstances. But I told myself that it would all be over in twenty-four hours. Millie would go to Anthony and Anthony would bring the money and I would be released. There was nothing I could do but wait and stay as calm as possible.

Discovering a narrow open space between two of the boulders, I slipped through and found myself on the river bank. The stream was shallow, not more than a few inches deep, clear, sparkling water rushing over a bed of small stones. The opposite bank was grassy, a few trees growing near the water's edge. I could smell moss and mud and the tangy smell of root. Pulling off my gloves, I moved down to the water and knelt in the sand, oblivious to the damage that might be done to my gown. I dipped the gloves in the water, wrung them out and bathed my face and arms.

The water was wonderfully cool and refreshing. I wanted to bathe all over. As I dipped the gloves again my hair came completely undone, its rich ebony waves tumbling over my cheeks. As I brushed my hair back and stood up, sponging my shoulders and the top of my bosom with the wet gloves, I heard someone approach. I didn't turn, for I was sure that he would follow me. He had risked capture in order to see me dance, and earlier on his manner had definitely been seductive. Now that no one else was around he was going to try to seduce me. I continued to dab at my shoulders, pretending I didn't hear those careful footsteps. I had known from the first that he wanted to make love to me.

But when I heard the spurs jangle, I whirled around to see Rico instead, standing a few yards away, staring at me with fierce intensity. I dropped the gloves. My blood ran cold as I saw what was in his eyes, as I realized what he intended to do.

"He—he'll kill you," I said.

"You think Rico ees afraid of him?"

"He'll kill you," I repeated.

My voice trembled. My heart was beating so strongly that I feared it might burst. I knew I shouldn't let him see my fear, but it was impossible not to. I stepped back, stumbling over a piece of gravel. Rico laughed, standing there with one hand resting on the butt of his gun, the wide brim of his hat tilting to one side. He still had the green silk neck scarf up over the lower half of his face, but I knew he was smiling a savage smile as he took another step toward me.

"We don't get the jewels," he said. "We don't get the gold. Ees all a waste of time. Rico doesn't like to waste time. I decided to make it worth my while."

"Don't—don't come any closer."

"You will scream?"

I nodded. The muscles of my throat seemed to be paralyzed.

"You won't scream," he told me in a rough, snarling
467

voice. "If you do, I will put a bullet through your heart. I will say you try to escape."

"You—"

"Take off the dress," he ordered.

I shook my head. Rico pulled out his gun and pointed it at me.

"You will take it off or I shoot."

His black eyes burned fiercely. I knew that he meant exactly what he said. He would shoot me if I didn't obey. Stark terror held me paralyzed, and I was horribly aware of the fragile texture of blood and bone and muscle, so vulnerable, so easily destroyed. One bullet could do it, simply, quickly. My knees were so weak, I felt sure they would fold up under me any second.

The hammer of his pistol clicked back. "I count to ten," he said. "One, two, three—"

Somehow or other I managed to move my hands behind me and reach for the tiny hooks in back of my dress. My vision seemed to blur, and there was a faint ringing in my ears, yet I could hear his breathing. He was breathing slowly, heavily, no longer counting. I fumbled with the hooks. There were so many, and my hands were shaking terribly. I tugged and fumbled, finally managing to undo the first few. The others came easier. The bodice of my dress fell forward. I slipped it down, pulling the sleeves over my arms, lifting my arms free.

"Too slow!" he snarled.

I couldn't seem to control my hands. They were fluttering like nervous white birds, and the ringing in my ears was louder now. I could see the man in the leaf brown outfit and I could see the glittering black eyes and the gun leveled at my heart, but it was all part of a hideous dream. The rough gray boulders, the sandy bank, the sparkling stream were the landscape of a nightmare, blurring in the haze that grew thicker and thicker.

"Off!" he cried.

I pushed the bodice over my waist, my hips, leaning forward to smooth it over the swell of my petticoat. The maroon satin rustled with a soft, silken whisper. The gown fell to my feet, and I stepped out of the crumpled circle of cloth, wearing only my black lace petticoat and chemise. The lace was finely spun, my breasts visible beneath the delicate floral patterns. Half a dozen black lace skirts lifted and billowed in the breeze.

"The rest!" he ordered.

I shook my head. I couldn't go through with it. I hadn't the will or the physical strength left. The haze shimmered, and the ground beneath my feet shifted. My bosom heaved, straining against the lace. I looked at him, shaking my head again and again, as he muttered in Spanish and took another step toward me, holding the gun stiffly in front of him. One quick jerk of the index finger and the bullet would fly through the air and it would all be over.

"I kill you," he said. "Not yet. After."

He laughed and, slipping his gun into the holster, came toward me, spurs jangling. He seized my wrist and jerked me into his arms. Pulling the green scarf down, he buried his lips in the curve of my throat. I struggled violently as his arms tightened and those hot, moist lips burned my skin, sliding toward my breast. I kicked. I tore the hat from his head and threw it aside and grabbed his hair with both hands, tugging at the black curls with all my might.

"Rico!"

He released me so abruptly that I almost fell, pushing me aside as he turned around. Black Hood stood several yards away, just beyond the opening between the two boulders. The silver of his gun caught the sunlight, reflecting it back in brilliant spokes.

"I mean no harm," Rico said, his voice now that of an amiable peon, higher pitched, whining. "We just have a bit of fun. She encourage me. She say Rico make her blood hot."

He laughed a jovial laugh and shook his head, and then his hand moved with blinding speed as he reached for his gun. There was a deafening explosion and he screamed, staggered and fell to the ground as bright crimson threads spurted from him. I didn't react at first. It wasn't real. It was part of the nightmare. Black Hood slipped his gun back into its holster and came toward me, stepping over Rico's body.

469

"It was inevitable," he said. "It had to happen. I suppose I knew that Rico was a mistake from the beginning."

The other two men came rushing around the boulders, pistols in hand, red bandanas flapping. When Black Hood picked up my dress and handed it to me and told me to put it on, I obeyed. He told one of the men to go fetch the trench tool that hung on Rico's saddle, and then he moved around to fasten up the back of my gown. I stood trancelike, numbed by what had happened, still unable to believe it. When Black Hood finished the dress, he led me toward the boulders. The man returning with the long, narrow-lipped shovel passed us.

"Make it quick," Black Hood said quietly. "I want to get to the hacienda before dark."

XLI

A particularly low-hanging branch loomed up ahead.
Black Hood held my waist tightly and leaned his body
forward, forcing me to lean forward, too, as we passed
under the branch. His cheek rested briefly against mine,
and I could feel the black silk of his hood rubbing
against my face. His body seemed to envelop me with
strength and warmth. He straightened up in the saddle,
drawing me back up with him, and I rested my head on
his shoulder once more, feeling wonderfully secure and
relaxed. Somehow I felt as if I had known him for a
very long time. It seemed natural for me to be with him.

"Where are your men?" I asked.

"They rode on ahead to give Juanita instructions.
They'll already be at the hacienda by this time. We're
almost there."

"Who is Juanita?"

"My housekeeper. She'll have everything ready for
you."

"I'd like a hot bath."

"You'll have one," he promised.

"My dress is ruined."

"We'll find something for you."

His voice was soft, gentle, a husky croon that was
like a soothing caress. I had been abducted by an outlaw who was holding me for ransom, yet I had never
felt so comfortable with a man. His manner was tender
and protective, as though I were something very
precious placed in his charge. He had killed a man over

me less than two hours ago. And though I was still shaken by the thought, any trace of fear I might have felt earlier had completely vanished. I was no longer even on the defensive. My icy demeanor and acid remarks would have been out of place now, as unnatural as fear. Why? What kind of spell had this bandit cast over me?

We had left the wooded area behind and were riding over a stretch of flat, grassy land that seemed to gradually drop away up ahead, and far beyond I could see a low rim of hills. I realized we were coming to a valley, and a few minutes later I saw it stretching out below us, large and beautiful, half of it bathed in the fading silver sunlight, that part nearer the hills covered with deep shadow. The sky was a pale silver gray overhead, streaks of soft gold and apricot tinting the horizon. I saw a sparkling ribbon of river, lofty trees, wide pastures, and a small valley isolated and enclosed. Black Hood tugged on the reins, drawing the horse to a halt so that I could appreciate the view.

"It—it's beautiful," I said.

"Like no other place on earth," he replied. "I've traveled all over the world. I've never seen a spot to compare with it."

There was a kind of reverence in his voice, and I could tell that he loved this valley. He touched the horse's flanks gently with the heels of his boots, and we started down the slope. The air was marvelously pure and laced with the scent of grass and rock and water. I could feel the magic of the place. It was almost tangible; an atmosphere of serene majesty enfolded the whole valley. I understood how he felt. I had the feeling that even I could live here contentedly for the rest of my life, the cares of the world completely forgotten.

When we reached the floor of the valley, I saw the hacienda in the distance. As we drew nearer I studied the pale beige walls and gracious archways, the verandahs and wrought iron balconies, the sloping reddish brown tile roof. The hacienda was built around a central patio, and there was a patio in front with a fountain spilling water over three tiers of basin into a small circular pond. In the gardens tall green shrubs and curious spiky plants I didn't recognize grew lavishly among trees with exotic fronds and hibiscus shrubs with large red-orange flowers. Several outbuildings stood beyond the house, and horses capered in a pasture nearby, enjoying the last rays of sunlight.

Black Hood urged his horse on, and a few minutes later we were moving around the circular drive. He pulled up the horse, set me on my feet and swung out of the saddle. The fountain made a splashing music. The spiky plants had a strange smell. A Mexican youth in loose white trousers and shirt came around the side of the house to take the reins and lead the horse away. The carved oak front doors opened, and a young Mexican woman stepped out onto the verandah. She smiled and moved down the steps toward us, her bare feet lightly slapping the tiles.

"I heard we were to have a guest," she said.

Her voice was low and musical, her English superb, the Spanish accent a subtle and lovely augmentation. A woman in her early twenties, she had a creamy tan complexion, gentle black eyes and a beautifully shaped mouth the color of pink camellias. Her dark black hair was pulled back tightly and braided in a long plait that hung down her back. Short, slender, she wore a white cotton blouse and a dark red skirt embroidered with rows of black, green and silver patterns.

"This is Juanita," Black Hood said. "Juanita, Elena Lopez. She will be staying with us tonight."

"Steve told me. I have everything ready."

"Juanita will take care of you, Elena. You'll have your bath, and I'll join you for dinner later on."

He walked toward the side of the house, the heels of his boots crunching on the crushed shell drive, and then he started up the stone staircase to the second story. Juanita, smiling, took my hand and led me into the house. We moved down a wide hallway with rooms opening on either side and then stepped out onto the inner verandah. The enclosed patio was tiled in black and white and red-brown, and there was another, smaller fountain in the center. A large old tree with spreading boughs grew to one side, baskets of plants hanging from several of the limbs.

"He has never brought a guest home before," Juanita remarked. "We are most happy to have you."

"I'm hardly a 'guest,' " I told her.

"He wants you to be very comfortable," she continued, ignoring my implication. "Steve told me that you were beautiful," she added.

"Steve?"

"My fiancé. He rides with Black Hood. He has blue eyes and dark-gold hair. He is as handsome as a young god. You would not have observed that, of course. He wore a hat and kept the bandana over his face."

Juanita smiled again, a lovely, gentle smile. There was an air of innocence about her, a childlike acceptance of things as they were. Though she knew what Black Hood and her fiancé did, she seemed to consider it a perfectly natural way of life. I said nothing more as we moved around the verandah. Strings of red peppers and onions hung from pegs on the wall, as did an occasional dried gourd, and plants in bright Mexican pots were placed here and there on the stucco bannister. Juanita finally stopped in front of a beautifully carved door and, pushing it open, led me down two steps into a long, spacious room with a low, beamed ceiling. The whitewashed walls were covered with deep shadows, and I could smell ancient wood and beeswax polish mingled with the scent of lemon.

"I will light the candles," she said.

At the fireplace, she took a long match from the jar atop the mantle and struck it, touching the flame to the wick of a candle in a brass holder. Carrying the candle from place to place, she used it to light candles standing in heavy brass candelabra that sat on intricately carved wooden chests. The room soon glowed with soft golden light, and I saw the dark red tile floor, the bright colored rugs hanging on the mortared white walls, the long tan sofa with a lovely black and white striped rug draped over its back. A small dining table stood at the far end of the room, chairs with high carved backs on either side. Windows looked out over the gardens, and an open archway at one end led into the bedroom.

"You will want to bathe at once," Juanita said.

"Your bath is waiting. I brought the hot water only a few minutes ago."

Still holding the candle, she led the way into the bedroom, and as she lighted the candles there, I saw that the room was dominated by an enormous brass bed covered with a beautifully woven blue spread. A large tin tub of steaming water stood in one corner, near a dark oak dressing table, towels, washcloth and a bar of scented soap on the stool beside it. Juanita unfolded a tall screen and placed it around the tub.

"Leave your clothes on the bed," she instructed. "I will see to them while you bathe."

She smiled once more and left the room. I undressed, stepped around the screen and climbed into the tub. I soaked for a long time, reveling in the luxury of wetness and warmth and scent, finally climbing out of the tub with great reluctance.

I dried myself off and, when I stepped around the screen, I discovered a pale blue dressing robe on the bed. I slipped into the robe and tied the sash securely, admiring its long sleeves that ruffled at the wrists, and the full skirt which was ruffled as well. Sitting down at the dressing table, I was pleased to see that Juanita had set out a brush, a comb and a small brass tray of hairpins. I had started to brush my hair when she came back into the room accompanied by a handsome Mexican youth.

"My brother Pedro," Juanita said. "We won't disturb you."

The boy grinned, clearly embarrassed. Juanita folded up the screen and handed soap and towels to Pedro, and then the two of them carried the tub out. I heard a splash in the other room. Pedro laughed. Juanita scolded. The door to the verandah opened, closed. I continued to brush my hair until it was completely dry and gleaming with blue-black highlights. Then I pulled it back and arranged it in a sleek, elegant French roll, turning my head to one side in order that I might inspect it in the mirror.

Satisfied, I examined my reflection thoughtfully. I didn't need make-up tonight, I thought, and I wondered what Juanita had been able to do with my gown. I

475

doubted that it could be salvaged, satin torn and stained, lace ruffles all ripped and covered with dust. I stood up as she entered the room. She was laden with boxes, and there was a sly smile on her lips.

"For you," she said.

Placing the boxes on the bed, she opened one and removed a white silk petticoat, skirts spilling out like the petals of a white rose. She put it down and took out a creamy white satin gown completely overlaid with exquisite lace, pale pink lace flowers scattered over the skirt. It was a sumptuous creation, and I knew it must have cost a fortune. Holding it up in front of me, I saw that it was going to be a perfect fit.

"There are undergarments, too," she told me. "Shoes as well."

"They just happened to be here?" I asked.

"He brought them back from San Francisco. A lady in one of the shops helped him, he said. He told her he was buying the things for his sister."

"I'm sure she believed it," I said wryly. "Just when did he do all this shopping."

"Over a week ago."

"I see."

I did indeed, and that put a whole new interpretation on that afternoon's adventures. He had been planning to abduct me all along, I realized, and he had purchased these things well in advance. Juanita gathered up the empty boxes and left the room. The mellow, sympathetic mood I had felt earlier was completely gone now. Black Hood had gone to an awful lot of trouble in order to have an evening alone with me. He had made very careful plans, had thought of everything. But he was going to be very disappointed.

I dressed slowly, carefully, filled with cool resolve. The gown was one of the most beautiful dresses I had ever worn, its pale pink flowers scattered over the skirt and delicately woven into the white lace. As I studied myself in the mirror, I knew that I had rarely looked more alluring. I wanted to be alluring tonight, if only to make his disappointment all the keener.

I stepped into the front room, my skirt rustling softly. Juanita had been busy in there, too. The dining table was set for two, china and crystal gleaming, wine chilling in a silver bucket. At least half the candles had been extinguished, leaving all but the dining area hazy with shadow. Very romantic, I thought. The only thing missing was music in the background. I had hardly stepped across the threshold before guitars began to strum in the gardens. I almost laughed.

"I've been waiting," he said.

His voice startled me. I hadn't seen him sitting there on the sofa. He got slowly to his feet and moved toward me, wearing a fresh outfit identical to the one he'd worn earlier. He carried a single pink rose, the velvety petals just beginning to open.

"For your hair," he said, handing it to me.

Accepting the rose, I fastened it over my right temple and looked into those dark brown eyes peering at me through the mask. I could understand why he wanted to keep his face hidden, but I wondered why he continued to disguise his voice with that soft, husky rasp. It suddenly dawned on me that I might have met him before, perhaps at one of the hotels, perhaps at the theater. I had been introduced to a great many men since my arrival in California. Many of the prominent men in each town felt obligated to come backstage and pay their respects. Black Hood might well have been one of them.

"The dress fits perfectly," I said. "Thoughtful of you to have purchased it for me. I wonder how you knew my size."

"I have means of obtaining such information."

"I'm sure you do," I replied. "I also wonder why you bought it over a week ago."

"You found out about that, I see."

"You planned to kidnap me from the first."

"Yes," he admitted.

"The money——"

"I know your manager had gone on ahead last night. I could have waylaid him quite easily."

"But you didn't. You wanted me."

"Surely you can't blame me," he said. The dark eyes seemed to smile. "What man wouldn't want an evening alone with Elena Lopez?"

477

"When Anthony brings the money tomorrow, you'll take it, though, won't you?"

He nodded. "I hate to, but I need it. You'll make five times that amount in San Francisco. You won't miss it."

"Bradford said you only hold up the exploiters, the men who've cheated and robbed the defenseless in order to achieve power. I see he was mistaken, or perhaps you consider me an exploiter, too."

"I'm making an exception in your case. I trust you won't blame me too much."

"You could have taken my jewelry," I said, truly confused. "But you didn't. I suppose I should be grateful for that."

"Indeed you should."

"You wanted an evening alone with me—well, you have it, but I might as well tell you that candlelight and guitar music and—and romantic atmosphere leave me cold. If you intend to sleep with me, you'll have to use force, and I promise you I'll fight like a tigress."

He chuckled softly, highly amused. "I've never had to resort to rape yet."

Tilting my chin haughtily, I moved over to the window to look out at the gardens. They were dark and shadowy, a few rays of moonlight gilding the exotic leaves. The musicians were invisible, and the music seemed to materialize of its own accord, lilting across the air, the Spanish melody soft and lovely. There were at least three guitarists. One of them was singing in a rich, low voice, the words barely audible. I could hear Black Hood uncorking the wine. A few moments later I felt him standing behind me. I turned. He handed me a glass of wine.

"Relax, Elena," he said. "Nothing is going to happen that you don't want to happen."

"You think I'm afraid?"

"I think you're extraordinarily brave. I also think you're the loveliest woman I've ever seen."

I sipped the wine, unmoved by the compliment, unmoved by the husky, caressing voice that was like a seductive whisper. The wine was rich and mellow with a taste that brought sunlight to mind. I finished the

478

glass. He stood very close, watching me with those luminous brown eyes that were really quite the most attractive eyes I had ever seen. Once more I wondered what the rest of his face looked like, and I longed to reach up and pull the hood off.

"Must you wear that?" I asked.

He nodded. The black silk wavered.

"I suppose you're afraid I'd be able to identify you later on. Or perhaps we've already met."

"Perhaps we have."

"So many men have come backstage to meet me. Rich and powerful and prominent men. They—they say you're prominent, too. They say you're a highly respected citizen when you're not marauding."

"I'd like to think so. But I own no gold mines. I do own this valley, or will as soon as I make the final payment."

He took my empty glass and led me over to the sofa. I sat down and arranged my skirts, while he went to fill my glass again. I smiled to myself. Obviously, he planned to get me drunk, hoping that would make me more susceptible to his masculine allure. I had to admit that he was appealing, his genteel manner and that caressing voice most pleasing, the black silk hood over his face adding a strange titillation. Appealing or not, he was an outlaw, and he was going to cost me twenty thousand dollars.

I accepted the glass of wine. Black Hood sat on the arm at the other end of the sofa, looking at me with tender brown eyes.

"Aren't you going to have any wine?" I inquired.

"I dined earlier, while you were bathing and dressing. I just came to keep you company."

"The table is set for two."

"Merely for symmetry."

"I see. Of course. You can't eat without removing your hood."

"Drink your wine, Elena."

I obeyed, sipping slowly. I felt very peaceful, at ease with him. I knew he was a villain. I had seen him kill a man before my very eyes. Somehow that made no difference.

479

"Why did you become an outlaw?" I asked.

"Out of anger and frustration, necessity, too. I arrived in California just a few months after the first gold strike. Like the others, I was struck with gold fever. I knew nothing about mining, but I became partners with a rugged old-timer who knew all the ropes. We bought provisions and went out to make our fortune. It took six months, six months of grueling work and incredible hardship, but we finally struck gold."

"Then why——"

"We filed our claim. We sold a few nuggets to buy equipment and hire some men. There wasn't much gold at first, just a small vein, just enough to make it profitable. Until one day Jake came tearing into the shed, so excited he could hardly speak. He took me into the mine, his hands shaking. We had worked it for days, and everyone was convinced the vein had played out."

He paused and shook his head, remembering.

"Jake handed me the candle and took up the pick one of the men had left behind. He began to hack at the muddy rock. It fell away in flakes, and in less than ten minutes I was staring at a wall of gold. Jake couldn't control his excitement. That night he went to the saloon and bought drinks for everyone and got very, very drunk and bragged about that wall of gold. We were going to be millionaires, he claimed. Our mine was going to be one of the biggest in California."

Again he paused, and I set down my empty glass, sensing what was to come. When he continued to speak it was quietly, without emotion.

"The big money men came in then. Our claim was discovered to be invalid, somehow. It hadn't been filled out properly, hadn't been filed correctly. Someone had gotten to the original document and substituted a forgery. We fought it, of course, but the others had too much money, too much power. Petty officials were paid off, and in the end we lost the mine. The night after we got the news Jake took down his rifle, went out to the mine and blew his brains out."

He was silent for a long moment, staring across the room without seeing, and then he sighed.

"What happened to me and Jake was an old story by

that time. A month before I had been on the verge of becoming a millionaire. Suddenly I was penniless and out in the cold. Literally. I vowed I'd get revenge. I vowed I'd get back at them somehow. I suppose you could say Black Hood was born the night Jake died."

"I—I'm glad you told me all this," I said.

"I wanted you to know, Elena."

There was a soft knock on the door. Black Hood opened it, and Juanita came in with a tray of food. She placed the dishes on the table, removed the lids and left quietly. Black Hood took my hand and led me over to the table. He sat across from me, watching me toy with the food. For some reason I was no longer hungry. The candlelight flickered, and the music continued to float through the windows. When he refilled my wine glass, I accepted it without protest.

"How is it you've never been caught?" I asked.

"Black Hood has many friends. Not one of them knows my true identity. Not one of them knows I work from this hacienda."

"What about your men?"

"They're unquestionably loyal. Each was victimized by the exploiters in one way or another. Even Rico. That's why I took him on. There's not a person in this valley who hasn't got strong reasons to hate the people I rob. That includes the household staff and everyone who works at the hacienda."

"Even Juanita and her brother?"

"Their father was a Spanish aristocrat, a widower who owned an unpretentious hacienda and two hundred acres of land. An up-and-coming politician took a fancy to the estate. But their father, Senor Hernandez, refused to sell. He had an unfortunate accident a week or so later, and the estate was appropriated. Pedro and Juanita were suddenly homeless."

"And you took them in."

He nodded. I could understand Juanita's attitude now, and I could understand why this man inspired such loyalty and devotion, why many considered him their champion. I felt bewildering emotions beginning to stir inside me, and I put down my fork, no longer pretending to eat. I wished the music weren't so sad and lovely.

I wished the candlelight weren't so soft and golden. I wished he wouldn't look at me with those luminous brown eyes that seemed to glow.

"What about you, Elena?" he asked quietly. "Are you happy?"

"Happy? I—I suppose I am. I have success and fame and I'm making money and—"

I hesitated, frowning. I didn't really know how to answer that question, perhaps because I didn't really know the answer. Was I happy? I enjoyed what I did, and I wasn't *un*happy, but still. . . . Sometimes there was an empty feeling inside, the old feeling that had caused so much anguish in the past. I took another sip of wine, remembering. Remembering wasn't good for me. It suddenly seemed that the past five years had been nothing more than a whirl of activity deliberately planned to help me forget an inn in Germany and the young man with a grim expression who drove away and left me alone.

"I'm happy," I said.

"Your eyes tell me otherwise."

"I have everything a woman could want."

"Love?"

I didn't answer the question. I got up from the table and walked over to the window. I gazed out at the gardens, angry with him, angry because I had allowed old feelings to surface, because he had been able to read them so easily. I stood there for a long time, and the anger melted and tremulous emotions replaced it. I heard him leave the table and turned to watch him step into the bedroom. He lighted candles there and then came back to extinguish the ones in the living room.

As he put out the last candle, the room became a haze of semi-darkness, a soft golden glow coming through the archway. I could hardly see him as he came toward me. He stopped in front of me and placed his hands on my shoulders, gently squeezing the flesh, and when I tried to pull back his fingers tightened. There was just enough light for me to see his eyes and see what was in them.

"No," I said.

"I want you," he told me. His voice was a soft murmur, a silken caress. "You want me, too."

"No."

He squeezed my shoulders and touched my throat. His thumb pressed the hollow of my throat, his fingers stroking the side of my neck. He murmured my name. Familiar sensations welled inside, and his hand slipped down to cup my breast beneath the layers of cloth. He squeezed the soft mound, and I tried not to gasp as the flesh responded, the nipple thrusting against his palm.

"I want you," he repeated.

He took me into his arms. It seemed right and natural. He looked down at me, the mask of black silk hanging loosely, dark eyes filled with tenderness and desire. I struggled. It was happening, and I had vowed it wouldn't. I tried to pull free, but his arms tightened and the music continued and the ache inside grew and I knew I was lost. I knew I wanted him as much as he wanted me. I wanted his warmth, his strength, his love. I grew breathless, poised on the brink of an abyss that beckoned, drawing me nearer and nearer the edge.

"I've dreamed of this moment," he said.

He tightened his right arm around my waist, drawing me against him, and he touched my cheek with his left hand, his fingers moving down to my mouth, his thumb gently stroking my lower lip. I closed my eyes, lost, approaching the edge, longing for the dizzying fall to commence. He lifted the hem of his hood and covered my mouth with his own, and I began to reel. His lips were firm and moist and warm, pushing, pressing, forcing my own to respond. I clung to him as his tongue thrust forward and filled my mouth.

He drew back. I looked up into his eyes. They seemed to glow darkly, luminous, lovely, silently telling me all the things a woman longs to know. He turned me around and began to unfasten my gown. I was trembling now. I thought I was going to swoon. The music came through the windows, sensuous and vibrating with passion, and it seemed to come from within me, seemed to fill me. His hands moved over my arms, pushing the sleeves down, and a moment later the dress fell to the floor.

I stepped out of the circle of cloth. He picked up the gown and tossed it onto the sofa and took me into his arms again and, raising the black silk hem, kissed me once more, tenderly, lazily, deliberately holding back the urgency that tormented us both. When he released me, I moved over to the sofa and took off my shoes and removed my petticoat. He stood in the shadows, watching, until I was naked. I removed hairpins and dropped them onto the sofa and shook my head and my hair tumbled down my back. The pink rose fell to the floor and petals scattered.

"I've never seen anything so beautiful," he murmured. "I love you, Elena."

"You—you don't have to say that."

"I love you," he repeated.

Taking me up into his arms, he held me against his chest and carried me into the bedroom. He lowered me onto the bed and stood back, looking down at me. He was like a demon lover dressed in black, the black hood covering his head, and I was naked and vulnerable and filled with an aching need that grew more and more urgent as those hidden eyes examined every inch of my body. The candle flames brushed the walls with soft gold light. Music still came from the gardens. He leaned over and stroked my breasts, ran his hands over my stomach, tightened his fingers about my waist, and I reached up to touch the hood.

Moving away, he stepped over to the candelabrum and extinguished the candles one by one until the room was in total darkness, velvety darkness that seemed to swallow me. I heard his boots clatter to the floor. He stood up, and I sensed his movements as he undressed. Moments passed, and as my eyes adjusted to the darkness I could see a faint outline as he approached the bed, naked now.

He climbed onto the bed and took me into his arms and kissed me over and over again, tenderly, tormenting me with kisses, his arms enfolding me, muscles tightening as his kisses grew more urgent, expressing a passionate need that mounted into furious demand. I responded with a violence that matched his own, clinging to him, shattered by sensations so intense I thought they must surely destroy me. Finally, he climbed atop me, crushing me beneath him, and I cried out as he entered me and thrust fiercely, driving deep and filling me completely with that one violent stroke.

I shuddered and dug my fingernails into his back. Flesh seemed to melt and expand and explode as he pulled back and thrust again and yet again. I had never known such fury, such splendor, such savage ecstasy. Every fiber of my being was shaken and shredded and I knew this had to be the height of all bliss, but it grew more and more intense and I seemed to be climbing and each rung took me into another realm of ecstasy, and I sensed it was the same for him. He paused. For one excruciating eternal moment he held back and left me suspended on the highest rung . . . until those ultimate thrusts sent me hurtling into a glowing oblivion.

XLII

A bird sang cheerfully in the gardens, and his song seemed to be part of a dream. I opened my eyes to see Juanita smiling. She was standing near the foot of the bed, wearing the white cotton blouse and embroidered red skirt she had worn the night before, her long black plait glossy in the sunlight. I sat up, gathering the sheet over my breasts. Sometime during the night we had gotten under the covers. Before he made love to me a second time? After?

"I will bring your clothes, and after you have dressed there will be breakfast," Juanita announced.

"What—what time is it?"

"After eleven," she told me. "You will be leaving at one. There isn't much time, but he said to let you sleep. I thought you might like coffee first."

She pointed to the tray on the table, smiled her gentle smile again and busied herself around the room. The coffee was strong and hot and delicious, and after the second cup the last vestige of drowsiness was gone. When I finished, the bed had been made and a complete new set of clothes laid out, undergarments, petticoat, a violet-blue riding habit. There was even a pair of black kid boots and a violet-blue hat with black and purple plumes spilling over one side of the wide brim. He had thought of everything, I told myself, slipping into the undergarments and petticoat.

I sat down at the dressing table and brushed my hair and put it up in a loose roll. There was no candlelight now, no sensuous guitar music, and I was not befuddled with wine. I felt cool and calm and appalled by what had happened, appalled that I had been so easily manipulated. He must be very pleased with himself. He had slept with Elena Lopez, and she had been all too willing. Had I wanted to I could have found all sorts of excuses for myself, but the fact remained that I had played right into his hands. Leaving the dressing table, I finished putting on the attire he had chosen with such care. The riding habit was a perfect fit, as were the boots, and the whole outfit might have been especially designed for me.

Juanita served breakfast in the other room, but I ate little. Returning to the bedroom, I put on the hat, adjusted the brim to the proper slant and stuck the long hat pin in place. Ten minutes later as I waited in front of the hacienda, I heard his boots clicking on the tiles of the outside staircase. I stared resolutely at the fountain, refusing to look at him as he joined me.

"You can ride, I trust?" he said.

"I can ride."

"Good. You look lovely, Elena."

I ignored the remark. He decided to ignore my icy manner. Pedro led two horses around the drive, Black Hood's chestnut and a lovely mare with a pearly gray coat and an English sidesaddle on her back. Black Hood helped me into the saddle. I wrapped my knee around the pommel and arranged the folds of the violet-blue skirt.

"No blindfold?" I inquired.

"I don't think that will be necessary."

"You're not afraid I'll lead the law back to this hacienda?"

"You won't," he said.

He climbed onto his horse, and a moment later we were riding toward the distant slope. My mare was gentle but strong. I found it quite easy to keep up with him. We climbed the slope and crossed the grassy stretch and went into the wooded area, riding at an easy canter. Leaving the woods, we moved over open country, vast and lovely and drenched in sunlight. A lonely hawk circled lazily in the sky, a speck of brown against the pale blue.

I tried not to think about the night before, but I kept remembering those moments of passionate splendor that had been the most shattering, the most magnificent I had ever experienced. He had held me in his arms so tenderly afterwards, stroking my skin, murmuring my name, that soft, husky voice the voice of a man deeply and irrevocably in love—or had I imagined that? Had the wine intensified and distorted everything?

An hour passed, two, and I was beginning to grow weary as we continued to ride. We had passed the lightly wooded clearing quite some time before, and I had averted my eyes from that mound of gray rocks, trying not to think about the scene of horror enacted down by the river. Could it have been only yesterday?

We reached another wooded area, and through the trees I could see the huge golden-tan boulders I remembered so well. Black Hood drew the chestnut to a halt and reached over to take the reins from my hand, looking at me with eyes that were completely inscrutable.

"You wait here," he said. "I'll be back shortly."

I climbed off the mare, and Black Hood dropped the reins, letting them trail. The mare began to graze contentedly on the short grass beneath the trees. Black Hood drew his pistol and moved the chestnut forward at a cautious pace, soon disappearing behind the boulders. I grew tense and nervous, afraid of what might happen. What if Anthony had brought the law with him? What if Black Hood walked into an ambush? He might be killed. Long minutes passed, five, ten, fifteen, and I didn't know if I could bear much more.

I kept staring at the boulders in the distance, and it was with a rush of relief that I saw him come around one of the largest and ride toward me. As he drew nearer I noticed a large burlap bag hanging from his saddle. There had been no shooting. Anthony had brought the money, and no one had been harmed. Black Hood paused beside the mare and leaned across to take hold of her loose reins. He stopped a few paces from where I stood. Bewildering emotions rose inside of me as I looked at him.

"Your friends are waiting for you," he told me. "It's a short walk. You'll find the coach beyond those boulders."

"I see you have the money. I hope you're satisfied."

He ignored the remark. A long moment passed, and then he tightened his grip on the reins.

"Goodbye, Elena," he said softly. "We'll meet again soon. Perhaps much sooner than you imagine."

He tapped his heels against the chestnut's flanks and rode away at a brisk gallop, the mare keeping pace behind. As I watched him leave, upsetting emotions continued to stir inside me. There was a feeling of emptiness, a sense of loss, that I couldn't understand. He disappeared, at last. Still, I stood under the trees for several minutes, deeply bothered, and then finally, I turned and started slowly toward the boulders.

XLIII

I stood at the front of the stage, hands on hips, eyes flashing. The poor musicians clutched their instruments nervously, waiting for the explosion, and the four male dancers who had been hired to accompany me huddled near the backdrop, afraid to breathe. The vast theater with its rows of empty seats was so quiet one could have heard a pin drop, until Anthony got out of his aisle seat and strolled breezily down to the orchestra pit, totally unperturbed. Had there been a gun in my hand I would have shot him without a moment's hesitation.

I had been perfectly reasonable, open to suggestion and patient to a fault. I was willing to work to the point of collapse in order to make this San Francisco opening special, but we had gone over this particular number at least ten times since noon, and Mr. Anthony Duke *still* wasn't satisfied. He still felt it necessary to carp and quibble and make ridiculous suggestions. The musicians were exhausted. The four male dancers were ready to drop. I was ready to kill.

"Let's try one more time," he said amiably.

That did it.

"You can go straight to hell!" I cried. "I don't intend to dance another step! I may never dance again for the rest of my life! I've had it up to *here,* Mr. Duke! I suggest you find someone else to ridicule and bully! Don't you *dare* try to humor me!"

"Now, luv—"

"Out! Everyone out! Rehearsal is over for the day!"

The dancers scurried off stage. The musicians quickly emptied the pit. In a matter of seconds Anthony and I were left alone. He looked up at me and sighed. I glared at him, still standing near the edge of the stage with my hands on my hips. Neither of us spoke. There were clattering noises backstage as dancers and musicians departed, and then, after a while, total silence.

"You're tense," he remarked.

He skirted around the orchestra pit and moved up the steps at the side of the stage.

"I meant what I said, Anthony. Don't try to humor me. I'm in no mood for your—your joviality."

"You were terrific, you know. I realize this new routine is difficult for you, and—"

"Difficult! Are you implying I can't—"

"This is the first time you've worked with other dancers. It isn't you I'm worried about, luv, it's them. Christ knows where Peterson found them. Members of a Spanish ballet troupe, he claims. They move like they've spent most of their lives roping steers."

"They're highly competent dancers."

"Hardly speak a word of English, either."

He strolled over to me, smiling, and tried to take my hand. I pulled away.

"Three more days until opening night," he said, "and every seat is sold out. We're going to make history. San Francisco has never seen anything like this. When they write books about these times, Elena Lopez is going to have whole chapters devoted to her."

"Do you think I care about *that?*"

"I think you're exhausted, Elena," he said. "I think you're nervous and distraught and need a little relaxation. You haven't gone out a single night since we got here. Besides, it's bad for business. People need to *see* you. Staying cooped up in your hotel room isn't helping at all. You've turned down every invitation."

"That's my affair."

"In some cases, I'm glad. That fellow Wayne, for instance. I'd hate to see you get mixed up with a chap like that, but when the Governor himself asks you to dine—"

"I'm weary, Anthony. I've never been so weary in my

life. I'm tired of theaters, tired of dancing, tired of being on show twenty-four hours a day. I'm tired of the strain, the upset, the—"

"You don't mean that, luv."

He wrapped his arms around my waist, drawing me to him and resting his chin on my head.

"You haven't been the same since that Black Hood incident. I realize it was an ordeal for you, but everything worked out beautifully. Even though we lost twenty thousand dollars, the publicity was worth ten times that much. The greatest showman on earth couldn't have arranged such a coup."

"I don't want to talk about it," I said stiffly.

"You're going to go to your dressing room and change," he informed me. "Then you're going to go back to the hotel and rest. Tonight I'm taking you out. We're going to the fanciest restaurant in the city. It'll do wonders for you."

"It'll also cost me," I snapped.

"*I'll* pay, luv. Don't I always?"

"You hand over the actual money. Then you deduct it from my share of the profits. It's listed as 'expenses.'"

"Tonight is on me," he promised.

He nuzzled my cheek with his and then stepped back. I was still irritated, but it was impossible to stay angry for long. He knew just what approach to use, just the right tone of voice to mollify me. I went backstage to my dressing room. Millie was out somewhere with Bradford, and it was just as well. I wasn't in any mood for her bright chatter. I washed and changed into a garnet taffeta frock, enjoying the silence and solitude. Anthony was right. Since my arrival in San Francisco almost two weeks before, I had been irritated, strangely dissatisfied and prey to a peculiar melancholy I couldn't seem to shake.

Everything seemed pointless. I had fame, modest wealth, a glamorous life full of color and excitement, and it meant nothing. I realized that more and more each day. Some performers thrived on glory, basking in their fame. As long as their egos received proper nourishment, that was enough. But I felt as if I were participating in some kind of insane race. I was well in the lead and the crowd was cheering me on, but I could see no finish line in sight. There *was* no finish line. For the past five years I had kept right on running. To what purpose? I had achieved incredible success, but in my heart I had to acknowledge that it was an empty success.

For some reason the encounter with Black Hood had brought all this to the surface. The dissatisfaction and melancholy had been there all along, carefully contained, but I had refused to acknowledge them. That was no longer possible. Black Hood had somehow or other touched a cord inside me and made me aware of feelings I could no longer ignore.

With a heavy sigh I turned away from the dressing table and put on the hat that matched my gown. The hat, a sumptuous affair of stiff garnet taffeta, dripped with frothy black plumes. Elena Lopez had to maintain her flamboyant air. The publicity I'd received in San Francisco was incredible. My abduction by the bandit had created a furor, and it seemed the city could think of nothing else. The newspapers were filled with sensational stories, and my refusal to disclose any information about my abductor had given rise to wild, romantic speculation. I was the heroine of the day, and I couldn't step out of the hotel without attracting a huge, admiring crowd.

Posters announcing my opening night were displayed on every street corner. But there was more. Several nights before, a theater on the waterfront had premiered *Elena and The Bandit*, a lurid melodrama that apparently had been written overnight and staged in record time. It was a nightly sell out. Incensed at first, Anthony threatened to sue, but then he decided the extra publicity was good for business. My own opening night was set back in order that a more elaborate production might be mounted. Male dancers were hired, new sets hastily constructed, and new costumes designed. Anthony thought it might be interesting to have the men dressed all in black with black silk hoods over their heads, a suggestion I immediately vetoed.

Now, I turned as he opened the dressing room door. Anthony would never think of knocking. Attired in dark blue jacket, gray suede top hat in hand, he was the picture of a perfect dandy, handsome and merry and vain, as he went over to the dressing table mirror and straightened his pearl gray neckcloth.

"Ready?" he inquired.

"I suppose so."

"We'd better go out the front way," he informed me. "I peeked out back, and there's a mob waiting for you. They must have found out about the rehearsals."

"There's always a mob," I complained.

"Your public. They love you."

"I feel like a freak."

"You'd attract a crowd even if you weren't Elena Lopez. You happen to be the most beautiful woman on earth," he said, "and San Francisco is starving for female beauty. The majority of women out here came in with the covered wagons, and most of 'em look as if they were up front, pulling."

"You're horrible."

He grinned and pulled on his gray suede gloves, and then, placing the top hat on his head at a jaunty angle, he took my arm and led me around to the stage and down the side steps. The theater still sparkled with newness, overwhelmingly red, walls covered with red brocade, seats of plush red velvet, balconies and boxes ivory white with gold leaf patterns. Sparkling chandeliers hung from the ornate ceiling. The bordello look was extremely popular.

"Hope you're feeling better," Anthony remarked as we moved up the aisle.

"I'm in a wretched mood."

"We'll take care of that later," he promised.

"I really don't want to go out tonight, Anthony."

"That's too bad. You're going out whether you want to or not."

I waited patiently as Anthony took out his key and unlocked one of the doors that led out from the lobby. We stepped out under the marquee, and Anthony locked the door and took my arm once again. People stopped and stared as we started up the wooden sidewalk toward the hotel. A crowd soon gathered, following at a discreet distance, exchanging comments about my gown, my hat, my complexion. I tried to pretend they weren't there.

"Lovely day for a walk," Anthony observed. "Ridiculous to hire a carriage for such a short distance."

"Seven blocks," I said, "all uphill."

"Exercise will do you good, luv."

"You keep telling me that."

Although I felt it necessary to make a token complaint, I was secretly glad Anthony was too tight to provide a carriage. The walks to and from the theater provided my only opportunity to observe the phenomenon of San Francisco—an incredible place, booming, bustling and expanding by the minute.

The whole city was throbbing with vitality. One could hardly turn a corner without seeing a new building going up. Stately mansions were beginning to bloom on the hills, and wooden shacks were giving way to blocks of fine stores. Gambling halls, saloons, churches, gaudily ornate hotels and an unusual number of fire halls—for fire was a constant hazard—multiplied with amazing speed.

The noise was deafening. Horses neighed and carriages rumbled. Bells clanged and hammers hammered. Men shouted heartily as piles of lumber were hoisted into the air on ropes and pulleys, and Chinese laborers chattered as they pushed wheelbarrows filled with bricks. The very air seemed to be charged with excitement. I longed for the freedom to explore freely and savor the marvelous atmosphere, but my celebrity made that impossible. As we reached the crest of the hill I could see the thick forest of ship masts in the harbor. Millie had told me that the waterfront was fascinating, wild and wicked and exploding with color, but I had yet to visit it.

"That fellow still sending you presents?" Anthony inquired as we drew near the hotel.

"What fellow?"

"You know bloody well what fellow. Wayne. Nicholas Wayne. He still sending you things?"

"Bouquets of flowers every day," I replied, "and an occasional diamond."

Anthony took hold of my elbow and helped me up

the steps in front of the hotel. His expression was sullen as we crossed the verandah.

"I hope you're not keeping them," he said.

"What does it matter to you?"

The lobby we entered was extremely large and showy, all rococo woodwork and luxuriant Persian carpets, potted plants in abundance. As Anthony led me over to the staircase, he took off his top hat, frowned, and glanced around to make sure that no one was within hearing distance.

"I don't like what I hear about the fellow, Elena. He's too rich, too powerful. He owns most of the gambling halls in the city, holds mortgages on those he doesn't actually own. He's counted a respectable citizen, very civic minded. He's on all the boards and committees, contributes to all the funds, even donated a new fire hall."

"I find that admirable."

"So do a lot of people, but there're others who aren't fooled by his façade. Steer clear of him, luv."

Continuing upstairs to my suite, I was both puzzled and intrigued by what he had told me. Why was he so adamant about Nicholas Wayne, a man he apparently had never even met? It would be nice to think he was jealous, but I didn't flatter myself. Anthony had never shown the least sign of jealousy when I went out with other men, had, in fact, encouraged me to go out with them if they were important and my being seen with them would make the papers. Nick Wayne was certainly important in San Francisco. It was rumored that he had political aspirations. I wondered why Anthony had taken such a strong dislike to him.

Nicholas Wayne had sent a bouquet of flowers to the suite the night I first arrived, along with an invitation to dine. Though I had refused the invitation, there had been more flowers, another invitation and a diamond pendant. I had torn up the invitation and returned the pendant. A third invitation, another bouquet, and a stunning diamond and sapphire clasp were delivered. The messenger boy had waited patiently while I read the brief message, then asked if there would be a reply. I shook my head and handed him the velvet box containing the clasp. With an exasperated sigh, he went on his way, only to return the next night with another note and another, larger velvet box.

Nick Wayne was persistent, to say the least, but I had no desire to meet him, or any other man for that matter. I had received dozens of other invitations. Everyone in San Francisco wanted to meet me, it seemed, but I was in no mood for social activity. The rehearsals were grueling, and after they were over I wanted only to rest. I hadn't even tried the hotel's dining room, but had my meals sent up to the suite instead, sharing them with Millie whenever she wasn't out with James Bradford. Which was seldom. Bradford had been monopolizing her time, and Millie quite clearly loved it.

As I stepped over to the window and looked out, I could see a patchwork of rooftops, a row of large brown warehouses and, beyond them, the crowded harbor. The sun, now a huge orange ball, made wavering golden streaks on the water and spread shadows over the rooftops. For some reason, I found myself thinking of the man in black, and that irritated me. Perhaps Anthony was right. Perhaps going out would do me good. Staying in and brooding about things wasn't going to help at all.

I had finished my bath and was tying the sash of my dressing gown when I heard the sitting room door open. Millie burst in laden with white boxes and aglow with vitality, her long golden curls all atumble. She dropped the boxes on the sofa, smiled her mischievous pixie smile and did a little dance step, lifting her dark pink skirt up over her petticoats.

"You must have had quite a day," I remarked.

"Marvelous!" she declared. "I think it might well be the best day of my life. He's hooked, Elena. Hooked good and proper. He finally asked me to marry him!"

"I assume you're talking about Bradford."

"I didn't think he was *ever* going to get around to it."

"And you've known him a good ten days."

"Don't be sarcastic. I'm in *such* a good mood. He was so serious about it. He took my hand there on the beach—we went to the beach today, two or three miles

498

down the coast, gorgeous country—and he looked into my eyes and said he wanted to settle down."

"What did you say?"

"I didn't say anything. I just looked demure and expectant. He told me he'd been saving his money to buy a small ranch and wants to take me there as his bride. He said he reckoned he'd fallen in love with me, reckoned I was the first woman he'd ever loved."

She moved over to the mirror and brushed a skein of golden hair from her temple, and when she turned around her eyes were pensive.

"I was thrilled, and touched, too. He really meant it. He really loves me. It isn't just sex, although he's terribly greedy in that department. Terribly good, too, I might add. He held my hand and looked into my eyes, and I actually felt like crying. I don't think anyone has ever really loved me before, not the way James does."

"You're lucky to have found him, Millie."

"I guess maybe I am. He's not what I had in *mind*, not by a long shot, but—I'm going to give it some serious consideration just the same. I've had to look out for myself ever since I can remember. I was out on my own by the time I was thirteen, nothing between me and starvation but sheer determination to survive—" As she paused to remember, there was a long silence, and then she shook her head and sighed.

"It might be nice to have someone else take care of me for a while. I may marry him. I just may do it."

"Did you tell him so?"

The engaging minx re-emerged. "Of course not!" she exclaimed. "I intend to keep him in suspense for a while. Can't have him getting *too* sure of himself. He's bossy enough as it is."

I smiled and asked her what was in the boxes.

"Well, beaches and scenery are all very well if you like that sort of thing, but after a while they begin to pall. James had been promising to take me to Montgomery Street so I could do some shopping, and I suggested we get back in the buggy and *go*. Montgomery Street's fabulous. The sidewalks are piled high with boxes of merchandise. You have to step out into the

499

street in order to get to the doors, and once inside the stores—"

She opened box after box, showing me the treasures she'd found and enthusiastically describing the wonders of San Francisco's shopping district. One could buy goods from all over the world, she said, and every store was like Aladdin's Cave.

"James was patient for the first couple of hours," she confided. "Then he grew more and more restless, and finally literally dragged me away! We must go together, Elena. Wait till you see the silks from Japan and the furs from Russia!"

While she put her finds back into their boxes, tissue paper crackling, I glanced at the clock and said that I had to start dressing. She looked surprised.

"You've finally accepted an invitation?"

"Not really. Anthony's taking me out to dinner."

"*That*'s certainly a novelty. I'll help you get ready. I've plenty of time. James is taking me down to the waterfront for seafood, but we aren't leaving until nine. I guess Anthony's had his fill of the gambling halls," she added as we left the sitting room.

"What do you mean?"

"He's been going to the gambling halls every night, ever since we got here."

"Really?"

I sat down at the dressing table. Millie picked up brush and comb and began to work on my hair.

"He's lost a bundle. At the tables, I mean. James and I saw him at The Golden Nugget a couple of nights ago. He was very dapper, very composed, but he was down to his last gold piece. He put it on black, and red came up. He pretended not to care, but I could see he was upset."

I shrugged. If Anthony wanted to squander his money, it was no concern of mine. Millie finished with my hair and stepped back to examine her handiwork. She had pulled it back in soft waves, arranging it in a sculptured roll in back.

"What are you going to wear?" she asked.

"I don't know. Something grand. He promised to take me to the finest restaurant in town."

Millie prowled through the wardrobe, a thoughtful look in her eyes as she examined the gowns. "What about the black velvet?"

"That'll do nicely. It's certainly grand."

Selecting a dark red lip rouge, I put on my make-up and was just reaching for the gown when someone knocked on the sitting room door. Millie hurried to answer it, and I heard the messenger boy's familiar voice.

"You again!" Millie said.

The messenger said something I couldn't hear, and then Millie came back into the bedroom with an envelope and a long black leather box.

"Nick Wayne," she announced. "He doesn't give up, does he? The boy says Mr. Wayne expects an answer."

I read the note aloud. " 'Is tonight the night I shall have the pleasure of your company? I'm hoping the answer will finally be yes. Nick Wayne.' "

"The poor man is obviously suffering," Millie observed. "Open the box. Let's sneak a look before you return it."

I snapped back the lid and removed the diamond bracelet from its nest of black satin. Over a hundred diamonds sparkled with rainbow-hued fires as I held up the bracelet.

"Lord!" Millie exclaimed. "Do you *have* to give it back?"

Dropping the bracelet back into the box, I closed the lid and handed her the box. "Tell the boy there is no reply."

I slipped into the gown and spread its skirt out over the rustling layers of red silk petticoats. Millie returned to help me fasten the back, a wistful expression on her face.

"No one ever sends *me* diamonds," she complained. "I'm lucky if I get a pat on the cheek. I hear that Nick Wayne is extremely good-looking, and he's thirty-five years old, and considered the best catch in all California."

"I've no doubt he'll make some woman very happy."

"You're not even *curious*?"

"Not in the least," I replied, affixing a short, curling

501

red plume on the left side of my hair and pulling on the long red satin gloves Millie handed to me.

"You're going to create a sensation," she announced. "People are going to drop their forks when you walk into the restaurant."

Gazing at my reflection in the mirror, I wondered at the glamorous creature I saw. Elena Lopez was the epitome of sophisticated allure, but the dark blue eyes were melancholy, the red lips discontent. I had been playing a role for so long, and most of the time I had enjoyed it, but the woman inside was growing tired of the part. I wondered how much longer I would be able to sustain it.

Millie gave me a hug, then gathered up her boxes, told me to have a marvelous time and left the suite. Anthony had gone back to the theater for a business conference with the management and hadn't been specific as to when he would come for me. I decided to go down to the lobby and wait for him there. I didn't want to be alone. I had spent far too much time alone of late, restless, bothered, thinking of that night at the hacienda and the man who had wooed me with such ease.

I moved down the hall toward the grand staircase. People would stare. Let them. I was prepared for it. I paused at the top of the stairs, smoothing one of my gloves, stepping into character. Elena Lopez was on again. I could feel the eyes of strangers, hear their murmurs as I descended the stairs. The vast lobby was crowded, but no one approached me as I left the staircase and moved to stand beside one of the enormous potted plants.

Several minutes passed. I was beginning to grow impatient as the clock ticked away and there was still no sign of Anthony. I brooded. Why couldn't he do anything properly? Why must he be so cavalier? I wouldn't be at all surprised if he didn't even show up. He'd better, I thought, tapping the toe of my shoe on the carpet. As I glanced around the lobby, I noticed a man in a dark beige suit standing across the room, staring at me with a calm, level gaze, and I realized that he had been doing so for quite some time.

502

Our eyes met. He didn't look away. He nodded politely and continued to gaze. He was very tall with a sturdy muscular build and thick reddish-brown hair neatly parted and brushed sleekly to one side. His eyes were a deep brown, his dark eyebrows straight, his features strong and perfectly chiseled. Not really handsome, he was nevertheless striking with the solid good looks that inspire confidence in men and give women a feeling of security. The beige suit was carefully tailored to flatter his physique and augmented by a brown brocade waistcoat patterned with bronze and darker brown leaves, and a bronze silk neckcloth. The entire ensemble signaled the wearer as a man of importance.

Discomfited by his steady gaze, which was neither rude nor blatant, I looked away, though I remained acutely aware of it as several more minutes went by and Anthony still didn't show up. I was just getting ready to go back up to my suite when Anthony hurried across the lobby toward me.

"Sorry, luv. I got held up at the theater on business. Will you forgive me? I've got a carriage waiting out front. Incidentally, you look smashing."

"Mr. Duke?"

Anthony turned. He tensed. Bright pink spots of anger flamed on his cheeks as the man in beige stepped over to us.

"I've been wanting to talk to you," the man said. "Would you like to introduce me to your lovely companion?"

"Not a chance!" Anthony retorted, taking hold of my elbow and propelling me toward the door with such speed that I found myself tottering. I didn't have to ask him who the man was. I already knew.

XLIV

Ordinarily I am jittery and on edge and unfit company for anyone on opening night. So, as I dressed to go to the theater, I wondered why I felt so cool, so calm, so . . . indifferent—that was the perfect word to describe the way I felt. I would do my best tonight. I would give my all, but for some reason success or failure no longer mattered as it had in the past.

It was eleven-thirty, and I was due at the theater at twelve. No lunch would be served today. All of us would snack lightly after the dress rehearsal on food sent in by the management.

As I prepared to leave, I thought about Anthony. He hadn't been at all himself for the past two days, not since we had gone to dinner together. He had been edgy and testy and impossible to get along with, snapping at everyone, brooding the rest of the time. I was concerned about him. Though I ignored his irritability, the constant worried look in his eyes bothered me a great deal. And when I finally asked him what was wrong he stormed at me, telling me to worry about my dancing and leave him alone. He apologized to me later on, giving me an affectionate hug and saying he hadn't meant to be such a bear, but the worried look remained in his eyes.

I knew I'd find out eventually what was worrying him, and then I would do what I could to help him. He'd probably made another ridiculous investment that had fallen through.

I walked into the sitting room to wait for Millie and Bradford who would take me to the theater in Bradford's rented buggy. Anthony had already left. Someone knocked and I opened the door immediately.

Nicholas Wayne looked surprised. He couldn't have been more surprised than I was.

"Good morning," he said. "I was expecting a maid to open the door."

"You're in luck, it seems. Had a maid opened the door I'd have told her to inform you that I was out."

"You know who I am?"

"I do, Mr. Wayne. And I'm very busy."

"I'd like to talk to you."

"You'd only be wasting your time," I informed him, "and, more importantly, mine."

"I don't think so," he replied.

Standing with my hand resting on the door, I gazed at him coolly. His reddish-brown hair was neatly brushed to one side as it had been the other night, and his deep brown eyes were calm, confident. He smelled of bay rum and leather, a clean, masculine smell that suited him perfectly.

"Have you brought diamonds?" I inquired.

"I'm afraid not."

"Not even a bouquet of flowers, I see. What is it you wish to talk to me about, Mr. Wayne? I'm really in a hurry, I'm due at the theater and—"

"May I come in?"

"Oh, I suppose so," I relented.

I moved aside to let him pass, closed the door and went over to sit down on the sofa. I didn't ask him to sit, deliberately omitting that courtesy. Sunlight streamed in through the windows, burnishing his hair and giving it a bronze sheen. I hadn't realized before just how large he was, how tall and sturdy. Nick Wayne seemed to exude power, and he had the kind of presence that would take him far if he did indeed go into politics.

"What is it you want?" I asked.

"I want to take you to dinner."

"You're very persistent."

"Very," he agreed. "I generally get what I want."

"Not in this instance," I promised.

506

He smiled a beautiful smile, warm, humorous and very persuasive. He thrust his hands into his trouser pockets, and his jacket bunched back, revealing more of the splendid waistcoat.

"Is taking you out to dinner so much to ask?" he inquired.

"I don't know you, Mr. Wayne."

"That's the whole point. I want you to know me. I want to know you. That's why I've been sending you gifts."

"I should think my returning them would tell you something."

"It told me that you're not the mercenary adventuress the papers have depicted. The Elena Lopez I've read about would have kept everything while conniving for more."

"The Elena Lopez you've read about doesn't exist, Mr. Wayne. I think you'd better go now."

"I understand you're very fond of your manager," he said.

"As a matter of fact, I am. Anthony and I have been together for years."

"Do you love him?"

"That's none of your business, Mr. Wayne."

My voice was like ice, but that didn't seem to bother him at all. I was beginning to lose my patience. Nick Wayne looked at me with those calm brown eyes, and then he shook his head and frowned slightly, reaching into the inside pocket of his jacket. If he intended to present me with a gift, his timing was definitely wrong. I was on the verge of ordering him out of the suite when he withdrew a sheaf of notes and glanced down at them, his frown deepening.

"You won't accept my diamonds, Miss Lopez. Perhaps you'll accept these instead."

He handed me the notes. I examined them. Nick Wayne observed my reactions closely. I could feel the color leave my cheeks. The first note was for five thousand dollars credit at The Golden Nugget, signed over to Anthony Duke by the manager. The second note was for two thousand dollars, the third for another three. There were eleven notes in all, and the total amount was

507

well over fifty thousand dollars. Anthony owed The Golden Nugget a small fortune, and there was no way he could pay it without using every penny of profit we would earn in San Francisco. The money was due in four days.

"I would never have allowed it had I known," Wayne told me. "These notes were brought to my attention only this morning. My man at The Golden Nugget assumed Duke had unlimited funds. He felt it would be all right to keep giving him credit."

"And he kept gambling it away?" I asked in a hollow voice.

"I'm afraid so."

"I can't believe it. I can't believe he'd be so foolish. There's no excuse—"

"I'm terribly sorry about this," Wayne said. "Men are going to gamble. I provide the facilities, but I try to keep a tight rein. I don't like to see anyone break themselves. When someone hits a losing streak and keeps on gambling, I cut off all credit. Your manager was foolhardy, and so was my man. He should never have permitted this to happen."

As I looked down at the notes in my hand, I felt a terrible sinking sensation. I was angry that Anthony could have done such a thing, but I was sad, too. I knew that this time it would be impossible to forgive him. I wanted to cry. It was all I could do to hold back the tears.

"The notes are yours, Miss Lopez," Wayne said. "Consider the debts cancelled."

I folded the notes in the palm of my hand, fighting back the tears. Nick Wayne was silent, and when I looked up he was still frowning, but his deep brown eyes were full of understanding. I knew now why Anthony resented him so intensely. He blamed Wayne for what had happened. Naturally. He hadn't the courage to accept the blame himself.

"I'm sorry," Wayne repeated. "I'll leave now. I think perhaps you'd like to be alone."

He left quietly, but I hardly noticed. I stood clutching the notes tightly, trying to decide what to do. The sadness was almost overwhelming, and I knew I had to stem it. Through the windows I could see that the light blue sky was gradually turning gray, clouds forming. At least ten minutes passed before I heard the footsteps in the hall outside. Millie opened the door, a look of alarm in her eyes.

"Goodness, Elena!" she exclaimed. "I thought something had *happened*. James and I have been waiting out front in the buggy forever. You're already late to the theater—"

She cut herself short and studied me closely. "Something's wrong," she said.

I didn't answer. I knew what I had to do. I drew myself up, my decision made.

"I'm not going to the theater," I told her. "Have Bradford take you there. Inform them that dress rehearsal is cancelled."

"But—"

"Do as I say, Millie. When you've finished, ask Bradford to come back here for me. I'll be waiting on the verandah. I'm going to need him this afternoon. I hope you won't mind."

Millie hesitated a moment, clearly disturbed and eager to question me, but she could tell that I was in no mood to explain. She gave me a nod and left. I went back into the bedroom, picked up my reticule and stuffed the notes into it, then went downstairs to the lobby to find the manager. He hurried over to me, all smiles, anxious to please.

"I'd like to have my jewelry box," I said. "It was placed in the hotel safe the night I arrived."

"Of course, Miss Lopez. Glad to be of service."

In his plush office, I tapped my foot impatiently while he knelt in front of the huge iron safe and began to twirl the dials, eventually swinging the heavy door open. He stood up and handed me the jewelry box. I thanked him politely and went on out onto the verandah to wait for Bradford. The sky had turned a brooding gray. The sunlight was a thin, pale white. A light wind caused my skirts to flutter. Rain was in the air.

Bradford pulled up in front of the hotel a few minutes later. The buggy was black, a two-seater with a black accordion top that could be drawn up in case of inclement weather. A sturdy dappled gray stood in harness, clopping his heavy hooves up and down impatiently. Bradford climbed down and informed me that he'd left Millie at the theater.

"I kinda thought you might not want her along," he drawled. "She said you needed my help."

"I do. I have to sell my jewelry, and I have to sell it this afternoon. Since you've spent a lot of time in San Francisco and know the city well, I thought you might have some idea where—"

"You want cash?" he asked.

"I must have cash."

"I reckon I know a place. It's not in the greatest neighborhood."

"That doesn't matter," I told him.

After Bradford helped me up onto the seat, he pulled the accordion top over the buggy and fastened it. The horse stamped restlessly. Bradford climbed up beside me and took the reins, snapping them to urge the horse on. Casually dressed as usual, Bradford wore scuffed black boots, a pair of faded gray cord breeches and a faded cotton shirt. His sun-streaked sandy hair flopped over his brow, and his expression was impassive as the buggy moved down the street, jolting and creaking with each turn of the wheels.

Because of the number of vehicles crowding the street, we had to move at a crawl. Drunks lurched in and out of the traffic, ignoring the rain. A bearded giant stumbled against the buggy and caught hold of the harness to keep from falling. He looked up with bleary eyes and saw me and let out a whoop, reaching his hand up to touch my skirts. I drew back, and Bradford calmly leveled his gun at the giant's forehead. The man whooped again and stumbled away, almost falling in front of a wagon loaded with large wooden barrels. Bradford kept his gun out, his face as impassive as ever.

We turned a corner. I could smell fish and tar and rotting nets as we passed a row of stalls. The rain was heavy now and the street had turned into a thick black mire. Bradford pulled up in front of a decrepit building that looked like a warehouse. Handing me the gun, he told me to fire it if anyone approached the buggy. Then

510

he alighted and dashed inside the building. I waited nervously, the gun in my hand, rain pelting on the accordion top and blowing in to splatter my skirts. The dappled gray stood patiently, his coat wet and sleek.

Ten minutes must have passed before Bradford returned carrying a large umbrella. He took the gun, placed it back in his holster and helped me down, leading me inside the vast, dimly lighted building filled with crates and barrels and smelling of sawdust. There was an office in the rear, and a heavy-set man in a dingy black suit stepped out to greet us. His face was fleshy, his dark eyes greedy, his bald dome fringed with thin hair. His name was Sykes, and he reeked of alcohol and damp talcum powder.

"I understand you want to sell some jewels," he said.

I nodded curtly, following him and Bradford into the small, cluttered office. Bradford took the jewelry box from me. He did all the bargaining, stern, tough, insistent, never once raising his voice, even though Sykes yelled and gave a convincing impression of apoplexy as Bradford turned down bid after bid, insisting on more money. They finally agreed on a figure approximately one twentieth the value of the jewelry. It was just enough to pay off Anthony's debts. Bradford looked at me to see if I was satisfied, and I nodded again. Sykes repeated his apoplexy routine when Bradford told him we had to have cash.

We left the building ten minutes later, Bradford retaining the umbrella, my reticule filled with money. As he helped me back up onto the seat, I realized I hadn't said a word since we'd left the hotel. Bradford climbed up beside me and took the reins in his hands. He didn't ask me any questions, didn't deem it necessary to discuss what had taken place, figuring I must have a good reason for doing what I had done. Millie was getting a remarkable man, I decided. Strong, capable, sure of himself in any situation, Bradford would always be calm and dependable.

"Where do you want to go now?" he inquired.

"Does Nick Wayne maintain an office?"

Bradford nodded, brushing a damp lock from his

brow. "He has an office in one of the buildings on Sansome and California."

"I'd like to go there."

Our progress was slow, for the streets had become treacherously muddy and almost impossible to navigate. Several vehicles had bogged down in the mire, horses thrashing, men shouting. The rain continued in a steady downpour, but the dappled gray plodded along, unperturbed by rain and mud, Bradford calmly guiding it around obstacles. It took us an hour to reach the building that housed Wayne's office, and by then the rain had slackened to a light drizzle.

"Want me to go in with you?" Bradford asked.

"I don't think it's necessary," I told him. "I'll be back out in a few minutes."

The building was new. Most of the area had been destroyed in the fire of '51, and new, sturdier structures had been erected. The lower floor housed a bank. A weary-looking clerk behind one of the mahogany desks pointed to the staircase and told me I'd find Wayne's office on the second floor. My skirt was spotted by raindrops, my hair damp and all atumble. I brushed it back from my eyes before knocking on the impressive door that had his name printed in neat gold letters on it.

A male secretary opened the door and showed me inside. The office was very large, panelled in dark oak, the carpet a golden brown. Prints of sailing vessels hung on the walls, and there was a leather sofa, a portable bar laden with crystal decanters, tall lamps with green glass shades. Wayne sat behind a beautiful Sheraton desk littered with papers. When he saw me he stood up immediately, pulling on the jacket that had hung on the back of his chair.

"Miss Lopez," he said, looking completely surprised.

He glanced at the secretary and indicated the door with a quick tilt of the head. The secretary left, pulling the door shut behind him.

"This is an unexpected pleasure," Wayne said.

"I've come on business, Mr. Wayne." I opened my reticule and took out the money. He watched as I counted it, his right eyebrow arched, a displeased look in his eyes. When I had the exact amount Anthony

512

owed, I folded the bills and held them out toward him. Wayne shook his head.

"I won't take your money," he told me. "I gave you the notes. The debts are already marked off the books."

"I must insist, Mr. Wayne."

He could tell by my tone of voice that I meant what I said. Frowning, he took the bills from me and dropped them on top of the desk. He studied me with puzzled brown eyes.

"What an unusual woman you are," he remarked.

"I believe the money is all there. You might count it."

"I don't care about the money."

"I thought you were a businessman. You've just made an enormous profit."

"Might I ask where you obtained the money?"

"From a Mister Sykes," I retorted.

"Sykes! You had dealings with a man like that?"

"I needed money quickly."

"What did you sell him? Your jewelry? You did, didn't you?"

"That's none of your business, Mr. Wayne. The only thing that need concern you is the money on the desk. Anthony's gambling debts have been paid in full. I'd like a receipt to that effect, if you don't mind."

Wayne frowned again and stepped behind his desk. He wrote out the receipt, tore it out of the book and handed it to me.

"You must love him very much to have done a thing like this," he said quietly.

"I do love him, Mr. Wayne. That's why I had to do it. I don't expect you to understand."

"Your jewelry was world famous."

"It was of no use to me whatsoever. It was merely a symbol—a symbol of a past I'm trying very hard to forget."

My voice was like steel, reflecting the cold tightness I felt inside. I clung to it. I had to. If I gave way now, I would never be able to get through the evening. Nick Wayne seemed to understand and his manner was warm and sympathetic.

"I feel responsible for this," he said.

"It isn't your fault," I replied, bending a little. "As

513

you said earlier, you merely provide the facilities. I must go now, Mr. Wayne."

"Let me take you back to the hotel."

"Someone's waiting out front."

"I see. At least I can walk you to the front door."

"If you wish."

We walked through the hall and down the stairs in silence. Although the clerk hadn't recognized me when I came in, word had obviously gotten round that I was in the building. All eyes were on us as we paused at the front door. The rain had stopped. The sky was clearing, a few feeble rays of sunlight straining through the gray. He stepped outside with me.

"Will I see you again?" he asked.

"I really couldn't say."

"I'd like to. I'd like to very much."

"We'll see," I said, and joined Bradford in the buggy to return to the hotel.

The theater was a blaze of lights. The street in front of it was congested with carriages. Sumptuously gowned women and men in formal attire were crowded together under the marquee, moving slowly into the lobby like so many privileged sheep, arriving early in order to have time for gossip and champagne. My show was the theatrical event of the year, and each one of them had paid dearly to be there. It took the driver of the carriage Anthony had hired for me a good ten minutes to make his way past the throng of carriages to the stage entrance in back.

As I approached the stage door, the doorman looked vastly relieved to see me. I had hardly moved past him when Anthony came dashing toward me.

"Where the hell have you *been!*" he cried.

But I ignored him and continued toward my dressing room. He followed me, so agitated his voice was cracking.

"Cancelling dress rehearsal! Disappearing like that! No one had the least idea where you were, not even Millie! I've been frantic!"

"I'm here, Anthony. That's all that matters."

"Christ! Pulling a thing like this, today of all days.

514

You have some explaining to do, luv. Do you realize the curtain goes up in—what? Less than thirty minutes!"

"I'm fully aware of that."

In front of my dressing room door, Anthony brushed a wave of hair from his brow and caught his breath. He was genuinely upset. I almost wanted to comfort him, and I despised myself for the thought. It took every ounce of will power I had not to touch his cheek and straighten his neckcloth and tell him everything would be all right. Clinging to the tightness inside, I willed myself to be hard.

"I want to see you after the performance," I said coldly. "There are some things we need to discuss."

"You bet your life there are! I don't intend to tolerate this, Elena. I didn't know *what* had happened. I've gone through absolute hell these past six hours, worried sick, and—"

"I'll talk to you later," I said, going into the dressing room and closing the door.

I had barely finished my make-up when the stage manager banged on the door. "Ten minutes, Miss Lopez!" he called.

Quickly stepping into a pair of gold slippers, I donned my costume. It was a gorgeous creation of yellow-gold silk, the low bodice held up by two thin, almost invisible straps. The flaring skirt glittered with thousands of golden spangles, a row of yellow-gold ostrich feathers edging the hem, which reached mid-calf. Beneath the skirt flounced six gauze underskirts in varying shades of gold and yellow. The total effect was dazzling. The woman in the mirror was truly the glamorous creature all San Francisco was waiting to see. She was not going to disappoint them. I was going to give the performance of a lifetime.

The overture had already begun to play when I stepped out of the dressing room. Anthony was standing in the wings, tall and lean and extremely handsome in his evening clothes, a sullen rake with moody blue eyes. A deep frown creased his brow. We didn't speak. He leaned his shoulders against a prop and folded his arms across his chest, scowling at me as I adjusted the bodice of my costume and reached up to make sure the curling

515

yellow-gold plume was securely fastened over my temple.

The four male dancers, waiting on stage, were dressed like Spanish caballeros in high-heeled brown boots, tight brown trousers flaring at the bottom, short brown jackets faced with bands of gold embroidery, and wide sombreros tied under the chin. All four stood in front of a backdrop that depicted a Spanish plain, painted in shades of brown and orange and yellow.

The curtain rose. The footlights illuminated the backdrop, turning it into a blaze of color. The effect was spectacular, and there was a scattering of applause as the dancers began their first number; a virile dance that conveyed their rivalry for the woman who had yet to appear. Although they had been good during rehearsal, they were nothing less than marvelous now, sizing each other up, snarling, stamping, shoving each other with carefully choreographed ferocity. The music swelled. Castanets began to click, dozens of castanets. The men turned, staring eagerly toward the wings, and I waited a few moments, deliberately letting the anticipation build.

I forgot Anthony. I forgot Nick Wayne. I forgot everything that had happened and became a seductive, flirtatious Spanish dancer on my way to meet my suitors on a hot Spanish plain. I let the music become part of me and, swinging my skirts, moved slowly on stage. The theater filled with thundering applause, but I paid not the slightest heed, disdaining the audience as I disdained the men. The dancers surrounded me, wooing me, and I condescended to dance with first one, then another, then all four, swinging, dipping, draping myself across muscular arms.

The men retreated to the rear of the stage, standing together, scowling unhappily as I told them through dance of another lover who surpassed them all. Gold spangles flashed as I swayed and swirled, describing the night of splender we had shared, and then each man in turn danced with me again, trying to convince me of his superiority. One wooed me with gentility, waltzing with me, and the next was severe and masterful, stamping out his dominance. The third implored me to take pity on him, pleading his case in movement and mime as the guitars strummed plaintively. The fourth dancer was sensual and seductive, stroking my arms and leading me in an erotic *pas de deux*.

Finally the four caballeros departed, leaving me alone on stage. The footlights dimmed, while behind me the backdrop glowed, sunset blazing bright orange through special lighting effects. I did my second solo, describing my lover once more, my longing for him. The sunset faded slowly and as I performed the final steps of the dance there was nothing behind me but a few orange blurs. The music stopped. The stage went dark. As the curtain fell I hurried to my dressing room, ignoring the applause that seemed to rock the whole theater. I would take no bows at the end of the first half, but would wait until the performance was over.

My orders were that no one was to come to my dressing room during intermission. I had refused a dresser, and I didn't even want Millie to help me. Hastily, I freshened my make-up and took down the second costume. It was identical in cut to the first, but made of rich black silk; the skirt, aglitter with black spangles, had six scarlet underskirts beneath it. I pinned a red velvet rose in my hair. The audience began filing back in to take their seats, talking noisily, but I didn't leave the dressing room until the second half overture had begun.

The first dances had been good, I knew that, but I had deliberately held back a little, saving myself for the second half. The male dancers passed by me in their gypsy attire. I smiled at them, told them they had been superb, and they moved on stage with new confidence. The backdrop depicted the same Spanish plain at night, the earth sable black, the sky above ash-gray with flickering silver stars. A gaudy gypsy caravan stood stage left, and three real fires burned. Specially treated logs had been set aflame in huge flat black iron platters that were invisible to the audience. Two of the dancers crouched before a fire. The third lounged on the steps of the caravan, and the fourth leaned against it in an arrogant stance.

As the curtain rose, the audience burst into spontaneous applause, so stunning were the stage effects, so real the gypsy camp. The two dancers by the fire rose and began a fierce dance of combat, murderous expressions on their faces as their lithe bodies moved to the clashing music. The dancer on the caravan steps joined in, separating them, ending the fight, and all three of them turned to glare menacingly toward the wings as another melody began. I whirled on stage, skirts lifting, black spangles glittering in the firelight. The applause thundered even louder this time. I ignored it as before, continuing my provocative dance and taunting the three handsome gypsies who watched with flashing eyes.

I did a *pas de deux* with each of them, and then I danced alone again.

One of the gypsies approached me. He handed me a pair of castanets, and we pretended to talk in conspiratorial tones as I fastened them on my fingers. We started to dance. The gypsy in the red silk shirt abandoned his post against the caravan, caught my partner by the shoulder and pulled him away, giving him a violent shove. Hands on thighs, he looked me up and down with eyes glowing. I smiled and clicked my castanets at him teasingly. He turned his back to me, folding his arms across his chest. I circled him, enticing him. Seductive, fully aware of my allure, I moved my body to the slow, sensuous music that gradually began to swell. He watched me angrily, nostrils flaring, desire beginning to stir, to burn in his eyes as I whirled and swayed.

It was the dance of love, the one I had danced so many years ago at a gypsy camp on the fairgrounds in Cornwall. Then, I had performed it with a youth named Juan, while Brence stood in the crowd, watching. I was eighteen years old, aglow with love, transformed by its magic. And now, as I danced on a stage in San Francisco, old memories swept over me, and the backdrop with its twinkling silver stars became the Cornwall sky, the fires the gypsy campfires, my partner the gypsy youth. . . .

My body became an instrument of passion, for I was dancing for Brence, in love with him then, in love with him still. I had become a dancer because of him, because I wanted to win him back, wanted him to see me and want me. I had never stopped loving him, never. The

518

loss, the pain was as great at this moment as it had been the day he abandoned me for good.

Memory and reality merged as the dancer came toward me and put his arms around my waist. As we swayed together, my body felt as if it were melting to the music as it had done that night in Cornwall when love was enchantment and the future a glowing promise. When the dancer released me, I whirled away from him, faster, faster, but he pursued me, clasping me to him in a fierce embrace as the music surged to a passionate crescendo and ended.

The curtain fell. The audience screamed, shouted, applauded madly. I joined hands with the dancers as the curtain came up again, two on either side of me as we approached the footlights and took our bows. The dancers retreated, leaving me alone on the stage. The audience was on its feet, going wild with enthusiasm. I took bow after bow, and ushers rushed down the aisles with bouquets of flowers, and I thought of Brence.

The audience continued to clap, to stomp, to shout in a frenzy of admiration, but without Brence it was a hollow victory. Accepting a bouquet of flowers, I smiled and bowed and let the tears spill down my cheeks as I realized at last that this mass adoration could never replace the love I had lost.

XLV

Brushing away the tears, I left the stage, though the audience continued to applaud madly. The backstage crew was waiting in the wings, beaming, applauding, too. I thanked them and smiled, trying to be gracious. They had worked very hard. A banquet and two cases of champagne awaited them, and soon they would be holding their own opening night celebration in the basement, as a treat from me. I apologized that I would be unable to join them and thanked them again. Handing my bouquet to one of the men, I asked if he would see that all the flowers were distributed among their wives.

"They're rioting out there," the stage manager said. "Don't you think you should take one more bow?"

I shook my head. "Mr. Duke is coming to my dressing room," I said. "Have you seen him?"

"I think he's in the office with Mr. Clark."

"When he returns, tell him I'm waiting, and—George, please don't let anyone else come backstage except Millie and Mr. Bradford. I'm not up to seeing anyone."

"Does that go for the press as well?"

I nodded and started toward my dressing room. The four dancers were waiting in front of the door, still in costume, and I forced myself to be enthusiastic for their sakes. I hugged each one, told them they had been magnificent, told them they had been largely responsible for tonight's triumph. Finally, bidding them goodbye, I stepped into the dressing room and closed the door behind me with considerable relief.

Emotions that I had contained far too long had swept over me during that final dance, leaving me shaken to the core. I had been forced to face the truth about myself. Glamor and glory and public acclaim were a poor substitute for what was lacking in my life. Without love, they were meaningless.

I had lost Brence and I would never get over it, but there had to be someone else. I must dare to love again. I must dare to give everything of myself, completely and fully, holding nothing back. As I stepped over to the dressing table I found myself thinking of the man in the black hood and that bewildering, magical night at the hacienda. I had given myself then. Once he had broken down the barriers, I had allowed myself to love without restraint. The experience had been shattering, and it had brought home to me the emptiness of the past five years.

As I changed, I posed myself for the ordeal ahead with Anthony. It was something that had to be done, and I knew I must be very firm, very strong. I forced back other emotions, willing the return of that tight, cold calm that had possessed me when I arrived at the theater. I wasn't completely successful, but by the time he sailed into the room I was able to look up at him with some semblance of composure.

"It was a triumph, luv!" he exclaimed. "A bloody triumph! You were magnificent!"

Anthony's cheeks were flushed, his eyes alight, and he looked like a little boy who has just received a box full of presents. He smiled a dazzling smile and took my hands and pulled me to my feet. I had never seen him so elated.

"You made theatrical history tonight, Elena. I mean it. San Francisco will never forget this night. You've always been good, always knew how to please your audiences, but tonight you were inspired! I've never seen you dance like that."

He smiled again and gave me a hug that almost broke my ribs. "I've never been so proud in all my life." He cocked his head, still grinning. "I've been a beast these past few days, luv." He lifted his hand and held it out in protest. "No, no, don't contradict me."

"I wasn't going to."

"I've been beastly, I know, but I—uh—I've had things on my mind. A couple of problems. That's all been solved now."

"Indeed."

He nodded. "I had a talk with Clark a few minutes ago. He wants to extend your engagement. We signed for two weeks. He wants us for another six, and, luv, he's willing to pay a fortune!"

"Is he?"

"Twenty-five thousand a week, and—this is the best part—he'll pay half of it in advance! All we have to do is sign. He's going to draw up the contracts tonight. Six more weeks, luv, and after that he'll probably want us to extend again. We could play San Francisco indefinitely! They love you here. You're not just a dancer, you're a bloody heroine! Before it's all over with they'll probably erect a *statue* of you!"

I sat back down at the dressing table and finished removing my stage make-up, deliberately stalling, listening to that rich, exuberant voice and dreading what I had to do. Anthony had grown eloquent by this time, making sweeping gestures with his arms, his face aglow. I knew further stalling would only make things worse. I put down my hair brush and turned around.

"Hurry up and dress, luv," he told me. "We're going to celebrate. I reserved a table at Delmonico's. It's the best restaurant in San Francisco, lobster you won't believe. A few chaps from the papers will be there, too. I told them I'd buy 'em some champagne, let 'em ask a few questions."

"They're going to be very disappointed."

"Hunh?"

"I'm not going, Anthony."

He had been so immersed in his own elation that he hadn't noticed my manner. But he noticed now and it worried him. He looked at me apprehensively. I stood up and reached for my reticule.

"Something wrong, luv? You've just had the greatest triumph of your career, and—"

"Something's wrong, yes. I think you might like to have these."

Reaching into the reticule, I pulled out the notes and the receipt Wayne had given me and handed them to him. Anthony studied them for a moment, and his cheeks turned pale. He looked up at me, shaken, not knowing what to say.

"Your debts have been cleared, Anthony. You don't have to worry any longer. You won't have to press Clark for an advance. Everything's been taken care of."

"Christ, Elena, I—"

"You don't have to explain anything," I said coldly.

"Elena, I—Christ, I never meant for you to know. I don't know what came over me. The first night I won a little and I thought—I thought I could keep on winning. I thought I could win enough to pay you back for what I lost in London on those phony stocks. I wanted to make it up to you. I wanted to—"

"It's over, Anthony."

"You—how did you get the money? How did you—"

"I sold my jewelry," I said. "A man named Sykes was happy to give me enough for them to pay off your debts."

"Your jewelry—"

His cheeks were ashen now. His blue eyes were dark with pain, and he shook his head.

"I'm not going to sign a new contract, Anthony. I'll finish this engagement under the terms agreed upon, and then—I don't know what I'll do then, but—"

"Elena—"

"I'm through, Anthony. After this engagement is over I'll never dance again. I'm tired of lonely nights in lonely hotel rooms, tired of playing a role I was never meant to play—"

"You don't mean that. You—you're upset now. Rightfully so. You've got every reason to be upset, but—"

"I've never been calmer in my life."

"Luv—"

"I mean every word, Anthony."

He shook his head, unable to believe what he had heard. His eyes were full of silent pleading, and he looked utterly lost, utterly bereft. His splendid attire somehow made him all the more pathetic—the dark suit with gleaming black lapels, the white satin waistcoat and silk neckcloth, so festive, his expression so lost. I thought my heart would break and, for a moment, I longed to take him in my arms and comfort him. There was a long, painful silence, and then he sighed and made an effort to pull himself together.

"I guess that's that," he said.

"I'm sorry, Anthony."

"I understand, luv. I don't blame you. You should have dumped me a long time ago. You don't need me. It—it's just that you're all I have."

He lifted his shoulders in a helpless shrug. A wry, resigned smile appeared on his face as he made a valiant attempt at the old jauntiness.

"Guess the chaps'll have to pay for their own champagne tonight after all. No point in me showing up by myself. Only make matters worse. I'll be seeing you, luv."

"Where—where will you go?"

"Might as well go back to The Golden Nugget," he said. "One thing's certain, my luck sure can't get any worse."

He sighed and left quickly, before I could reply. I stood very still, staring at the door he had closed behind him, and it was one of the worst moments of my life. Several minutes passed. I could hear sounds backstage, hearty voices, laughter, a faint rumbling as the gypsy caravan was moved offstage. Feeling numb, I turned and took down my clothes.

Slowly, I slipped into my petticoat, pulled on my dusty rose silk gown. I sat down at the dressing table and applied a touch of pink to my lips, rubbed a suggestion of rouge onto my pale cheeks. My eyes were dark with grief, so dark they seemed more black than blue, the lids etched with natural mauve-gray shadows.

But now as I stared at myself in the glass, I no longer saw my own reflection. I saw a merry young man lounging in a theater seat, saw his engaging grin and mischievous blue eyes. I saw a fierce bully, prowling a large studio, casting thunderous glances and promising to throttle me if I didn't get the dance right. I saw a handsome rogue with a playful smile as he came naked to my bed and pulled me roughly into his arms. I tried to shut the images out of my mind, but they continued to haunt me, making the pain all the sharper.

I kept telling myself that I'd done the only thing I could do under the circumstances. But it didn't help. He had looked so forsaken, so lost, and then he had smiled that cocky smile, even as his world collapsed around him. "You're all I have," he had said. What had I done? What in God's name had I done? I was all he had, he claimed, and it was true. It was true. Anthony was all I had, too, and I had flung him away.

The dressing room door flew open and Millie whirled in, resplendent in a gold silk gown, her golden hair pulled back and worn in dangling ringlets in back. Bradford was right behind her, looking uncomfortable in formal attire. Millie's cheeks were flushed, her blue eyes sparkling. The long gold ringlets bounced as she pulled Bradford into the room.

"I thought we'd *never* make it!" she exclaimed. "Everyone in the immediate area is trying to force their way backstage, matrons in velvet and men with silver hair! Men with more flowers, young men with lovesick eyes! You've never seen such a crush! James had to knock a dozen people down before we could reach the door!"

"Only one or two," he drawled.

"They're still out there!" Millie continued. "Your carriage is waiting in front of the theater and the horses have already been unharnessed—a dozen men ready to pull you through the streets. There must be at least four hundred people waiting for you to appear."

"I went and got my buggy," Bradford said calmly. "I brought it around to the stage entrance in back, just as a precaution. I thought you might not want all that fuss tonight."

"Thank God."

"I've never seen anything like it!" Millie vowed. "The whole city's gone mad over you, Elena, and no wonder! You were electrifying! Marvelous! That final number—I still can't get over it!"

She shook her head and glanced around the dressing room.

"Where's Anthony?" she asked.

"He—he left."

"I'm not at all surprised! Just like him. One of the biggest nights of your life and he disappears! You'd think he could at least take you out to dinner! Not our Anthony! It might cost him a dollar or—"

Millie saw my expression. She cut herself short, changing her manner abruptly. "Is—is something wrong?"

"I'm all right."

Millie didn't believe me. "You're exhausted," she said quickly, trying to hide her concern. "Of course you are. It's only to be expected after all that tension and strain. We—James and I will take you back to the hotel."

"Thank you."

She took my hand and squeezed it. "Don't just stand there, James! Open the door. Thank goodness the buggy's waiting in back of the theater. You're in no condition to face that mob."

We left the dressing room, Bradford in front of us, Millie holding my hand firmly. She kept glancing at me with concern as we moved down the hall toward the stage door. Did I look so bad? Was it so obvious? The doorman saw us coming and leaped up to open the door for us. The night air was cool and damp as we stepped outside. I hesitated on the metal step, suddenly unable to move. I gripped Millie's hand so tightly she winced in pain.

"Millie—"

"Elena! My God—"

A premonition swept over me like a dark cloud, engulfing me, and for a moment I thought I might actually faint. Something was going to happen. I felt it in my bones. I felt it in my blood. Through a swirling haze of blackness I saw something dreadful, something bright and blurry and terrible. The sensation was like a physical blow, jolting me, leaving me stunned, and I began to tremble. Millie gathered me in her arms, terrified.

"James!" she cried. And he was suddenly at my side, his arm around my waist.

"I'm all right now," I said.

"You're sure?"

"I—I just—felt a little weak."

"Good lord, you gave me a turn!" Millie exclaimed. "I thought you were going to pass out. Your face was white as a sheet, and your eyes—the look in your eyes was absolutely frightening!"

"Shut up," Bradford said curtly.

He handed her up into the buggy and then helped me up beside her. Millie moved over a bit to give me more room, while Bradford stepped around the back of the buggy and took his place on the other side of her. We could hear the noisy crowd in front of the theater. They were cheering, calling my name.

"We'd better go on down the alley and take the side street," Bradford said.

As the dappled gray started slowly down the alley, the buggy shook gently from side to side, creaking with each turn of the wheels. Suddenly, I knew what I had to do. I leaned forward to speak directly to Bradford.

"Do you know how to get to The Golden Nugget?"

"Reckon I do," he said.

"The Golden Nugget!" Millie cried. "Have you lost your mind? You're going straight back to the hotel!"

I ignored her. "Will you take me there?" I asked.

"If that's where you want to go."

Millie opened her mouth to protest further, but Bradford silenced her with a stern look. As we pulled out into the street, he reached under the seat and took his gun from its hiding place. He placed it on the seat beside his thigh. Millie recoiled. Though she was very upset, she kept silent. She took my hand and sat back, her gold silk skirt rustling.

Everything would be all right once I found him. I would ask him to forgive me. He would sulk a while, but eventually he would condescend to accept my apology and then he would grin, and put his arm around my shoulder and say 'We're a team, luv,' and everything would be all right. Later, at the hotel, we would make love and I would hold him to me, hold him fast. He was all I had. Millie was going to marry Bradford, and she would leave. Anthony was all I had.

I loved him. I didn't love him the way I loved Brence —I would never be able to love anyone else that way, but what I felt for Anthony was just as real. He was a thorough rogue, exasperating and mercurial and impossible most of the time, but I loved him just the same. I remembered the premonition, and I squeezed Millie's hand, consumed with fear.

"Please—please hurry," I begged.

"Can't go any faster down these muddy streets," Bradford said.

"Are we almost there?"

"It's not much further."

The sidewalks were crowded as we passed restaurants and saloons, more respectable-looking than they had seemed in the afternoon. Several carriages moved along the street, men on horseback as well. The thick, treacherous mud made our progress agonizingly slow, and it seemed to take us forever to reach the area lined with plush, expensive gambling casinos. Torches in stanchions burned in front of each establishment, illuminating the gaudy façades.

Music spilled out into the street, accompanied by the sounds of revelry. Several men in evening clothes paraded up and down the sidewalks, peering into the windows, trying to select the right place to lose their money. I looked anxiously at the signs and finally spotted The Golden Nugget half a block ahead of us. As the horse trudged forward, I saw the white doors swing open. A tall, slender man in formal attire stepped out, pausing under the portico. He shook his head and reached up to shove a brown wave from his brow, and then he moved over to the edge of the sidewalk, peering up the street.

"There's Anthony," Millie said.

"Thank God," I whispered. "Thank God—"

"He's probably lost his last cent," she remarked. "Honestly, luv, the things you put up with. I'll never understand it if I live to be a hun—"

Suddenly, out of nowhere, three men on horseback came tearing down the street, shouting raucously, firing their pistols wildly. A window shattered. A woman shrieked in terror. The gunfire was deafening, explosion

529

following explosion, as shards and splinters went flying in all directions.

As the riders raced past, Bradford stopped the buggy and grabbed his gun. I cried out. Up ahead Anthony looked up, startled and confused as the horsemen tore past him. Then, clutching his chest, he reeled forward, stumbling into the street, and fell to his knees as a vivid red stain spread across his white satin waistcoat.

Millie tried to hold me back, but I tore free and leaped from the buggy. Slipping and stumbling in the mud, elbowing my way through the gathering crowd, I ran to Anthony. He was still holding his chest, that same startled expression on his face.

"A doctor," I pleaded. "Please get a doctor."

"Elena," he said. "Is that you? Elena?"

"It's me, Anthony. I'm here."

"Don't know what happened. I was just standing there, looking for a carriage, and—"

He gasped and closed his eyes. The wet red stain grew. He tried to say something else, but he couldn't speak. Sitting down in the mud, I pulled his head and shoulders onto my lap. He opened his eyes and looked up at me. I smoothed the hair from his forehead. His cheeks were a deathly white, as he looked up at me with glazed eyes. He frowned, unable to understand why I was holding him, why all those people were gathered around us.

"Must be dreaming. . . ." he muttered.

"Anthony—"

"Elena? What are you doing here, luv? Elena! Christ —something hit me. What hap—"

"Don't try to talk. They've gone to get a doctor. Everything is going to be all right. You were hurt, but—"

"Hurt? I—I can feel it. Elena—you came. Knew you couldn't stay angry with me, luv. I have something to tell you. I—"

He gasped again, his eyes widening. I held him tightly, my tears falling onto his face. He grimaced as the pain increased, and then he sighed and looked exasperated with the whole thing.

"What I meant to say—been meaning to for years,

530

luv—what I want to say is—What are we doing out on the street? Who are all these people? You're getting your gown all muddy, luv. Just look at it. What's going on? Did—am I going to—"

"Hush," I said. "Hush, my darling."

"I love you. That's what I meant to say. It was always you. I never told you before because—I didn't want you getting any—big ideas. I could never settle down, and—"

Gazing up at me with wide blue eyes that could no longer see, he tried desperately to focus, and after a moment he recognized me again. He started to say something else and then he went limp in my arms. I cradled him, holding him against me while my tears splattered on his face. He could no longer feel them. Anthony was dead.

XLVI

Nick Wayne helped me down from his carriage with the same thoughtful concern he had shown every day over the past five weeks. He was a polite, attentive, kind gentleman and I felt completely at ease with him. He seemed so capable of handling any situation that I had come to depend on him. Certainly, I would never have been able to get through the period after Anthony's death without him. He had taken over, arranging the funeral, settling with the theater management, doing everything he could to make things easier for me. And though I owed him a great deal, Nick had never indicated he wanted anything in return. During all this time he hadn't so much as attempted to kiss me goodnight. I was grateful for that.

"It's rather a steep climb," he said. "Think you can make it?"

"I'm not an invalid, Nick. I wish you'd stop treating me like one."

He smiled his attractive smile, which was both warm and humorous. Nick Wayne was born to dominate. The full curve of his lower lip suggested a hearty sensual appetite, and his powerful build indicated unusual prowess. Any woman would feel fortunate to have him, I knew that I could. Of course he was merely biding his time. And I wondered what I would do when he finally made his move.

"Climbing hills outside the city isn't my idea of the perfect afternoon outing," I remarked.

"Wait till we get to the top. The view is spectacular."

"I've worn the wrong shoes. I can see that already."

Nick smiled again and took my hand as we started up the rocky, chaparral-studded hill, one of several that rose beyond Stockton Street. Rocks and scrubby brush and coarse grass made the climb difficult, and a brisk wind didn't help matters. The skirt of my dark blue dress billowed up over the ruffles of my white petticoats, and strands of hair fluttered across my temples as the wind tore at my French roll.

I stumbled over a rock. Nick gripped my hand firmly, supporting me, and we continued to climb. Though I pretended to be put out, actually I was enjoying myself. It was a glorious afternoon, the sky a clear light blue, sunlight sparkling, the air laced with the aroma of wild plants and soil. Since Anthony's death, Nick had kept me engaged almost every evening, and several afternoons we had gone for rides along the coast in his open carriage. Despite his attentions, I had spent far too much time alone in my hotel room, grieving, filled with remorse. It was good to be out in the open, to be moving about.

"How much further to the top?" I inquired.

"We're almost there."

"Does this hill have a name?"

"Officially it's called Fern Hill, but a number of very wealthy men have been buying lots up here—society people—and a lad in the land office refers to it as snob hill. Only he doesn't pronounce the 's.' So, folks are beginning to call it Nob Hill."

"Enchanting," I said.

We reached the top of the hill, and Nick let go of my hand. I brushed the strands of hair from my face, only to have them fly back a moment later. My skirt lifted and billowed, and the green scarf around Nick's throat whipped against the lapels of his suede jacket. His reddish-brown hair, burnished by the sunlight, had taken on a bronze hue. His size and strength made me feel very vulnerable, very feminine. I was extremely grateful to this man who had devoted so much time to me, who had helped when I most needed help.

"Here it is," he said.

Looking around at the scrub-covered land, I was at a complete loss. "Why would anyone want to purchase lots up here?" I asked. "There's no way you could build, no way you could get the materials up the hill."

"Strong wagons and mules could make it, particularly if some system of pulleys were installed to help. San Francisco is growing by the minute, Elena, and it's bound to grow in this direction."

"You own some land?"

"I own the land we're standing on. I'm going to build a house here, a grand mansion. I already have an architect drawing up plans. In a few years Nob Hill will be the most exclusive area in the city."

"Impossible to reach," I added.

"We'll work something out. Turn around, Elena."

As I turned, I caught my breath. The view was spectacular indeed, all San Francisco spread out below us, hills sloping and leveling all the way down to the shoreline, great clusters of houses and buildings and intersecting streets bathed in brilliant sunlight, rooftops jutting up at different angles, water and ships beyond. It was beautiful and somehow inspiring. I saw immediately why Fern Hill might become a desirable location for homes of the wealthy. A man would feel like a king standing there on the steps of his home, surveying the city below.

"It was worth the climb," I said quietly.

"How do you feel about San Francisco, Elena?"

"I—I don't quite know what you mean."

"Do you think you could be happy here?"

"Happy? I no longer think in terms of happiness."

"I could make you happy," he told me.

He was standing next to me and he took hold of my arm just above the elbow, drawing me back against him. I wanted to lean back, to rest against that large, sturdy body, forget all my cares and let him take command. He wanted to, and it would have been so easy to let him. It would have been nice to let someone else take care of me. But I stood very still, refusing to lean back, not yet ready to make that decision. His fingers tightened slightly on my arm. His deep, beautifully modulated voice was husky in my ear.

535

"You know I want you, Elena."

"I know, Nick."

"I've been very patient."

"I realize that and I appreciate it."

"I wanted to give you time. I know Duke's death was a terrible blow, and—"

"I don't want to discuss it, Nick."

"You made no effort to leave San Francisco. You've made no plans at all, as far as I know. I thought perhaps you were staying because of me. I'd like to think so."

"You've been—very good to me, Nick. It was marvelous of you to settle with Clark. I know he intended for me to fulfill my contract, but I—I could never have done it. After that night . . ." I hesitated, a tremor in my voice. "I know you had to pay Clark a great deal of money to buy out my contract."

"I did so willingly."

"You've been kind and attentive and—I don't think I would have made it if it hadn't been for you. I'm grateful, Nick, but I'm not in love with you."

"Not yet," he said.

His strong arms inched around my waist, drawing me against him, and I didn't try to resist. As I rested my head against his shoulder, I could feel his warmth, and I could smell the masculine odor of his body. I felt fragile and weak, knowing he could crush me in his arms, but I felt secure, too, knowing he wanted to cherish and protect me.

"I thought you would leave," he said. "Every day I was afraid you would tell me you'd packed, that you were going home."

"I have no home. There's no place to go back to."

"Make your home here, Elena. With me."

"Nick—"

"I know why you turned down all my gifts," he continued. "You thought my intentions were dishonorable, and they were. I might as well admit it. I wanted to sleep with you. I thought I could win you with jewels— have the famous Elena Lopez as my mistress. It would have been a great coup. Every man in California would have envied me. I still want to sleep with you, Elena, but I want to do it legally. I want to marry you."

He tightened his arms around my waist, holding me fast. I closed my eyes, giving way, too weary to argue, too weary to protest. Nick rested his cheek against mine.

"I'm already a wealthy man, and I'm going to be a very important man, too. I'm selling the gambling halls. I have plans to get into politics. In a few years I might well be governor. I want you at my side, Elena. I want to make you First Lady of California."

He turned me around in his arms so that I was facing him, and I tilted my head back to look up into those sober brown eyes. His expression was serious. I could feel the power he exuded, but I sensed his ruthlessness as well. I had been aware of that from the first. A man would have to be ruthless to achieve what he had achieved, to reach the goals he planned to reach.

"I love you, Elena," he told me. "I know you loved Duke. I know you haven't gotten over his death yet, but I think I can make you love me. I think I can make you happy."

His lips covered mine, and he kissed me for a long time, tenderly, carefully, deliberately holding back the urgent passion that possessed him. It was a chaste kiss, but only because he exercised the greatest control. As his mouth continued to caress and savor my own, I sensed that Nick Wayne would be a vigorous, masterful lover, and I was not immune to his physical attractions. I just wasn't ready to succumb to them.

He released me and looked into my eyes, looking for an answer. Finding none, he sighed heavily. "I won't press you, Elena. I know you need time. I just want you to promise me you'll consider my proposal."

"I'll consider it, Nick."

"That's enough—for now," he said and smiled. "I intend to be very persuasive in days to come."

"No diamonds," I said lightly.

"No diamonds," he promised, "but after you marry me, I'm going to cover you with jewels and you'd damn well better like it."

The smile played on his lips, his eyes fond and full of humor, and then he pulled me to him and kissed me again, wrapping his arms around me. The kiss was brief, breezy, affectionate, and I enjoyed it immensely. I liked

537

Nick Wayne a great deal. Perhaps in time I would be able to love him.

"I guess I'd better get you back to the hotel," he said. "I've got to attend a committee meeting at three. We're going to discuss a new sewage system."

"Fascinating."

"Necessary," he retorted.

"I need to get back, too. I promised Millie I'd go shopping with her. She's probably waiting."

He gripped my hand tightly and led me down the steep slope to the carriage, and I only stumbled once, catching my skirt on some spiky brush. Nick unfastened it, smiling broadly, clearly pleased with the way everything had gone. I felt very good myself as we drove back to the hotel. Today, for a while, I had been able to put my grief completely aside. Thanks to Nick I was beginning to feel better, to acknowledge that life must go on.

When we reached the hotel, I placed my hand on his arm and could feel the hard muscle beneath the sleeve of his suede jacket as I kissed his cheek and said, "Thank you, Nick."

"I'll see you tonight," he informed me. "I'm going to take you to a Chinese restaurant."

"Oh?"

"It's just a tumbledown shack with a triangular yellow silk flag hanging in front, but the food is sensational. Afterwards we'll wander around the Chinese district. I might even buy you some firecrackers and a paper fan."

"I'd love that."

We said goodbye, and I went on up to my suite. I had barely finished freshening up when Millie arrived, looking lovely in a sky blue dress, her golden curls falling to her shoulders in the usual shiny cascade. She had hired a carriage to take us to Montgomery Street, and she was in an unusually serene mood as we rode along. There was a pensive look in her eyes; a few casual remarks took the place of her usual bright chatter. I could tell by her manner that she had something important to tell me, but she wasn't ready to blurt it out. We spent a good two-and-a-half hours in the large, jumbled stores, leaving only because the driver had promised to pick us up at five-thirty.

538

The boardwalk was piled high with crates and teeming with people, and it took some maneuvering to get to the corner where the driver had let us out. Millie clutched her parcels as we made our way through the congestion.

"I don't see our carriage," I remarked.

"He'll be here," Millie promised. "I gave him an enormous tip. Did you really like the dress I bought?"

"It's a lovely shimmery yellow, like sunlight. It looked marvelous on you. A perfect fit, too."

"It's going to be my wedding dress," she confided.

"I rather suspected that."

"We're going to be married next Tuesday. This morning James drove me out to his ranch. He'd just bought it. It's small and neat and—well, *James* likes it. It has bunkhouses and barns and an adorable house, white frame. It cost a fortune."

"Oh?"

"You're wondering how he could afford it," she said wryly. "So did I. I thought he must have robbed a bank. He didn't. He merely took it out of his account. Would you believe the scamp is *loaded*? When he came to California he was practically penniless, the blacksheep of the family. A very fine old southern family, I understand."

"I'm not terribly surprised," I confessed.

"Two years ago an uncle of his died—this uncle had been a blacksheep himself, and he was fond of his errant nephew—and he left James everything. Everything was almost a hundred thousand dollars! I was absolutely livid when James told me!"

"Why should you be livid?"

"To think he's been living in a sordid boarding house, taking me to the cheapest restaurants. And me thinking he was a poor vagrant with nothing but his ability with a gun going for him, I imagined a future of dire struggle and beans five times a week. I thought I would have to raise chickens and save my egg money and— Do you know what he said when I asked him why he hadn't told me about his landfall before? He said he wanted to make sure I was interested in *him* and not just his money!"

"I imagine you set him straight."

"I almost broke off the engagement then and there! We had a terrible fight. Right in front of the bunkhouses. But . . . making up was divine. He kissed me and kissed me and kept on kissing me until I was too flustered to fight any more. I just wanted to purr. Lord, Elena, sometimes I think I must be the luckiest woman alive."

Our carriage came rumbling down the street then, wheels churning in the mud. Quickly, we climbed inside and a minute later we were on our way, the carriage rocking shakily as we started up the hill.

"What about you?" she asked. "What are you going to do?"

"I'm not sure, Millie."

"You can't just stay on at the hotel. You could take another engagement. . . ."

"I swore I would never dance again, and I meant it. Without Anthony it—it wouldn't be right. I couldn't. That part of my life is behind me."

"And the future?"

I hesitated for a moment, gazing out the window at the shopfronts, not really seeing them, before I said, "Nick Wayne asked me to marry him today."

"I imagined he'd get around to it eventually. Are you going to accept his proposal?"

"I should. He's wealthy and prominent and—and he would take care of me. He plans to build a fine mansion on Fern Hill. He wants to be governor and have me his First Lady of California."

"I've no doubt he'd do just that. Nick Wayne generally gets what he wants."

"You don't like him, do you?"

"Not particularly," she said carefully. "He's a bit too smooth for my taste, a bit too calculating, but he's been very good to you. I can't fault him there. He's the most eligible man in California, terribly attractive as well."

"I wish I loved him."

"Perhaps you will in time."

"Perhaps," I said. "You—you've been very fortunate Millie. I'm elated for you. Your dream has come true but mine. . . . Well, mine was destroyed a long time ago For years I refused to admit it. For years I held on to

540

the shreds of my dream, hoping it would materialize again."

Millie took my hand. "I know," she said quietly.

There was a silence, and when I spoke again my voice held a steely undertone of resolve.

"The last shreds have faded away," I said, "and there's nothing left to hold on to. The dream is gone, and I suppose I have to face reality now. If reality is Nick Wayne and a fine mansion and a future of security, I have to make the best of things."

"If you waited you might eventually meet someone else who—" Millie began.

"I can't afford to take that chance," I told her. "Nick loves me. I may not love him, but he knows that. There's no dishonesty involved. I'll make him a wonderful wife. He won't be sorry he married me. I'll see that he isn't."

Millie didn't say anything, but I could tell she was disturbed by my tone of voice. At the hotel, Millie accompanied me to the door of my suite.

"I'd better hurry. James is going to stop by for me early. We're going out to celebrate—at another cheap restaurant, no doubt. To hell with him! I'm going to order the most expensive thing on the menu and in*sist* on champagne."

"Nick is taking me to Chinatown."

"You'll enjoy it. It's ever so colorful. Have a good time, and, Elena—" She hesitated. "Whatever decision you make, I'm sure it will be the right one. I'll see you in the morning."

Inside, I stood for a moment in the sitting room, trying to fight the grief that swept over me whenever I was alone. It was an almost tangible thing, catching me unawares, tormenting me. After several very bad minutes, I managed to gain control. I pulled the bell cord and, when the maid appeared, ordered a bath. The hot bath helped, and later on, as I put up my hair and applied my make-up, I knew that I was going to be all right. I would never forget Anthony. I would never get over his death, but I could go on now. I had spent enough time in this dreadful limbo of loss and indecision.

I was going to marry Nicholas Wayne.

Nick was attractive and wealthy and sure of himself,

and he did love me. I was certain of that. He would cherish me and protect me, and I would have a life of ease. There wasn't an unattached woman in all California who wouldn't leap at the chance to marry him. But why did I feel so ambivalent about it? Why did I keep thinking of an enchanted hacienda and strumming guitars and a man in black?

I sighed and got up to dress, selecting a gown of rich burgundy taffeta. As I passed the door to the sitting room I thought I heard someone at the hall door. But I had locked the door as I came in. I decided I must have imagined the noise and gave it no more thought as I dressed. I would have to dress differently as Mrs. Nicholas Wayne, I reflected. The Elena Lopez wardrobe would be replaced by one equally as grand but considerably more subdued. It wouldn't do for the future First Lady of California to display quite so much bosom and shoulder.

When I finished dressing, I glanced out the window. There was a curious orange glow in the distance, soft and hazy in the darkness. No doubt it was a bonfire at one of the construction sites at the foot of the hill. The accumulated rubbish had to be disposed of somehow. There seemed to be an unusual amount of noise in the distance as well, but San Francisco was always noisy.

I walked into the sitting room, which had only one lamp lit, its circle of light casting the rest of the room in shadow. I lighted another lamp and turned to glance at the clock. I saw him then, and my heart seemed to stop beating.

"I didn't mean to startle you," he said.

"You—" I whispered.

"I told you we would meet again, Elena."

He spoke in that low, husky voice that was half whisper, half seductive caress. The black silk hood covered his head, but he wasn't wearing the black outfit I remembered so well. Instead, he wore a dark blue suit and waistcoat of pale blue brocade. I realized he couldn't have risked entering the hotel in his usual attire. He must have slipped the black hood over his head after picking the lock to enter my room.

"Don't be afraid," he said.

542

"I'm not afraid."

"We have to talk, Elena."

"What—what is there to talk about."

"Your future."

As I stared at him, all the emotions I should have felt were curiously absent. I had thought of him so often, had been thinking of him only minutes before, even as he stood in the shadows, waiting for me to come into the room, and now that we were face to face I had a sense of unreality. I seemed to be standing far away, observing the two of us from a distance. Through the window behind him I saw the orange glow. It was much brighter than before. That didn't seem real either.

"You shouldn't be here," I said. "Someone might—my fiancé is due to arrive at any minute."

"Your fiancé?"

"He mustn't find you here. You must leave at once."

"You can't marry Nick Wayne, Elena."

"How—how did you know his name?"

"I know he's been seeing you almost every day since Duke died, but I had no idea it had gone so far. I've kept you under very close observation, Elena."

"Have you?"

"I've never been too far away. I should have come sooner, after your manager was murdered, but I only found out about that this afternoon. I knew he had been shot, of course, but I didn't know it had been deliberate."

His words didn't seem to register. I stared at him. His dark brown eyes were grim.

"It was no accident, Elena. It was carefully planned. Those horsemen had been stationed down the street for over an hour, waiting for Duke to appear. They had been given specific instructions. They were to make a big ruckus, shoot out some windows, cause a lot of commotion and murder Anthony Duke."

I remembered how the horsemen had seemed to come out of nowhere, firing wildly, and I shook my head, refusing to believe it. The sense of unreality grew stronger. Black Hood stood there quietly in front of the window, watching me, and behind him I saw the orange glow blazing brightly, spreading, staining the sky. I

543

could hear distant shouting. The hotel was filled with noise. None of it registered.

"He planned it, Elena. He wanted you, and he believed he had to get rid of Duke before he could win you."

"No. No. Please."

"It's true. One of the horsemen got drunk a couple of nights ago and began to talk about it. At first no one believed him, but word got back to me just the same and I came to San Francisco immediately to check. . . ."

And then I remembered what he had said in his office that afternoon, when I told him how I had sold my jewelry to pay Anthony's debts. He had said I must love Anthony very much to have done a thing like that. And I had said that I did. But he hadn't understood what I meant. All he could see was that Anthony was serious competition that had to be eliminated . . . and that night Anthony had been shot in front of one of Nick's gambling halls.

Black Hood continued: "I told you once about the man who stole my mine, caused my partner to blow his brains out. That man was Nick Wayne, Elena."

"I was going to marry him," I whispered.

"I would never have allowed that, Mary Ellen."

The husky whisper disappeared and he spoke in his natural voice. I stared at him, unable to believe what I heard. Mary Ellen. He had called me Mary Ellen. I knew then. I think I had known from the first. Not consciously, perhaps, but my senses, my soul had told me what my mind had been unable to admit. In my heart, I had known, and now everything fell into place. It had been so right. It had been so beautiful. It had been like that first time on the moors, and now I understood all those feelings that had been so bewildering, that had haunted me for so many weeks.

"It—it can't be."

"Yes, Mary Ellen."

He reached up and pulled the black hood from his head. Holding it for a moment, he looked down at the limp cloth in his hand, his dark eyes thoughtful and grave, and then he tossed it onto the carpet. He was still standing across the room, in front of the window.

544

He looked up at me, and I examined that handsome face I knew so well, the stern jaw, the full pink mouth, the taut cheekbones with faint hollows beneath them, the jet black hair so rich and unruly.

I stared at him, unable to speak. Brence was silent, too, gazing at me with cool self-possession, and in that moment of silence both of us became aware of the commotion in the hotel. It was louder than ever, and it seemed incredible that we had been so involved that we hadn't paid any attention to it before. Excited shouts and the sound of heavy footsteps echoed down the hall. Brence frowned, puzzled, and I suddenly realized that the orange glow had completely filled the sky. In the window behind him, I could see flames and clouds of smoke.

"Brence! Fire! It—it's right outside!"

He whirled around. What had been a hazy orange glow at the foot of the hill only a short while ago was now a raging, monstrous, crackling conflagration devouring everything in its path. The whole block was on fire, flames leaping, licking, dancing wildly in the wind, almost upon us. I could see the building at the corner burning, and the building next to the hotel was certain to be next. Smoke rose in the air like great black clouds. Even as we watched, the rooftop next door cought fire, rivers of flame rushing over the shingles, spreading. Not more than thirty seconds had passed since I first cried out.

Brence turned to me, but before he could say anything the door burst open, and Nick charged into the room. His face was ashen, his cheek smudged, his eyes wide with alarm and concern. When he saw me standing beside the table, he gave a cry of relief.

"Thank God! I had to fight my way up the stairs! You can't believe the confusion down there! The street's a mob scene! Fire spreading—hotel's going to go up any minute!"

He started toward me, but then he saw Brence and he stopped abruptly. Though I felt a terrible need to say something, no words would come. As Nick stared at Brence, he seemed to forget all about the fire. His clean-cut features hardened. His large hands curled into

545

fists. Brence was alarmingly calm. He might have been standing idly in a stuffy drawing room, bored to distraction. Nick noticed the hood on the floor. He stepped over and picked it up, examining it carefully, rubbing the black silk between his fingers, and then he dropped it. When he looked back up at Brence, his face was like granite.

"Brence Stephens," he said.

"It's been a long time, Wayne."

"You! You're the one who's been hiding behind that hood! I should have guessed it."

"You should have, yes, but then there were dozens of other candidates, dozens of other men you and your kind robbed. It didn't feel so good when you were paid back in kind, did it, Wayne?"

Nick didn't answer. He stared at Brence for a moment, his hard brown eyes filled with hatred, and then, with one quick movement, he reached under the flap of his jacket and whipped out a small pistol. I screamed, but Brence didn't blink an eyelash. For a long, terrible moment the three of us seemed frozen in an incredible tableau, Brence cool and unperturbed, me with hands clasped in horror, Nick standing with his legs spread wide, the pistol leveled at Brence's head. Until smoke began seeping into the room. . . .

Nick's lips lifted at the corners in a terrible smile that chilled my blood. He cocked the pistol, took careful aim. I screamed again, flinging myself at him, seizing his arm. As the gun fell to the floor and skittered across the carpet, he gave me a brutal shove that sent me reeling backwards. I fell, knocking the side of my head against a chair, and I must have blacked out for several minutes. When I opened my eyes my head was throbbing painfully and the room was rapidly filling with smoke. Through the curling gray swirls I could see the two of them fighting, swaying together in a deadly embrace, arms locked around each other.

They staggered back and forth across the carpet. They reeled, toppled, crashed to the floor. Nick was on top. He wrapped his hands around Brence's throat, fingers tightening mercilessly, that chilling smile on his lips. But Brence reared up, flinging Nick to one side. The smoke grew thicker. I began to cough, taking hold of the chair to pull myself to my feet. There was a deafening shatter as the windowpane burst from the heat and gusts of swirling gray-black smoke poured through the opening.

Nick was on his side, Brence behind him, an arm wrapped around Nick's throat, his legs locked around Nick's. The pistol wasn't more than three feet away. Nick grunted, straining, reaching for the pistol as Brence continued to strangle him. Nick's fingers curled around the pistol. He raised it, and with one mighty thrust rolled over backward, trapping Brence beneath him and breaking the hold. The smoke billowed, thicker now, so thick I could hardly see them thrashing and rolling, the pistol still in Nick's hand as he tried to position the barrel against Brence's chest.

I heard the shot. I held my breath, too terrified to breathe, and I backed against the wall as I saw one of the men rising, the other sprawled at his feet. Dear God, I prayed, dear God, don't let it be Brence. Don't let Brence be the one on the floor. Nick staggered, looking for me through the smoke. He started toward me, took three steps, moving heavily, and then flung his arms out and fell face forward. I screamed, and I was still screaming as Brence climbed to his feet and hurried toward me.

He seized my arm, but I pulled away from him and screamed again. He slapped my face with savage force, and he started toward the door, dragging me behind him. The hall was full of smoke, too, but it wasn't nearly as thick as it had been in the room; a fine gray haze filled the air. My cheek stung painfully and the side of my head throbbed, but I was coming to my senses now.

"The back stairs!" he cried. "They're closer!"

We raced down the hall, Brence holding my hand in a crushing grip. I coughed as swirls of smoke rose up the stairwell. There were no flames. Not yet. There was no carpet on the stairs and our footsteps rang out loudly. As we reached the first landing, the smoke was so thick I could hardly see him. My eyes were burning, I couldn't breathe, and my lungs seemed about to burst. Brence scooped me up into his arms and raced down the last flight of stairs, across the wide hallway, and through the door that led out into the alley behind the hotel.

I was unsteady on my feet as he put me down. The alley was narrow, and the building on the other side of it was already ablaze, the wall facing us a burning mass, the flames leaping voraciously, devouring the wood. Pieces of burning wood fell into the alley, and the whole wall began to tremble, tilting toward us. Brence must have been as terrified as I was, but he gave no indication of it. He hesitated only a moment, then swung me up into his arms again and started running down the alley as blazing lumber tumbled all around us, shooting up fountains of sparks.

A terrible rending, crunching noise followed us and we cleared the alley only seconds before the wall collapsed entirely and filled it with blazing rubble. Brence kept on running for a few moments more, stopping finally when we were clear of the burning building. He set me down. I clung to him still, sobbing, and I felt his chest heaving. He put his arm around me, stroking my hair with his free hand.

"It's all right," he said. "It's all right, Mary Ellen."

When I managed to control my sobs, he ceased stroking my hair and dropped his arm from my shoulder. Looking up at him, I saw that his face was grim with unspent anger. There was a bad scrape on his left cheekbone. His eyes were remote. I remembered Barivna. He had rescued me then, too, and he had killed a man, just as he had done upstairs in the sitting room. He had seen me to safety and then abandoned me. Was he going to abandon me again? I couldn't stand that. Better to have perished in the fire than to be abandoned again.

"Brence—"

"There's no time for talk. I must help. They'll need every man they can get to put out this fire."

"But—"

He took hold of my hand and started around toward the street in front of the hotel. Hundreds of people were rushing about, shouting. Horses reared and whinnied in panic as the fire wagons tried to get through the crowd. Men were spraying the hotel with water from the huge cisterns on the backs of wagons, and a congested river of humanity moved up the hill away from the path of the fire, urged on by the volunteer firemen in their shiny red hats. Plump matrons in evening gowns tottered along beside scrubwomen and Chinese laborers. Men in ragged attire shoved against gentlemen in top hats, and excited children darted about, the whole scene illuminated by the advancing flames.

"Up the hill! Up the hill!" a volunteer shouted. "Hurry! We're going to blast!"

Brence and I stood on the corner, jostled by the crowd as he searched for some way to help. I heard someone call my name, and saw Millie struggling toward me, pushing people out of her way. Her dress was smudged with soot, her hair all atumble. She stumbled forward to clasp me in her arms, hugging me tightly as tears brimmed over her lashes.

"You're all right! You're all right! James and I were on our way to the restaurant when the fire started. I told him we had to come back to find you! Thank God you're all right!"

Bradford was right behind her. He and Brence exchanged looks and he explained that they were going to try to block the advance of the fire by blasting the building in its path. They hoped to contain the fire to the immediate area. Kegs of gunpowder were waiting, but more volunteers were needed to help with the blasting. Brence nodded curtly.

"You women go on to the boarding house," Bradford ordered. "It'll be safe there. It's blocks away, on top of the hill. You know where it is, Millie."

"No, you're not going to help them blast! I won't let you—"

"Start moving!"

Millie's cheeks were pale, tears streaming down them, but she managed a meek nod and took hold of my hand. Brence was already heading toward one of the wagons loaded with kegs of powder. Bradford started after him. Millie bit her lower lip, fresh tears brimming over her lashes.

"He'll be killed. I know he will. Blasting's the most dangerous job of all. That's why they can't get anyone

549

to help. Oh, Elena, I don't know what I'll do if anything happens to him."

"He'll be careful," I said. "Come on, Millie."

She brushed the tears from her cheeks, and we joined the stream of people trudging up the hill. One block, two, and it was still as bright as day, the street illuminated by the flickering orange glow. Three blocks, four, climbing steadily, shoes sinking into the mud. The crowd began to thin, people turning off onto side streets, standing in clusters to look back at the inferno. Clouds of smoke drifted our way. The noise in the distance never ceased, loud shouting accompanied by the horrible crackle of flames and the crunch of collapsing roofs.

We walked on for several more blocks and had turned down a side street, when we heard the first explosion, a deafening rumble like a clap of thunder. The ground seemed to shake beneath our feet. Millie stopped walking and gripped my hand fiercely. The rumble was followed by a tremendous crash as the first building toppled.

We moved on. The side street slanted upward, too, and my knees seemed about to give way, bone and muscle straining to the limit. It was six more blocks to the boarding house, a ramshackle white frame structure with a wide verandah. People stood in the shadows of the verandah, talking in hushed voices, watching the distant flames. There was another blast as Millie and I climbed up the steps.

Explosion followed explosion. Neither of us felt any inclination to go inside. We sat down on the steps, huddling close together. From where we now were the fire didn't seem to cover so large an area—not more than six or eight blocks at the most. It burned furiously, a glowing orange patch surrounded by miles of darkness. The sky directly over us was a clear blue-black, sprinkled with stars. Millie squeezed my hand, worried sick about Bradford. I thought about Brence and prayed he wouldn't be hurt. I prayed he would come back for me. We sat on the steps as the hours passed, watching the fire grow dimmer, waiting.

XLVII

Stella stood with hands on hips, watching, an expression of disapproval on her plump, moon-shaped face as I finished drying the dishes and put them away. Two hundred pounds if she was an ounce, wearing a frilly white apron over her pale green work dress, her hair an extremely improbable shade of yellow, done up in sausage curls, her eyes brown and bossy, Stella was a wonder. Although she had been up since the crack of dawn, starting the stoves, heating the water, cooking a hearty breakfast for her boarders and serving it with customary vigor, she looked fresh and full of bustle, outraged to have found me in the kitchen.

"There," I said, putting away the last plate. "I'm all finished. Is there anything else I can do?"

"You can get out of my kitchen!" she snapped. "The very *idea* of you doin' the dishes! Where's that Agnes? Daydreamin' somewhere, no doubt. I run the best boarding house in San Francisco and that means the best in the state, and it ain't because I put my guests to workin' scrubbin' floors and such! I got help for that, though Lord knows Agnes isn't much."

"I need to keep busy, Stella, and since you won't let me pay for my room—"

"You think I ain't honored havin' a bloomin' celebrity stayin' here? I should be payin' you. Get on out now, let me fetch a cup of coffee and rest for a minute. I don't wanna catch you dustin' the parlor furniture, either, you hear?"

I smiled. Stella was a saucy, outspoken, lovable tyrant, and during the past four days I had grown very fond of her, a feeling Millie failed to share. Stella nourished a huge affection for Bradford and made no secret of the fact that she'd have married him in a minute if she'd been twenty years younger and a hundred pounds lighter. Yes, ma'am, she'd have bowled him over, and no flighty minx like Millie would have stood a chance. Such remarks hardly endeared her to Bradford's intended.

I hugged Stella's shoulders and, leaving the kitchen, went on upstairs to my room. The boarding house was large and airy and spotlessly clean, anything but sordid, as Millie had described it. Stella had given me a big room in front on the second floor, near James Bradford's. Millie had been consigned to a tiny attic room, which she bitterly resented. She could hardly wait to get away from the place. She and James were going to be married in two days, and they would leave for the ranch immediately afterwards.

I still had no idea what I would do. I had money in banks in New Orleans and New York, but not a penny in San Francisco. James had insisted that he wanted to loan me some, and perhaps I would let him. I had borrowed enough to buy a couple of new dresses, at least. Millie and I had gone back down to Montgomery Street the day after the fire, but everything was gone. Both of us had lost everything we owned. Millie blithely purchased a new wardrobe with her future husband's money, including a yellow silk gown identical to the one she had bought to be married in, but I had limited my purchases to the bare necessities, shoes, undergarments, a new petticoat, two simple cotton frocks, the dusty rose I was wearing and another of navy blue. Cleaned and mended by the Chinese laundry down the block, my burgundy taffeta would do for the wedding on Tuesday.

Perhaps I would allow James to loan me enough money to get me to New Orleans. From there I could journey on to New York and then take a boat to England. I couldn't stay in San Francisco, not with Brence so near and so obviously never intending to see me again. He knew where I was staying. James said he had given him the address. The two of them had worked together throughout the night of the fire, helping set up powder and fuses. The fire had been contained and finally put out sometime after dawn, so that by ten o'clock that morning James had been able to return. He had trudged wearily up the steps of the boarding house, sandy hair covered with soot, shirt and trousers badly singed.

But there had been no word from Brence since he had left James four days before.

I stepped over to the window and looked out over the city. It was a beautiful morning, the sky a dazzling white only faintly stained with blue, sunlight spilling down in radiant beams. James and Millie had gone to buy provisions for the ranch. They wouldn't be back until late in the afternoon. I wondered how I was going to spend the day. Stella was adamant about my not doing housework, but I knew I couldn't stand to stay shut up in my room.

I rested my hands on the windowsill. A gentle breeze caused the fresh white window curtains to billow up on either side of me. I found myself thinking of that night of horror, living it anew. I saw the curling smoke, the flames at the window, the robust man in the gray suit pointing the pistol at Brence's head. I remembered their struggle over the gun, my uncertainty about who had been shot when the gun went off, Nick getting up and staggering, falling at my feet. I shuddered, forcing the image out of my mind. According to the San Francisco *Herald*, Nick Wayne had died a heroic death while trying to help evacuate the hotel. Brence and I were the only ones who knew the real story.

Stella's boarding house was situated on one of the highest streets in the city, and, peering out the window, I could see in the distance the six blocks that had been destroyed by fire. One would hardly guess there had even been a fire. Incredible as it might seem, most of the rubble had already been cleared away and new buildings were already springing up, tents crowding all the vacant spaces. The area was alive with activity as construction crews went about their business. I was amazed, but San Francisco was an amazing city.

I decided to take a walk, and I started to turn away from the window when I caught sight of a carriage coming down the street toward the boarding house. It was a splendid open carriage, pulled by a beautiful, smoothly muscled prancing bay with rich auburn coat. The driver wore tall black knee boots and a pair of navy blue breeches, his fine white shirt open at the throat, collar fluttering in the breeze. He wore neither jacket nor vest.

As I turned away from the window, I felt no great rush of joy, no stir of excitement. I wouldn't allow myself to feel them. Instead, I stepped over to the mirror and adjusted the bodice of the dusty rose cotton, smoothed the full skirt out over my petticoats. I brushed a lock of hair from my temple, glad that I had washed it the night before. It was loose, flowing to my shoulders in silky waves that gleamed with blue-black highlights. He had come at last, but I didn't know the reason and I wasn't going to raise my hopes only to have them brutally dashed as they had been so many times in the past.

When Stella came puffing into the room, her eyes full of lively curiosity, I tried to appear unconcerned.

"There's a man to see you!" she exclaimed. "He's waiting downstairs in the hall."

"Oh?"

"Handsome devil, too. Tall and lean and moody-lookin', made my heart dance a jig. He says he wants to speak to you."

"Thank you, Stella."

My nerves were all atremble, and the emotions I refused to feel rose dangerously near the surface. I firmly suppressed them, willing myself to be calm and studiedly indifferent as I moved slowly down the stairs. Brence stood in the hall, watching me descend, his dark brown eyes as indifferent as my own.

"Hello, Brence."

"Mary Ellen."

"How nice of you to call."

"You're looking well," he remarked.

"Thank you," I replied.

It was so stiff, so formal. We might have been casual

acquaintances, forcing ourselves to be civil. There was no warmth on either side, only a great deal of strain.

"I thought you might like to go for a ride," he said. "It's a fine morning. Are you busy?"

"Not particularly."

"You'll come?"

"I suppose. I have nothing better to do."

He frowned. I could sense anger just beneath the surface. Stella, who had started down the stairs, stopped midway to observe the scene. When I told her I was going out for a ride, she looked thrilled. As Brence turned and moved to the door, she gave me an encouraging wink, gesturing to me to go after him, to grab him while I had the opportunity.

Neither of us spoke as Brence headed the carriage down the street. Fifteen minutes passed, and then I noticed he was taking a road that led out of the city. A few minutes later San Francisco was behind us and we were riding along the coast, steep rocks on our left, waves crashing below.

"I assume you have plenty of time," he said.

"I've plenty of time," I replied. "I'll need to be back at the boarding house in time for dinner."

We drove along the coastal road for thirty minutes or so, then turned inland. The sky arched above us, clear and lovely, the air laced with a salty tang. Red-brown hillsides stretched into the distance on either side, stark and lovely. The horse cantered along briskly, his coat gleaming in the sunlight. I fervently wished I hadn't agreed to come with Brence. It was agony to be so near to him and yet so far away.

I fought the emotions rising up inside. I wasn't going to cry. I wasn't. I would hate myself forever if I allowed him to know how I really felt about him. I wasn't going to give him that satisfaction. Another quarter of an hour passed in silence. The land was gradually changing; an occasional tree appeared; flat, grassy slopes replaced the red-brown hills. There was no formal road, but the horse moved confidently, as though he had come this way many times before.

"What have you been doing since the fire?" I forced myself to ask.

"I've been busy. They needed help clearing the rubble away after the fire, setting up tents, hauling in lumber. I felt it was my duty to lend a hand."

"I find that very admirable."

"And you? What have you been doing?"

"Making plans. I—I plan to go to New Orleans and New York, then to London—maybe Paris, I'm not sure. I plan to live very quietly."

"I see."

He didn't give a damn. I could tell that. Why had he come? I was utterly miserable as ten minutes stretched into twenty, twenty into forty and the terrible silence continued. It had been at least two hours since we left San Francisco. We had been driving over grassy plains for the past half hour or so. I noticed a lightly wooded area up ahead that looked vaguely familiar, but I was too upset to pay it much heed. Finally, I felt compelled to break the silence.

"I suppose *you*'re planning another hold up," I said. "I imagine you have your black hood stashed away somewhere."

"As a matter of fact, I do. I'll keep it as a memento. Black Hood has permanently retired, Mary Ellen."

"Has he?"

"I had no intentions of becoming a bandit. I came to California from Germany after my diplomatic career was ruined. I wanted to make a new start, and California seemed like the best place for it. I had some money and I became partners with Jake in a mining venture. You know the rest."

I was silent, looking at the grassy stretch before us. Brence stopped the carriage. I felt a tremor inside as I realized where we were. He put down the reins and turned to me, a grave expression on his face.

"I became Black Hood because I had to. I believe in justice, Mary Ellen. The law wouldn't provide it, not for me or for any of the others who had their mine stolen or their land sold out from under them."

"So you took the law into your own hands."

Brence got out of the carriage and came around to help me down. A gust of wind caused my skirt to flutter as I stepped to the ground. He didn't let go of my hand.

out held it firmly, as he led me across the grassy stretch.

Speaking in a deep voice as we walked, he explained, 'I robbed only men like Nick Wayne, men who had acquired their wealth through treacherous means. I returned it to the people who had worked for it. I kept only what I felt I was entitled to keep."

"You abducted me and held me for ransom. You took twenty thousand dollars from me. Does that come under the heading of justice, too? Because I had ruined your career? Because you wanted revenge?"

He didn't answer at once. We reached the edge of the slope. The valley was as lovely as I remembered it, peaceful and serene, touched with magic. I saw the waving grass, silvery in the sunlight, the lofty trees, the sparkling ribbon of river, and near the foot of the low mountain the pale beige walls and red tile roof of the hacienda stood half in shadow. Seeing the gardens with their exotic plants, the fountain splashing in front of the drive again, I remembered the night we had spent together, and I had to fight to hold back the tears.

"I wanted revenge, yes," he said. "And I blamed you for all that had happened to me. I thought I hated you, Mary Ellen."

He took hold of my shoulders and turned me around so that I was facing him. "When I saw you again, I realized I didn't hate you at all. I realized what I felt— what I'd felt all along—was the exact opposite."

"Yet you took the money."

"That was my last official act as Black Hood. I took the money, and I made the last payment on the land. The valley and the hacienda are mine now—and yours."

"Brence—"

"I love you, Mary Ellen. I've loved you from the first day I laid eyes on you. You were wearing a dress very much like the one you're wearing now, and your hair was blowing in the wind, as it is now. I'd like for this to be our new beginning."

I didn't say anything. I was afraid to speak.

"I've learned a great deal about myself, and I'd like to think I've finally become the man I was meant to be. Can you forgive me, Mary Ellen? Can we begin anew? Can you love me in return?"

"I've never stopped loving you," I whispered.

Pulling me into his arms, he held me loosely for a moment and looked into my eyes. Then he smiled and kissed me with incredible tenderness, murmuring my name as his lips touched mine. This was the way it was meant to be. This was the destiny Inez had foretold for me so many years ago in the gypsy camp. As I put my arms around him, I knew at last that dreams can come true.

THE BEST OF THE BESTSELLERS
FROM WARNER BOOKS!